FLOOD

A GREAT SMOKY MOUNTAINS ADVENTURE: BOOK 1

DAVID SAFFORD

BEAN TREE PRESS

Contents

A Note From the Author

Flood: A Great Smoky Mountains Adventure is a work of fiction set in Great Smoky Mountains National Park in Tennessee and North Carolina. Each year, millions of visitors come to enjoy the incredible beauty and adventure this place has to offer.

However, all visitors need to take precautions prior to experiencing all that the Smokies has to offer. The importance of those precautions, and the wisdom behind them, is the heart of this book.

While *Flood* is not based on actual events, its scenes are inspired by real-life occurrences in which visitors to the park have been injured or killed. Please prepare for any outdoor adventure by packing the "10 Essentials" to ensure you and your loved ones safely enjoy the rare beauty of the Smoky Mountains. As always, please adhere to the tenets of "Leave No Trace" so that future generations can enjoy the miracle of our wild treasures.

All characters in this book are entirely fictional, and any resemblance or similarities with real persons, living or deceased, are coincidental. There are a large number of people to whom I am extremely grateful for their example and assistance with this project, and their names can be found in the Acknowledgments.

If this book inspires you to visit Great Smoky Mountains National Park, or any other outdoor location, please remember the following principles of responsible stewardship:

- Pack out any trash.

- Bring plenty of water, even if the weather is not currently hot.

- Bring rain gear, even if it's not currently raining.

- Pack a flashlight that isn't your phone.

- Bring a map and/or compass that isn't your phone.

- Boil or filter all water taken from the park.

- If hiking or camping, always share your itinerary with a loved one.

- A "fed bear is a dead bear." Do not approach or feed wild animals.

Enjoy the book, and enjoy your next adventure in Great Smoky Mountains National Park!

To Ken and Sue

*for introducing me
to the mountains
and their Creator*

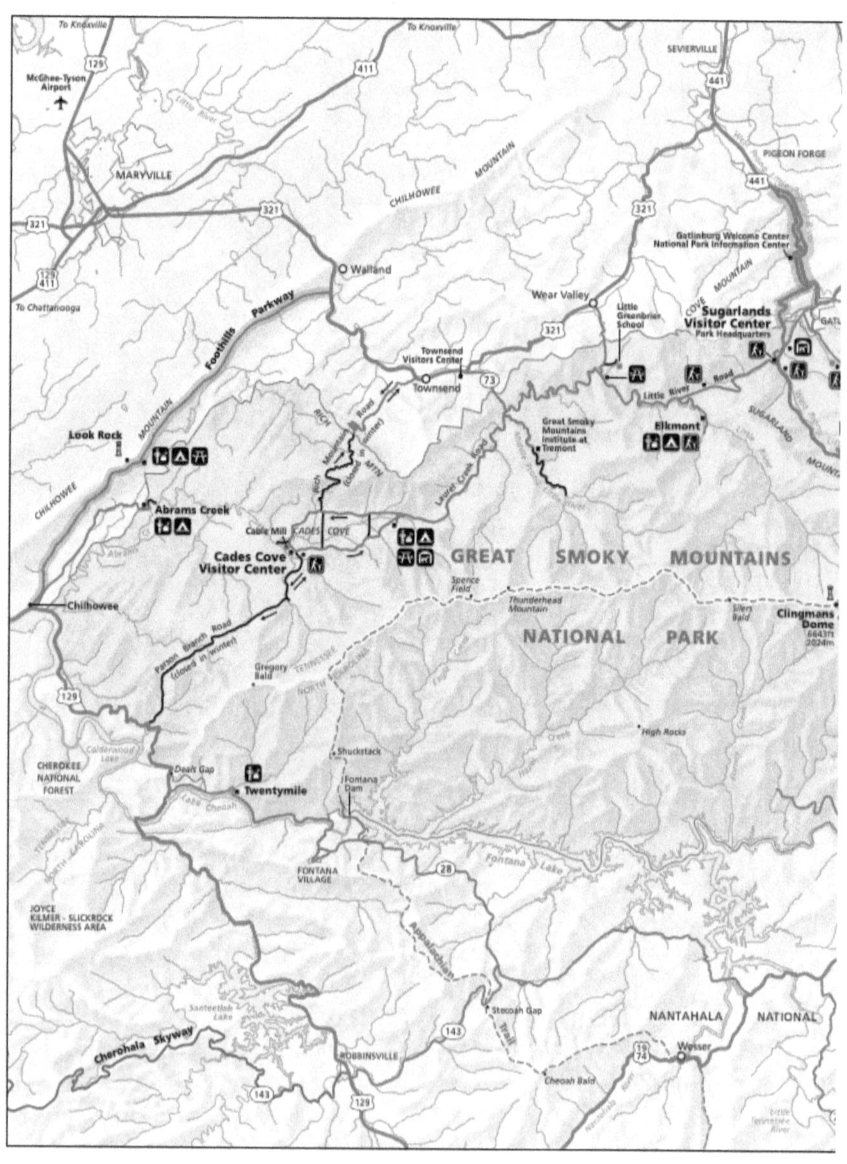

To Knoxville
To Knoxville
SEVIERVILLE
129
411
441
McGhee-Tyson Airport
PIGEON FORGE
441
MARYVILLE
CHILHOWEE
MOUNTAIN
321
321
Gatlinburg Welcome Center
National Park Information Center
129
411
Walland
To Chattanooga
Foothills Parkway
Wear Valley
321
Little Greenbrier School
COVE MOUNTAIN
Sugarlands Visitor Center
Park Headquarters
GAT
Townsend Visitors Center
73
Townsend
Great Smoky Mountains Institute at Tremont
SUGARLAND
Look Rock
Little River
Elkmont
MOUNTAIN
Little River
RICH MOUNTAIN
MTN
Road (closed in winter)
Laurel Creek Road
CHILHOWEE
Abrams Creek
Cable Mill
CADES
COVE
GREAT   SMOKY   MOUNTAINS
Cades Cove Visitor Center
Abrams
Spence Field
Chilhowee
Thunderhead Mountain
Silers Bald
Clingmans Dome
6643ft
2024m
NATIONAL   PARK
Parson Branch Road (closed in winter)
Gregory Bald
TENNESSEE
NORTH CAROLINA
High Rocks
129
Calderwood Lake
CHEROKEE NATIONAL FOREST
Deals Gap
Shuckstack
Creek
Twentymile
Fontana Dam
Lake Cheoah
TENNESSEE
NORTH CAROLINA
FONTANA VILLAGE
28
Fontana Lake
JOYCE KILMER - SLICKROCK WILDERNESS AREA
Appalachian
Stecoah Gap
NANTAHALA   NATIONAL
Santeetlah Lake
143
Trail
19
74
Wesser
Cherohala Skyway
ROBBINSVILLE
Cheoah Bald
Little Tennessee River
143
129

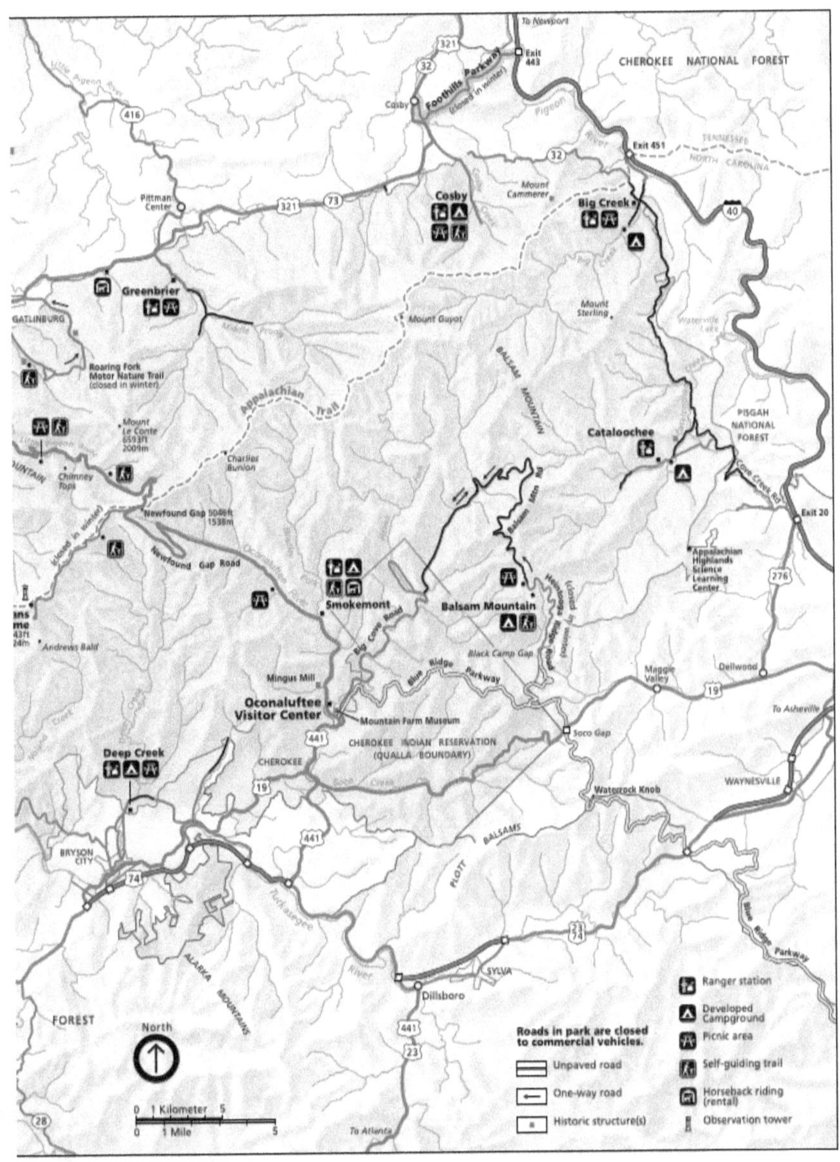

Source: https://pom-static-national-park-trips.s3.amazonaws.com/public/
SmokyNP-official-map.pdf

He replied, "You of little faith, why are you so afraid?"
Then he got up and rebuked the winds and the waves,
and it was completely calm.

- Matthew 8:26

FLOOD

1

WATERS RISE

ONICA'S FINGERS SHOOK AS THE FRIGID WATERS CRASHED beneath her. Hanging from a wire suspended over the raging river, Monica reached for the winch securing her to the cable, shoved it forward, and covered the last half-dozen feet to the shore. Her trembling hands fumbled with the catch connecting the cable to her harness and swung it loose. She dropped a few inches onto dry land, teetered a moment, then stood on two trembling legs, her feet sinking into the thick mud.

Monica Greene caught her breath and glanced heavenward. "Thank you," she whispered.

She turned and faced the chasm she had just crossed. The Little River lay at the center of a beautiful gorge through Great Smoky Mountains National Park. Normally it was a serene paradise; after several days of tropical rains, it was a swollen chute of powerful floodwater.

"I'm on the ground," she said into the radio clipped to her uniformed shoulder.

It crackled in response with a female voice. "How'd the wire hold up?"

"Not bad," she answered.

Across the gap, her fellow ranger and friend Allison Blaze wore a typical yellow search and rescue helmet, but her red hair spilled out the borders of the headgear. She flashed a thumbs up.

A vicious *crack!* ripped through the valley. The trees upstream writhed back and forth, their trunks groaning under the windy strain. Monica's heartbeat pounded in her ears. Blaze swung her head upstream at the sound.

"Any trees coming down?" she said.

Monica studied the forest as it continued its dance, but none of the trees seemed to be succumbing to gravity yet.

"We're good for now," Monica said.

Blaze stood and gestured toward the river. "I can come over there if you think it'll help."

"No," Monica waved. "Stay put. I don't want any of us exposed out there."

"Okay," Blaze answered, "but hurry. These kids are crying for their mom."

Monica exhaled at the reassurance that Blaze would not cross the river and put herself in serious peril. In the short time Monica had been a Great Smoky Mountains ranger, she had really bonded with only one person, and that was Blaze.

Monica turned back to her side where a final victim was in need of rescue. A few yards up the trail, a female hiker huddled on the ground, shivering from the cold. The ranger jogged up to her and knelt.

"I'm Monica," she said. "I'm here to help you. What's your name?"

The woman's lips quivered, already thick and purple. "Puh-Puh-Patricia," she said, teeth chattering.

Monica smiled. "Hey, Patricia. I'm going to help you get back to your family."

Patricia's eyes took a look at the foaming waters, then she fiercely shook her head.

"I know you're scared," Monica said. "I am, too. We'll go together, one step at a time."

Patricia buried her face in her arms and didn't move.

Monica wasn't phased. This kind of fear was normal. Heck, she felt it herself.

"I'll be with you every step of the way," Monica continued. "You'll be completely safe."

She held up a black and yellow harness like the one she was wearing. "You don't have to go into the river at all. We'll pull you over on a cable." Then she unclipped a spare helmet from her belt and set it before Patricia. "You can wear one of these. It's essential that we protect our heads out here."

Patricia lifted her eyes, exposing cheeks streaked with tears. She was a middle-aged woman, her long, braided black hair was draped over her shoulder, and her skin worn with exhaustion. While her eyes were battered with weariness and fear, they seemed to alight with hope of safely crossing the deluge and holding her kids again—

Another *crack!* split the air and Patricia hugged herself more tightly, retreating into her own personal cocoon.

Monica bit her lip and glanced across the river as it spewed and raged, throwing white plumes into the air while the forest shook with fury. Blaze waved at her.

"Give me a minute," Monica said.

"We don't have a minute!" Blaze answered, the radio crackling.

Monica laid a hand on Patricia's knee.

"It's okay to be scared," she said, "but we have to go now. If we could helicopter you out, we would. But we can't: there's too much wind. This is the only way."

Without waiting for permission, Monica took the harness and began threading it around one of Patricia's mud-caked boots.

"I need you to put this on," Monica said. "Come on—"

Another loud burst filled their ears and Patricia nearly leapt in the air.

"It's okay," Monia continued, her chest about to explode as adrenaline shot through her arteries. "We're perfectly safe, I promise."

Patricia lifted her legs just enough to let Monica shimmy the straps the rest of the way.

"Okay, let's get you up," Monica said.

Monica grasped Patricia's hands and pulled, bringing the woman staggering to her feet. Monica yanked the harness up and arranged it around Patricia's hips and clicked the two plastic ends together.

"Look at you," Monica said, smiling. "Ready to go!"

Patricia's eyes were wide, her skin white as milk. "A–almost."

"Just one more thing," Monica said. She held out the helmet again, the inside thick with gray foam.

For an agonizing moment, Patricia remained frozen in fear. But something within the terrified woman seemed to discover courage, and she slowly extended her hands to accept the helmet like a gift.

"You're so brave," Monica said as Patricia raised the helmet and placed it on her thick hair. Monica snapped the chinstrap under the woman's jaw, then gently pulled it tight.

"Okay," Monica said. "This way."

She took Patricia's hand and led her to the safety cable. The radio squawked with Blaze's voice: "You ready?"

"Yes, we are," Monica said boldly. She turned to Patricia. The woman was staring at the river, her mouth hanging open. Monica's heart dropped into her guts.

She's not going to budge.

"Just a few steps more, sweetheart," Monica said, taking the harness strap in hand.

"No," Patricia said, shaking her head.

"I know it's not easy," Monica said. "I promise you'll be safe."

"No, no!"

"We're almost there. I just need you to step this way—"

"*No!*"

At that, Patricia fell backward and the harness strap slipped from Monica's fingers.

"Patricia, please!" Monica said. "We're all waiting for you!"

"I can't!" the woman cried, tears streaming down her cheeks. "I'm sorry, but I can't!"

As hot blood flooded her ears, Monica knew she had to do something. It was never wise to force someone to cross a river like this, but there wasn't time to delay. Monica leaned over, grabbed the harness, and hauled Patricia back up. Monica suddenly felt fiery pain burning over her arms.

Patricia was clawing at her!

Monica let go and the woman flopped to the ground like wet spaghetti, then lay panting and coughing.

The radio burst to life. "*Monica!*"

She whirled and gasped; Blaze had attached herself to the rescue line.

"No, stay there!" Monica cried.

"I'm coming over to help you," Blaze insisted.

"Allison, I'm fine—"

"Don't try to move her yet. Just wait for me."

Her friend kicked off from the shore and began sliding over the water. When her momentum stopped, Blaze began pulling herself hand over hand as the white waves boiled below.

Monica spun back to the poor, terrified individual on the ground. "Patricia," Monica said, "I'm sorry for grabbing you, but we have to get you back to your family."

"Don't touch me," the woman whimpered. "Please don't...."

"I won't, I won't," Monica said, the words flying from her quivering lips. "How about this? You tell me something about yourself and I'll get you across this river. It'll be easy."

The woman shook her head.

"It's going to be okay," Monica said. "Where is your family from?"

But Patricia shook her head, protesting every bit of it. "I don't want to, I don't want to!"

As if on cue, another *crack!* cut through the forest like a gunshot. Monica turned just in time to see a mighty tulip poplar tree begin a slow dive into the creek.

"Blaze!" Monica cried.

The enormous trunk slammed into the waters with a thundering boom, launching geysers high in the air. The dislodged water hovered a moment, spattered a few thousand leaves, then rained down. Monica shielded her eyes from the torrent and watched as the trunk slid along the path of the river, inching toward Blaze dangling on the safety line.

"Get out of there!" she screamed.

Blaze took a quick look at the oncoming threat with enormous eyes then began hauling herself across, her thick arms flying over her head. The tree teetered on a lip of rock and rolled with a series of deep thuds, then jammed into a clump of debris that was choking a narrow passage. It no longer moved.

"Allison, go back now!" Monica said into her radio.

Blaze shook her head, and hastily pointed toward the cowering hiker.

Monica cast a suspicious glance at the tree, water bubbling under and over it where it had stopped.

"Hurry, then," she muttered, then crouched beside Patricia once more. "You can do this. Just tell me where you and your family are visiting from."

"L–London," Patricia stammered.

"You came all this way?" she said to Patricia. "Is this your first time in the Smokies?"

Patricia nodded, her breath heaving as she continued to stare at the river. Monica glanced at it and Blaze was still moving, her body swinging back and forth as the cable swayed under her effort.

"Well," Monica said, "you've definitely been on quite the adventure."

Patricia sniffed loudly and began wagging her head back and forth. "I'm not going," she moaned. "I'm not going, I'm not...."

"Hey," Monica said, laying a hand on Patricia's arm. "We'll be with you all the way. I promise."

Patricia shook her head. "I'm a terrible mother," she whimpered, her voice barely audible below the roar of the water.

Monica swallowed. "That's not true. I'm sure you're a great mother."

"I left my children," she sobbed, wiping her eyes. "And now I'm too scared to go to them!"

"You did what was best," Monica said, squeezing her arm with a gentle grasp. "You made sure they were safe first."

"I shouldn't have even brought them here," Patricia wailed. And then she fell into a bout of loud weeping.

Monica began to speak but stopped herself. Patricia wasn't wrong. She *shouldn't* have brought her family here. For nearly a week the region had been under threat of a tropical storm. Dozens had ignored the advice and sojourned into the backcountry anyway; and when the rains came and the waters rose, they were cut off.

Monica swallowed and turned her attention back to Blaze.

She wasn't moving.

Instead, the ranger hung from the wire, rubbing vigorously at her face. "What's wrong?" Monica radioed.

Blaze shook her head, then pointed furiously at her eye. She groped at the radio on her uniform until her broken, static-ridden words broke through: "My eye—damned rock or something—hurts like a—"

The transmission cut to silence, and for a moment Monica watched her friend jam a finger into her eye socket.

Then the forest erupted again. Snapping branches popped all around her like the *rat-tat-tat* of a machine gun. The colossal tulip poplar trunk broke through the wall of debris and spun over the water, a rolling pin of bark and branches. It jammed on another precipice under the surface, then slid onward with an earth-shaking crash, moving right toward Blaze.

"Allison!" Monica screamed.

Blaze blinked as the toppled tree rolled and bobbed down the river, speeding toward her. She looked to the far shore and back toward Monica, as if in a cry for help. Then she reached for her harness and began working furiously at the catch.

The wall of wood raced toward her.

"Blaze!" Monica shouted. "Move!"

The fallen tree barreled forward, accelerating until it slammed like a battering ram into a protruding stone. A calamitous *boom!* stung every ear deaf as the two forces collided. The giant poplar wobbled over the stone, surged upward in the current, and thudded over with an earth-shaking splash.

Then Blaze disappeared.

Monica blinked as the tree tumbled under the safety cable down the mountain. Only a thin metal wire remained where Blaze had been.

Her friend was gone.

2

PREVENTION

TWO WEEKS PRIOR TO THAT MOMENT ON THE RIVER, MONICA sat in her boss's office, chewing the cap of her pen. A month of service had come and gone, and it was time for a standard thirty-day review with the Emergency Manager.

For Monica, this meeting needed to be anything but standard.

She sat and waited, gnawing the plastic covering and rehearsing her request in her mind. The purse strings around here were tight, but there had to be a way to loosen them. It was the only way to save lives.

She peered out the narrow window where the well-mown lawn of the park headquarters grew soft and lush under the morning sun. Highway 441 lay beyond, a black-topped strip choked with cars. Monica tried to ignore its blight upon the green tranquility, and she smiled as a chipmunk skittered across the grass, pausing to nibble a tiny morsel in its paws before darting away to the safety of the overgrowth. It was so peaceful, so serene. Yet that apparent peace masked the reality of a wilderness fraught with risk, and many of the Park's guests seemed ignorant of the danger—

The drawl of her boss's voice echoed through the hall, bouncing off the World War II-era cinder block. Monica took a long, slow breath, bit down into the black cap with a snap, and pulled her gaze from the beauty beyond the window.

"Mornin', Monica!" the man said as he entered.

Mike Ownby bustled through the open door to his worn cedar desk, a cup of coffee wobbling in his hand. The Emergency Manager plopped the mug on his desk calendar and black liquid dribbled over the lip, sliding down the white ceramic.

"Good morning," she replied.

Ownby leaned back in his chair and crossed a leg. A handsome Appalachian man of fifty-five, Ownby spoke with a pleasant accent seasoned by a lifetime of living in East Tennessee. He smiled, his eyes bright blue, and said, "You feel like you're gettin' to know the park well enough?"

Monica nodded. "Yes, sir."

Ownby jerked a thumb toward the window. "Blaze said she took you 'round in her truck the other day. You two hit it off pretty good, right?"

"We had a good time sharing stories," Monica said. "It's nice to click with someone so quickly."

Ownby grinned. "She's quite the spitfire. We love the energy she offers." Then he leaned forward and added, "I have no reason to think we won't get the same from you."

Monica felt her cheeks flush. "Thank you, sir."

Ownby nodded. "You're welcome. What did you think of our park?"

"Oh, I'm quite familiar with the Smokies, sir," Monica replied. "I grew up here."

Ownby snapped his fingers. "That's right! This is home for you. Your father's Cherokee, right?"

"Half, yes."

"Y'know, my great-grandpa was Cherokee himself," Ownby said. "There's a whole exhibit about him in the museum over in the Qualla Boundary."

Monica nodded, but her smile was falling. She wasn't here for the small talk.

"Did you have a chance to read my proposal, Mr. Ownby?" she said.

"Please, call me Mike," he said, pursing his lips together. "As for your proposal, I gave it a good look. I'm sure you know that we've been underfunded for decades now. Our visitor numbers are through the roof and—I'll be honest with you, Ranger Greene—we're barely able to keep our facilities up to standards as it is. I went ahead and forwarded your paper to D.O.I., and we can pray that maybe they'll come to their senses and send a few of those taxpayer dollars our way. But," he said, cocking his head with a sad half-smile, "I wouldn't bet on it."

The pen had found its way back to her mouth. Her teeth had dug a series of grooves in it. She lowered it, a bit embarrassed of her childlike habit.

"I know money is short," Monica said. "It always is. But people's lives are at stake here."

"I understand," Ownby said, his hands adjusting the items on his desk, "and the park does the best it can. It's always been this way, and people know the risks."

"I don't think they really do," Monica said.

Ownby frowned. "Is that so?"

"Yes," she said. "We put too much faith in common sense these days. God bless the families that come here, Mr. Ownby, but these people, even the parents, don't realize what they're getting themselves into."

"We have plenty of warnings in place," Ownby said, shrugging. "I trust you've seen the signs at each major waterfall."

"They're not enough," she said. "This August a man drowned in Big Creek, despite a sign about the risks. Just last week, the backcountry search and rescue team had to carry a family out of Forney Creek simply because they didn't pack any water, got confused at a trail junction, and went three miles in the wrong direction."

She paused to take a breath and Ownby's fingers began to cradle his freshly-shaved chin as if in deep thought.

Perhaps there was a chance.

"I think," she continued, "we need to assume that most of our visitors, more than ever perhaps, don't know what they're getting into. They watch something on the internet, or think that because they ran a 5K in Orlando last month that they can tackle Mt. Leconte on a July afternoon. *With their children.*"

"I know," Ownby said. "But people are still free to make their own decisions, Monica."

"We need to help people make *better* decisions," she countered. "Besides, we're going to spend the money either way."

"Either way?" Ownby said, an eyebrow flicking up.

"Either we spend it on prevention, or on a dangerous search and rescue."

Ownby drew a long breath through his sizable nose and exhaled. "You're not wrong, Ranger Greene," he said. "Not wrong at all."

A flinch of hope tugged at her cheeks, and Monica wanted to smile. But Ownby lowered his head, shaking it slowly.

"Here's my fear," he said. "We can invest in all kinds of prevention. Heck, we already do. But we're still gonna be out there, hackin' through the forest to find some poor soul who lost their way or couldn't make it to camp before dark. It's just going to happen. And we have to be prepared to pay for it, no matter what."

Monica crossed her arms. "When we pay for rescue, we don't pay just with money. We pay with human lives."

"I know that," Ownby said, nodding. "And I know about what happened at Grand Canyon last year. I'm terribly sorry about those rangers of yours—"

"I think I've made my point," Monica interrupted, and with a burst in her legs she stood and turned to go.

"Wait a minute, now," Ownby said. "I hear you."

The words caught her like a lasso and she paused, turning back to him. "Do you?"

"Yes, I do," he said. "Now please sit."

"You said yourself there's no money. What else is there to talk about?"

"Monica," Ownby said, his pitch rising, "do you really want to start your time here like this?"

She stopped, guilt churning in her middle.

He's right.

She turned back to him, head bowed. Ownby was looking at her with a face that seemed to exude nothing but goodwill, and Monica sensed the furious air leaving her body. She placed her hands on the chair back and leaned against it.

"I'm—I'm sorry, sir," she said, stammering. "When everything happened out west, I almost quit. I don't—I *can't*—go through that again."

"I dare not imagine it," Ownby said. "There's nothing worse."

"No, there isn't," she whispered.

"Now, about your proposal," Ownby continued. "Nothing you're saying is wrong. It makes perfect sense. But something unique about us here at the Smokies is that we don't charge an entry fee. We never have, and never will, thanks to some bylaws. Now, there's a chance we can generate some revenue through a parking pass system, but that's years off. We have to do our work in an imperfect system, and we have to make the best of it. That's all I'm tellin' you."

"Okay," she said.

"I'm sorry, Monica," he said, his voice raspy. "It ain't like out west here. You'll have to get used to a few things, but they aren't all bad. But please understand that it's not personal, or careless, when the answer's gotta be 'No.'"

Monica nodded, her face still warm with rushing blood.

"I understand," she said. "And it wasn't all rosy out west, either. I just thought that the Smokies, being the most frequently attended national park, would have access to more resources."

At this, a laugh popped out of Ownby and he immediately covered his mouth as if he'd sneezed.

"I'm sorry!" he cried. "That wasn't you. Just—just the idea of us gettin' a little extra love from Washington—well, that just tickled me!"

She frowned, unable to hide her annoyance with his folksy approach to all of this. Hadn't she made her point clear? This wasn't a hypothetical. Backcountry accidents were claiming lives, including those of rangers. The evidence was more than sufficient: the public had to be brought onboard with a sensible approach to enjoying the raw beauty of the wilderness. That meant a campaign, and that meant funding.

Her phone awoke with a vibration and ear-splitting ding. Glancing at it, she saw a simple, poorly written message:

Hurry they're trying to kill me!!!

Monica swallowed as hot bile shot up her throat.

"I have to go, sir," she said.

"Anything wrong?" Ownby said.

"My father needs me."

"Is he okay?"

She nodded even though her phone was vibrating again.

"He's fine. He just—he overreacts to his doctors."

Ownby crossed his arms. "Caring for family can be quite the stressor."

Monica kept her answer simple, in spite of the flood of emotions. "Yes," she said, her voice weakening. "It can."

"Before you go," Ownby said, hoisting his cup of coffee and taking a sip, "I'll make you a deal. Why don't you print off some waterproof signs and post 'em at the major trailheads. I don't know if you've heard the forecast, but some tropical storms are brewing in the Atlantic that might come our way."

Monica allowed a frail smile to work its way over her face. "Thanks. What's my budget?"

Again, Ownby laughed.

"Just make sure you do it on the office copier."

Monica nodded. "Will do."

She turned and marched through the door, down the hall toward the parking lot. Once again, the phone shuddered as more messages poured in.

But she didn't read them. Instead, she pushed the building door open, stepped into the bright, beautiful sun, and whispered, "Give me strength."

She lowered herself into her small sedan and started the engine. Peeling out of the parking lot and racing up the highway toward Knoxville, she whispered a prayer and asked God for the power to endure whatever trials were about to come.

She was going to need it.

3

BLAZE

THE SIGHT OF THE BROKEN TREE CRASHING INTO HER FRIEND carried a surreal horror that wrapped its hands around Monica's neck and squeezed with all its might, and for a moment she thought her throat had swollen shut. It had all been so fast, like the tree had been hurled down the mountain by some furious giant far above and she was helpless to stop it. Now, against all her training, experience, and desire, she couldn't move.

A sudden piercing shriek snapped her back to reality and Monica whirled to face Patricia, whose face was aghast. She had seen what happened, too.

"Stay here!" Monica commanded, and then leapt into the rhododendron thicket. She immediately felt the stinging wrath of the wooden talons. She shoved her way forward but the gnarled den of roots ripped at her boots, nearly tearing the gear off her body. She kicked her legs backward and yanked them free from the tiny snares. With a few swings of her arms, she managed to crawl out of the vegetation and stumble to the riverbank.

"Blaze!" she cried. The quivering cable hanging over the river remained empty, devoid of her friend's presence.

Monica turned to the far side of the river where another ranger was standing. He, too, was staring in horror into the swirling depths, trying to see where Blaze might be.

"Do you see her?" Monica radioed.

The thickly bearded ranger on the distant shore shook his head.

"No!" he called.

Christian "Wilde" Webber was rushing and weaving through his own mess of trees and bushes, stopping to scour the surface of the river for any sign of Blaze. He leapt over a jutting root, only to land on a patch of mud and slide into the water.

"Wilde, careful!" Monica called.

He immediately twisted his upper body and caught the long tentacle of a root, working himself back onto land.

Monica maneuvered back into the bushes, moving steadily downstream. The low ceiling of emerald rhodo forced her to crawl like a cat, weaving through the nest of branches and narrow trunks. The canopy above her blotted out so much daylight that she strained to see the ground right in front of her face.

She emerged from the patch of woodlands, her knees were throbbing in new pain, long threads of scarlet blood dribbling down her shins. Monica ignored the bleating pangs and located a break in the overgrowth along the river's edge. She stumbled in, the water immediately swirling around her calves.

"Blaze!" she called again.

No answer.

Where are you, Allison!?

Fifty yards away, the lumbering mass of the fallen tree continued its downhill trek, smashing into rocks and other broken timber in a cacophony of cracks and thuds. Allison had to be in here somewhere. There was no way she was still under that tree, even if she had been trapped beneath it—

A yellow-helmeted head bobbed to the surface, right in the middle of the foaming flume.

"Blaze!" she cried.

Monica squinted to see Allison's condition, but almost as suddenly as she appeared, her head vanished into the spraying water once again.

"No!" she yelled, and her eyes darted in nearly every direction. Blaze was in there, somewhere. She'd seen her and somehow had to get to her.

Monica turned upstream, where the rescue cable was still strung between the two banks. It was nearly thirty yards away, too far to use.

She looked down at her gear. Did she have a life vest?

Yes.

Monica twisted the valve to automatically inflate the small flotation device that was strapped around her synthetic shirt. With a hiss it puffed into shape, squeezing her chest. She reached to her back, tugged at a velcro strap, and pulled a retractable hiking pole loose.

She stepped into the depths.

Nothing she had felt in her life could compare to the fierce muscle of the current. Even in low water, the Little River was swift enough to topple a sure-footed hiker, but this torrent was something else entirely. The force of millions of gallons of water was funneling into a solitary chute, and the river had great and powerful hands that took hold of her legs like vices and pulled with all their might, yearning to hurl her down and drag her along the rocky course for miles and miles.

Monica wavered under the assault and jammed the hiking pole into the dark water. It caught and she found her balance. Only then did she lift her foot and take a step. Just as her boot left the streambed, the current grabbed it. She yelped and tightened her grip on the trekking pole with a shivering hand.

How was she ever going to get to Blaze?

Monica lunged forward and planted her foot. She looked up, searched for a sign of Blaze, but found nothing.

"Go, go" she urged herself, and marched forward, one slow step at a time.

A yell sounded from across the river—it was Wilde, running back up the bank, his long beard flapping in the wind. He reached the end of the security cable and began removing it from the tree.

He's moving it toward us, she thought, and a warm rush of hope surged through her.

She took a careful step just as another violent *crack!* sounded up the river, and Monica turned her head in time to see a dead branch the size of a stepladder careening down the flume straight at her. Its bark was black and laden with broken, spiked arms—

Monica drew a breath and ducked under the surface. The current hit her full in the face, but she twisted away and shot out her arms, grabbing for anything to pull herself down. Her fingers found a swollen rock and hauled her body down while the branch skidded right over, its jagged edges scraping at her helmet. Monica waited until it passed, then erupted from the depths, gasping. She wiped her eyes and saw the log pinballing downstream, slamming into one rock after another until it disappeared entirely.

She pushed herself onward with all her strength, working against the drag of the current. Jab with the pole, she thought. Test its hold. Step once. Step twice. Repeat.

"Allison!" she called.

Jab. Test. Step.

Yet another eardrum-piercing crack exploded upriver. Succumbing to the relentless abuse of the last few days, a thick tulip poplar plummeted to the earth. Before it could smash into the water and chase them away, the trunk slid into the tight 'V' shape of two other trees on the far shore, and the stout body settled into a black bridge spanning the width of the river.

Monica exhaled, the corners of her vision dark with oxygen loss.

Keep going.

She gasped her way toward a pair of rocks that protruded from the raging cascades like gray fingers.

"Blaze!" she called.

Monica stole a moment to glance at the far shore where Wilde was still at work. He had successfully moved the cable anchor downstream. The rescue wire hung low and precarious over the water, given the great width between its endpoints. Wilde clipped himself in and began to test the wire and whether it would hold him high enough over the water or not.

Panting with effort, Monica reached the first rock. The side was impossibly slippery, and the current shoved her along, and her feet nearly gave out on the slick, mossy stones strewn along the creek bed.

Jab.

The trekking pole continued to hold strong, and Monica steadied herself as she ducked under the slab.

Then she cried aloud.

Leaning against the other side of the monolith, her trembling fingers barely holding onto the wet surface, was a person. It was Allison Blaze, and her face was streaked with blood.

Monica immediately drove the hiking pole deep into the soft, muddy bottom, and propped herself against it, adding a little leverage against the rushing river. She hooked Blaze's armpits with her hands and hoisted the limp body, trying to keep her head out of the water.

"Allison, I'm here!" she said, pulling her friend's body close to hers.

At first, the woman appeared to float freely in the current. But as her face rotated into clearer view, she could see that Blaze was conscious, her eyes blinking and staring up at the sky as if stunned.

"Allison, can you hear me?"

Blaze blinked and a bulb of red blood dripped down her cheek.

"Hi," she said, the corners of her mouth twitching as if to smile.

"Can you move?"

Blaze's lips quivered and the smile vanished. "I– I– I think so."

"Okay," Monica said. "Let's get you out of here."

Monica bent her knees and shoved upward. The water rushed past her, but Monica pushed back against the relentless torrent. A splash hit them and Monica shook the drops out of her eyes in time to see blood running off Blaze's face, revealing a purple cut under her left eyebrow. A fresh bubble of crimson appeared again.

"Can you put pressure on that?" she said, pointing to the wound.

"Yeah," Blaze answered, her voice distant.

Monica dug her boots into the riverbed, twisting each foot to gain even a little leverage, and pushed upstream. "I've got you," she said, her voice hoarse with effort.

"I'm dizzy," Blaze moaned, her hand falling from her head.

"Hold that!" Monica said, grabbing Blaze by the wrist and forcing her hand back to the wound. "Hold it tight!"

Blaze yelped in pain, but kept her palm in place.

The forest once again burst into deafening noise with another *crack!* and Monica looked just in time to see a tree plunging into the river. It was one of the two forming a 'V' around the tulip poplar. The trunk crashed down, sending a geyser high into the air, but this time it was jolted forward as the second tree, the one it had been supporting moments ago, tumbled after. The two bobbed a moment, buoyed by the rushing waters, then began to slide right toward them.

"Wilde!" Monica shrieked, turning to the shore.

He was already midway along the cable, winching himself along in their direction. At the explosive sounds, Wilde let out a little slack on the line connecting him to the security wire. He slid a short way, then swung to a stop.

Thud!

Upriver, the first of the two poplars slammed into the remains of a beaver dam and wedged to a halt.

"Hurry!" Monica cried.

Wilde lowered himself to the surface of a dead tree, its bark bright with slimy moss. His boot slid right off like ice and he wobbled in the air, then kicked to propel himself forward.

Blaze moaned. Her entire arm was red from holding the horrible cut. Monica gritted her teeth and felt her friend's mass increase as she surrendered to the menace of the current.

"Just a second more, Allison!"

Blaze mumbled, but Monica couldn't hear or understand it over the roar of the wild stream.

With a high whining sound, Wilde floated overhead, the winch crying against his weight. He set his feet on the slab of sandstone and crouched, extending his arm.

"Give me your hand!" he yelled.

Monica put her lips right by Allison's ear and said, "Reach up!"

Blaze's arms twitched with effort, but fell to her side.

"Come on, Ranger!" Monica shouted. "Put your hand up!"

Lifting her friend's lifeless appendages, Monica hoisted her as high as she could. She felt a drizzle of water as Wilde slapped his hand around Blaze's wrist, closed his fingers, and pulled.

Blaze hardly budged.

"Help me with her!" Wilde yelled.

"I am!" Monica answered.

Yet again, a vicious *crack!* split the air.

Monica didn't need to see it to know what was coming. Beneath her, tiny vibrations signaled that the whole tonnage of the two trees was careening down the valley straight toward them.

"On three!" Wilde called.

He counted, and at his word they both lifted, screaming in effort. Blaze rose only a foot out of the water and sagged back down, nearly slipping out of Monica's grasp and under the surface.

"What are we going to do!?" she yelled, gazing up at Wilde who was now in terrible danger just as Blaze had been. If he couldn't get free, he too would be mowed down by the wooden bulldozer driving straight toward him. Where would that leave her, holding Blaze as she bled out?

"Try again!" Wilde answered.

"No time!" Monica yelled. "Get out of there!"

But Wilde reached down again. "One more try!" he said. "Tell her, one more for me!"

Monica brought her mouth to Blaze's ear.

"Pull with everything you have left, Ranger!" she commanded. *"Everything!"*

Blaze moaned but the sound was silenced by a sickening *boom!* as the logs crashed closer.

"One!" Wilde yelled.

She squatted to lift Blaze's knees.

"Two!"

"Give me strength, Lord!" Monica whispered.

"Three!"

Dipping under the water for a moment, Monica pushed against the creek bed with every bit of remaining power, shoving Blaze's legs out of the river.

"Come on!" she heard Wilde shout.

"Grab him!" Monica cried to Blaze. "Grab his hand!"

Then her arms started to give under the terrible strain.

She closed her eyes and prayed.

I can do all things through Him!

Above the banshee hiss of the river, another explosion of lumber and stone blasted their ears. The trees were about to crash right into them.

She stumbled a moment, nearly falling forward. Then everything became shockingly light.

Her burden had vanished!

She opened her eyes to see Blaze's boots sliding onto the stone slab. Wilde crouched over her, a thick carabiner in his hand. He tossed Blaze's exhausted body over his shoulder like a bag of cement, spun, and leapt off the jutting rock into the air back toward the shore.

For a moment they seemed to float there, suspended seven feet above the violent, squalling stream, as if they might never fall to the Earth again. Monica stared, open mouthed, waiting. The world slowed to a crawl, if only for a moment.

Then Wilde began to fall like a missile and the safety tether caught with a neck-jerking snap and the two swung forward, sliding over the tightly woven cable. Blaze remained draped over his shoulder, her head hanging and arms limp.

Are they clear? Monica thought.

The oncoming projectiles rushed into view and she twisted and dove toward the underside of the enormous slab. The impact shook the entire world and her ears burst with a tinny whine while the sediment plate shuddered and beat against her helmet. She ducked under the swirling rapids as the trees rolled over like the treads of a tank, their massive black surfaces churning and carving in a relentless march. For a moment the world was complete darkness, and she held her breath in the murky depths. Monica wondered if this was, indeed, the end, and whether all her efforts to be wise and safe had been for nothing.

Then the mighty trunks hung in the air after careening over the ramp-like rocks, spinning in a patient gyre, until they slammed back down with such tremendous force that the ground shook as if from the footsteps of a dinosaur.

Monica broke from the surface, leaning on her hiking pole, gasping. She wiped the spray from her face, turned toward the shore, and smiled with joy. Wilde and Blaze were safely on the ground, and her friend was sitting up and conscious, holding the wound above her eye as Wilde prepared a bandage.

"Thank you, Lord," she said.

But she quickly fell to shivering from the power of the river, and sidled up to the boulder and leaned against it, shaking.

"I–I'm so cold," she moaned, her teeth chattering.

Would Wilde be able to make a second journey out here to help her? Could Blaze be left alone for that long?

The sound of the high-pitched whistle of the wire met her ears again and she lifted her trembling head to the sky. Wilde hung from the safety cable just above her. He lowered himself, crouched on the rocks, and offered a hand.

Monica took it and felt herself lifted to safety. By the time Wilde had clipped her to the cable she was crying, and she did not stop even when her feet returned to the earth.

4

—— • ——

DEAD RANGERS

I T TOOK A SECOND TEAM OF RANGERS ANOTHER HOUR TO safely cross the river and convince Patricia to leave her haven on the far shore. After much resistance, Patricia finally allowed her rescuers to connect her to the safety cable. With incredible, heroic patience, the rangers performed the crossing and the forest saw fit to spare them any additional brushes with disaster, and soon Patricia was surrounded by her family, embracing them and weeping with joy.

Monica watched the rescue from the ground, sitting beside a patch of wildflowers and wrapped in a silver emergency blanket. She sat a few feet from Blaze, who was being tended to by a medical team. Wilde stood over her, his arms crossed in frustrated worry. He watched with an anxious frown as the medics bandaged Blaze's numerous wounds, and when it looked to him that one of them had committed an oversight, he crouched and quickly snapped off a correction.

Monica smiled and turned back to watch the river, its waters still raging white with spewing foam. She sipped an insulated mug of hot tea, trying to warm herself. It wasn't just the river that had chilled her like sleet. This rescue was the kind of event she had feared, the very thing she had warned Ownby about several weeks prior. A ranger had almost died, and the extent of her injuries was unknown. Monica had put herself at great risk to salvage the situation and if Wilde had been a microsecond slower, he could have been struck by the last barrage of trees, and all three of them would likely be headed to the hospital.

Or the morgue.

Once Patricia had safely arrived on the near side of the creek, a wave of exhaustion blasted Monica to her bones, and she closed her eyes. But she had barely begun to push out the pallid light of day when a rushing wind shook the treetops and a loud creaking reminded her that the forest was still threatening to throw projectiles down at them. Monica crawled to her feet and stood behind the medics as they secured a collar around Blaze's head, stabilizing it for the bumpy journey back to civilization.

"How is she?" Monica said.

"Definitely a concussion," one of the medics said. "Lost a decent amount of blood, too."

Then Blaze's raspy voice croaked from below, "I'm fine."

Monica peeked around the rescuer. Blaze was staring up at her with a clean face and a large rectangular bandage covering her eyebrow.

"The heck you're fine," Monica replied.

Blaze raised a hand and shooed her with a playful wave.

Monica chuckled, a throb of pain piercing her own head, and she winced.

"You okay?" said a deeper voice this time.

It was Wilde, his arms still crossed, the bottom of his beard touching his hands.

"Yeah," Monica said, massaging her temples. "Just a headache from all that."

"You should get checked out," Wilde said.

"I will, don't worry."

"I'm not worried. Just get it checked."

She leaned toward him, closing the gap between their faces only a fraction. Her movement had the intended effect, and he lifted his gaze to meet hers, and for a moment, their eyes locked.

"Thank you," she said.

He nodded. "Of course."

"Really, thank you," she added. "You saved my life. Both of our lives."

He looked away, and she immediately sensed he was wishing she had just left the matter alone. She had only known Christian Webber a few days and could already tell he was rather closed off, even if he didn't mean to be. According to some of the rangers, including Blaze, Wilde rarely let his emotions break through his professional exterior. Some blamed it on his numerous years in the Army; others said it was due to a personal matter.

Either way, she couldn't help but wonder what he was thinking. Was he judging her for her choice to go into the river? Or was he admiring her courage and willingness to put her own life on the line?

Wilde's gray expression remained rigid. With a quick nod, he flashed a muted smile.

"No problem," he said.

He crouched again to get a closer look at Blaze.

Monica pressed her thumb and forefinger into her temples. The sharp pains were getting worse, and no amount of rubbing could alleviate the discomfort.

She needed something to do, somewhere to put the remaining adrenaline that was making her entire body shiver with energy.

With that, she began to walk down the trail, away from the scene of near-death.

The Little River Trail was a pleasant path to walk, level and smooth. It was an old railroad bed, a remnant of the logging days that inspired Horace Kephart to campaign for a national park. The wind sang a frightful hymn in the timbers, blowing through the leaves like reeds, and it sent chills through Monica's body. Should she be walking alone right now? At any moment another tree could come down right on top of her. But she wanted to be far from the river, far from the sight of an injured Blaze and the harsh glare of an emotionally distant Wilde. She needed space.

Calm.

Peace.

Everything had happened so suddenly and violently. Her heart was pounding yet, her chest a parade drum, and she had no idea how to settle herself.

Pray, Monica.

She slowed to a leisurely walk, as if enjoying a stroll on a beach, and placed her hands in her wet pockets.

Thank you, God, she began.

And for nearly a hundred calm paces, Monica gave thanks for the miracle of their deliverance from the raging waters. A verse came to her, this from the happy conclusion of the story of Noah.

I will establish my covenant with you: never shall there any more be a flood to destroy the earth.

She stopped, drawing a deep breath as the boughs hissed above her. She placed a hand on her chest.

Calm.

"Thank you," she whispered.

Then she continued her walk until the rumble of a vehicle began to rise from the trail below her. It was a utility terrain vehicle, or UTV, and it appeared around a bend with a flatbed loaded with stretchers, first aid kits, and duffel bags of harnesses and gear. Layers of cords held the goods in place and they jostled back and forth over the bumpy path. The transport purred toward her, then the engine gargled into an idle.

Mike Ownby removed his hands from the wheel and set them in his lap.

"Are you alright?" he said, his eyes heavy.

The question stung, and she looked past him into a clump of blooming trillium. "I'm still here," she muttered.

Ownby bit his lip, his head shaking gently. "Everyone else okay?"

At this question, Monica couldn't help but draw a deep, angsty breath, and released it with a huff. "We don't know yet."

"Hop on, I'll give you a ride," Ownby said, jerking his thumb to the empty seat beside him.

But Monica didn't move.

"It was bad. Wilde barely got us out before more trees came down. You nearly had three dead rangers on your hands today."

The man nodded as she spoke, his gaze shifting up the old railroad bed as if he could see the events unfolding before him. "I'm sorry, Monica," he said. "I'm terribly sorry."

Monica sniffed. "This didn't have to happen, sir."

"No," Ownby said. "It didn't."

"We can do more."

Ownby nodded again. "Yes, we can."

For the first time in weeks, a hopeful lightness filled her body. Monica's mouth parted. "Do you mean that?"

He turned to her, one of his dark eyebrows jutting skyward. "Of course I mean it. I never disagreed with you. I just don't see where the money's gonna come from. But," he continued, "I think we have to. I still don't know how we're gonna pay for it. But we will."

She wanted to shake his hand. To hug him. To do *something* to express her gratitude that her boss had agreed that preventive search and rescue was a priority before more rangers had to pay the ultimate price.

Instead, she just smiled. "Thank you, Mr. Ownby."

"Monica," he added, shaking his head as if ashamed, "I've told you more than once: Just call me Mike. Everyone does."

"Okay," she said. "Thank you, Mike."

"Thank *you*," he said, his face serious. "From what they're telling me on the radio, you put it all on the line out there."

"It was a team effort, sir."

"Of course it was a team effort, but it was one that you led, despite the risks. Now, Ranger Greene," he pivoted, "you need to get in and stop walking. Medical will be evaluating you at the trailhead."

"Yes, sir."

"Mike," he repeated.

Monica sighed. She was too tired for this, even though it was in many ways a relief. "Okay," she added weakly.

She hoisted herself into the empty passenger seat, dizziness tossing her head each way.

"Ready?" Ownby said.

Monica nodded.

She sat in silence as he drove to the scene of the near-tragedy so they could pick up Blaze and Patricia and give them rides as well. Wilde, as he was known to do, flatly refused a ride and opted to walk back by himself in total solitude, leaving the remaining rangers to head back on their own UTV.

Ownby swung the vehicle in a tight circle and began heading downhill, chattering the whole way back to Elkmont about the tightness of funding, the budget loopholes he'd come to know in his years as Emergency Manager, and what he knew about effective preventive measures. While Monica listened, her mind wandered with a sleepy lightness until she found that she could hear nothing but the growl of the motor.

5

PSAR

AFTER EVERYTHING THE RIVER THREW AT HER, MONICA ENDED up with only a dozen bruises. One was particularly broad and dark, painting her knee a sickly purple color, but otherwise she had come away with little physical damage. In her mind, it was nothing short of a miracle.

Ownby insisted she take a few days off.

"You've gone above and beyond," he told her over the phone. "If you don't rest, none of us will either."

Weary beyond words, she obliged, taking the time to read her Bible and enjoy binging a few shows. She was alone, but for Monica it was no punishment to partake in solitude. She was used to it, the only child of a doomed marriage between a dashingly handsome man of Cherokee descent and a strong-willed woman from East Knoxville. And since neither parent had remarried or borne more children, she remained the only fruit of the ill-fated relationship.

That solitude was broken, however, when her father began to repeatedly call at unthinkable hours of the night. Each time the phone lit up, her stomach flip-flopped as if she'd just consumed old fish, and she took the device in weary fingers to answer.

"What is it, Dad?" she'd say.

Then came the complaints. They came in an endless stream of verbal vomit over every imaginable aspect of his medical care, and at times Monica could do nothing but set the phone on her bedside table, roll over, and close her eyes as he continued to ramble on and on.

The interruptions were particularly bad the night prior to her return to work, and she had to beg him to trust her, to just take the prescribed doses and turn off his television—though he complained he needed it to sleep. He finally relented and she fell into a tenuous, sweat-soaked imitation of rest. When her alarm sounded at six, she wondered if she should even bother getting up at all.

Yet the call of the forest was louder than the longing for more rest. The work of Preventive Search and Rescue had to begin.

WHEN SHE PULLED INTO AN EMPTY PARKING SPOT, Wilde was standing next to his truck waiting for her. His arms were folded across his muscular chest and a pair of sunglasses wrapped around his face.

"Hey," he said as she opened her door.

"Hey," Monica answered.

"You ready?" Wilde said, jerking his head toward the passenger seat.

"Ready for what?"

"Game plan," he said. "Ownby wants us to tour the major trailheads and lay out a PSAR strategy."

Monica glanced at the windows of the park headquarters, wondering if Ownby was watching them from his window. She strolled over to Wilde's passenger door, climbed in, slid into the seat, and tucked her feet up against a mound of filthy camping gear: A dirt-smeared tent bag, a wadded up sleeping bag, plastic bags stuffed with god-knows-what, and several pairs of boots emitting a pungent smell like onions and old trash.

"Nice," she said, scowling at the debris.

"Sorry about the mess," Wilde said. "You can thank the people who left this at Campsite #38 last night," Wilde growled. "I had to chase off a family of raccoons to clean it up. As for the tent and the sleeping bag, I thought I could wash them. It's always nice to have spare gear."

Monica eyed the pile once more, narrowing her gaze. "And the boots?"

Wilde shrugged. "Those are mine."

She wrinkled her nose. "They smell *great.*"

"How do yours smell?" he quipped back.

She smiled. At least Wilde could take a joke.

"So where are we going?" she asked.

"I thought we'd start in this area while traffic is lighter, then loop clockwise around the park. You good to work late?"

At the sound of the word 'late,' Monica yawned. "Can I sleep while you drive?"

"Sure," he said. "Long night?"

"Sort of. It's nothing."

Wilde nodded, all business again. "Okay."

THEY CLIMBED UP HIGHWAY 441, the only road to cross from Tennessee to North Carolina through the Smokies. As Wilde had predicted, traffic was relatively light, slowed only by an assortment of wide-eyed onlookers and recreational vehicles heaving their way up the mountain. To the southeast, the hulking massif of Mt. Leconte loomed over the valley and a pair of breathtaking overlooks grabbed Monica's gaze as they passed. Further up the road after a pair of sharp switchbacks, the twin towers of Chimney Tops watched over the trees like ancient fortresses.

"This is our first stop," Wilde said.

He pulled the truck into the narrow parking area which was already lined with dozens of vehicles. Families with small children were preparing for the short but arduous journey, shouldering backpacks and lacing boots. Wilde found a spot and cut the motor.

The moment the truck fell into silence, Monica heard the pleasant sigh of the Pigeon River as it rushed toward Gatlinburg. Though the waters had receded since the storm passed, the streams were still flowing high. She stepped onto the asphalt sidewalk and fell into step behind Wilde until they reached a single display board.

"Okay, Monica," Wilde said, stopping and turning to face her. "This is a prime candidate for dehydration and sprained ankles. What did you have in mind for preventive search and rescue?"

Monica surveyed the scene. The trailhead was shallow, hugging the parking lot where a set of stone steps led to a dirt path that immediately fell toward the gorge and the first crossing of the river. Little space was available for more signs and displays. The existing billboard already taught visitors about a number of matters: Leave no trace, the importance of treating water from the stream, and a broad notice that the very top of the trail was still closed, allowing the mountain to recover after the apocalyptic fires of 2016.

"Let's walk," Monica said.

"We have a lot of stops today," Wilde said, frowning.

"I think better when I'm moving," she said, and without waiting for him, began the descent into the valley.

She found a brisk pace down the slope, her mind already hard at work. The sound of Wilde's heavy boot steps crunching behind her let her know that her colleague wasn't deterred.

"Okay," he said. "We're moving. What do you think?"

They rounded a sharp switchback and passed a family coming the other way. Three little kids, a boy and two girls, smiled at the neatly uniformed rangers.

"Good morning!" Monica greeted them.

Wilde tipped his wide-brimmed hat and mumbled, "Morning."

The trail ran swiftly to the water where a bridge spanned the creek. The two quickly crossed, smiling at even more tourists snapping pictures of the beautiful water cascading over a thousand smooth stones. In the midst of the river, a fly fisherman whipped his line in the air like a spider thread.

"Here's the problem," Monica said. "People don't read the warnings we post."

"Really?" said Wilde, his voice stained with disbelief.

"Really," she said. "You may see people taking a look at these signs, but very few actually internalize the information."

"I disagree."

"Come on," Monica said. "If everyone read and followed the wildlife signs, then no one would feed bears or stalk the elk across Oconaluftee. If everyone followed the anti-vandalism signs, no one would carve their names into the cabins in Cades Cove."

"People will always break the rules," Wilde said.

"Of course they will," Monica answered. "And that's the problem."

They reached the next bridge spanning the creek and made quick work of its length.

"So you want to fix human nature?" Wilde said as they reached the far side.

"Not exactly. Do you know how we did preventive search and rescue out west?" Monica said.

"Yes," Wilde said.

"Do you know why it won't work here?"

"No."

She stepped aside to let a young couple pass them on the trail. They wore matching shirts that read "Bride" and "Groom," but their heavy, sweat-soaked faces betrayed a lack of marital bliss at the moment.

"At Grand Canyon, our work was straightforward," Monica explained. "The trails are long, steep, and exposed, but there are checkpoints and relief stations along the way. We also had the benefit of simplicity: The majority of hikers enter Grand Canyon from one of three entry points, each of which is amply staffed. And due to the distance, hardly anyone actually attempts the route from the north because it's so long and difficult. Only the most seasoned and well-equipped hikers tackle it, and they're rarely the ones we end up rescuing."

Monica paused again as they came to a stretch of shadowed trail, the rhododendron forming a complete tunnel over their heads. The fatigue of last night's lack of sleep was hitting her, and she stopped to catch her breath in spite of the relative ease of the footpath.

"Our model for preventive search and rescue required human resources," she continued. "And with only two main stretches of trail, we could accomplish that. We built a team and rotated schedules."

"Let me guess," Wilde broke in. "We have too many trails for that."

Monica's cheeks tightened as her mind formed an answer. "Sort of," she said.

"Sort of?" Wilde echoed, incredulous.

"It's not so much the number of trails, or even the mileage of them," Monica said. "It's the layout. The distribution. Out of the nearly six hundred miles of trail in Grand Canyon, most people only hike thirty-five of them, and they access them from only three trailheads." Then Monica swept her hand out. "How many trailheads do we have here? And how many remote corners of the park do they access?"

"Dozens," Wilde nodded. "Hundreds, even."

"Hundreds," she repeated.

"So it's a logistics problem."

"Yes."

"There are just too many trailheads to staff."

"Trailheads *and* trails," Monica corrected. "To execute our model of PSAR at Grand Canyon, rangers would hike in pairs loaded with food, water, lightweight shelters, and first aid kits. Whenever they encountered a hiking party, they'd ask a series of basic questions. 'Do you have enough food and water?' 'Does someone know where you are?' 'Do you have the necessary gear to build a shelter if necessary?' And then the rangers would teach and equip them as needed."

"How many trailheads did you have to service?"

"Three," Monica said.

"Three," Wilde repeated, glaring skeptically up the trail.

Monica smiled. *He's beginning to see the problem.*

"And remember," Monica added, "Grand Canyon charges an entry fee."

"Okay," Wilde said, nodding.

"So out there, we only needed three teams at a time. They would head out on Bright Angel, or the North or South Kaibab Trail, and that was it," Monica said. "Out here, God knows how many teams we'd need."

Wilde murmured something under his breath, but nodded and adjusted his hat.

Monica jerked her head back the way they had come. "Let's go back. I need to move again and come up with solutions."

Wilde laughed softly. "I think I do, too."

They marched back up the trail, crossing the sturdy bridges and smiling politely at a number of visitors. Before long the parking lot was in sight, just up the wall of the valley, but they came face to face with a large throng of tourists, all of whom were empty-handed and wearing cheap flip-flops.

"'Morning," Monica harkened.

Most of the people in the group continued chatting with one another as they gazed in amazement at the river.

"Good morning," Wilde said, raising a hand as if he were a police officer. "You all headed to the Chimneys?"

"We sure are!" answered a man with sunglasses and a bright blue bucket hat.

"Do you have any tennis shoes or boots with you?" Monica asked.

The man looked around and laughed. "Nope!"

She frowned and saw Wilde's eyebrows narrow.

"How about water or food?" he said. "You got anything like that?"

Blue Hat shook his head. "No."

Monica took a deep breath and yelled, "Anyone here got some snacks or water?"

Every head in the group shook side-to-side, *no.*

"Hey," Blue Hat replied, "don't worry. We'll be alright."

Then he waved at everyone, gesturing for them to gather close to him, and grinned at the rangers.

"Can you take our picture?"

Monica scowled. With a sour glance at Wilde, she held out her hand. Blue Hat chuckled and said, "Thanks!" and plopped his phone in her palm.

She snapped a few quick pictures and nearly tossed the device back at him. "Go get some supplies," she said. "You're really taking a risk going out there without proper gear."

"Like I said," the guy smiled as his group shuffled past him, talking excitedly about the peaks looming overhead, "we'll be fine."

Monica watched them hobble away, her face fraught with tension. "I hope you will," she finally muttered.

Wilde sighed. "We should swing by a gas station and get a case of water," he said, his voice grim.

"Yeah," Monica said. "Good idea."

6

— ◦ —

WILDE

T HEY STOPPED BY ALUM CAVE TRAIL AND NEWFOUND GAP, two popular visitor stops. At each, WIlde rattled off details about infrastructure and notable trail features while Monica took notes in a spiral-bound book. After a slow drive through the Newfound Gap parking area, Monica asked, "What about Clingman's Dome?"

"We'll hit that later," Wilde said. "There's a gift shop near the parking lot that's permanently staffed. I'd consider it a low priority."

Monica scribbled a hasty note on a new page labeled *Clingmans.* "Any major incidents out there recently?"

"Yes," Wilde said. "A few years back a woman and her daughter got separated coming back from Andrews Bald. The Wilderness Area Search and Rescue unit found her body three days later. She'd gotten disoriented in the dark and wandered four miles down the Appalachian Trail before falling into a ravine. Terrible tragedy."

"Was the gift shop staffed at that time?" Monica said.

Wilde frowned. "It closes at five."

"So it's not *permanently* staffed," Monica corrected. "Meaning anyone who is running behind could be in trouble if it gets dark."

"That's true."

"Was that the case with this mother and daughter?"

Wilde glanced at her, his gaze dark. It fell into complete shadow as he navigated his truck through a short tunnel along the edge of the mountains.

"I know where you're going with this," he said. "We do the best we can with the resources we have."

"I'm not judging you," she said. "Just answer me so we can make a plan."

Wilde drove in silence. Then, after a deep breath, he said, "There are multiple signs posted at each trail junction. It's possible she missed the one pointing her to the parking lot in the dark. I don't think we can post a ranger there, twenty-four seven. Do you?"

"Of course not," Monica said. "I told you, I'm not judging anyone here."

"We can't stop every tragedy. It's just not possible."

"I know that. But answer this: Were any rangers in danger during that rescue op?"

Wilde was silent again. "Injuries are always a possibility."

"That's what I'm trying to prevent," she said. "If fewer visitors get in trouble, then our rangers don't end up hurt."

This seemed to satisfy him, and he let the truck rumble down the mountain without another word. Monica let her gaze fall on the scrolling roadside. Everywhere she looked, garbage peppered the shoulder and ditch. Beer cans, soda bottles, chip bags, candy wrappers, tissues – even a diaper. An unspeakable number of blights lay everywhere, poisoning their treasured natural resource.

People need to care, she thought.

But if they don't care enough to protect themselves, how could they be convinced to care for the world around them?

Monica lowered her pen and closed the notepad. It wasn't fair to paint so broadly. People *did* care. Millions did, in fact.

But enough of them did not, or at least not in ways that made a difference. That created a yawning gap between safety and danger, life and death.

"I don't know what the answer is," she said. "But I'm going to figure it out."

Wilde nodded. "Let's grab some lunch. You think better when you walk, but I think better on a full stomach."

Monica smiled. "Sounds like a plan."

THEY PICKED UP SOME BARBEQUE from Calhouns, an East Tennessee favorite, and devoured it as Wilde drove through the Roaring Fork Motor Trail. Named for a noisy branch of the Little Pigeon River, Roaring Fork emptied the western flanks of Mt. Leconte and trickled through a lush valley. The land was now young forest where expansive orchards once stood, and a number of the Smokies' most popular trails explored the area.

Wilde set a half-eaten brisket sandwich on his leg and pulled into yet another parking area. "Ever hiked Rainbow Falls?" he asked.

Monica swallowed her own bite of pulled pork. "Nope."

"Long trail," Wilde said. "Lots of rocks and roots to twist an ankle on. Plus it's one of the longest and steepest 'tourist' hikes in the park."

"What makes it a 'tourist' hike?"

"Waterfall," Wilde said. "You search the internet for cool hikes in the Smokies, you get waterfalls. Rainbow is one of the harder ones to reach."

Monica nodded and wiped her hands on a napkin, then made another note in her book.

They continued along the motor trail, passing a route to another waterfall, the beloved Grotto Falls. This one was remarkable because the trail passed behind the falls, providing a unique experience—and plenty of risky photo opportunities.

"At least once a week, we have to carry somebody out of there," Wilde said, shaking his head. "That one could *definitely* use some advisories about the dangers."

After the trailhead for Grotto Falls, traffic slowed to a crawl. The afternoon sun was rising and Monica began to fan herself with the notepad.

"Doesn't this thing have air conditioning?"

"Oh," Wilde said, "I forgot to turn it on."

He leaned forward and began cranking the window. The glass slid down with a squeaking whine.

Monica scowled. "Are you serious?"

Wilde smiled and took another bite of his sandwich, brown globs of barbeque sauce dripping into his beard.

She hunched over and worked the handle until her own window gave and stubbornly sunk into the door. Thick September air came rushing in, along with the exhaust from the cars in front of them.

Monica sighed, took another bite of her own sandwich, and wondered if she was being punished.

THE NEXT STOP WAS THE GREENBRIER REGION, home to Dolly Parton's ancestors. One of its trails, the route to Ramsey Cascades, frequently caused headaches for the rangers.

"I don't consider this a tourist hike, but everyone else does," Wilde explained as they bounced along the narrow two-track.

"Why is that?" Monica asked.

"Most tourists never make it," he said. "They hike a while then reach a sign that tells them there's still two-and-a-half miles to go. And that's when the trail turns into Army training."

"Is it worth it?"

Wilde shrugged. "Ramsey is the tallest waterfall in the park, and in my opinion, the most breathtaking. For some folks it's worth the suffering, but this trail definitely needs a clear warning about what awaits people here: Snake bites, wasp stings, sprained ankles, heat exhaustion, you name it."

She uncapped the pen and began to scribble, her handwriting jerking each direction as the truck jostled along the potholed road.

They pulled into the dirt lot. It was a sloping dirt bench where drivers jammed their vehicles into whatever spot was still available. Wilde double-parked and killed the motor.

Monica let herself out, already weary with the road trip. Clearly each trail in the Smokies posed its own unique hazards and risks, few of which were being taught to the casual visitor. This was a place that expected its guests to be well prepared, but did little to oversee the preparation.

"Ramsey Cascades - 4.0 miles," Monica read off the trail sign. "That's all it says?"

Wilde nodded. "That's all."

He walked past it and led her to the wooden bridge spanning the creek.

"Any thoughts?" Wilde said.

Monica leaned against the railing of the bridge. Water ran over smooth stones, its flow singing a peaceful song.

"I have a few ideas," she said, not entirely sure if it was true. Then she turned to him. "What do you think we need to do?"

Wilde crossed his arms. "No one cares what I think. I just want to keep people safe."

She studied him, lowering her eyebrows. He turned and his eyes found hers for a brief, unsteady moment, then fled to the safety of the creek.

"I don't believe that," she said. "People respect you."

Wilde shrugged, staring into the creek.

Monica continued. "Well, here's what I think. I believe PSAR can keep people safe if our whole team commits to it. That means reorienting our whole approach to overseeing this park."

Wilde sniffed. "I don't think people care about safety. They care about getting a good picture so they can post it to social media."

"Yes," Monica said, "but maybe we can make that picture completely safe."

Wilde turned back to her. The muscles in his forehead pulsed, and he no longer frowned with the same intensity as before.

"You want to know what I think?" he said. "The Smokies will never be safe. It's a massive wilderness. The idea is great, but I don't think it can work."

"Maybe you're right," Monica answered. "The Smokies will probably never be completely safe. But we need to help people make better choices out there. If those hikers hadn't been on the other side of the Little River, you wouldn't have had to save us. But you did, and it's a miracle you're alive."

"I don't blame the storm," Wilde said. "You can't control nature."

"You can plan for it."

"Bad things happen, things outside your control," Wilde continued, his voice growing more aggressive. "You have to move forward, even if you feel you did all you could to prevent them."

Her eyes narrowed. The vagueness of this remark struck her as curious, and she said, "Well, we did prevent them. Right?"

Wilde shrugged and looked away again, his eyes flying over the river and into the invisible depths of the mountain.

"Sure," he said after a long silence.

She stared at him, hoping he'd look away from the haven of the river and offer more clarity. But he didn't, inhaling slowly and letting it go with a raspy whistle of his nostrils. He bowed, his thickly bearded face masked by a shadow that seemed to pass over his entire world.

Then he stepped away, moving back toward the truck in silence. Monica watched him go, her thoughts racing with questions.

Was it something she had said? Had she accidentally disrespected him without knowing it?

Monica sighed, alone with her thoughts on the bridge. With another glance at the beautiful river, its gurgling waters shimmering like panes of glass, she turned back toward the truck and tried to focus on her mission to protect her fellow rangers, and not on whatever was troubling her colleague.

7

— • —

MESSAGES

N O MORE WAS SAID ABOUT THE ODD EXCHANGE, AND MONICA utilized the strained silence to write notes in her book and turn the question of Preventive Search and Rescue over in her mind. Tackling the challenge of the Smokies' multitude of trailheads was beyond anything she'd imagined. How could one create and sustain an engaging message across dozens of widely separate regions?

Monica once again began to chew her pen. To make a message relevant, it needed something powerful. Visual. Something that stimulated the mind *and* heart. That was another thing Monica had taken from her experience as a classroom instructor: Video and images had incredible power.

Monica once hoped to change the world as a teacher. Straight out of college she accepted a position in the cash-strapped public schools of Detroit. The experience quickly proved to be too much for her patience. It wasn't because the children were the little devils everyone warned her they would be. It was the administration, the district, and even the State of Michigan itself that drove her to righteous anger. Changing the world, she quickly learned, wasn't going to be easy.

She threw herself into the work. Perhaps grit and determination could be the difference-maker. Single and bereft of any relationships outside work, Monica spent her evenings tutoring kids with 'F's and giving them rides home after. The sound of gunshots frequently accompanied their trips through neighborhoods where every other house was abandoned or falling apart, prime targets for drug addicts to build nests and roost. Her patience reached its breaking point when gun violence claimed a student's life for the fourth time in a single semester. The next day she tendered her resignation and packed her apartment. After pouring out her body and soul for three years, she had nothing left to give.

The truck rattled as it hit a pothole with a loud *ka-thunk.* Monica's head shook and her eyes snapped back to the world of East Tennessee. Wilde turned onto the highway, heading east toward the small town of Cosby, the ancient home of rampant moonshining. Home to innumerable hollers, dens, and caves that were nearly impassable, Cosby had been the perfect hiding place for outlaws and their stills. Today it was home to a campground and a small web of trails, some of which were considered the park's most grueling.

It was a twenty-minute drive to the campground and Wilde didn't speak a word the whole way. That was fine in Monica's view, and she continued to jot down ideas.

Visual stimuli, she wrote. *Go viral.*

Of course she didn't intend to "go viral" with any of her PSAR efforts. But the principle of online virality had been useful out west to guide the writing of brochures, billboards, and park signs, and she wondered how they could wield its prowess in the Smokies. She would have to come up with a way to rapidly teach people about the dangers of hiking unprepared, and with minimal funding and manpower.

As they pulled into Cosby, Monica yawned and massaged her temples while the truck sauntered up to a roadside trailhead with practically zero space.

"Hen Wallow Falls," Wilde said. He went on to detail the distance, altitude, and dangers.

Monica listened, but realized she had already made up her mind. A uniform approach would be needed. It wasn't as if the danger of breaking an ankle was much more severe on one trail than another. Sure, there could be specific notes based on mileage or altitude gain, but in general, each advisory would require the same information.

Wilde pulled into the campground and parked next to another trailhead.

"Low Gap," he said, his voice falling into a monotonous drone. He, too, was obviously bored. "While not a popular hike for families with small children, it's on the list for would-be adventurers. Very steep and rocky. Lots of injuries and heat exhaustion on this one."

He glanced over and caught her mid-yawn.

"Am I boring you?" he said.

"No," she said, wiping her eyes. "I think I get the picture."

"What picture?"

"You have lots of trails and lots of risk. There are far too many of them to staff, which means we need a self-sustaining, automated approach."

"Fine, where do we go from here?" Wilde said.

"I think a list of trailheads would be sufficient."

Wilde frowned. "I think we should hit more locations. The terrain in North Carolina is far more rugged and remote. We should definitely get a look over there."

"Can it wait a day?" Monica said. "I'm exhausted, and I think I have enough to go on."

"Ownby said to make sure you saw Deep Creek."

"That's hours away."

"I know," Wilde said. "I told you it was going to be a long day."

He drummed his fingers on the steering wheel. She could tell this was making him impatient, that he longed to be doing something else as well.

"Fine," she said. "I'll try to nap on the way."

Wilde maneuvered the truck out of the campground without a word. Monica leaned back and tried to let the scenery blend into a beautiful, sleepy mirage that would put her down for the long journey around the eastern edge of the Smokies.

She closed her eyes, but her mind continued to work. It amazed her that Wilde thought they could hit so many destinations in one day. The Great Smoky Mountains took an enormous amount of earth.

The truck crossed another threshold in the road with a few loud bumps and the suspension squealed. Monica opened her eyes, glanced around to make sure the vehicle was still in one piece, then lay back again.

Suddenly a vibration erupted in her pocket, accompanied by a loud beeping sound. It was her phone, meaning they had regained cell phone coverage.

Monica took the phone from her pocket. Her mouth fell.

Why aren't you answering me?

Monica please pick up

She scrolled on. There were more messages.

I'm so lonely, I want it to be over

Monica where are you????

She swiped through the deluge of texts, then opened her voicemail. Five unheard recordings awaited her, each more than two minutes long.

"Oh, God," she moaned.

Wilde glanced over. "What is it?"

Her eyes couldn't leave the screen. The messages kept coming in a terrible stream of ear-piercing sounds.

They are trying to kill me!

I know it's for real this time

I'm not paranoid, I know what you're thinking

Where are you? Pick up now!!

Hello???

"Wilde," she said, her voice trembling, "I need to get back to my car."

"What's wrong?"

What is wrong with you? Don't you love me?

I'm your father for god's sake!!!
"Please," she said. "Take me back. It's my father."

Thankfully there was no arguing. Wilde swerved into a broad, roadside gravel patch and aimed the truck toward Gatlinburg and the park headquarters.

Monica kept scrolling.

Fine I've had enough

I'm going to end it all

Goodbye

She turned the phone over so she couldn't read anymore. Wilde pressed the accelerator into the floor and the engine roared as if the truck could sense Monica's panic.

The phone buzzed again, but she just clenched her fingers around it. Monica closed her eyes and began to pray.

8

FATHER

SHE CALLED HIM BACK WITH THE HOPE THAT SHE'D BE ABLE TO sneak in a word or two. The phone rang once before her father's voice began to flow through the receiver, mid-sentence.

"Where have you been?" he said. "I need you to tell them—I need you to—I need you to talk to them and tell them to stop. They can't keep changing my prescriptions without my permission, because I can't— I can't deal with it!"

She sighed, out of breath even though she hadn't yet uttered a word.

"I'm on my way," she said.

"But—but—you're not *here!*" he said, the phone crackling at the burst of noise. "I need you here but you're not. You're not here, Monica. I'm your father and I need you and—"

"Dad!"

At once he stopped.

"I told you, I'm on my way," she said. "I can't get there any faster, so just be patient."

"I don't know, Little Bear," he said, picking up the cadence again. "They sent this man here, this man who says he's a nurse but I just don't know about that and I really think they're out to do it this time, so I need you to—"

"Dad, listen to me," she said, cutting through the wall of words. "You need to calm down. Don't do anything until I get there and I'll—I don't know, but I'll figure it all out."

"You're coming?" he said.

"Yes," Monica replied. "As soon as I can."

"Oh, good, because I just can't—"

But she ended the call with a jab of her finger, leaned over, folded her hands between her knees, and bowed her head.

Why did the hospital keep sending new people? She had asked them to use the same nurse each time because her father's memory was getting worse, and when he skipped his meds—which was happening quite often—he couldn't remember important details. The doctor had also taken up a hobby of rotating prescriptions, so the names were never the same. This triggered her father's swarming paranoia and with each passing week the house would fill with orange, rattling bottles that he'd toss to the floor like dirty socks.

Several minutes rolled by as she hung her head, praying her father could keep it together until she was able to reach him. It was only when they came to a red light that Monica realized her chauffeur had kept silent, graciously giving her the space to process things as she needed. She lifted her head and glanced at him.

"Thank you," she said.

"Sounds stressful," Wilde said. "I'm sorry."

"We all have something, don't we?"

Wilde nodded, locking his gaze on the road ahead.

When they reached Park HQ, he mumbled, "Good luck."

"Thanks," she said, and leapt out the door.

It took Monica the better part of an hour to reach the house. Her father's narrow two-story home sagged low and gray like a mound of broken rubble. The shutters were once bright blue, painted by Monica's mother in the days when she took care of such things. Since then, however, they had lost their color, and were now pale and flecked with white specks of ashen primer.

The century-old wooden floorboards groaned under her feet as she marched through the kitchen and up the stairs to her father's bedroom. As she reached the landing, the bedroom door opened and a tall, thin man who was not her father slipped out. His face was pale.

"Can I help you?" Monica said.

"Are you Miss Greene?"

"Yes. Is my father alright?"

"Yes," he said. "My name is Andrew. I'm a nurse from UT. Your father called us several times so the hospital sent me to check up on him."

Monica sighed and glanced through the narrow sliver of the open door. "Thank you. What's he doing now?"

"Painting," Andrew said. "It seems to help him stay calm."

"It does," Monica said.

"I have to get back to the hospital," Andrew said. "Let me know if you need anything."

He turned and slipped past her, but Monica reached out an arm.

"Has he eaten anything?" Monica said.

Andrew gave the door at the top of the stairs a quick look. "He ate some toast and drank a little water. It took me an hour to convince him it wasn't poisoned."

"I'm sorry."

Andrew shrugged. "I'm used to it," he said. "Doesn't make it easier, though."

Monica smiled. "Thank you for helping him. I really appreciate it."

Andrew nodded and hurried down the stairs, possibly to avoid any further questions that might delay his exit. Monica swallowed and finished the climb, then stood motionless before the door.

Just breathe, she thought.

She stepped inside Joshua Oaken Greene's bedroom and spied him sitting in a homemade wooden chair, one of many pieces he'd built several decades ago. His long, black-and-gray hair was threaded into two tattered braids that fell onto his shoulders like burnt ropes, a tribute to his Cherokee father. He didn't seem to notice her, leaning intently over an oak desk he'd also built. It was a natural extension of his body, firm and dark like ancient timber. At the sound of her footsteps, Joshua turned his boxy head and smiled.

"Little Bear!" he said, his voice high and thin. "What a wonderful surprise!"

"Surprise?" she said. "I told you I was coming."

"You did?" he said. "I didn't know that you were—"

He doubled over in a fit of coughing. Monica knelt beside him and rubbed his back as he hacked into his fist. He cleared his throat with a violent sound and spat into a cup beside him.

"It's a miracle I'm still alive, you know," he muttered. "Not because I'm sick, of course. They tried to give me some new, deadly pill. You can't trust these people, Monica. I looked it up. This thing can kill you."

Wiping his mouth, he rotated back to the desk, dabbed his paintbrush in a small pool of brown acrylic, and began coloring a canvas with wide, sweeping ovals. Monica glanced at it, then said, "The nurse told me you had some toast."

"Mm, hmm," he murmured.

"Have you had anything else? Something more substantial?"

"No. I'm working."

"You're working," she echoed.

"Yes," he said, rinsing the brush in a cup of water.

She glared at him. "Why did you blow up my phone, then?"

"Blow up your *what?*"

She opened her phone and thrust the stream of messages in his face. "Look," she demanded.

Joshua flinched and moved his head away. He swirled the brush in a small circle of peach paint.

"Dad, come on!" she said.

"What?" he whined. "Let me work!"

"Let you work?" she cried. "What about me? What do you think I'm doing all day when I'm not here?"

He lifted his head and scowled. "I thought you moved here to take care of me, to protect me from these—these murderers!"

"I do take care of you," she said, her heart panging. "What about the meals I cook and freeze for you?"

"They take too long to thaw," he said.

"No, they don't! And you need to stop worrying about the doctors. I'm on the phone with them constantly. If they prescribe something, I've told you: trust them and take it. If there's a problem afterward, I'll deal with it."

"I'm sorry," he said, shaking his head, "but I just can't trust them."

She grit her teeth. How was she supposed to deal with this kind of obstinance?

"Dad," she said, "where's the new prescription?"

"Huh?"

"The new pill that—" she paused, unsure how to phrase it, "—that you think can kill you."

"The trash," he declared, lifting his nose proudly. He jerked his thumb toward the tiny bathroom attached to the bedroom. "You can look if you insist."

Monica balled her firsts and stepped into the cramped water closet. She immediately wrinkled her nose. A moldy black ring encircled the toilet bowl like a devil's halo. The translucent shower curtain was flecked with brown and the sink held a dozen or so prescription bottles and an open toothpaste tube. At her feet, the small white garbage bin was filled with tissues and spent toilet paper rolls. A number of faded vials lay in the depths, and she plucked them out and began to read the labels.

"Which one is it, Dad?"

"Don't start, Little Bear," Joshua said, his voice high and whistling again. "I've told you: We can't trust these people. What use do they have keeping an old man like me around? I'm just a bother to them, after all."

"Stop it," she said, her eyes scouring the bottles. "I'm trying to read the label."

"Do you remember that horrible woman they sent last week?" he continued, undeterred. "She stuck me ten times before finding a good vein. Ten times!"

Monica squinted at the label.

Angiotensin-converting enzyme inhibitor.

"Is this for your kidneys?"

"Is what for my kidneys?" he muttered.

Take two times daily with food.

She lowered the bottle and frowned across the room. "You need to take these. If they gave you these, it means your kidneys need help."

"No, no," he said, "I won't do it. I don't trust that medicine."

"You need it."

"No," he repeated, turning back to his desk and scooping up the paintbrush. "It made me horribly sick. It's poisoned, Little Bear. Poisoned, or—or there's something in it, something in it that I'm allergic to."

A pocket of steam was forming in Monica's forehead.

"It's not poisoned," she said. "You just need to take it with food."

"Take it with food? How am I supposed to remember that?"

"I don't know," she said, slamming the bottle on his desk next to the canvas. "Write yourself a note? Or maybe set a reminder on your phone. Have you tried that?"

She let herself sit on the edge of the unmade bed, the sheets reeking of sweat. She could at least give them a wash, she thought. Then she turned back to her father, and the piece of artwork that had his full attention. He was now lightly marking a large oval with accents like flecks of dark chocolate.

"What are you painting, Dad?" she said.

With a slow drag, as if the very words brought him pleasure, he said, "Mama Bear."

Monica wavered on the edge of the mattress, suddenly dizzy. She swallowed and blinked.

"Why?" she said.

Her father smiled at her, mischievous.

"She's coming home soon," he said, his face once again high and proud. "You should be here to greet her. You know how much you mean to her."

Monica bowed, her hands folded between her knees once again. The surging sickness in her belly threatened to overflow like a geyser, and for a moment all she could do was continually swallow to hold it down.

"No, Dad," she whispered. "She's not coming home."

"Really?" he mumbled. "And whose fault is *that?*"

She felt drunk, a wave of dizziness nearly blowing over. She grabbed the back of his chair, her knuckles white, and took a long breath.

"Okay," she sighed. "I'll try to be here."

She gazed weakly over the man's shoulder, past his long salted hair. His hand continued to work, and with perfect precision he added a rosy touch where a woman's cheekbones might be. Then Monica blinked and it was nothing more than a rough canvas stained with smelly paint.

She sighed, turned around, and began stripping the yellowed sheets from her father's bed.

9

Shock Value

"NICE LAPTOP," WILDE SAID.

Monica buckled her seatbelt and opened the device. "Thanks."

"What's the plan?"

"Let's finish our tour," she said. "But don't be offended if I'm working on this most of the time."

"You know we won't have signal most of the time," Wilde said.

She booted the device and the screen glowed. "I know. I won't need it."

"What are you doing, then?"

Monica glanced at him and found him eying her curiously.

"Solving our problem," she said.

They spent the morning and early afternoon traveling the rest of the park, venturing deep into North Carolina along several bumpy, winding dirt roads that turned Monica's stomach. They hit a half dozen stops in Bryson City, Fontana, and the remote outpost known as Twentymile before circling back through Tennessee. By the time they pulled back into headquarters, Monica was smiling broadly for the first time in nearly a week.

"You're back!" Ownby exclaimed as they walked through the door. He was leaning against the pale cinder block walls, a mug of coffee in his hand.

"Afternoon, Mike," Wilde said.

"And you, Christian," Ownby replied. "Monica, how'd it go out there?"

"Good," she said. Then she pointed at her computer and added, "I have some sketches I'd like to show you."

"Sketches?" Ownby said, his eyebrows forming thick arcs. "Let's take a look."

He led the way down the hall to his office. Monica helped herself to the available chair and set her laptop on Ownby's desk.

"Alright, then," Ownby said as he plunked down in his own cushioned seat. "Let's see what we've got."

Monica rotated the device so the screen was facing her boss. "Meet Helpless Henry and Ready Ryan," Monica said.

On the left side of the screen, Helpless Henry sat on the ground, cradling his swollen, red ankle while a tear fell from his cheek. Meanwhile, Ready Ryan was walking by in his hiking boots with good ankle support, a smile on his face and his thumb extended in approval.

Ownby leaned forward, squinting. Then his face fell.

Oh no, she thought.

The Emergency Manager's lips seemed to disappear as if he were sucking them into his mouth in frustration or complete befuddlement. He nodded slowly with a quiet "Hmph."

"What do you think?" Monica asked.

Ownby crossed his arms. "I think I get it," he said. "Show, don't tell, right?"

"Yes. If I learned anything at Grand Canyon, it's that people don't read signs."

"They sure don't," Ownby said, his frown still fixed in place. "But here's the thing: The second one—what was his name?"

"Ready Ryan."

Ownby nodded. "Right. This Ryan fella looks like a jerk. He's just walkin' past this other guy like it's the road to Jericho. You know what I'm saying?"

Monica leaned over the desk to see the image as Ownby saw it. To his credit, he was right. Ryan *was* trekking along with nothing but a stupid grin on his face, all while a very sad Henry sat alone and wounded on the trail.

"So get rid of Henry and focus on Ryan's good behavior?" she asked.

Ownby rubbed his chin, humming softly. Then he shook his head. "No," he said. "Keep Henry. Get rid of Ryan."

Monica frowned. "Get rid of Ryan? He's the one we want people to be like."

Ownby's heavy expression morphed into a smile.

"Yes," he said, "but that doesn't tell our story. I think we've got to make this fella look like the fool he is and give our guests something to think about."

"I get it," Monica said, the picture crystallizing in her mind. "We want them telling each other, 'I don't want to be *that* guy.'"

"Peer pressure," Ownby said, nodding. "I'm all for positivity, but there's something powerful about a negative example. Packs a good dose of shock value. Know what I mean?"

"I know exactly what you mean."

Ownby leaned back and waved at the computer. "Did you draw these?"

Monica smiled nervously. "I did."

"They're very good. It looks like they're animated—you know, in motion. Amazing."

"Thank you. I've always enjoyed making art, and I created a lot of my own materials when I was a teacher."

"Good for you," Ownby said. "So is this it? Or do you have other scenes?"

Monica tapped a key to change images. A new one appeared in which Helpless Henry, soaked in sweat with a scarlet forehead, had fallen on the side of the trail. Below him were red, bold words, "Got enough water?" Ready Ryan had already passed Henry and was sipping from a bottle.

"I'll get rid of Ryan," she said. "What do you think of Henry in this one?"

Again, Ownby was smiling. "I like it, Monica. I really like it."

"Thank you, sir," Monica said. She kept her voice subdued, but she wanted to jump out of her chair with excitement.

Ownby pointed at the screen. "Let's pilot these at our most popular trail-heads," he said. "Send me your designs and we'll get 'em made."

"Sir," Monica said, her lips trembling, "Thank you—"

"Please," Ownby said, waving away the emotional response. "I'm just happy we can make the park a little safer and have some fun doin' it."

"I'll get to work," she said, reaching for the laptop.

Ownby nodded. "How about you spend the rest of the day working with Allison at her desk?"

Monica glanced back to the hallway, then to her boss. "Allison's back?"

Ownby flicked a finger toward the cluster of offices where the law enforcement rangers often worked. "You bet. She came back this mornin', all healed up."

Happiness began to surge through her like a geyser of hot springwater. She tucked the laptop under her arm and she smiled at Ownby, who gazed back at her with a paternal glow.

"Thank you, sir," she said.

He offered a quick nod, his eyes beaming. "You're welcome, Ranger Greene."

Monica turned and rushed down the hall, her feet moving more swiftly than ever. She darted into a large office that was jammed with small desks, filing cabinets, and desktop computers from the Nineties and early Two Thousands. At the far end of the long space, Allison Blaze sat at one of the workstations, her bright red hair pulled into a ponytail that was threaded through a white baseball cap. Monica slipped into the room and crept up behind her.

"Hey," she said.

Blaze twisted in her chair. "Monica!" she exclaimed, and swiftly rose from her chair.

"How are you?" Monica said.

"Oh, I'm fine," Blaze said. She pointed to the jagged black line above her eyebrow. "Check out my souvenir!"

"Wow," Monica said. "I'm so glad you're okay! I still can't believe that tree didn't kill you."

"For a minute I thought it did," Blaze said. "Here, sit down."

She gestured to an empty desk chair, and Monica took it.

"It definitely knocked me out," Blaze continued. "I remember looking at you on the shore, then at the tree. Somehow, I ended up in the river."

"I was terrified it ripped you in half," Monica said.

"Too bad it didn't," Blaze said, grinning. "That would have been an awesome way to go!"

"Allison!" Monica cried.

Blaze shrugged as if the whole episode had been nothing more than a stunt. "What? I would have been a legend. I'm doing better now, though. Still, you shouldn't have jumped in after me like that."

"Why not?"

"It wasn't worth the risk," Blaze said.

"There wasn't any *'it,'*" Monica said, her voice friendly but still correcting. "There was *you,* and that was all I cared about."

Blaze offered her a quick smile. "Thank you," she said. "I mean it. My husband told me to cook you a meal to say thanks, but that's not really my thing."

"Don't worry about it," Monica said.

"How about I buy you a drink?"

Monica shook her head, her eyes getting hot. "No thanks. I don't drink."

Then an idea came to her, and she set the laptop on the desk next to Blaze's topo map. "Maybe," she said, "you can help me with something else."

IN LESS THAN TWO HOURS they were marching back to Ownby's office with a handful of renderings, hoping for his approval. While some of the sketches didn't make the cut, the majority of them did. Ownby only suggested one major change, and Monica and Blaze agreed to it without any pushback: The name had to be changed.

The truth was that Henry wasn't helpless, but foolish. The last thing Monica and the rangers wanted to do was give the impression that he was doomed to his unfortunate situation by nothing more than bad luck. It was his shortsightedness and recklessness that got him where he was, and the viewer needed to see that Henry's choices led to his dangerous and painful circumstances.

In other words, he wasn't helpless.

But what was he?

As they searched for the new name, the team knew that they had to tell an honest story. The character couldn't get off too easy and just sprain an ankle.

Nor could they depict him in the jaws of a hungry bear, sowing seeds of fear, mistrust, and even violence against the mostly-gentle beasts. They had to show what was most likely to happen. Lost, hurt, starving, freezing, or exhausted hikers always ended up stranded, leading to the need for a rescue operation.

So it was Blaze who said with a proud glimmer in her eye, "Stranded Steve!"

Monica raised her hand and the two rangers high-fived, while Ownby nodded as if to bestow his blessing.

They drafted the campaign in full: Stranded Steve would appear at major trailheads in a variety of ghastly situations no reasonable explorer would ever wish on himself or his worst enemy. The meeting adjourned and Monica and Blaze left the Emergency Manager's office.

"Want to come to my place for dinner?" Blaze said. "Travis is grilling pork chops."

At the offer, Monica's heart leapt. She and Blaze had clicked from the beginning, but never spent time together outside work. In fact, it had been nearly six months since she'd relaxed with others her age, and her heart was longing for the safety of friendship.

But Monica felt her phone vibrating, and her head fell. She sighed and laid a hand on her pocket to quiet the trembling device.

"I'd love to," she said. "But I'm caring for my father right now and he's—he's not doing well."

"Well, damn," Blaze said, her face sinking. "We'd love to have you."

"I'd love to come," Monica quickly replied. "Maybe this Friday?"

Blaze nodded. "I'll check with Travis. The offer stands, though."

Monica thanked her again for both the invitation and the outpouring of great ideas. Then, frustration drilling through her guts, she trudged outside, head hanging. She dropped into the car, started it up, and withdrew the phone from her pocket.

Then she gasped.

The texts weren't from her father.

Heard from Mike about the Steve character. Sounds like a great idea. Good job, Greene.

Then a second message appeared:

This is Wilde, by the way.

Monica exhaled, then laughed. Throwing open the door, she flew from her car and rushed back inside.

"Blaze!" she called, nearly falling over as she rushed into the office.

Allison was shoving her laptop into a messenger bag. "Yeah?" she said.

Monica grinned. "Change of plans!"

10

— • —

DINNER

THE BLAZE HOUSEHOLD WAS A SIMPLE RANCH DWELLING tucked in a hollow outside Pigeon Forge. Technically it was a Sevierville address, but the creeping waves of development had swollen the borders of old "Stringtown" and now the two municipalities were almost one and the same.

Following Blaze along the backroads to avoid traffic, Monica pulled into the narrow driveway after her host who parked alongside a colossal fishing boat and trailer hitched to a bulky black Dodge. She stepped out and heard the trickle of water running down the gully alongside the road.

Blaze led the way onto a shallow front step into a prefabricated baby blue house. "You can leave your boots on," she said, holding the door. Monica stepped inside and gently closed the door.

"Travis?" Blaze called.

A voice rang out somewhere beyond the walls: "Out back!"

"He must be getting the grill going already," Blaze said. "Want a beer?"

"No, thanks," Monica said.

"Oh, that's right!" Blaze said. "You don't drink. Would you like anything else?"

"Do you have any tea?"

"Of course," Blaze said, opening the refrigerator and pointing to a half-drunk gallon of dark liquid. "It's locally made, by the way. Not the stuff from chain stores that tastes like medicine."

Blaze handed her a glass.

"Thank you," Monica answered, pouring until the cup was only half full.

"Fill it up, honey," Blaze said. "You're my guest."

The sugar quantity didn't exactly thrill her, but Monica didn't want to be rude and reject the southern delicacy that was sweet tea. In her time out west she'd fallen out of drinking most sweetened beverages, mainly due to the genetic risks she'd inherited from her father. For her, the drink of the day was always water with electrolytes.

Blaze uncapped a beer with a hiss. "You sure you don't want one?" she said, wiping her lips. "No pressure, it's just so good after a long day."

"No, thanks."

Blaze nodded, took another swig, and then said, "Family?"

Monica absorbed the question with a stammer and mumbled, "Yeah, you could say that."

"I hear you," Blaze said. She leaned against the sliding door that led to the back deck. She didn't open it, lingering a moment longer than Monica expected. Then Blaze turned, found Monica's gaze, and locked eyes with her.

"I'll be honest with you," Blaze went on, her voice suddenly heavy. "My father was a worthless drunk. He got mean as the devil when he drank, too, which was all the damned time. That's how I learned to fight men twice my size."

She paused. For a moment Monica couldn't tell if Blaze was actually speaking to her, or to the haunted memory of her old man. Then her focus crystallized and she continued, "What about you? If you don't mind my asking."

"Me? No, I don't mind," Monica said. She leaned against the kitchen countertop, sensing she'd need a little extra support before continuing.

"You don't have to say anything," Blaze continued. "Me, personally, I can't keep my mouth shut and I don't like to waste time pretending to talk when we're not actually, you know, *talking.*"

Monica smiled. She had to hand it to Allison. While the abrupt nature of the conversation was discomforting and dug at pieces of her life that she preferred to keep buried, she couldn't help but respect Blaze's approach to human discourse.

"It all happened a long time ago," Monica said, forming her words slowly. "I haven't seen her in years. I don't know if she's even alive. And even if she is, there's no relationship. No communication, nothing."

Blaze nodded in silence, letting Monica finish unraveling the web of her thoughts. Then she asked, "Who is *she?*"

Monica swallowed. "My mother."

Blaze exhaled and let the acknowledgement sit a moment. Then she stepped forward and laid a hand on Monica's shoulder, giving it a good squeeze. She held the muscle firmly, and Monica knew what she had meant by having the strength to fight men twice her size. The woman had a grip of steel. But its strength wasn't brutal or cruel, instead gently working through layers of tension and defense to reach the softer parts within, the parts of a person that need to be held with the utmost tenderness.

"I'm sorry," Blaze said, rubbing her arm. "I can't imagine what that's been like for you."

"Thanks," Monica whispered.

Blaze softened and a smile crept onto her face. "I don't blame you for keeping your guard up. It's hard to be the new kid. I figure you haven't had much of a chance to, you know, let loose."

"Not really," Monica admitted.

"Come on. Let's see what Travis is cookin'."

Monica smiled. "Sounds good."

They stepped through the sliding door onto the broad porch. The construction was relatively new, as it still smelled of fresh cut lumber and hadn't grayed with years of cold and water. Blaze strolled over to Travis who turned from drenching a pyramid of charcoal with lighter fluid. He was tall and stocky with a luxurious red beard, the kind that a man grows while hiking the Appalachian Trail for six months. He beamed at the sight of his wife and wrapped his arms around her.

"Allie Girl!" he exclaimed. "You hungry for pork chops?"

"You bet I am," Blaze said. She turned back to Monica and added, "You're in for a treat. Travis's pork chops are to die for. He's got an apple cider marinade that tenderizes those babies right up."

"I heard we were havin' company," Travis said, nodding politely to his guest. "I'm Travis."

Monica smiled and extended a hand. "Monica."

Travis removed his grilling glove and slid his nobby, calloused hand into hers with a welcoming shake.

She glanced at the hands, noting their rugged texture. "You a fisherman?" she said. "Or lumberjack?"

He smiled. "Fisherman. I've put these mitts through a lot."

"Do you charter?"

Travis sipped his own bottle and nodded, jerking his head in an easterly direction. "Yes'm. Out on Douglas."

The three of them seated themselves around a patio table in well-cushioned chairs while the coals began to smoke. Travis raised the table's umbrella to shield them from the glowing sun still burning bright in mid-September, then lifted his beverage.

"Before I forget," he said. "How about a toast to the woman who saved my wife's life?"

"Hear, hear!" Blaze cried, raising her own bottle.

Monica wanted to disappear at this sudden show of attention. She lifted the glass of tea, flashed an obligatory smile of gratitude, then took a quick sip.

"Just doing my job," she murmured.

"The heck you were," Travis scoffed. "That was heroic. Plain and simple. You didn't have to do any of that."

Blaze leaned over and laid her head on her husband's shoulder. "Monica was the Emergency Manager at Grand Canyon National Park," she said. "She's got some amazing ideas for us."

"Really!" Travis said, though he didn't sound surprised. "Grand Canyon, eh?"

"Yes," Monica acknowledged.

"You think she's gunnin' for Ownby's job?" Travis said, his face twisting with devilish delight.

Blaze gave his arm a decent smack. "So why'd you leave Grand Canyon?" she said.

"My father," Monica answered.

"To take care of him?"

She nodded.

"That's a big sacrifice. You gave up a major position at a huge national park. Your father's lucky to have you."

"Thanks."

"How's that workin' out, by the way?"

Monica frowned. "Taking care of him?"

Blaze covered her mouth to stifle a burp. "Yeah."

"We're figuring it out. He's convinced the doctors are trying to kill him. He doesn't trust people."

"Neither do I," Blaze replied, shrugging.

On the surface, Monica knew that her father's fears weren't crazy. Many people were untrusting. But there was a reason he had been given the middle name "Oaken" by his father. He was stubborn as a tree. When Monica was a girl, her parents would often take her to visit the Qualla Boundary and their distant relatives would comment openly about how hard-headed Joshua could be.

Monica sighed and sipped her tea, wincing at the hit of sugar. An impulse flashed in her mind, and she quickly rotated in her chair.

"Allison?" she called.

Blaze paused, halfway through the sliding door. "Yes?"

"I was wondering," she said. "Do you have any red wine?"

Blaze smiled. "I sure do."

Monica raised her hand and formed a small pinching symbol with her thumb and forefinger, as if to say, *Just a little.*

Blaze hurried inside and Monica leaned back once more.

Yes, she was new and a relative stranger. Yes, her life was filled with anxiety over her father and regret about the things that happened at Grand Canyon.

But she couldn't live a life ensnared by fear. That was also one of her father's attributes: Paranoia.

Yet rubber bands of tension were pulling at all the muscles in her arms, her forehead and cheeks, and deep in the chambers of her rapidly beating heart. Joshua Greene had shown his daughter how to be afraid throughout her entire life. Yet his words and faith tried to cry out, *Fear not.* It was a torturous contradiction, and she felt its palpable sting up and down her body.

The glass of wine hit the table with a *clink!* and Blaze slipped into her own chair with a crisp bottle of suds.

"Cheers," she said, raising her drink.

Monica took the goblet, swirled the red liquid, and studied it suspiciously. There was probably no worse way to relieve stress than alcohol. But then again, this wasn't just alcohol. It was a glass of wine, a gift from a friend.

She didn't have to be afraid.

So Monica lifted it high, smiled, and tipped it back.

11

— • —

ABRAMS FALLS

WITHIN A FEW DAYS, THE FIRST *STRANDED STEVE* SIGN WAS ready.

Steve would make his first appearances around major waterfalls, illustrated as trapped and drowning underwater with bloated cheeks filled with dwindling oxygen. Above his head was a thought bubble that read, "I thought I was a strong swimmer!"

With a little help from the internet and a few bilingual rangers, Monica printed the message in several different languages in smaller letters at the bottom of the sign. Finally, in bold white letters against a midnight black background, Monica printed a firm warning: "Don't be next!"

The message was stark and grim. There were already a number of park signs with red lettering advising park guests that people had drowned. But the signs were outdated, limited to English, and devoid of any imagery. The picture of Stranded Steve was admittedly upsetting, and several staffers at Headquarters argued that it was in bad taste and would turn visitors away. But Monica stuck to her guns, and in a final review meeting with Ownby and the park superintendent, she reminded everyone of the power of images.

"We're not a Florida theme park," she'd said. "We don't traffic in magic or illusions. Our attractions are real. There are no safety nets, no lap bars, no fences beyond what is absolutely essential. If Stranded Steve scares a family away from Laurel Falls or Ramsey Cascades, then perhaps we did them a great service. It's quite possible they would have been our next rescue op."

Ownby and the park superintendent approved the designs and had them printed on a waterproof composite wood. The next task was to install them, one at a time, at each major waterfall trailhead and destination. Since it had been her idea, the mission was assigned to Monica.

As the sun rose on a Wednesday, Monica loaded up a Park Service truck with one of the signs wrapped in protective plastic, a six-foot wooden post, a post-digger, pickaxe, bolts and hardware, and a leather toolbelt stocked with all the necessary devices to accomplish the work. From there she would drive to Cades Cove and pick up a horse and trailer to assist in transporting the heavy materials to the falls.

"Hey, stranger!" she heard a voice call.

Monica slid a post-digger into the back of the truck, slammed the gate home, and turned. It was Blaze.

"Good morning," she said.

"Want some help?"

"I'd love some," Monica answered. "Does Ownby know?"

Blaze shrugged. "Sort of. He asked me to patrol Cades Cove for illegal parking and make sure visitors aren't getting too close to the wildlife. I figured you and I could team up."

"I like it," Monica said. "Hop in."

After double-checking that all the proper items were safely stowed in the truck bed, Monica started the engine and piloted the vehicle onto Fighting Creek Road, the east-west track that followed the old railroad routes along the Little River toward Cades Cove.

The first Stranded Steve sign had an important job: prevent tragedies at Abrams Falls. The most recent drowning in the park had occurred there. Its waters thundered over a broad ledge into a deep pool that was popular for summertime swimming. While most visitors instinctively kept a respectful distance from the flume, some tempted fate and got too close.

When the rangers reached the entrance to the cove, Monica steered the truck into the gravel parking area of the Cades Cove Riding Stables. A trailer was already waiting for them, loaded with a pair of horses. A wrangler with a tan fedora stood beside and waved as they pulled up.

"You'll be riding Rocket and Peanut today," he said, slipping a sugar cube through the trailer windows for each horse. The treats disappeared into the geldings' great mouths, and the wrangler reached in and ran his fingers through their manes. "Take good care of 'em, will you?"

Monica nodded and laid her hand on the nearest horse's nose, stroking it. "I think they'll be taking care of us," she said with a smile.

Monica heard the clattering of chains as the wrangler lowered the trailer's coupler over the ball hitch and Blaze secured the carriage to the vehicle. The wrangler gave the go-ahead and they pulled out onto the paved loop and began the slow crawl around the cove. With the sun shining bright in her rearview mirror, Monica looked over the valley and smiled.

Cades Cove was a geological marvel. It lay between the Smoky Divide and a series of small mountains to the north, protected and hidden from the outside world like El Dorado. Its people lived a rugged life; the cemeteries alone tell the story of the daily struggle for survival. Next to every adult headstone there seem to be two or three marking the resting places of little children.

It took twenty minutes to reach the Abrams Falls Trailhead on the far end of the loop, as the single-lane path was already packed with creeping cars and trucks filled with eager-eyed tourists. Every visitor to the cove hoped to spot a mother bear with its cubs feeding in the fields. This morning, the only animals in sight were white-tailed deer nibbling grass along the forest edge, chewing peacefully and afraid of nothing.

They pulled to a stop in the gravel parking area and set about preparing the animals and their loads.

A little girl in a bright pink Minnie Mouse t-shirt walked up with her parents. "I like your horse!" she said. "May I pet him?"

"You sure can!" Monica said. "This is Peanut."

The child grinned and caressed the coarse neck fur as Monica draped two saddlebags over the mount. The sign barely fit width-wise in one of them, and she had to bungee it across the horse's flank. In the other bag she placed the grooved handle of the post-digger and strapped its curved blades to the sign with another cord. With Peanut loaded and ready, they turned to Rocket and loaded his bags with the post, pickaxe, and other tools. They wished the little girl and her family a fun, safe day, and set off across the bridge and down the trail.

A wide, heavily-used footpath, the trail enabled the rangers to pass hikers with room to spare. They reached the halfway mark of the trail, Arbutus Ridge, and looked down on the Abrams Creek valley below while taking quick sips of water. It was here that the river ran against the impenetrable fortress of the ridge, then swung south, ran a circular course around the base of the stony rib, and took up its original course all the way on the other side. It formed a perfect horseshoe and both curves of the creek could be viewed from the overlook. Monica smiled, then spurred Peanut down the hill.

They passed several more eager hikers until, after another mile, they made the final climb up a rocky cliffside until the roar of the falls could be heard far below. The horses descended, crossed a feeder stream, and led the rangers to a side path to the iconic falls. Monica dismounted, gave Peanut a sugar cube, and began unloading the saddlebags.

"Where are we putting it?" Blaze said, standing beside the existing sign with a hand on her hip. It's brown surface was inscribed with a firm message of caution:

WARNING
Climbing On Falls is Hazardous

Stay On Constructed Trail
Closely Control Children

Monica rotated, inspecting the triangular trail junction, and pointed to a small patch of dirt. "There, across the way."

Blaze jammed her fist into her hip and stared at the existing sign. "You'd think this would be enough."

Monica laughed as she leaned the new Stranded Steve against a tree.

"You would," she said, grunting with effort. "But you'd be wrong. Notice everything that sign *doesn't* say?"

"Don't do anything stupid?"

"Well, there's that," Monica said. "How about, 'Don't swim near falls.' If it doesn't say not to do it, people will."

Blaze scowled. "People never think the worst will happen to them. It's always someone else."

"Exactly," Monica said, hoisting the post-digger over her shoulder. "Hopefully Steve will show them that tragedy *can* happen to anyone."

Blaze unstrapped the long wooden post that would hold the new sign.

"You know," she said, a hint of attitude spicing her tone, "you sort of just described yourself there."

Monica lifted the post-digger and jabbed it into the ground. Its blades barely pierced the surface. She'd need the pickaxe.

"Yeah?" she teased. "How so?"

"You jumped in the river like you were a superhero," Blaze said, arching her eyebrow playfully. "Didn't you worry that tragedy could happen to you?"

"Hey, I was just trying to save your butt."

Monica readied the pickaxe, but a sudden thought came to her and she lowered it, smiling at her partner.

"You know, I *did* save your life, didn't I?"

Blaze raised an eyebrow. "You did."

Monica thrust the pickaxe at her.

"How about you loosen this dirt for me?"

Blaze shrugged, then quickly redid her ponytail to make sure each ginger strand was tightly secured.

"Okay," she said. "More muscle for me."

She took the pickaxe, and with furious determination, aimed the first strike at the ground.

THEY TOOK TURNS WORKING THE GROUND, and after just a few minutes their foreheads streamed with sweat that dribbled into their eyes and stung like fire. A half an hour of attacking the ground led to a sufficiently loose pile of dirt, and Monica switched to the post-digger.

"How many of these are you planning to install?" Blaze said, sitting near the trail with her arms on her knees.

"You don't want to know," Monica huffed, slamming the tool downward and pulling up small chunks of crumbling rock and orange clay.

"I don't know if this is worth the effort," Blaze said, glaring over at the large pool where the water from Abrams Falls steadily gathered. Monica gave it a quick glance and saw a pair of swimmers in its midst, splashing one another with loud shouts of glee. One was relatively close to shore, but the other had ventured deeper and closer to the chute of thundering water.

"Oh, goodness," Monica said.

"You gonna talk to them?" Blaze said dryly.

"Maybe," Monica said. "Can you take a turn for a minute?"

"Sure," Blaze said. "I'm only sweating like a feral hog down here."

Wiping her face with a bandana, Blaze stood and stepped up to the work site and began driving the digger up and down again, removing bits of rock and soil. Monica turned back to the falls and began walking, sizing up the situation.

In all, there were four families on the shore, perched on rocks and broken tree trunks. There was little room to spread out and enjoy the water's edge, thanks to decades of rocks breaking loose and trees collapsing and crashing down into the river. Still the pool was wide and calm, especially when viewed against the roaring white spectacle of Abrams Falls. Millions of gallons spilled over its edge by the minute, the force of every creek in the Cades Cove drainage filtering to this one point where gravity and inertia exploded into one violent cascade.

What visitors didn't see, but every Smoky Mountains ranger knew, was that all of Abrams' power didn't disappear once it slammed into the pool below. It flowed down into a well of swirling currents no one could see. Hidden in the depths, spinning through a nightmarish wren of emaciated tree branches that had been pounded into the deep, were dark claws that trapped wayward swimmers and drowned them. Under the remarkable beauty lay a remorseless beast that knew nothing of family, dreams, social media, anything else.

"Hey!" Monica called.

The visitors near her turned at the sound of her voice, but the two swimmers, a young couple by the looks of them, either didn't hear her or were ignoring her.

She waved her arms. *"Hey!"*

This got their attention. The young man, closer to the shore, propelled himself around and peered at her.

"What?"

"Don't swim so close to the falls," Monica said. "It's very dangerous."

The man ingested this message for a moment, then turned to his partner, a blonde woman treading water several yards further out. She was still a good fifty feet or so from the bubbling feet of Abrams, but Monica could see that the girl was drifting little by little toward the pulsing base of the falls.

The man turned back to the ranger. "We're good!" he called. "Thanks!"

But Monica shook her head. "Your friend is too close! People have drowned from where she is!"

"She's a good swimmer, lady!" the man yelled. "We'll be fine!"

Monica grit her teeth.

Lady.

"You've got to come closer to the shore! It's for your own safety!"

Again, the young man gave his girl a look, likely one of blatant annoyance, and turned back to shout, "Leave us alone, okay?"

"Yeah!" the girl shouted in a taunt.

The guy laughed, clearly impressed with his girl's way of sticking it to an authority figure.

Frustration burning in her ears, Monica balled her hands into fists and yelled one more time, "Please be safe out there! Don't be the next statistic!"

With that she turned and marched up the short access path until she found Blaze working the post into the newly dug hole. Her face was red and her ranger uniform was soaked through with sweat.

"Thank God you're back," Blaze wheezed. She immediately stumbled backward and leaned on her horse's saddle.

"They didn't listen to me," Monica said.

"Well, that's on them," Blaze said, uncapping a bottle for a drink.

Monica scowled. "I want to feel that way, but I can't. If something happens, it's a tragedy and I'm partly responsible."

Blaze finished a long gulp and swallowed. "When smart people get screwed by bad luck, that's a tragedy. When foolish people do dumb things, that's karma."

"I don't believe in karma," Monica muttered, scooping dirt into the hole around the sign post.

"You know what I mean," Blaze said, waving her hands as if to indicate some balancing of scales. "Fairness. Justice. That's what we're talking about."

"Okay."

"It's not fair for the families when their loved ones do stupid stuff," Blaze continued. "It's wrong that divers have to fish their bodies out of the muck and put themselves at risk. These people—" she said, waving toward the rippling pool, "—are only going to get what's coming to them. Save your grief for those who deserve it, Monica."

"I'm sorry, but that kind of apathy won't get us anywhere," Monica said, packing in the dirt as tightly as possible. "It ignores the danger to our rangers, and I will *not* let something like that happen again."

Once these words were said, Monica realized she'd probably spoken too much. The ensuing silence from Blaze proved it. Monica sighed, sat up on the ground, and wiped her forehead.

"I lost two good men at Grand Canyon," she said. "Husbands. One was a father to three little kids. And why? Because a bunch of college kids thought it'd be fun to kayak the Colorado River and post it on social media."

Blaze's mouth opened as if she were going to answer, but she just listened in silence.

"I feel like there are a thousand things I should have done to prevent that. Little things like clearer warnings and stronger enforcement of the rules. But I didn't, and now those men are dead. Those men reported to me. They were out there on my orders, searching for bodies in Class Five rapids."

She blinked and a tear fell from her eye, but she quickly wiped it away. "I'll be *damned* if something like that happens again, Allison," she said. "That's a tragedy. That's *my* tragedy. And I'm responsible for it."

Monica bowed and massaged the thudding headache that was swelling in her head. She inhaled through her open mouth, feeding her brain oxygen, and then hobbled to her feet.

Blaze continued to stare at her, listening in silence. It was rather unnerving, in fact, how the normally talkative Blaze had suddenly fallen into a zenlike state of—

"It's not your fault," she said at last.

"I disagree."

Blaze shook her head. "There were too many factors. Too many things out of your control."

"I had to knock on those widows' doors, Allison," Monica said. "I was the one who told them their husbands were never coming home."

"I can't imagine," Blaze said.

"Do you know what those men looked like after we pulled them from the river?"

Blaze nodded. "I've had to do that, too."

Monica began to run her hands in and out of one another, as if struggling for warmth. "They—they didn't even look *human* anymore. Their flesh was so pale. Like—like paper."

"It's horrifying," Blaze said. "I know."

"Never again, Allison," Monica said, continuing to shake. "And I wasn't going to do it that day on the Little River when you went in."

"Thank you," Blaze said. She inched across the ground until they were side-by-side, then wrapped her arms around Monica's shoulders and pulled her close for a long, powerful hug.

"I can't keep watching people die, people who didn't do anything wrong," Monica said.

"You won't have to," Blaze whispered, rubbing Monica's back.

The sound of raucous giggling broke the peaceful air, and the two rangers parted. Monica flicked away some fresh tears just as the oncomers appeared. It was the young man and woman, both clearly in their early twenties, dripping wet and wrapped in towels.

"See?" the girl said, sneering proudly. "We're fine."

The guy nodded like a bobble-head and proudly grinned. "We told you so," he proclaimed.

"Good for you," Monica muttered.

The guy reached into his girlfriend's pink backpack and withdrew a candy bar, and peeled back the wrapper. The two scooted past and the girl shot another sassy glance the rangers' way.

"Bye... *Mom,*" she scoffed. Then she grabbed the snack from her boyfriend and gnawed a bite before they disappeared around the corner, their laughter still cackling through the underbrush.

Monica felt a rising lump in her throat. She swallowed, her throat burning.

"Come on," she said. "Let's finish this sign."

12

SNACKS

I T TOOK THE BETTER PART OF AN HOUR TO SECURE THE brightly colored board to the post, level it by packing more dirt into the hole, and pile small stones around the base. Monica smiled in satisfaction and gazed at poor Steve's inundated situation, hoping it would prevent passersby from joining him.

"Thank you for your help," she said, patting Blaze on the shoulder.

Blaze leaned against Rocket, her form somehow filled with swagger after all the labor. She stroked the horse's mane and nodded. "You chose the right partner," she said.

"Oh yeah?"

"Mm-hmm. Wilde would be gassed by now."

Monica laughed and immediately knew it wasn't true. Wilde had a reputation for always volunteering extra hours during the most grueling SAR operations, especially when the target was determined to be off-trail. She would be sure to recruit his help when he was done with his current assignment tracking and relocating bears in the Big Creek area.

They loaded the saddlebags with the tools and post-digger, and after giving each horse an additional sugar cube to reward their patience, they mounted up and spurred the steeds up the trail.

The midday sun hovered high above, cooking the two rangers as they rode back toward the road. Coupled with the heat, the work of erecting the sign made Monica think she could fall asleep right on the horse's back.

"Help me stay awake, Allison," she said. "Tell me a scandalous story from your life."

"My whole existence is a scandal," Blaze quipped, glancing behind her with a sly smile. "And I'm not telling you. That's privileged information."

"I'm sure I could find out. Aren't you from around here?" Monica asked.

For a moment, there was only the clop-clop of the horse's hooves.

"That's what the rumors say," Blaze said. Then she turned around and grinned. "I'm kidding. There're no rumors about me. I don't allow them."

"Oh?"

"How can there be rumors when you tell everyone everything?"

Monica laughed as Peanut followed Rocket around a large group huffing its way up the trail. Each hiker wore an identical neon shirt, indicative of a large family reunion or some kind of youth group trip. The rangers tipped their caps as the children paused to wipe the sweat from their faces and reach out to pet the horses.

"Sure, you're an open book," Monica said, "but that doesn't mean I know your story."

"Fair enough," Blaze said. "If you must know, I'm from Pittman Center."

"Did you always want to be a park ranger?"

"As long as I can remember."

"Why?"

At this, Blaze stretched out an arm toward the river. "Look at this place. Why *not?*"

Monica couldn't agree more. God's creative genius was certainly on display along every inch of the Great Smoky Mountains. But it still didn't answer the core question.

"I'm still wondering why park ranger was your first choice," she said. "There are so many other ways to take it all in. Photographer. Tour guide. One of those vloggers who gets sponsored by all the big brands. But park rangers work harder and probably get paid less than all of those. So why this?"

This inquiry earned her more silence, as Rocket clip-clopped on one step at a time, carrying his burdens without any sound. Then Blaze spoke, her voice drained of its playfulness.

"It's the only thing I know."

"How do you mean," she said.

"I don't know how to explain it," Blaze said. "I've just—I've always loved it out here. I want to care for this place, to tend to it. You know, like a mother tends its babies."

Her words struck Monica right in the ribs, and she immediately pondered them. Blaze's use of the word 'mother' was especially intriguing, and Monica couldn't help but wonder if it was a slip of the tongue. She had noticed that there had been no signs of children at the Blaze household. It certainly wasn't a requirement for a married couple to have children, but Monica wanted to indulge her curiosity and ask Blaze why. Yet they still had two miles and a long car ride to endure, and if Blaze took the matter poorly, there was no way of stuffing the awkwardness away—

"Stop!"

Out of the serene quiet, a sudden noise jarred Monica from her thoughts. Rocket whinnied loudly, rearing up and sending the post-digger flying out of the saddle bag. Peanut did the same, shaking his mane in fury.

"What's wrong?" Monica said.

She leaned forward and soothed the horse, stroking its neck. Peanut continued to stir, shaking and grunting at some disturbance.

"Look," Blaze said, her voice a hushed whisper. She pointed up the trail with one hand while rubbing the neck of her own mount with the other.

She couldn't see at first, as Peanut had sidled to the edge of the trail, obviously perturbed by the other horse's terror. But as Monica spurred him along, she strained her neck to peer down the path.

Then she gasped.

An enormous black bear was right in the middle of the broad dirt track, busily chewing something in its jaws.

And lying between its feet, ripped wide open, was a pink backpack.

YOU'VE GOT TO BE KIDDING ME, Monica thought.

The bear had clearly been there for some time, feasting on the banquet of sugary snacks. Past the massive creature, perhaps twenty or thirty feet down the trail, a small crowd had gathered in an excited clump, watching and snapping photos.

Monica lowered herself from the saddle and stroked Peanut's mane.

"It's okay, big guy," she said, soothing the troubled horse who was still stamping his hooves and snorting. "You're gonna be fine." She reached in her pocket, found a sugar cube, and slipped it into Peanut's mouth. He accepted it gratefully and the treat seemed to calm him for the moment.

They had stopped near the creek along a straightaway of moist dirt. A handful of visitors stood motionless watching the bear and waiting for it to move.

Monica peered at each face. The plucky girl and her shallow boyfriend were nowhere to be found. Monica stepped through the crowd of onlookers, inching closer to the bear. With one enormous paw, it held the pink pack against the ground and pulled at something inside with the other. It lifted its head, revealing the metallic shimmer of food packaging. The bear stuck a claw into the object, and pulled with a sudden ripping noise.

It was a bag of chips.

As if it knew exactly what to do, the bear raised the bag to its mouth and stuck its tongue into the opening. Right away, the loud crunch of snapping snack food filled the air. In less than three seconds the bag fluttered to the ground, emptied of everything but tiny crumbs.

Monica shuddered. How much had it already eaten? Was it willing to approach the onlookers, hungry for more?

"What do we do?" she said, turning to Blaze who was still sitting atop Rocket.

Blaze frowned and crossed her arms. "Dart it," she muttered.

"You think the crowd will be a problem?"

Blaze turned to the side and spat. "To hell with the crowd."

"Okay," Monica said, nervous at the palpable spite in her partner's voice. "We have to do it now, before she bolts."

"She's trying to stock up for the coming cold," Blaze said, her voice low. "Look at her. She's hardly got any good fat on her."

Blaze's scowl hung like an executioner's blade over the crowd as Monica looked back and forth between her and the bear, which had buried its head in the pack to get at something hidden deep within.

"You think she took it from them?" Monica suggested.

"No," Blaze said. "They probably dropped it and ran. Cowards."

"Well, they're gone now." Monica sighed. "Let's just get this over with."

Monica turned back to Peanut and opened the saddlebag. Inside was a standard-issue pistol for all rangers working in the backcountry. It fired tranquilizer darts for the express purpose of sedating a bear that needed to be relocated for its own safety. The same kind of thing was necessary out west when brown bears would stumble upon a poorly-kept campsite or an open trash can. She'd darted plenty of animals during a brief stint at Yellowstone. It was how things worked when man and wild tried to coexist. Man always got his way.

Monica unsnapped the leather protector, withdrew the firearm from its embossed holster, and checked the chamber. A single dart lay within. She rolled it to glance at the label, guaranteeing it was the correct compound, dosage, and date for use.

It was.

She would have loved to simply scare the creature off and be done with it. Scaring bears was a basic skill in the Smokies, practically an essential like starting a fire or filtering water, and all she and Blaze would have to do was make themselves big and loud.

But the bear had already enjoyed a buffet of highly-processed human food, all under the approving eyes of a dozen people, none of whom were acting threatening. It was tasting and enjoying the same kind of treats campers brought when they stayed in the backcountry. This bear would forever crave the potent sugars and starches of modern carbohydrate-rich diets, and it wouldn't be long before the bear, in spite of its own reclusive nature, ended up hurting a human being.

Or killing one.

It had to be removed, and that meant hitting it with the tranq dart as soon as possible. Monica closed her eyes and drew a deep breath. Then she slipped through the crowd.

"Everyone, step back!" she cried, cutting through the din of excited chatter.

The throng of wide-eyed visitors didn't move. A few watchers even shot her annoyed looks. A man's shoulder leapt out of the group and shoved Monica to the side as he jostled for a better view of the feasting bear.

"Ladies and gentlemen," Monica yelled, "I am a National Park Service ranger! This situation is incredibly unsafe and we need to sedate this animal for relocation!"

She raised the pistol and began aiming toward the bear.

Her movement had the intended effect. Around her, faces fell at the sight of the weapon.

"What are you going to do?" a woman said.

"Don't kill it!"

"What is wrong with you!?"

Monica raised her other hand, hoping to calm the crowd before it became a mob.

"This bear has tasted human food," she announced. "If we don't relocate it immediately, this animal will become a danger to everyone in the park, and ultimately to itself."

Believing the matter settled, Monica rotated and extended the pistol toward the bear. It was lying on its side now, pawing at a large brown bag. Brightly colored candy began to tumble out and the bear opened its mouth to begin lapping up in the tasty morsels with its long tongue.

Monica lifted the pistol, the muzzle quivering.

"You better not shoot that bear," someone behind her said.

"I'm not *shooting* it," Monica scowled, turning to face a mustached man. "I'm sedating it. This is just an air pistol, and it's loaded with a single dart that injects the animal with a tranquilizer. Once it's asleep, we can move the bear to a safe location."

"You think my son wants to see someone shoot a bear?" the man said. The hair on his upper lip was shimmering with sweat. Monica felt her muscles seizing as she looked at him, and his steely stare reminded her of a guy who'd tried to take liberties with her in her younger years. She swallowed, steadying her gaze.

"Then tell your son to look away," she said.

Monica turned back to the animal. She lifted the pistol once more and aimed at the bear's haunch, the ideal injection point where the meaty muscles met the top of the hind leg. Assuming a clean hit, she'd have to wait until it was surely down, then hurry in and deliver a second, smaller dose that functioned more as a nerve-suppressant to keep the animal calm, sleepy, and pain-free. Given the size of the behemoth in front of her, though, it could be a few minutes before it felt the full effect—

Suddenly, she felt firm pressure bore into the small of her back, like an enormous metal thumb jammed against her spine. She instantly knew it was a handgun.

"What the hell are you doing?" she said, turning to see the mustached man's face leering behind her.

"Put that down," the man said.

Then she heard the hammer cock.

13

STANDOFF

THIS WASN'T THE FIRST TIME SHE'D HAD A GUN POINTED AT her.

The first was long ago as a child, when she and some of her friends stumbled upon a back alley business arrangement to which they were not welcome. The second was in the halls of her Detroit school when a fifteen year-old threatened to kill her and her colleagues for "ruining his life." He then turned the weapon on himself in a scene that Monica still endured over and over in her nightmares.

The third and most recent time, at least until now, happened outside a grocery store in Arizona. A would-be purse-snatcher waited until she stepped between several parked cars, then sprung from the shadows and knocked her to the ground. With his hand in his jacket pocket, the attacker claimed to have a gun and demanded she give him her purse, wallet, phone, and everything else. Pretending to oblige, Monica reached to the back of her belt and unholstered her own loaded firearm and leveled it at the assailant's head.

So as the thick steel barrel pressed against her on the Abrams Falls Trail, Monica exhaled and said, "You should put that away."

"It's my right," the man said.

"Think about what you're doing."

"I'm protecting that animal," the man said.

"No, you're not. *I'm* protecting that animal by getting it away from all these people. *You* are threatening a law enforcement officer."

She felt the pressure from the barrel lighten.

"As for your son," Monica continued, "use this moment to teach him. Make sure he understands how vulnerable bears are when millions of tourists come through this park, what with their campsites and coolers and destructive habits." She paused and took a breath, continuing to fight the urge to whirl on him and disarm him in an instant. "Trust me," she added, "I'm going to save this bear, but only if you'll put that thing away and let me do my job."

For a moment the muzzle clung to her back. But the force slowly vanished and she turned back to the mustached face and saw it was still glaring at her as if she was somehow an enemy of the very nation the park stood to represent.

"Do the smart thing," she said, her eyes flitting to his hand where the gun still lurked, "and stow that. You're allowed to carry, but drawing with intent to fire is a felony."

"I'm a law-abiding American," the man began, "and I'll draw this weapon whenever and wherever I want—"

A blur of olive green clothing flashed straight toward them. The man barely had time to turn his head before a red-faced Allison Blaze knocked the gun from his hand with one hand and snagged a fistful of his collar with the other. The weapon flew into the weeds and disappeared.

"That's enough!" she snapped.

"Hey!" he hollered, twisting away from her and toward his fallen weapon. "How dare you—"

"How dare *I?*" Blaze thundered. "How dare *you* draw a gun on a park ranger? She's trying to save this bear's life! Are you out of your damned mind?"

Then Blaze unleashed a salvo of curses at him, taking advantage of the full width and breadth of the English language. Every face in the crowd stretched taut with shock. And when she finally paused to catch her heaving breath, Blaze was clutching the man's shirt while her other was tightened into a fist, cocked back and ready to strike.

"Allison," Monica said, laying a hand on Blaze's shoulder.

"No, Monica," Blaze said, panting hard, "this jerk is the reason we have these problems to begin with. How's he ever going to learn if we don't send a proper message?"

"*Allison!* Stand down."

Then Monica heard the bear begin to groan, likely for a sore belly. She squeezed Blaze's arm, as a mother to a daughter. "Stand down," she repeated.

"I'm sick of it," Blaze seethed, refusing to unlock her gaze from the man. "I'm sick of people like *you.*"

"His son is watching."

Blaze narrowed her eyes, the anger fading. With a sharp sneer, she turned, released the man's wrinkled shirt, and marched through the crowd to her horse. The man stumbled backward, then retreated to the bushes to fetch his gun as a pale-faced boy and a rather embarrassed-looking wife watched.

Monica exhaled, the crisis seemingly resolved. She turned to Blaze, who was leaning on Rocket again, scowling at the man with the mustache.

"Cover me while I dart the bear," Monica said.

Allison nodded and Monica stepped into the open. The bear had risen to its feet and was looking around for an exit route.

Monica raised the pistol. The bear walked a slow circle, taking in the onlookers and options.

Then it turned and bolted toward the hillside.

"Now," Blaze said from her place on Rocket. "Do it."

The bear halted a moment, clinging to the steep incline, and glanced back at the watchers. Monica's aim quivered, adrenaline continuing to pump through her arteries. She had to act fast, but she couldn't risk missing the bear and possibly hitting a bystander.

"Do it!" Blaze said.

Monica squeezed the trigger, clenching her fingers until the fluttering pistol bucked in her hand. A puff of compressed air hissed out and evaporated in a tiny cloud. She gasped and squinted toward her target.

The bear sauntered onward, clambering expertly up the slope and through webs of rhododendron and stinging nettle.

Had she missed?

The bear paused and growled, stopping to paw at its side as if a wasp were repeatedly jabbing it. Then it sat down with a grunt. It groaned, looking back and forth as if lost, and then laid down.

She'd hit it.

Monica exhaled, releasing a rush of tension. For a moment she thought she might topple over, dizzy with relief.

Blaze said, "Great shot," and Monica nodded. She shuffled back through the crowd to Peanut's side so she could stow the tranquilizer pistol.

"Alright everyone, it's time to move along!" Blaze shouted, beginning an attempt at crowd control. Still, the stiff-necked throng lingered to peer curiously through the undergrowth at the sleeping bear. Monica leaned against Peanut, caught her breath, then followed Blaze as she crept up the ridge beside the bear. Blaze knelt, inspecting it. She removed a syringe from her pack, and with quick, careful aim, injected the bear with the second dose of sedative.

"Show's over, ya'll!" Blaze hollered again, glaring at the onlookers through the trees.

But the crowd refused to disperse. Monica watched as Blaze stowed the spent needle, looked the bear over, then clambered back down to the trail.

"Show's over," Blaze repeated, frowning at everyone in sight. "She's just fine up there. Move on, now."

This finally seemed to make an impression, and the large congregation began to make its way up the trail. That was, everyone except the mustached man and his family. Arms folded with a scowl firmly affixed to his hairy visage, the man stood erect as if on sentry duty. Was he suspicious that they were going to hurt the bear? Was he just carrying on the role of the great American watchman, overseeing Liberty's natural resources by his own volition? Or was he hoping to come face-to-face with the rangers' supervisor and weave an elaborate, though not entirely false, tale of their wrongdoing?

He held vigil along the trail for nearly two hours, during which Monica radioed for help and kept a close eye on the bear's vital signs. They also bagged the pink backpack and candy for analysis, and steered oncoming hikers away from the noticeable scene upon the slope.

Just as Monica suspected, when the Utility Terrain Vehicle arrived and one of the regional managers was aboard, the man with the mustache stood by and delivered a monologue for the ages, all while Monica, Allison, and two other wildlife rangers labored to care for the bear.

First they blindfolded it, pulling a large black rag around its head and gently affixing the ends with Vecro. They monitored its breathing and heart rate, making sure that the animal was never at risk for side-effects to the sedative. Then they undertook the tricky task of transferring the sleeping creature into the "cradle," a kind of blend between a stretcher and a basket. Finally, inch-by-inch, they maneuvered down the hillside, often sliding over the loose carpet of slick brown leaves, and hoisted the bear onto the vehicle where a set of safety straps awaited to keep it secure for the duration of its relocation.

By the time they finished, the sun was casting a crimson hue over the west end of the park. The regional manager had taken three pages of incident notes and promised to give them due diligence. And with the bear still snoozing in the small payload bed, the UTV sputtered off down the trail, leaving behind two incredibly weary rangers and their equally sleepy horses. When Monica reached into her pocket for a sugar cube to reward Peanut for his patience, her fingers found nothing.

"I'm sorry, big fella," she said, stroking the horse's mane. "I'm all out."

Blaze sighed as she climbed onto Rocket. "You think that guy will be held accountable?"

"I hope so," Monica said, offering little more than a leaden smile. "But I'm more worried about us."

"You mean me," Blaze said, a weak smirk slung between her cheeks.

With the blood orange sun disappearing over Abrams Creek, the pair spurred their horses with quiet whistles. The mighty beasts trotted along the trail, their steps slow and exhausted as ever.

14

— • —

FIGHTING STUPID

O N THE ROAD BACK, NEITHER OF THEM SPOKE.

Plenty had already been said throughout the day, so Monica navigated in silence, trying to enjoy the ride. The quiet gave her time to think. The confrontation with Mr. Mustache had set her ill at ease, a creeping bitterness rising from her tired spirit. There was no chance the man was actually going to shoot her. He'd been an absolute lunatic to pull his weapon, and as a gun owner he had to know the law would not be on his side. But even that knowledge couldn't ease the throbbing tension in her guts.

She piloted the truck around a bend into the darkened Sugarlands valley, the only visible light glowing orange from the visitors center parking lot. As her foot held the pedal and slowed the truck to a crawl, Monica shuddered. What was Ownby going to say about her first day with Stranded Steve? It was quite possible he was going to crush the program immediately. Of course the standoff had had nothing to do with the installation of the sign, but a headache was still a headache, and Monica didn't want to be perceived as the cause of one.

Breathe, she told herself.

She took a tight left turn and parked in a lot cloaked in harrowing shadow. Other than Monica and Blaze's vehicles, only one other was present: Ownby's Jeep.

"The boss is still here," Monica said.

"Of course he is," Blaze muttered.

"You think he got that report from our friend on the trail?"

Blaze nodded. "You bet he did."

Monica took a quiet breath. Something had been stirring in her, something that she didn't want to vocalize. Her relationship with Allison was still fresh, crisp, easily snapped off and broken. Yet a friendship without honesty was no friendship at all. She swallowed again.

"Thank you for backing me up," she said. "That was—No one's ever had my back like that before."

"Hey," Blaze said, staring at Ownby's Jeep, "anytime."

"But here's the thing: You really went off on that guy."

"Of course I did."

"It's just—your temper is something else."

"You noticed?" Blaze said, smiling weakly.

"I'm glad you have the courage to share how you feel," Monica continued. "But sometimes your anger, your words, they can be—extreme."

"Extreme?" Blaze said, shrugging. "You mean I swear a lot. Look, I've been a hotheaded potty mouth my whole life."

Monica laughed softly. "Hey, I swear too, it's just—"

"Well, you *are* the churchy type," Blaze interrupted. "Am I right?"

It was Monica's turn to shrug. "I'm a person of faith, if that's what you mean."

"Religious, judgmental," Blaze said, flashing a mirthless frown. "Got it."

Monica killed the motor and they opened the doors, the hinges creaking in protest.

"It's not just rules and all that," Monica said. "It's a relationship. It's about putting your trust in God, and not in worldly stuff."

Blaze turned and snapped, "I said I got it."

Monica froze. "I didn't mean anything."

But Blaze continued, a wry, matter-of-fact look on her face. "I figured you were a church-goin' girl. Well, I hope you enjoy bein' all perfect and holy all the time."

Then she leapt out of the truck and slammed the door.

Monica's mouth opened, but no words were there. She jammed her hands in her pockets and muttered, "I never said I was perfect."

Blaze ignored her, marching toward her car. She reached the driver's side just as the doors to the Park Headquarters flew open. Ownby stood like a spector in the backlight, his frame nothing but a shadow.

"Y'all come here a minute," he said, then disappeared back inside.

Blaze sighed, threw her keys in the air, caught them, then stuffed the jangling mess back into her pocket.

"If you'd like, I'll go ahead and swear now," Monica said.

It was an olive branch, and for a moment it seemed to work. Blaze glanced at her and the corners of her mouth twitched, as if the comment were pulling at them with invisible strings.

But she donned her scowl again and marched to the HQ doors without a word. Monica sighed and followed after her.

SHE ASSUMED OWNBY WOULD REAM THEM OUT.

She was half right.

Monica crossed her leg and began biting a scab on her knuckle as Ownby leaned over his desk, jabbing his nubby index finger at Allison Blaze. For her part, Blaze took it like a carefree punching bag, unfeeling and without comment. She simply let her palms rest on her thighs and stared back at her boss with a face flatter than pavement.

He wrapped up with some equivocation, mumbling, "I'm glad you had Monica's back, because that fella was certainly out of line right then."

But he immediately returned to berating her for physically and verbally assaulting a park guest, reading from a list of alleged quotes. At the recital of her words, Allison let out a quiet giggle. Ownby's eyes snapped up, narrowing until nothing was visible except the tiny black pupils.

"This isn't funny, Allison," Ownby said.

Blaze shrugged. "Are you done?"

"Get out of my office," he ordered. "Take tomorrow off."

Blaze slapped the arms of her chair and shot out of her seat. "Fine. I could use the rest."

It all occurred so suddenly, and Monica realized that there might be something said on her friend's behalf. She opened her mouth, but like so often occurred for her, the words weren't ready to share. She uttered something guttural, possibly the phrase, "She didn't hurt the guy," but it sounded more like she was choking on a biscuit.

Then Blaze was out the door, her boots thundering over the carpet.

Ownby exhaled, shaking his head. He ran his hands through his dark, thinning hair, and leaned back in his chair.

Monica swallowed, waiting for her turn. Yes, the man in the mustache had been in the wrong. But she felt there had to be an angle to it in which she was at fault and going to be punished. She couldn't afford a suspension. Would Ownby drop such a hefty penalty on her? Or would it be worse? Was this the moment she would be relieved from duty and sent back out west where her ideas and approaches were apparently more tolerable?

Ownby took a toothpick and began digging at his gums. Then he shook his head again.

"This isn't how it was supposed'ta go," he said.

"What do you mean, sir?" Monica said.

He gestured toward the window. "Your Preventative Search and Rescue. The whole point was to stop this kind of foolishness. And look what happened."

"Sir," Monica said, "my signs had nothing to do with the incident with the bear. The two are completely unrelated."

"I know that," Ownby said sharply. He closed his eyes and ran his hand over his face. "I'm sorry," he added, his voice more gentle this time. "Long day."

"It's okay, sir."

"I meant this isn't how it was supposed to go for *you*," he continued. "We haven't had someone with your optimism in quite some time. Look," Ownby said, laying his hands on the table, "today was a long day for all of us. You especially. Why don't you take tomorrow off, get some rest, then come back fresh and install a few more of those signs? From my point of view, it doubles as trail patrol. Just keep an eye out for safety concerns and wildlife issues as you work."

Monica nodded, exhaling slowly, and her thoughts returned to the topic of her PSAR signs. She had hoped to install two today, but only managed one. She was behind. It wasn't just a matter of meeting arbitrary deadlines. In her eyes, every trail that didn't have Stranded Steve there to warn against reckless behavior was a ticking bomb, waiting to explode into more rescue operations that put her and her colleagues at risk.

She instantly shook her head. She couldn't take tomorrow off.

"Thank you, sir," she said. "I appreciate the gesture, but I need to keep working. Our visitors and our staff can't wait any longer. I'll be here."

"Monica," Ownby said, "you don't have to be a hero. I like your Steve character, and I think he'll help a couple people here and there not do somethin' stupid. But folks will still get lost, dehydrated, hungry, exhausted, heat stroke, and so on. It's bound to happen. So take your time. When it comes to fighting stupid, you have to play the long game."

Then he chuckled at his own witticism. Perhaps it was an adage Ownby had picked up over the years, or one he'd coined himself as the overseer of emergency rescue. However, it wasn't a maxim Monica would be adopting.

To her, it wasn't about trying to "fight stupid." It was about teaching and transforming. The perfect way to inoculate the public against stupidity was to boost its intellectual immune system. That was what worked with her vulnerable students in Detroit, and what worked with many hikers out in the west.

It had to work here.

"Thank you for the advice, sir," Monica said. Then she pushed herself up out of her seat. "If you need me, I'll be finishing my work at Abrams tomorrow morning."

Ownby shrugged. "I'm telling you, take a day if you need it. The offer doesn't come often."

Monica nodded. "I know, and thank you."

"You're not going to take it, are you?"

"I can't. Not when there's so much to do."

The emergency manager sighed once more, his hands working on his scalp again. "I suppose. Just remember what I said."

Monica nodded. She'd remember. But she knew it was only a matter of time before she or her friends were put in another life and death situation. With it being hurricane season in the tropics, the next storm could pop up at any time. Stranded Steve wasn't just a bunch of signs; it was the lives of people she cared about.

"Thanks, Mike," she said. "I'll remember."

She excused herself to the hall without waiting for any more of Ownby's cleverness. It was going to be a long drive home under the oppressive, starless cloak of night, and she didn't want to waste any more time on small talk.

Monica turned the corner toward the doors when she heard a phone ring, its mechanical drumroll reverberating in the silent, empty corridors. Ownby's voice answered, the words inaudible.

She pressed on one of the double doors and it refused to budge. Sighing, Monica fumbled with the latch until it swung clear and the barrier gave under her pressure.

"Monica!"

She turned and found Ownby staring at her, breathing heavily.

"What?"

He pointed toward his office.

"The hospital just called. It's your father."

15

—·—

E.R.

T HE AUTOMATIC DOORS SLID OPEN TO LET HER PASS, BUT IF they had been a second slower she might have rammed right through and knocked them off their tracks. She stumbled to a stop before the reception desk.

"Joshua Greene," she blurted.

The receptionist had a phone against her cheek. She held up a finger.

Monica beat her palm on the countertop, then turned to avoid the rising glare from the receptionist. The room was crammed with stiff-backed chairs and sour-faced patients waiting their turn to be seen. In the far corner under a mounted television, a woman bounced a wailing baby on her knee.

"Ma'am?"

Monica whirled. "Joshua Greene, please," she said. "I'm his daughter."

The receptionist nodded and leaned over her desk, the glow of a computer screen reflecting in her eyes. She glanced up at Monica and stood.

"This way."

Monica's heart thundered as a pair of silver security doors emblazoned with "Do Not Enter" insignia swung open.

She jogged through the yawning portal into a bustling hive of gurneys and blue-scrubbed nurses and surgeons. Machines cried out in loud, incessant beeps. Monica scanned the large, crowded space, hoping she might somehow find her father in the chaos, but to her great gratitude, a stocky woman with a mushrooming hair net stepped out of the frenzy, a clipboard in her hand.

"Greene?" she said.

"Yes."

"Follow me. Watch your elbows, we're busy tonight."

The nurse proceeded through the hailstorm of wheelchairs, carts, IV trees, stretchers, and empty hospital beds lined against the walls. Monica tried to make herself small, yet it seemed that objects were coming at her from every direction as the enormous room throbbed with sound.

They rounded a corner into a hallway. It was walled on one side and lined with curtains on the other, a network of rails dictating the boundaries between each patient's space. They passed a half dozen sections of curtain until the nurse stopped at one and pulled it back with a flick of her wrist.

Monica closed her eyes. Could she possibly prepare herself for whatever was awaiting her on the other side? Would he even resemble the man she knew, the man who had bounced her on his knee and sang her his favorite children's songs, ancient melodies bequeathed to him by his Cherokee father? Or would he be a shriveled prune of a thing, drained of the full-blooded vitality with which he approached every task life threw at him?

The withdrawn curtain revealed a single hospital bed, its back slightly inclined. A man lay upon it, his body hidden by drab blue bedsheets and a thin salmon-colored blanket. A face seemed to be where the man's head was, but it was obscured by the thick tentacles of tubes feeding oxygen and medicine to the ailing body. A machine wheezed like a collapsing lung, and with each raspy sigh the man's chest rose just a little under the meager coverings.

Monica stood tall but immobile, her body holding its place like a cracked stone column. Her first reaction had been denial. That *couldn't* be her father. There had been a mistake. The denial seeped down her legs and hardened like cement and she found herself unwilling to move closer, for moving any nearer to the man would enjoin her to confirm the horror.

But it *was* her father. There was no practical reason it shouldn't be. She only had to accept it and rearrange the bricks of her life accordingly. Denying it would achieve nothing. Heck, denial was what had put the man here in the first place. Denial that his kidneys were failing, denial that his blood pressure was an unpredictable carnival ride, denial that his mind was losing its power.

She lifted her leg from the floor and took the few long steps across the partition until she was bedside. She looked upon him and felt her middle collapse.

His eyes were closed, sunk deep in the sockets as if they could jostle loose at any time. The light brown cheeks hung frail and sallow. All she could see of one of his arms were tubes and dark spots marking his flesh. Skin was certainly there, covering the innards, but it was hardly noticeable. Her father had been reduced to a Halloween decoration.

How long had he been like this? Had she not noticed? She knew he had been losing weight, skipping meals to keep painting. All sick people lost weight. Just how much, though, she couldn't guess.

She drew a deep breath again as the full scope of his illness finally came into focus, and suddenly she found she could no longer stand. Her knees hit the floor beside the bed and her forehead tunneled into the sheets just in time to muffle the sobs.

It was only when her joints began to throb in sharp pain that she stood, wobbling like a toddler, and found a corner of the bed to sit on. Just then the curtain withdrew and a thin, dark face appeared.

"Miss Greene?"

Monica stood. "Yes?"

A woman in a white lab coat entered and closed the curtain behind her. "I'm Dr. Watt."

The two shook hands and the new arrival gestured to the spot where Monica had been resting. "Go ahead and sit," she said.

Monica obliged, finding her way back into the narrow spot.

Dr. Watt was a thin, athletic woman with skin the color of fresh coffee. As she sat herself on a small stool several feet from the bed, her thick, natural hair came into view and Monica smiled.

"I like your hair," she said.

"Thank you," Dr. Watt said. "I like my hair, too."

She sat on a stool and leaned back, folding her hands in her lap. "I think you know that your father's health is not very good."

"I figured as much."

Dr. Watt's expression hardened.

"I don't think you realize just how bad it is. His kidneys are barely functional."

Monica bowed. This news was a long time coming, but hearing the words had the effect of a sledgehammer to the gut. "Okay," she said softly.

"Some time last night, between his scheduled physical therapy—which he has refused to attend for the last few days—and this morning, he lost consciousness. One of our nurses came by the house to deliver his medication and found him."

"Thank God," Monica said.

"The good news," Dr. Watt continued, "is that his pulse has remained strong throughout his whole time here. His kidneys may be starting to fail, but his heart is not."

"What about his blood pressure?"

"One-thirty over ninety," the doctor said. "A little high, but safe."

That was a miracle. For all Monica knew, the man subsisted off sodium-laden microwave dinners and fast-food delivery. He had never known how to cook, nor had he gone to the trouble to learn. In Monica's first weeks back in Knoxville, she had labored each night to prepare meals that could be frozen and reheated, like lasagna and casseroles and meatloaf. But when she arrived to check on him, all the meals were still in the freezer, hard as granite.

"Now, about his medication," Dr. Watt said, "he hasn't taken it in over four days."

Monica nodded. "I know. I get on him about it, but he's pretty stubborn."

"Has he shared why?"

She threw a glance at the unconscious man beside her, yards of tubing coiling in and out of his motionless body.

"He doesn't trust doctors," she said, sighing in embarrassment.

Dr. Watt smiled. "That's what he told me."

Monica turned back to her. "He talked to you?"

"Briefly," the doctor said. "After we stabilized him, he was awake for a few seconds. He was... vocal," she said, pausing to select the kindest word possible. "But I gathered that he wasn't very fond of me and my colleagues, even while we were saving his life."

Saving his life.

Monica shuddered.

"So," she said, "what's next for him?"

"We'll keep him here for a few more days to assess the proper course of treatment. I'm guessing you've figured this out, but your father will need dialysis in order to replace the functionality of his kidneys."

"Wait," Monica said. "Are you saying he has no kidney function? Like, *none?*"

She bit her lip, bracing for the worst, and the look on Watt's face confirmed her fear. A sharp pain cut into her stomach.

"I can't definitively say, 'none,'" Dr. Watt answered. "But it might as well be."

Monica's head fell.

"I'm sorry, Miss Greene. If he'd taken his medication, we could have gotten more time. The whole purpose of the prescribed treatment was to assist his endocrine system as it flushed waste out of his body. Instead, it built up to the point of becoming toxic. There is little his kidneys can do on their own at this point."

Monica sighed, her abdomen pulsing, but felt the warmth of a hand on her knee. She looked up.

"Hey," Dr. Watt said. "We'll get through this."

Monica nodded. "Thank you," she whispered.

Still, she wanted to walk away and weep. She'd tried so hard to help her father, yet nothing she did was working. She'd lost count of the number of talks she'd had with him, or the number of times she'd looked up a drug's ingredients to prove it was safe. Despite everything, he had still ended up here.

Monica drew a breath. "When he's released," she said, "how often will he need dialysis?"

Dr. Watt glanced quickly at her clipboard. "It's hard to tell," she said, her voice somewhat stilted. "We'll assess that during his time here and then share a treatment plan with you."

Monica bit her lip, and found Dr. Watt looking back at her with a much softer expression again. It was like she was looking into the face of an old friend.

"I promise we'll get through this," she said. "But I won't lie to you. His kidneys don't have long. Even with dialysis, he'll need a donor."

Monica blinked. "A donor?"

Dr. Watt lowered the clipboard and locked gazes. "Yes, a kidney donor," she said.

"Is there a waitlist?"

"Oh, yes," Dr. Watt said. "A very long one."

Monica shook her head, her mind filling with tension thick like haze. She licked her lips.

"Is there any hope, then?"

Dr. Watt continued to stare at her. "That depends," she said. "Can I ask you a question, Miss Greene?"

Monica shrugged, exhausted. "I guess."

The doctor laid her pen on the clipboard, her eyes narrowing. "Tell me," she said coolly. "What's your blood type?"

16

Papa Bear

H ER FATHER REMAINED UNCONSCIOUS THROUGH THE LONG, lonely night, even as they moved him several floors upstairs to a regular room.

Monica followed at a distance, trailing like a wind-beaten kite behind the entourage of nurses. She nearly missed a turn to another hall and through a set of automatic doors, but one of the nurses, a tall man with a strikingly handsome face, checked for her in time to hold the doors and call her name. She snapped her head up, her mind still lost in a dense fog, and let him guide her through the hard-edged labyrinth until she found herself in a cramped, dark room that reeked with that artificial metallic smell of too much sanitation. She seated herself in the rigid chair, and watched as the staff hooked up all the necessary wires and plugs to keep her father alive just a little longer, and let her head fall against the wall. As they exited, one of them draped a blanket over her. She remembered hoping it was the good-looking one, but was asleep before her eyes could find the strength to reopen and check.

When Monica awoke, the sun was shining its scintillating gold through the parted window curtain. She massaged the side of her face and sat up with a groan. Her back was stiff, rigid with the hours bent at a wildly unnatural angle.

Then a soft voice spoke in the hopeful light.

"Hey, Little Bear."

He was sitting upright, the back of his hospital bed inclined to let him reach the breakfast that had been placed on his bedside table. He smiled and shoveled a dollop of applesauce into his mouth.

"Dad," she said.

"Have you seen the sunrise?"

"Yeah," she said, still groggy. She rubbed her eye socket, loosening the muscles. "It's great."

"What a beautiful morning," he said, his contented smile still set in his face.

"Sure is," she said. "I'm glad you're here to see it."

He spooned another glob of applesauce into his mouth and nodded slowly, his ragged gray locks falling over his shoulders. "I am too, Little Bear."

Monica sighed and rotated herself to face her father full on. "Why do you still call me that?" she said, not hiding her annoyance.

"Because," he said, his tone salty, "you're my little girl. My adventure partner. My *buddy.* How many times did we go out there and have a ball in the wild? A hundred? Two hundred?"

Monica didn't answer, instead squeezing her forehead with her fingers.

He laughed softly and then coughed. "We were so close, Monica. That's why I still call you that."

"I was just a kid," she said.

"Of course you were. Please let me have this, while I have time left. Those were the best moments of my life. Just you and me, sitting beside a warm campfire, telling stories and jokes until we cried laughing." His cheeks spread wide in a boyish grin. "God, what I'd give!"

Monica clenched her teeth together and held back what she wanted to say. Then she scolded, "Why didn't you take your meds, Dad?"

His face fell.

"How could I?" he whined. "You know I can't trust them. That crap could be poisoned for all I know."

"No," Monica said, "the poison was in your freezer, all that frozen food you eat. The medicine was meant to help you get rid of it properly."

"Don't judge me," he pouted. "I'm an adult."

"If you're an adult, why do I have to keep checking up on you? And why, while I'm busy at my job, do the nurses find you half-dead on the floor?"

"I wasn't half-*dead,*" he said, waving a hand toward the door as if he could shoo the hospital staff away somehow. "I was just asleep, deep in a dream with your mom in the old days—"

"Enough!" she screamed.

Suddenly the room was silent, save for the methodical, soulless beeping of her father's heart monitor. He gazed at her, a deepening sadness welling in his eyes, then looked away. Monica could only glare at him, fury bordering on madness flaring within her.

"You can't change the past, Monica," he said softly.

"Don't do this."

He shrugged. "I still love her."

"You're changing the subject."

"No—"

"You're changing the subject because you don't want to tell me the truth about your health."

Her father leaned over the rail of his bed, his eyes bright. "No, Little Bear," he said. "I'm not changing the subject. Your mother is *always* the subject."

She raised a hand, perhaps to say something that wasn't quite ready to be spoken, and balled her fingers in a tight fist.

"Please," she sighed. "I want you to listen to me. Whatever they tell you to do in here, just do it."

Her father's lips quivered, then tightened. "I'll try."

"No," she said. "Don't try, Dad. Do it. Whatever they tell you."

"Monica—"

"If they give you a pill," she continued, "swallow it. If they poke you with a needle, deal with it. If they ask you to get up and run laps around the building, suck it up and do it. You can complain all about it later."

His face melted like ice cream on a July afternoon. "You trust these people?" he whimpered.

"I trust them a whole lot more than I trust you. Don't you understand that everyone here—*everyone*—cares a heck of a lot more about you than you do yourself?"

Her father absorbed this without answering, his chest rising and falling in slow waves.

She swallowed. If he was going to let her talk uninterrupted, then perhaps it was time to drop the hammer.

"Here's the thing, Dad," she said, tossing up her hands. "You're dying."

He stared. She stared back, her eyes burning.

"You're dying, Dad," she repeated. "Did they tell you?"

His eyes fell.

"Yes."

"So you know?"

"They told me," he said, obviously wounded. "That doesn't mean it's true."

"It's true," Monica answered. "Your kidneys are dying. They'll be paperweights soon. *Rocks.* Does that make sense?"

"I'm fine."

"No, you're not!"

Hardly a second passed before the room's door opened with a rattle and a female nurse strutted in, an unwelcome smile pasted on her face.

"Good morning, you two!" she burst.

"Good morning to *you,*" her father said, his expression transforming into a glowing smirk.

Monica watched as the newcomer checked blood pressure, oxygen levels, temperature, and more as her father soaked up the attention like a sponge. Disgust flooded her mouth like battery acid. Crossing her arms, she cast him the most revolted visage possible until the nurse left. The door closed with a click.

"What was that?"

"What?" he said, feigning innocence.

"Maybe we need to limit your medical staff to young, attractive bimbos," she said. "Would you trust *them?*"

"I was being nice," he said. "What is it with you?"

"What is it with me?" she scoffed. "I'll tell you what it is. I moved across the country to take care of you, to make sure you got the care you need. And now that I'm here and I go out of my way to help, you ignore my advice at every turn."

"That's not true, Little Bear—"

"Let me finish," she continued. "So after you throw my help and my advice back in my face, things go wrong. And when they do, and you're in pain and fear, you call me and completely blow up my life, screaming for help. And what do I do? I come running! I always come running for you, because you're *Papa Bear.*"

At this, any remaining strength in his face evaporated until a weathered, wrinkled palette of flesh was all that remained. Monica glanced at him, to see if his huge, wet eyes would be staring at her, ready to offload a heap of guilt. He turned away, staring at the window in silence, the yellow light still shining through the blinds.

Monica swallowed and clenched her fingers into a fist, back out, and in again.

Had her father figured it out? Had he somehow deduced that she, his own daughter, was the only donor available? That her blood type, physical condition, and overall health put her in the position of being the sole individual with the power to make such an important sacrifice?

She sniffed and closed her eyes.

"Please forgive me, Dad," she said.

"No," he rumbled, staring at his lap. "Forgive *me.*"

She wiped her eyes and hurried to him. He put his hands on her back and she felt surprising strength from them, just like he had when she was only a few feet tall. She closed her eyes and buried her head in the crook of his neck. And even though he smelled of something foreign, there was still the distant hint of sweet tobacco and ripe cologne, the two smells by which she knew him best.

"Please don't let me go," he whispered, squeezing her.

Monica exhaled a deep gust, the heaviest breath she'd ever held, and knew it would come back to her soon and hold her prisoner once again.

"I won't," she said.

They sat together for a long time on the thin, hospital mattress, holding one another close. After a few minutes, she couldn't help but notice that her side was nudged up against his, right at the hip where the cold tubes meandered like snakes in and out of the man's fading body.

She inched away, and didn't say a word about them.

17

FORECAST

IT TOOK SOME ASSURANCES, BUT JOSHUA GREENE PROMISED that he would do good by his daughter, and he would do it by listening to his doctors, taking them at their word, and following their instructions.

"Every pill," Monica said.

"Okay."

"Every dietary restriction."

"Monica...."

"You're dying, Dad," she declared. "Your kidneys are failing."

At this he nodded with a ragged sigh.

"Fine. I'll eat whatever cardboard they give me."

"Good."

As she pressed him to agree to the entire list of non-negotiables, Monica chose to keep the possibility of giving him a kidney to herself. It was too emotional a topic, and she needed her father to prove he could be responsible with it. What good would a single healthy kidney be if he refused to eat well, take his medicine, and do what his doctors told him? Trapped in the confines of his toxic endocrine system, the precious organ would wither in only a few months.

So as her father lay back in his bed for a late afternoon nap, Monica decided to head home for a much-needed shower. She steered her car out of the parking garage and saw her phone lighting up. It was Allison.

"Hey, you," Monica answered. "What's going on?"

"The weirdest thing," Blaze answered, her drawl unmistakable. "You know how people post their hiking videos on social media?"

"Sure," she said, finding her way toward the interstate.

"This guy just published a video claiming he's found an abandoned mine in the park. Based on what he says, it's loaded with precious minerals," Blaze continued.

Monica laughed. The idea that a gem mine existed in the Smokies was absurd. Sure, there were a half-dozen tourist traps playing on the idea. And yes, it was true that White settlers had gone rabid when they heard even the slightest rumor that there was gold in the misty Cherokee hills.

But few precious minerals had been found within the park boundary, despite local names like Goldmine Trail or Goldmine Loop. There were no gem mines in the Smokies, period.

"He's full of it," Monica said.

"Apparently not," Blaze said, her voice dry. "He showed the goods in his video."

"The goods?"

"Handfuls of stones," Blaze said. "Gold, diamonds, copper, cobalt. Even an emerald. It seems real enough."

Monica sighed. "I don't know. It sounds suspicious to me.

"Well, suspicious or not, Ownby wants us all at HQ by seven so we can figure out where he filmed this."

"Does he give a hint in the video?"

"Nope. He only said the tropical storm exposed a mine that's been forgotten since before the government bought the park, and he's paying us back by telling everyone that this treasure trove is out there."

Monica shook her head, still wanting to laugh. But she kept it inside this time and simply said, "That's the stupidest thing I've ever heard."

"Exactly," Blaze said. "The guy's a fraud and I can't wait to expose him. But Ownby is worried that the autumn crowds might take him seriously and start looking. He wants a robust response, followed by our own social media campaign."

"Okay, I'll be there," Monica said before hanging up.

Monica navigated the miles back to her apartment in silence, trying to quiet the voices in her head: Blaze and Ownby, and this idiot treasure hunter, and as always, her father.

When she finally arrived at home, she stumbled up the steps and nearly slept walked through her shower, slowly rubbing her bath loofah over her hip. When she finally hit the pillows, she instantly fell into a dreamless sleep.

IT WAS SEVEN O'CLOCK when Monica zoomed up the Gatlinburg Parkway into the national park, and seven-oh-five when she pulled her car into a space beside HQ. She sipped her coffee and hurried into the conference room. Ownby was already there, as were Wilde, Blaze, and several lead rangers who managed various regions and departments across the Smokies. She settled into an empty chair next to Blaze, took a pen from a cup in the middle of the table, and immediately began gnawing on the cap.

"Good morning, everyone," Ownby said. "I know you've all probably seen it, but let's watch the video one more time."

He clicked a button on his laptop. Immediately an online recording began to play.

It was hectic from the start. The camera was handheld, shaking wildly. Clearly the filmmaker had used his phone. Monica looked away on instinct as the violent cinematography sent her stomach spinning right away. Squinting, she opened an eye to continue watching.

"You guys are *not* gonna believe what happened!" the man said, jogging through a poorly-lit tunnel. He wore a medical facemask and a black beanie hat. Only his eyes were visible, and they were dark and hard to discern. "I was hiking in the Smoky Mountains, and found an entrance to an old mine. Check this out: It's wide open!"

The camera panned each direction, but the poor lighting made it nearly impossible to make out any distinct features.

"The tropical storm that just hit triggered a ton of landslides," the guy continued. "That's how I got in. The crazy thing is, you can too! Check out what I found!"

The camera spun and the image shook, as if the holder was about to drop it. Then it went still, focusing on an outstretched hand. Lying in the palm, dusty but still glittering, were an assortment of jewels. Then the picture whirled once more, distant backlight flaring against the lens.

"Would he stop shaking the camera?" Monica muttered, covering her mouth.

"Friggin' kid," Blaze growled.

The frame found the masked face again.

"This is just the beginning," the man said. "If you want a piece of this for yourself, then come out to the Smoky Mountains National Park."

"It's the *Great* Smoky Mountains!" Blaze yelled at the screen.

"Do your research, people," the guy continued in the video. "The truth is out here. Why did the government buy all this land, huh? Why did they dispossess thousands of people?"

Yet again the image churned with terrible violence and Monica felt her throat spasm. The camera settled and zoomed in on the handful of colorful minerals. His voice boomed a final time.

"This can be yours, ya'll," he proclaimed. "Come out and get it."

Ownby tapped his laptop again. The screen went dark, killing the video.

"So there it is," Ownby said. He pressed a button and a map of the Smokies appeared on the wall behind him, its green terrain littered with red dots. "This is a map of all known historic mining operations in the park," he said, pointing at the sea of crimson symbols. "As you can see, there are a lot of them. However, based on what you just saw, this mine is large. It's tall enough for a man to walk in without ducking." He clicked once again and three-fourths of the dots disappeared, leaving four that changed color to green. "That eliminates most contenders, thankfully," he continued. "These four are all that remain when you factor in those criteria."

Blaze leaned over. "You know what I'm gonna do when we catch him?" she whispered.

Monica shook her head.

"Feed him to the wild hogs," Blaze said, grinning.

"Today," Ownby continued, pointing at the green icons, "I want you to investigate each of these sites. As far as the Park Service knows, these mines are all abandoned and off-trail. I don't know if their entrances are buried or blocked, but your GPS should let you know if you're in the right place."

Across the table, Wilde raised his hand.

"Yes, Christian?" Ownby said.

Wilde cleared his throat. "Is there any chance that these mines have entrances that weren't recorded in our files?"

Ownby shook his head. "Highly unlikely. The Park Service's sources are extensive, and many of them are unavailable to the public for safety reasons. Besides, our guy says he found it and walked right in."

At this, Wilde frowned and began to scribble notes.

"Do you think you know where he was when he filmed this?" Ownby said.

Wilde finished his writing, then leaned back with a sigh. "I have a guess."

"Where, then?"

"I don't know where he was, but I know where he *wasn't*."

Monica leaned forward to hear more of Wilde's deduction. Ownby cocked his head and wrinkled his lips. "Huh?" he said.

Wilde shrugged and pointed at the map with his pen. "There's no way he filmed this in our park. It's a hoax."

"A hoax?" Ownby echoed.

"I'm telling you, the guy was never here," Wilde said. "I think he's trying to get internet traffic and be the next big deal."

"What's your evidence for that?" Ownby asked. He pinched his chin, and Monica couldn't tell if he was critical or genuinely curious.

Wilde smiled, running his fingers through his lengthy beard. "It doesn't look like a mine to me. It looks like he found some place that resembles a mine and decided to pull an elaborate stunt. He's not here."

The boss crossed his arms. Monica bit deep into the pen cap.

"You might be right," Ownby said. "We all know how often you are. But I can't just dismiss this out of hand. We have to respond. Let's cover our bases."

Now it was Blaze's turn to raise her hand. Monica glanced at her with a smirk as Ownby said, "Yes, Allison?" his voice tinged with slight annoyance.

"We're not filming this, are we?" she asked.

Ownby laughed. "Goodness, no. As far as the general public knows, these mines don't exist and I'd like to keep it that way."

Blaze smacked her tongue against her teeth. "Then how will we prove anything?"

"We'll hold a press conference. I expect all of you to be there," Ownby said. "I know it's dull, but the last thing we want to do is be vague. This video is a trail of breadcrumbs, and who knows how many would-be adventurers are out there willing to look for it."

"We're going to hold a press conference," Blaze sneered. "That's all?"

"Yes, Allison," Ownby said. "That's all."

Clearly the water was not completely under the bridge between them. Monica shifted in her seat, swallowing nervously. Blaze continued to stare Ownby in the face.

"Wow," she said, not at all impressed. "That'll be—that'll be *awesome.*"

"I don't know what else you expect," Ownby said. "We'll do the best we can and hope the world doesn't lose its damned mind in the process."

He tapped his computer once more, and the map of the Smokies vanished. In its place, the entire eastern coast of the United States appeared.

"One more thing," Ownby added. "This is today's radar."

An enormous coil of clouds swirled over the blue waters of the Atlantic, veering toward North Carolina.

"Oh, come on," Blaze said.

"That's right," Ownby said, his voice heavy. "Another tropical storm is headed our way. This is just a projection, of course. The storm could do any number of things, and hopefully the worst we'll see is some rain. But if it *does* come this way, we need to be prepared."

"When's it going to get here?" Monica asked without raising her hand.

Ownby squinted at the screen, peering through his reading glasses. "Two, three days," he said. "Again, that's just the forecast. It could be longer, shorter, or not at all. But we need to be ready."

"Of all the times for this jerk to go viral," Blaze grumbled. "Couldn't he wait until hurricane season is over?"

"We would all love that, Allison," Ownby said. "But we don't get to choose our crazies. And you're right to call it a hurricane. This one's already a Category

2, and it could reach Cat 4 by the time it makes landfall. It'll never maintain that strength all the way here, but it could still get nasty."

"Great," Blaze sighed.

Ownby ended his presentation and turned on the conference room lights. "Let's get out there and put an end to this 'Treasure Hunter' nonsense so we can focus on storm prep. Wilde, I want you to review the likely mine sites and assign teams. Blaze, do what he tells you."

"I will," she said, turning to Monica with a smile.

But Monica was raising her hand. At the mention of the coming storm, her heart jumped as a deep panic began to rise. "Sir?" she said.

"I know what you're going to ask," Ownby said. He shook his head. "I'm sorry, but I need you on this."

"What if Wilde is right and it's just a hoax?" Monica said. "Then this is just an enormous waste of our time, especially with a potential disaster on the way."

"Maybe, but how much worse will the disaster be if there are a hundred treasure hunters out there when the storm hits?" Ownby said. "How many tragedies will that cause?"

"Come on, Mike," she said. "Could people really be that foolish?"

Ownby's eyebrows leapt to the top of his forehead. "When did *you* get so rosy on the common sense of mankind, Greene?"

With a teasing smirk, he handed Wilde a stack of papers and topographical maps.

"Wilde is in command, followed by expedition leaders," Ownby declared. "Follow their orders, locate these mine sites, and get answers."

Then, with a paternal glance at Monica, he added, "*Then* you can get back to Stranded Steve."

18

— · —

ROAD TO NOWHERE

"FOLLOW ME," WILDE SAID.

He marched out of the conference room and the rangers trailed after. Monica leapt into motion, trying to match his swift pace.

"Hey," she said. "You said yourself this is a hoax. Please let me out of this."

"That's not my decision," he answered.

"You heard what Ownby said," she continued. "A hurricane is coming. We need preventive measures in place at every major trailhead, campground, and entrance to the park."

"Yes, we do," he said, pushing the door to the parking lot open and holding it for the train of staff behind him. "We need to figure out what this 'Treasure Hunter' guy is doing, and stop him. Then we prepare for the storm."

Monica shook her head. "Could Ownby be wrong, though?"

Wilde turned to her, a frustrated glare sunk deep into his face. "Just follow the orders. I hope I can count on you for that today."

Monica narrowed her eyes. "Of course you can count on me," she said. "Don't question my professionalism."

Then, to her surprise, Wilde smiled. She couldn't remember if she'd seen his sullen face ever do such a thing. And yet somehow she'd gotten it out of him, and at this moment of all times. Was he mocking her?

"What?" she asked accusingly.

"Nothing. I like your spirit, Greene," he said.

She instantly found the comment annoying. Now wasn't the time for this. Thankfully there wasn't time for more chitchat as the last of the rangers filed into the parking lot and assembled near a row of Park Service vehicles. Wilde tossed another quick glance Monica's way and strode with powerful steps across the lot into the midst of the men and women.

"Four teams," Wilde announced. "Rangers Blaze, Curtis, Shields, and I will lead." He held up the stack of papers and maps he'd been handed by Ownby.

"These are the alleged locations of four mine sites that are considered closed, buried, or possibly lost to history. Apparently this joker found one."

He handed one set of documents to Allison. "Blaze, take three rangers with you to the Cane Creek drainage and move to those coordinates. There's an old gold and copper mine near the riverbed."

Blaze nodded and immediately tapped the closest three teammates to begin reviewing their assignment.

"Ranger Curtis," Wilde announced.

A short, solidly built fellow with short blond hair stepped forward and took the next set of papers.

"Balsam Mountain," Wilde said. "Approximately five hundred feet below the current campground, there is an entrance to a very old mine. Pre-Civil War, according to our Cherokee sources."

Adam Curtis nodded, stepped away and began reviewing the map with his own team.

"Shields," Wilde said.

Krista Shields appeared out of the crowd, a woman of significant height.

Wilde handed her a packet of documents. "This is a long shot, but there are still credible records of Perry Schultz's gold mine on Greenbrier Pinnacle. Exact coordinates are unknown, so you'll have to sweep these proposed areas."

"Yes, sir," Shields said.

Finally, Wilde turned to Monica. "That leaves you and me."

Monica didn't smile. "Lucky me."

He glanced at her, a quick shift of the eyes, but returned his stare to the folded map in front of him. "We're taking the Road to Nowhere."

"Nowhere?"

Wilde smiled again. "Forney Creek, actually. But to get there, we'll have to take the Road to Nowhere."

He tapped two remaining rangers on the shoulder, said, "You're with me, too," and then turned to face the loosely gathered teams.

"I want regular check-ins every fifteen minutes. Do not lose sight of one another. And remember: No one is out there waiting to be rescued. This is just a treasure hunt. Do not take any unnecessary risks."

The teams climbed into the park vehicles and rolled out. Wilde watched them go one at a time, then motioned toward one of the remaining trucks.

"Greene, you're the praying type, right?" he said.

"Yes," she said, unsure where he was going with the question.

"Go ahead and whisper one for us," he said. "I don't want anything to go wrong."

She climbed into the passenger seat next to him. Wilde put the truck in gear, hit the gas, and sped out of the parking lot.

Monica, meanwhile, bowed her head.

THEY CLIMBED HIGHWAY 441 TO THE TOP OF THE MOUNTAIN, then coasted down the other side where Cherokee and Bryson City were waiting for them. As they traveled, Wilde explained the route they would take down Lakeview Drive, and then cover the rest of the way by UTV.

The Road to Nowhere was a six mile strip of winding pavement that terminated at the entrance to an abandoned, graffiti-stained tunnel. After the creation of Fontana Lake during World War II, the National Park promised to build a road across the north shore of the new lake, enabling displaced residents to visit their ancestral lands and the final resting places of their deceased loved ones.

Yet the project hit a fatal snag when the blasting of ancient Anakeesta sandstone began releasing toxic chemicals into the water. Dead fish bobbed to the surface of the creeks leading down to Fontana, while plantlife wilted in the path of the poisonous runoff. The Park Service realized how devastating the project would be to the environment, as thousands of tons of rock would have to be blown open to make room for the road, turnoffs, service areas, and more. Added to this were the challenges of building a highway through the uneven, remote wilderness. The costs began to far outweigh the benefits, and by the early Seventies the project was abandoned. The displaced residents were furious.

Monica felt the bumpy road rattling beneath her as the roar of distant engines echoed off the exposed stone walls. Wilde cleared his throat in disgust and rolled his window down. A cluster of sports cars, the kind that kids buy and soup up on their own, were parked by the pylons blocking access to the tunnel. Their drivers stood in a huddle, laughing loudly and dragging on vape pens. Wilde glared at them, flared the truck's emergency flashers, and blasted the siren with a quick, jolting chirp. The kids startled and immediately rushed into their vehicles. The cars screamed to life and tore down the road, disappearing with a screech.

"I wish we'd post a ranger station here," Wilde said. "This place is a mess."

"Why don't we?" Monica asked.

"Money," Wilde said with a sigh. "Always, money."

He pulled off the road onto the grass, then killed the motor. He threw open the door. "Greene, can you help Mullens and Metcalf with the UTV?"

Monica leapt out of the vehicle and circled back to the trailer where a thick-wheeled Utility Terrain Vehicle sat. The two other rangers on their team followed and started loosening the straps securing the UTV to the large flatbed. Ashlyn Mullens was a tall woman with short blonde hair, the tips dipped in bright orange. As she bent to jerk one of the straps loose, the sun caught the colorful crop and made it look like a flickering fire. The other ranger, a man in his mid-twenties named Dylan Metcalf, ducked under the front of the four-wheeler and removed a large silver hook and chain. He coiled the links around his muscular arms and laid the loop on the floor of the trailer.

"What can I do?" Monica asked.

Mullens looked up, her hair glimmering, and shrugged. "We're good," she said. "Want to drive?"

Not particularly, Monica wanted to say.

Perhaps sensing Monica's reluctance, Mullens jerked her head toward the captain's chair. "Go ahead, it's fun."

"Yeah," Metcalf added, leaning against the passenger's side. "We'd love to see how you handle it. Wilde's driving lives up to his name."

Monica laughed. "Okay," she said.

"I heard that," Wilde called, his head stuffed into the truck. He emerged with a load of backpacks on his arm. "She can drive, but I call shotgun."

Monica slipped into the pilot's chair, twisted the key, and carefully backed down the ramp. When she hit the ground, Mullens and Metcalf raised the trailer ramp and climbed into the back row. Wilde threw the packs into the back cargo area.

"Ready?" Monica said.

"I'm in," Wilde announced, sliding in beside her. "Let's go."

Monica hit the gas and the UTV shot into motion toward the abandoned tunnel. Immediately the harsh neon stains of graffiti met her gaze. On one hand, some of it was rather artful, a few pieces even beautiful. But much of it was profane, crude, and self-serving, the kind found on overpasses and truckstop bathrooms.

"You're right," she said to Wilde. "We do need a presence out here."

He nodded and said, "Headlights."

Monica burned the blinding halogens just as they rumbled into the tunnel. The lights illuminated a family in the midst of the long chute, the children running about. The parents quickly gathered the little ones in their arms and stood to the side as the UTV lumbered past, the roar of the engine deafening as it reverberated against the curved tunnel walls. With the pedestrians safely behind, Monica opened the throttle. It seemed like they had hardly entered the long, dripping tube before the blinding horizon rushed up to meet them and they shot into the open under the green canopy of forest.

The old highway continued for about two hundred yards. Then, as if one could visualize the moment the crews realized the true scope of the challenge, the two-lane passageway of cracked asphalt funneled into a narrow dirt path, just like so many other Smoky Mountains trails. Monica slowed their pace to navigate the twists and turns as the path clung to the side of the mountains. Wilde held his phone in his lap, glancing occasionally at a topographical map with a blue dot which was inching along like a tortoise. Monica glanced at it, then returned her eyes to the road. It grew more rugged and the vehicle's tires thundered over old roots and timeless boulders exposed by erosion.

They continued along the meandering path until a trail junction appeared, the unmistakable brown rectangle of a Smoky Mountains trail sign smiling at them in the distance.

"Keep to the right," Wilde said.

Monica steered the UTV toward the desired path and continued their journey north, deeper into the valley cut by Forney Creek. It was a beautiful river and it had caught the eye of early settlers, including miners. While all the mines along Fontana's north shore were closed and sealed off, there were a few that the Park Service hadn't taken notice of in decades, mostly because they were so far off the beaten path that hardly anyone knew of their existence. One of them, known only as "Slab Camp Mine," was a confirmed worksite from the late 1800s. However, it closed when the financier went out of business, likely due to poor prospects.

They turned off the meandering Lakeshore Trail onto a narrow path that skirted the Whiteoak Branch. The going was relatively slow as Monica took care to navigate each obstacle and not sicken her crew or damage the UTV. When they came to the titular creek, its foaming waters feeding the main creek, Monica turned to Wilde, who seemed to expect her hesitance.

"We'll be fine," he said, then nodded to the rushing stream. "Take us in."

Keeping her foot on the brake pedal, Monica steered the UTV into the creek with a pair of great splashes that sprayed their faces. The tires, pocketed with deep ravines of tread, grabbed hold of the bottom and pulled. A few inches at a time, Monica powered them through the hissing water as the UTV wobbled over boulders below them. Then she hit the gas and the vehicle responded by climbing up and out of the creek, its engine still muttering proudly.

"Good work, Ranger," Wilde said. "Not far from here."

They forged ahead, even passing a pair of hikers and pausing to check in on their preparation and conditioning. It wasn't long before they rumbled through another trail junction.

Wilde kept his eyes forward. "Just ahead," he said.

A few more curves brought them to the union of Forney Creek and another feeder stream, its white water cascading down the thin crevice between two towering mountains high above.

"Here," Wilde said.

Monica pulled the UTV to a stop and looked at Forney. It was a deep, rushing torrent. Could the off-road vehicle manage it?

Yet Wilde seemed to answer that question by unbuckling himself and leaping out, his boots hitting the ground with a loud thud. "Gear up, ya'll," he ordered.

Monica took another look at the waterway before them. Brown, bottomless water rushed from right to left, hurrying down the mountain with all speed and force. She watched it for nearly a minute, and the sound of Wilde and the others removing gear from the back of the UTV faded into the loud whisper of the wild. Her eyes stared into the glimmering pool, and suddenly she blinked and saw a horrible sight.

"No!" she gasped.

Her eyes beheld Blaze standing on a rock, just as a colossal tree was about to crush her. Monica nearly screamed, rubbed her eyes, and looked again.

The waters were crystalline and innocent, simply hurrying on their thoughtless way. No one was in their midst.

Monica exhaled slowly, her stomach churning.

"Hey, Greene!" Wilde shouted.

Monica turned to him, already exhausted with this whole operation.

"What?" she said.

"If you ever want to get back to PSAR," he said, "let's get going."

She turned off the UTV's motor and let go of the steering wheel.

It was time to get in the water again.

19

TREASURE HUNTER

MONICA SECURED HER CHINSTRAP, FIRMLY ATTACHING THE bright yellow helmet to her head.

Wilde had already stepped into the creek, its gentle waters reflecting the emerald treetops and azure sky. It was quite serene, given the impending forecast of doom brought about by the coming storm, and Monica couldn't help but sigh as she lowered her own boot into the cool waters.

Monica sank to her thighs and studied the creek bed, its bottom littered with boulders, their smooth brown surfaces poor places to rest one's weight. She swept around them, aiming for soft mud or hard limestone, then paused to look upstream.

The sun emerged through the trees in thin, radiant slices of halcyon, and a soothing breeze whistled through the air. The first hints of orange were beginning to show in the foliage, and when the leaves shuddered their colors exploded like a bushel of peaches and apricots. The trees held firm and not a sound could be heard except the melodies of rose-breasted grosbeaks and winter wrens perched upon the boughs above. Nothing here warned of tragedy. Could she afford to take a deep breath and relax, even on a frustrating mission like this?

Monica exhaled again and closed her eyes. How wonderful it would be to let go for a moment, to let the crushing beauty of God's splendor and creation wash over her, cleanse her, and make her new. To baptize her in sun and river and color. To shut her mind to the suffering of the world without worrying about it, if even for an hour or two.

"Look alive, Greene," Wilde called from the far shore. Monica turned back and found her fellow rangers climbing the narrow bank, the edges choked with rhododendron and dogwood. She grabbed an outstretched hand and climbed onto solid ground.

They stood at the corner of two creeks on a tiny plot barely large enough for their four bodies to cram together side-by-side. The Slab Camp Branch gurgled along a thin, cramped crevice into Forney Creek. Peering through the thick overgrowth, Monica squinted up the narrow path carved by the Slab Camp. How could this be the site of anything accessible by humans? The stream cascaded down stairsteps of moss-smeared rocks under the diagonal, zigzagging carcasses of dead trees. One could barely follow the white waters more than twenty feet before any signs of them vanished into the shadowy murk of the holler.

"This way," Wilde said.

"Have you been here before?" Monica asked.

"No."

Then he stepped into the splashing belly of the Slab Camp, the waters spattering his legs, and launched himself upstream around a densely snarled rhodo bush.

"You're kidding," Monica scoffed.

"Just stay close to me," Wilde said. "I can see the path."

"What path?"

Wilde ignored her, flattening his body against a boulder abutting the stream and shimmying alongside it.

Ashlyn Mullens shook her brightly colored head. "I don't see it either," she said.

Monica shrugged as if to say, *I think he's crazy, too,* and turned back to the gilded aura of Forney Creek. She wanted nothing more than to return to its middle, find a suitable stone to sit upon, and to take a moment to soak in all this beauty. But the mission was calling.

Monica turned and followed Wilde's creative footing, ascending into the claustrophobic nettles.

THERE WAS NO PATH.

There wasn't even a manway, an abandoned trace from decades past. There were only roots, boulders, unyielding debris, and unforgiving branches stronger than a football team pushing back in one's face. Monica had hardly taken ten steps before the first thorn raked her cheek. She touched the spot and her hand came away bloody.

"Watch yourself, Greene," Mullens said.

"I am," she replied.

Wilde continued to lead the way, cutting through the suffocating foliage. After ten minutes, they could no longer see or hear the creek below. They might as well have been in the jungles of Brazil, plumbing the depths for El Dorado.

Broad leaves smeared their faces while enormous spiders guarded the way with their muscled white webs. Wilde brushed them all away without a second look, but Monica couldn't help but swat at them to make sure they were clear. The uphill grade steepened until she could only cling to vines so she wouldn't tumble backward. Her boots barely clung to the narrow shelf of earth, its severe angle threatening to dump her into the rocky stream below. Monica propelled herself upward, trying to climb with one arm while holding elastic azalea bushes to the side so they wouldn't swing back like a paddle and strike the ranger behind her. Thorns covered the slope like knives, their blades more than an inch long. They easily found weak spots in the stitching of her pants, sinking their points into her flesh. One of them found its way into Monica's calf and she shrieked in pain.

Following the back of Wilde's boots in the blinding foliage, Monica clambered up an eroded lip of wet rock and suddenly found her feet on flat ground. Gasping in relief, she straightened up and stretched her back. They had come to a hollow barrel of valley where the stream spread into a narrow pool. Monica peered at her surroundings until her gaze settled on the north wall of rock, its sheer face worn down by eons of trickling water. She turned and saw Wilde looking in the same direction.

"There," he said.

"I think you're right."

The rock face was cut as if by a giant's ax from top to bottom, revealing a dark space within. She fell in step beside her fellow ranger and waded through the shallow, cool creek toward the distant cliff.

"How'd you find the way through all that?" she asked. "I couldn't see any sign of a path."

"You have to know what to look for," he said. "I was trained to find POWs in the caves of Afghanistan. Believe me: Finding this old mining route was a hell of a lot easier than tracking terrorists through the desert."

Monica considered the stark difference and simply nodded. For all her years in the Detroit school system, and the many days and weeks she *felt* like it was war, she hadn't actually served in the armed forces.

"What branch were you?" she asked.

Wilde stepped out of the waters onto a small patch of pebbled sand.

"Army," he said softly. "Ranger corp."

Rangers.

No wonder Wilde didn't seem phased by the challenge. Rangers, *Army* Rangers, had a different definition of pain and suffering than the rest of the human race.

Wilde stepped into the shadowed gap between rock walls. The surface was covered with old leaves and little else. Wilde crouched and traced a faint, footlike shape on the ground.

"Boot," he said.

"You think it's our treasure hunter?" Monica asked.

"Couldn't say," Wilde answered. "Lots of hikers go off-trail, especially locals. This could be anybody."

He glared into the gloom of the narrow pass, then stepped into it with cautious steps. The ground was level at first but quickly angled up as the accumulated dirt and runoff from above rose to form a slippery ramp. As the thin chasm climbed it emerged upon the gray rock buttress topped with loose soil. Fraser magnolias clung to the stones, their roots spreading like a hundred snakes squeezing life out of the primordial granite.

Monica crept up beside Wilde. "See anything?"

He pointed once more and she peered into the understory. Beneath the mess of leaves, the dull, speckled red of rusted metal lay silent and forgotten. Monica leaned out and ran her finger along its eroded surface.

"Rail," she said. "From the mine?"

Wilde nodded. "Probably."

Monica stood and bent her neck to behold an incredible spectacle. A broad wall of stone rose like a skyscraper, its innards exposed after centuries of erosion like a freshly cut cake.

Monica leaned forward on all fours and scrambled up the slope behind Wilde. As they approached the wall it rose higher and higher like an ancient ruin filled with archeological treasures, booby-traps, and sarcophagi. Wilde crested a half-buried boulder rising out of the dirt like a shark fin, and leaned against it.

"I found the entrance," he said.

Monica scrambled along the sheer surface, her lungs burning. She could barely see over the newly grown shoots rising green and lush from the mounds of earth, but it didn't take long to spy exactly what Wilde had found.

A black teardrop lay at the base of an endless crack in the wall, the rocks broken open and propped up by pitiful, rotting timbers. Even as she stood fifty yards away, an icy wind nipped at her cheeks, bringing with it a musty, sour smell that reeked of decay and ancient damp. Monica wrinkled her nose and turned to Wilde.

"We're not going in there, are we?"

He glared at the entrance with skeptical eyes. "Not for long," he muttered. "And not far."

Mullens and Metcalf ran up from behind, both gasping. "Is that it?" Metcalf wheezed.

"Yeah," Monica said.

"I can smell it from here," Mullens said, waving her hand in front of her face.

"Me, too," Metcalf said. "Still, I can't believe it's actually here!"

"Let's be careful," Wilde said. "No need getting hurt just because some guy has a social media account."

With that, the four of them crawled the remaining distance, as if in homage to some heathen god waiting for them in its temple.

THE MOUTH OF THE MINE was a jet black portal to a world of demons and darkness. Monica instantly wanted nothing to do with it.

It was clear that it had been recently exposed after years of burial, just as the Treasure Hunter had said. The timbers, while rotting, were surprisingly well preserved. Their exteriors were dotted and smeared with the kind of multi-colored mold that grew in dark, moist seams far out of the sun's sight. Clearly these beams had been hidden away, providing the perfect narrow channel for trickling runoff from the quarry above. Whatever mounds of earth had covered them were all gone now, and the wooden planks remained jammed awkwardly in place as if the operation were still up and running.

Wilde, too, was studying the black maw, a grim frown on his face. His beard seemed to hang lower than usual, its golden hue graying as he stood before the mouth of the cavern. He leaned into his radio.

"HQ, this is Wilde," he said. "We've found the site."

The radio was silent for a moment, then Ownby's twanging voice cut through in a blaze of static. "Any sign of our guy?"

Wilde squatted again, inspecting the ground. "No prints," he said.

"Any way to seal it off?"

"We have caution tape. That's all."

"Do it," Ownby said. "Can you see anything inside?"

"We haven't gone inside, sir."

"Why not?" Ownby said.

Wilde glanced up at Monica, then at Metcalf and Mullens. "It's not safe."

"That's fine," Ownby said. "You think it's what our Treasure Hunter found?"

Wilde turned and scowled into the abyss. His eyes narrowed, and Monica instinctively followed his gaze.

"Can't say for sure. Were there wooden beams propping up the cave entrance in the video?" Wilde asked.

Mullens stood and removed her phone from her pocket. "I'll check it."

The radio crackled, then Ownby said, "He was inside the whole time. He didn't show the entrance."

"Not from the outside," Wilde said. "But he panned around. There was light in the background for a second."

The radio crackled. "What?" Ownby said. "Can you repeat that?"

Wilde sighed, bowing his head in annoyance. Mullens, meanwhile, was leaning over her phone, her face twisted in investigative intensity.

"The guy panned his phone," Wilde repeated. "We saw the light from the entrance behind him. Were there wooden supports there?"

"Hell," Ownby grumbled, his voice even more ragged through the airwaves. "I don't know."

Monica looked away. It was tiring to listen to people struggle to communicate. She took a few slow, calculated steps until she was abreast of the timbers, the black jaws of the mine ready to close on her. She snapped on her headlamp and squinted into the murk. The light illuminated a relatively flat surface littered with forest debris and orange powder. With each step, the stench grew more intense, like sulfur and burning metal.

"Greene!" Wilde snapped. "Stay away."

"I'm fine," she replied. "Just figure things out with Mike."

She turned back to the mine. The last thing she needed right now was to be supervised. It wasn't like she was a liability, after all. She was a former Emergency Manager of one of America's largest and most popular national parks. Besides, she was beginning to feel like a fifth wheel on this expedition.

Suddenly she sensed movement behind her and whirled.

It was Dylan Metcalf.

"Sorry," he said, smiling. "Didn't mean to startle you."

"It's fine," she said, her heart pounding. "Creepy place."

Dylan ran his gloved fingers over the thick layers of moss coating the timbers. "Yeah. You think this is the place?"

Monica shook her head. "Heck if I know."

"Can you imagine working here back in the day?" he said, clicking on his own headlamp. "Crawling in here, trying to find a chunk of rock big enough to buy food for tomorrow?"

Monica couldn't help herself and let a playful smirk spread over her face. "That'd be something."

"They probably camped down by the creek," Metcalf continued, "near where we crossed. I bet they worked themselves to the bone every day. God knows what's down there."

He stepped past the beam and angled the headlamp around the tight walls, trying to see what secrets the mine was hiding from them. Monica looked back toward Wilde and Mullens, still smiling. She couldn't tell if Metcalf's small talk was just the honest thoughts of a history nerd, or casual flirting. It was as if the abandoned mine, with its icy, haunted breath whistling in their faces, was the proverbial water cooler of park rangers.

A shout broke the quiet air from below, as Mullens said, "Wilde!"

She handed him her phone.

"Tell me what I'm looking at," he said.

She pointed at the corner of the screen. "He's panning really fast here, so it's blurry. But that light looks like the entrance behind him."

Monica stepped down from the black ingress and joined the pair of rangers. They squinted at the phone, its small screen struggling to emit a bright enough image to counter the sun. But she saw what Mullens had spoken of, and the sight of it was unmistakable.

It was a clear, unobstructed sphere of light. No wooden beams. No teardrop shape.

It wasn't this mine.

If anything, it looked like a culvert, the kind of big drain pipes that ran under a highway.

"Thank you," Wilde said, handing the phone back.

"We still have to block this off," Monica said. "Anyone could follow our trail here, especially now that four people have beaten the manway to death."

"I know that," Wilde muttered, then leaned into the radio again. "Ownby, come in."

"Ownby here."

"We just analyzed the video," Wilde said. "It's not the same site."

"Are you sure?"

Wilde glanced at Mullens, who was shaking her head.

"We're sure," Wilde said.

Then, with a crackle, Ownby replied, "Extract immediately. Note GPS co-ordinates so we can send in a team to install blockades."

Wilde rose to his feet. "Ten-four. Extracting now."

He threw out his arms into a stretch. "What a great use of our time," he grumbled.

"Hey," Mullens said, pocketing her phone, "at least we confirmed the location of an abandoned mine. Now we can secure it."

"I suppose," Wilde said. "Greene, you ready to go?"

Monica nodded. But as she did, something was bothering her. It felt as though someone was watching her from the shadows, a presence she hadn't accounted for. She lifted her head up, suddenly suspicious of the entire situation. As she surveyed the steep flanks of the mine entrance, she confirmed what her brain had been telling her: They were still alone. There was no boogeyman hiding in the woods, no Treasure Hunter to catch in the act.

But why did she feel so strange all of a sudden?

She whirled and faced the entrance to the cave, its black mouth empty and silent.

"Where's Dylan?" she said.

20

The Mine

SHE SPRINTED THE DISTANCE TO THE MINE.

"Dylan!" she called.

Her voice careened off the rippling stone walls and returned with a hollow, metallic ring.

"Dylan Metcalf!" Monica called again.

Wilde and Mullens rushed along behind her.

"Any sign of him?" Wilde asked.

"No," Monica said.

"Metcalf!" Wilde shouted.

They waited, the echoes of their voices fading quickly. No answer came.

"Did anyone see him go into the forest?" she said. "Perhaps to use the bathroom?"

"No," Wilde said, clutching one of the timbers and leaning into the darkness. "The last I saw, he was next to you."

Mullens leaned into the mine. "Dylan!" she called.

Still, no answer came.

Monica shed her backpack, tore open the top zipper, and reached for her medical mask. It wouldn't be enough to protect her from any toxic fumes for very long, but it would have to be enough for a quick rescue.

"What are you doing?" Wilde said.

"I'm going in to get him," Monica said.

"No," he answered, and he reached out and grabbed her arm.

The power of his grip jarred her. It wasn't often that another person latched on in such a fierce manner, and she instantly glared down at the hand then up at his face.

"Take your hand off of me," she said.

Wilde's fingers twitched for a moment, but he heeded her command and withdrew his hand, leaving her flesh cool where his grip had been.

"I'll go," Wilde said, reaching into his own pack. He took a mask and placed it over his mouth and nose.

"And what about you?" Monica said.

He threaded his arms back into his pack. "I'll be fine."

"Are you sure?"

"Yes," he said.

"But what if something goes wrong? What if one of us has to go in after you? Then what?"

Wilde bowed his head and sighed. "Fine. We'll both go."

Monica turned and laid a hand on Mullens' shoulder. "You stay here and maintain contact with Ownby. Update him on the situation. Do *not* come in after us."

"Okay," she acknowledged, her voice faint and wrought with fear.

Wilde unclipped the radio from his shoulder and handed it to Mullens. "Make the call to Ownby."

Mullens took it, her hand shaking. Then Monica and Wilde turned toward the gaping jaws of the mine.

"Please," Mullens said, "come right back."

"We will," Monica said. Then she fell into step behind Wilde and moved into the darkness of the cavern.

THE STENCH IMMEDIATELY KNIFED THROUGH THE MASK into her nostrils. It was a sour smell, like rotten eggs tinged with hair-raising notes of hot metal. Her eyes began to water and she blinked to clear them so she could see in the murky darkness.

The walls narrowed until they had to walk single file between the bent iron rails at their feet. At first the path gently climbed, but after ten feet it crested at a small platform where the walls had been dug out on each side.

"Dylan?" Monica yelled.

Her voice clattered along the rough rocks, but no answer came in reply.

The small landing gave way to an abrupt descent, and Monica grabbed the wall to steady herself as the floor seemed to disappear beneath her.

"Dylan?" she called again.

Nothing. The shaft narrowed and the roof dropped so suddenly that Monica almost bumped into it with her helmet. She crouched and crept into the slim chute. The odor thickened and a wave of dizziness nearly threw her backward.

"It's hard to breathe," she said, gasping through the mask.

"Let me go first," Wilde said, squatting behind her.

"No," she answered. "I'm already in front."

The shaft's steep decline eased into a more gradual descent. The cold air tickled her exposed skin, and the wretched smell slithered further into her head, filling every cavity with its hellish stench. She stumbled a moment, then caught herself with a trekking pole.

"How did he make it this far?" she said with a cough.

She took another step and the stone roof vanished above her head. Her light shone into a seemingly endless abyss, the middle of a vast subterranean hall. They had reached the first depth of the mine.

"He has to be here," Wilde said. "Check the walls."

A ripple of adrenaline swept through Monica's body just as another surge of foul air hit her brain. The dizziness struck once more and she wobbled like she'd had a few drinks.

"Dylan?" she called, her mouth fumbling with the syllables.

"Dylan!" Wilde roared.

Monica felt her way through the dark. It was as if all her lamp could see was the endless fog. She whirled about and saw nothing but an orange-gray mist. She doubled over, then squinted to see any kind of wall or marker she'd already passed.

Her headlamp swam through the murk, then she barely spied the dark opening where they'd entered. She stumbled toward it until she fell before the small, shadowed tunnel and threw her arms against the cold rocks. Sweat ran like rain over her fingers. Despite the harsh halogen glare of her headlamp, the dark chewed up the light like a terrible leviathan in the blind depths of the sea.

Monica drew her shaking hand away from the wall. Wilde was practically invisible now, his body a mere spectral form in the moonlight of his own lamp. She clawed at the walls, the wet stone slippery to the touch.

"God help me," she whispered.

She was alone. In an instant she could fall and Wilde would never find her corpse and she'd be lost in this catacomb forever.

She blinked and took a slow breath through the mask. Her lungs were boiling and she swallowed, the taste of lead on her tongue.

"Don't give up, Monica," she whispered.

She rose to her feet, pressing into the wall. The world wobbled, dizzy and sick, and she took a lurching step forward.

Monica closed her eyes to clear her head, then opened them as she lowered her light to examine the ground about her feet. There was only dirt. She took two halting steps, clasping the wall with her iced fingers. The light swung wildly.

Her boots scuffed the surface with another step. The light danced, revealing dirt and more dirt, and she gulped with sickness.

Don't give up....

Her head sagged, the light falling to her feet. She blinked and as if by magic a large, contorted object appeared crumpled against the wall. She crouched, squinting at it until her weary mind realized she was staring at mud-smeared khaki pants—

"Wilde!" she cried. "I found him!"

Her partner's heavy bootsteps thundered in the hollowed space until he knelt right beside her.

Dylan was lying on his side, motionless. Monica braced his neck with her hand and rolled him to his back.

"Dylan, can you hear me?" she said.

The man didn't answer. His eyes were closed as if he were sleeping. She shook his shoulder with gentle shoves.

"Dylan, wake up!"

"Any idea what happened to him?" Wilde asked.

"I don't know," she said. "He's unconscious."

"Any head trauma?"

She leaned over the young man's head and ran her fingers through his hair, scanning for blood or lacerations.

"No," she said.

"Then it must be the air," Wilde said. "I can barely breathe."

"Me, too."

Wilde crawled to Dylan's head, hooked his hands into the young man's armpits, and hoisted him up. "Help me," he said.

"You think we can move him?"

Wilde steadied the slack body and rose to a crouch. "We don't have a choice."

Monica hated the idea of moving him. There were so many risks associated with lifting an unconscious victim. But as she wrapped her arms around his legs, another wave of stunning dizziness hit her and her vision went black. She bent over, catching herself with her hands before she hit the ground.

"Greene?" she heard Wilde say. His voice seemed distant, muffled, as if he'd already crawled back up the tunnel.

"I'm fine," she gasped, trying to breathe in thin sips.

She rubbed her eyes and found the world was just as she'd remembered a few seconds ago—dark, suffocating, and perilous. She grabbed Dylan's legs and lifted.

They stood, hoisting the deadweight body between them. He was extraordinarily heavy, as if the thick, venomous air had soaked him through like a sponge. Monica took three backward steps, wobbling with nausea. She steadied, started again, and immediately caught her foot against an embedded stone. She flopped backward and felt her head smack the Earth.

Her vision swirled and stars sprinkled in the night sky of blunt trauma. She reached for her skull, expecting to feel hot blood, but instead found the cold fiberglass of her rescue helmet. Even with the protection, her brain was losing it.

She rolled to her side, heaving and choking for air.

"Greene, get out," Wilde said, his voice an underwater garble. "I'll take care of him."

She shook her head.

"No, I can help...."

Her sight began to spin like a carousel from Hell. Then the vomit came, a rushing surge of lava up her throat. She grabbed to remove her mask but her hand was too slow, and she violently threw up into her mask and hot bile sprayed into her eyes.

Her world became fire. The acid flared like the surface of the sun and she screamed in blinding pain, ripping the mask off and wiping furiously at her face.

"Greene, go!" Wilde shouted.

Two powerful hands grabbed the back of her shirt, hauled her to her knees, and forced her forward in the dark.

"I can't—see," Monica gasped.

"Just crawl!" Wilde yelled. "Go straight and don't stop!"

She pawed at the ground, dragging herself forward, still unable to see. She dared to pry an eye open, but the pyre of Satan ignited and sent white hot coals deep into her skull. She yelped and wiped her face, but it seemed to do nothing. There would be no navigating out of this, no wits or wisdom in the thick of danger. Just moving forward, fleeing on one's belly from death and darkness.

Monica crawled onward, doing as Wilde commanded, trusting he had set her in the right direction. But every breath brought more nausea, more wild whirling to her head. How could she know she was going straight? Then there was the pain, the screaming agony.

Monica clawed forward. Her lungs burned and she gagged. Then she threw up again.

I can't die like this.

She reached out, her arm trembling. Her fingers clamped on the smooth floor and pulled but raked back brown crumbles of dirt. Her body didn't move. She reached again but her arm fell flat.

Stay... awake....

Monica pushed with her toes, the tips of her boots scraping, but she couldn't move. She was blind and paralyzed and trapped in a chamber of toxic gas.

Don't give up, Monica!

She reached again, groping for something, anything, to give her leverage. Her fingers splayed wide and slapped at the ground. There had to be something, a rock, a root, an old railway....

Monica panted, her mouth desert dry. Every breath was a labor. Every motion a dreadful effort.

Monica went limp. She took a sharp breath in and found it catching in her throat. Then a new darkness began to find her, one much deeper and fuller than the shooting pain in her eyes. It was the darkness of unconsciousness, the darkness of a body in surrender.

No, she protested, groping at the earth.

Her head fell to the ground and for a moment a vision flashed before her. It was the countenance of a woman, a subdued smile set on her lips. She looked much like Monica, and yet very different. It was a face she hadn't seen in many years.

Monica blinked and reached for her, but the darkness took her and she saw no more.

21

DROWNING

S HE WAS IN A CANOE.

The vessel rocked gently in the waters of a calm river. She grabbed the gunnels and pulled herself to a seated position, her bottom resting on the damp hull of the canoe as it wobbled in the water.

"Hello?" she called.

Her vision was fuzzy and she couldn't quite make out more than the river around her, pocked with stones and murmuring water. It was just her and the river and the canoe, and nothing and no one else.

Monica looked around again, terribly puzzled. If this was a dream, it wasn't behaving like one. She lowered her hand and dipped it into the river, hoping to let the cool, refreshing stream bring her back to reality.

She rose to her knees, and as she did the world around her seemed to shudder, ripple, and then come into clearer focus.

The Obed River.

There was nothing defining about the scene around her. With vision still obscured, Monica could only gather bits and pieces of trees and boulders and bare, exposed cliffsides. But she knew for sure where she was, because she had gone canoeing here with her parents years ago in the canyons of the Obed Scenic River.

That meant they were here, too.

But where were they?

"Dad?" she said. "Mom?"

Her voice felt weaker, thinner with youth. She could see herself as if in a movie, and she no longer had short, confidently-cropped hair, but a mess of elementary school curls she hadn't figured out what to do with yet. She was scrawny and pimpled, unsure and ever-anxious.

She gripped the gunnels with white fingers.

"Dad? Mom?"

A new sound hit her ears. She spun and grabbed the other rail, sending the boat rocking like a cradle. Someone—no, two persons—were flailing in the water, swinging their hands and sending up a spray with loud cries.

"Help!" one of them hollered.

She leaned over the edge, the boat teetering dangerously.

A man's head broke through the surface, his long graying hair matted to his flesh.

"Daddy!" she cried.

"Monica!" he shrieked. "Help me!"

She turned and searched the boat for an oar or life jacket, but the canoe was empty.

"Hold on!" she yelled.

She leaned over the edge and drove her hand into the water. But the moment she touched it, the cool, refreshing liquid had been replaced with terrible scalding water. She winced and stared helplessly into the waters.

"Monica," her father said, his voice interrupted by a mouthful of water as he dipped under for a moment, "I need you!"

"Daddy, I can't!" she whined.

"I'm drowning!" he said. "You have to help us!"

The sound of the word *us* struck her like an icy blast, and her blood seemed to turn to sleet in her veins. Her gaze veered to the other person in the river, a woman treading water, bobbing up and down. The woman stared back at Monica. Then, as if she had waited there long enough, the woman smiled and slipped below the surface.

"Monica!" the father shrieked. "Help her!"

The little girl squeezed the gunnels and screamed.

"Do something!" her father hollered. "Save her!"

She shook the boat and tried again, wanting nothing more than to scream for help. Someone had to do something to save them. Wasn't there anyone else nearby who could help these people?

"Monica...," her father moaned. His eyes fell dark, the light and hope leaving them.

If only she could get to him! She cried, "Daddy!" and for a moment he seemed to regain the will to fight, to kick with all his remaining strength, and the water about him bubbled with life. She reached again, straining to make her arm long enough to grab his hand and pull him to safety.

But once again he disappeared, and all that remained was a churning spray.

No! she tried to scream.

She couldn't lose him. He needed her, and she was letting him down.

Monica lunged toward the place where they had vanished and hit the water like it was a slab of sidewalk.

It was no longer a boiling cauldron. The water was cold and sick with green spores, the whole river bottom infested with filthy weeds and vines. Before she could react they wrapped themselves around her arms and legs, tightening against her flesh.

She tried to scream, thrashing, but they dragged her down, deep where there would be no breathing or sunlight.

Monica fought, and by some twisted logic of the nightmare, tore loose and started pushing through the water toward her parents. The filth and mire passed away and she was alone again.

Then she saw them. Their bodies were lifeless, hanging limp in the murky suspension, the tiny green algae floating about their skeletal heads like demon faeries.

She again tried to scream, but there was no sound, and no reaction from them. They were already rotting, already long lost in this inundated prison.

Then the weeds returned with their long ropey arms to coil themselves around her arms and legs and face and drag her down, down into the clouded darkness of failure and loneliness. She closed her eyes, shaking with the sobs of the drowning.

All sunk into darkness, and she did not wake for a long time.

22

— • —

FORGETTING TO BREATHE

S UNLIGHT SPILLED THROUGH THE BLINDS, WARMING THE GRAY interior of the small cabin sleeping quarters. Monica sat in a bed, her back propped up by pillows as she sipped coffee from a ceramic mug, her eyes silently watching the steam rise.

She drew in a long, slow breath, her core muscles burning. She held it, counting to twenty. Finally, after her head started to tingle, she exhaled through pursed lips, letting the air out. She closed her eyes and took a quick drink. Then she repeated the exercise.

A knock rapped on the door and it opened. Medical Officer Jack Brown, nicknamed "Chief" since he was the son of a Cherokee elder, poked his head into the room.

"Ownby's here to see you."

Monica nodded, still staring at the wisps of steam.

"You doing okay?"

She shook her head. "Not really."

Chief glanced behind him. "I can have him come back later, if you want."

She smiled at the gesture. "It's okay."

"Alright," Chief said. "I'll send him in."

He stepped out of view while Monica let her head fall against the pillows. She turned to gaze toward the window. There was little to see through the curtained portal, but it was worth trying. To afford the rangers some privacy, the residence bedrooms faced the forest and not the meadows of Ocanaluftee where the cabin was located. Otherwise might be able to spot some elk as they grazed.

She had been here two nights. They first took her to the hospital in Cherokee, but all she needed were electrolytes and some oxygen. They released her on orders of bed rest, and for the last twenty-four hours she'd been at the staff cabin in North Carolina, a small and weak medical patient.

Monica exhaled as the sound of the door opening broke her thoughts. Ownby appeared and paused in the doorframe. She glanced at him, then turned back to the window.

"I'm sorry, Monica," he said.

Monica swallowed, her throat still sore from the vomiting.

"I overreacted," Ownby continued. "The threat was something we had to address. The video had ten thousand views, and many of the comments indicated people were going to go looking for this place."

"It's the internet, Mike," Monica growled. "Everyone's a superhero in the comment section."

"The internet touches our world all the time. What would you have done?"

She closed her eyes and shook her head. For a moment, she saw scenes from her nightmare and shuddered, opening her eyes again. "Waited," she said. "I would have waited."

"Waited," Ownby repeated.

"Yes," she said, giving him the courtesy of eye contact once more. "To see if he posted more. The video gave no specific details. Wilde was right from the beginning that it was an obvious hoax. I don't think it was worth sending our best rangers into harm's way when there wasn't much of a credible threat."

Ownby grunted to clear his throat. "You may be right. Still, we had to act based on the information we had."

"Well, you asked what I thought," she said, and took another sip of coffee.

"By the way," Ownby continued, "we found him."

"Who?"

"The Treasure Hunter," Ownby said. "Wilde was right. It was just a kid from Sevierville trying to boost his social media platform."

"Well, there you go," Monica said. "I hope he's willing to pay my hospital bill."

Ownby stuffed his hands in his pocket and bowed, a bald spot on his head catching the orange sunlight. "You know the park service will take care of you," he mumbled.

At the thought of her infirmed situation, Monica suddenly remembered the whole reason she and Wilde had ventured into the mine.

"How's Dylan?" she said.

"Metcalf? He's fine, thank goodness," Ownby answered, looking up with a weak smile.

"What happened to him?"

"He passed out from the fumes, but a lot faster than you did," Ownby said. "Between the old exposed minerals, the mold, and the decaying remains of whatever managed to get in there and eventually die, he breathed it all in. He must've fallen down the shaft and tried to crawl out, only to go the wrong way. That's where you found him."

Monica nodded. She'd been waiting a day to hear about Metcalf's condition, but Chief hadn't been able to give her a solid answer.

"And Wilde? How's he?"

"Wilde's fine," Ownby said, laughing softly. "He carried Metcalf before he went back for you."

Monica nodded, though a sheen of shame felt like it was running over her skin at having to have been rescued.

"Listen," Ownby said, his tone sharpening to a professional point, "Chief says you'll be good to leave any minute now. When you do, I want you to go home and rest."

At first she wanted to agree. But a lingering thought was nagging at her, and it materialized almost immediately.

"What's the weather forecast?"

"It doesn't matter," Ownby said. "You need more rest."

"Mike," she said, sitting up straighter to bore into his eyes. "What is the forecast?"

He flinched and looked at the floor. "It's—we're not one hundred percent certain—"

"The storm is coming," she said, picking the low-hanging fruit Ownby was pathetically dangling before her.

He sighed. "We believe it is, yes."

"How long do we have?"

"Monica, you've just barely survived a life-threatening accident—"

"Ownby! How long?"

"Thirty-six hours."

"Thirty-six hours?" she repeated. "That's not enough time."

Ownby held up a hand. "Don't think so little of me," he said. "You know what I've had our team doing while you've been here?"

"I don't know," she said, risking an air of sarcasm, "installing my signs?"

Ownby nodded, unable to contain his pride. "Actually, *yes*. Stranded Steve is now standing guard at Alum Cave and Chimney Tops."

"Great," she said. "Where else?"

Ownby's face fell. "What do you mean, *where else?* That was a significant allocation of human resources."

"What about Laurel Falls?" she said. "Elkmont, Ramsey Cascades, Porters Creek, the A.T.?"

"We don't have time," Ownby said. "We had to choose."

Monica tried to hide her frustration. She had hoped the list would go on longer. How many people had he put on this? She could have done those two by herself in that amount of time!

"Well, at least I've got thirty-six hours," she said, throwing the sheets aside on her bed.

"Whoa," Ownby said, holding up both hands to stop her. "You're not cleared to leave yet."

"Cleared to leave?" she scoffed. "By who? You?"

"Chief," he said.

She lifted her chin and bellowed, "Chief! I'm ready to leave!" Then she lowered her gaze to her boss. "I've got work to do."

"I'm ordering you to rest, Greene," he said, his eye's narrowing.

"And I've been ordered by the National Park Service to save lives," she snapped.

"Monica," he said, "I'm worried about you. Don't do anything rash."

Monica ignored the remark and swung her legs over the side of the bed. At her motion, Ownby stepped toward her, hands out as if he was going to restrain her.

"Don't touch me," she snapped. "What is it with you people and touching?"

He recoiled, face contorting in shock. "I—didn't mean anything—"

"It doesn't matter what you *meant,*" she said. "Don't touch me."

"Okay," he stammered. "I—I'm sorry."

"You know something?" she said, standing. "I'm surprised you're the man with this job. When things go south, where are you? Huddled in your office? Riding on a golf cart? That's not leadership, Mike."

She coughed, her throat simmering with savage pain. But she swallowed and continued, "I'm going to do my job the way I know best, and you better not send me off on any more ridiculous errands."

Ownby's face turned to rigid stone. His shock from before seemed to morph into restrained anger, his cheeks flush with rushing blood. Would he tolerate this act of blatant disrespect? Monica wondered for a moment as she sat on the bed's edge, ready to bolt past him at Chief's signal.

But something in the Emergency Manager was softening, and his face fell and sighed.

"Like I said, Monica," he said. "I'm sorry."

He turned toward the door and opened it, about to let himself out, then placed his hand on the wall, head bowed.

"By the way, your father has been calling," he said.

"Why?" she barked. "Is he having another meltdown? Is he in the E.R. again?"

Ownby took a long breath. Then he turned to her, the same grievous expression hanging on his face. "No," he said. "He's wondering how you're doing, and he wanted to thank you for coming to see him in the hospital."

Monica blinked, forgetting to breathe again.

Ownby shrugged. "That was all. You might consider calling him back."

Then he let himself out, leaving her stunned and alone, shame continuing to seep over her skin like cold sweat.

23

— . —

DONOR

T HE PHONE RANG JUST ONCE.

There was the usual scuffling noise, as if the man had to wrestle the phone to the ground before answering it. Then his high-pitched voice said, "You're there! Are you okay?"

"Hey, Dad," she said.

"It's been two days, Little Bear!"

"I know," she said, trying to hide the sniffle in her sinuses. "I—we had a tough mission in the backcountry."

There was a prolonged silence. She rubbed the corners of her eyes and exhaled slowly.

"There's a new nurse coming to see me," he said suddenly. "I like her."

"Really?"

"Yes," her father answered, perhaps a bit too forcefully. She could tell he was trying to hit all the right notes, like a child promising to never steal treats from the pantry. "I think the medicine is helping, too."

"Good," she said. "Remember, if you don't take it, your—"

"—my kidneys will fail," he said, finishing the sentence for her. "Yes, yes, I know that."

"Okay, good," she said, her hand instinctively flying to her hip, and she began to massage the tender flesh.

"You know," he continued. "Dr. Watt phoned to talk about my treatment."

The hair on her neck stood at attention. "She did?"

"She asked if you'd made up your mind," he continued.

"Made up my mind?" she repeated. "About what?"

"About the kidney donation."

In an instant, her blood turned to sleet. The phone nearly slipped from her fingers and she fumbled to regain her grip.

"What did Dr. Watt tell you?" she said, breathless.

"Well, I mean, I *think* she meant—"

"Dad," Monica said, cutting him off. "What did Dr. Watt say?"

"She couldn't get ahold of you," her father said. "Neither could I. So I asked her what treatment options there were, and she said you were a match for a donation. Would you really do that for me?"

Monica lay back on the bed, her forehead throbbing. Why had Dr. Watt told him about it? What had she been thinking!?

"Little Bear?" her father said. "Is it true?"

"It's true that I'm a match."

"Oh, Monica," he said. "That would be—but of course you can't—"

She rubbed her forehead as an intense ache was forming there. "Dad, can we talk about this later?"

"Yes, yes," he stammered. "Just know that I'm not asking you for anything, I know that's too much—"

"Dad," she snapped.

He immediately ended his rambling. She knew how this was going to go. It was a dance, the kind of tango between the sober and the drunk, the willing and the captive. He would say whatever was necessary to placate her. He would believe his own words, too. But under it all, beneath every compliment and denial, would be his insatiable insistence on Monica giving up her kidney to save his life. It had been that way with her mother, decades ago. Now her father was the addict in her life, a junkie for control.

"We'll talk about this later," she said. "Are you taking your medication?"

There was a brief silence, but he answered, "Yes."

"Are you going to your dialysis treatments?"

"Of course," he said. "The nurse picks me up and drives me to the clinic—"

"Good," she said. "I don't know what I'm going to do, Dad, but I can't be a part of this if you're not committed. You put yourself in this position. Not me. And I want you to prove you can make good choices. Okay?"

"Yes, I agree!" he gushed, again perhaps too forcefully to be completely believed. "I love you, Little Bear. So much."

Just as she thought, he was playing it up to satisfy her. Yet his eagerness had a soothing effect. He was still her father, and she had to admit it felt good to hear him be passionate about his own health.

She swallowed. "I love you too, Papa Bear."

At this, another silence fell between them. She cleared her throat.

"Dad, things are going to get busy here," she said. "There's a storm coming from the Atlantic that could make my job really hard."

"I heard," he said. "The nurse said I should get water and batteries."

"Yes, that's right," Monica said, rising from the bed and beginning to pace across the room. "Can you order groceries for delivery?"

"I think so."

"Do it," she urged. "I'll pay for whatever you need. Just get plenty of water and non-perishable food. Not that frozen junk. You can't microwave when the power's out."

"I know that," he said.

"I just want you to be prepared, Dad."

"Okay."

She put the phone on speaker and began to dress in her freshly laundered uniform.

"I've got to get going," she said. "You stay safe, okay?"

"Sure," he said, his voice growing urgent. "Any chance you could come by today? Or maybe tomorrow?"

"I'd love to," she said, "but we need all hands on deck here. Apparently this tropical storm will be here soon."

"The news said it could turn south."

"Hopefully," she replied. "Either way I promise I'll come see you once it passes."

"Okay."

She opened the door to her room and saw Chief standing in the middle of the sitting area, his hands in his pockets. He looked up from the floor, his broad jaw rigid with concern.

Something was wrong.

"I've got to go," she said. "Love you, Dad."

"I love you, too."

She ended the call and slid the phone into her pocket.

"What is it?"

Chief took a breath. "If you feel healthy enough to leave, you can."

"Okay, great."

"With that, I have to ask," he said, his eyes heavy. "Are you on duty?"

"What?"

He jerked his head toward the room. "I overheard part of your talk with Ownby. I know he wants you to take some time, but are you choosing to remain on duty?"

"Yes," she said. "Why?"

"We just got a call from Smokemont. An elderly man has gone missing, and they need all active duty rangers to assist in the area search."

Monica stared at him. "You're kidding me."

He shrugged and grabbed a radio from a nearby rack on the wall. "We don't get to pick our spots, Ms. Greene."

He extended his hand, offering her the device.

She scowled, stared at the radio, then lifted her arm to grab it. A vision of dark, swirling storm clouds flashed in her mind. Then she saw the river, the falling tree, and Allison Blaze vanishing. A shiver convulsed her body and Monica swallowed, her throat dry.

Her hand trembled and she closed her eyes, trying to drive the image away. But in the recesses of her mind, the face of her father appeared again as it plunged into the filthy depths, her nightmare living on. Monica exhaled, and her arm tightened like a rubber band and she pulled her hand back.

"I can't," she said.

Chief's eyes went wide. "What do you mean?"

"I can't help you," Monica said, looking at the floor. "I have to prepare for the storm."

"A man is missing, Ranger. We have to find him," Chief said, his voice heavy.

Monica lifted her eyes and met his dark gaze.

"Then go get him," she said.

24

— · —

RAMSEY CASCADES

MONICA CLUTCHED THE STEERING WHEEL WITH BONE WHITE knuckles.

What is wrong with me?

She wasn't a person to walk away from someone in need of a helping hand. Throughout her life, everyone who knew her would loudly gush about how generous and selfless she was.

Yet that was exactly what was eating her. Why was it always her who had to drop everything and help? And why was she always made to feel shamefully guilty about it when she had the slightest resistance or excuse?

Monica grit her teeth as she flew past Newfound Gap, its parking lot stuffed with vehicles and tourists peering eagerly into the horizon.

Yes, she was generous. Yes, she was selfless. But why? Was it even out of genuine love, or just a fear of being judged? DId these people in her life truly know her? Or had she successfully tricked them?

Did she even know herself?

Monica's foot weighed heavy on the accelerator as she powered over the crest of the Smokies and gladly rode the bumper of an RV descending the Tennessee side of the park.

She pulled into the Alum Cave Trail parking area with a screech of the tires and ran across the bridge to check the sign that Ownby's team had apparently installed. It was right where she would have wanted it.

Score one for Ownby.

Finally, someone had considered her priorities.

Then she gasped, her mouth hanging open.

Stranded Steve lay miserably at the base of a waterfall, his body broken and face smeared with tears. A wooden bridge stood beside him, clearly identifying the place as Laurel Falls.

It was the wrong sign.

"Are you kidding me?" she exclaimed.

How could they make a mistake like this? There were no waterfalls on the Alum Cave Trail! Had Ownby sent a bunch of kids up here, interns who didn't know their right foot from their left?

Monica planted a hand on her hip and stared. Not only would this have to be dug up and removed, it would have to be replaced, essentially doubling her workload. She bit her lip, her fury growing. Then she ducked her head in shame.

Anyone could have easily made that mistake. The Steves were her idea, her creation. The people who installed the sign had done a fine job of it, too. They'd just grabbed the wrong one from the barn at HQ where she'd stacked her materials, and they probably didn't know there were unique signs for different trails.

She turned and walked back over the bridge, her boots thudding as they hit the boards. She didn't want to be angry. Anger was corrosive to the heart and mind. All it did was intoxicate one into thinking they were always right in spite of all facts to the contrary.

As she laid her hand on the truck's door handle she closed her eyes, took another long breath, and climbed in.

Take your time.

And she could take her time. As she fired up the truck, the LCD clock glowed: 10:30.

"I've got all day," she said, daring to smile. Then she put the truck in gear and steamed down the mountain toward Headquarters.

When she got there, there would be no mention of the faulty Alum Cave sign, no passive-aggressive remarks about how other people performed their jobs. She would just collect the necessary materials for another trail sign, install it, and then perhaps treat herself to a cheeseburger somewhere in town. Maybe Blaze could join her.

As Mt. Leconte rushed by, she rolled the windows down and let the air swim over her. Aside from the overcast skies and raucous winds, it was a beautiful day complete with a cool breeze. The first leaves of autumn were just beginning to show their pumpkin colors and a few were fluttering to the ground as she rolled down the road.

All didn't have to be doom and gloom.

At Headquarters, Monica piled everything high in the bed of her truck: Signs, posts, tools, and even gear to work long into the night if necessary. She would put in her hardest day of work yet, and while her body was spent in effort she would pray for the missing man and his family. If she couldn't be his means of rescue, she could at least call on God to help in her stead.

The first stop was Elkmont, a popular campground and hiking hub. It was where she and Wilde had rescued Blaze from the Little River. Small, temporary signs stood at the trailhead indicating that hikers and backpackers should take caution due to high water. Yet these precautions had done little to prevent the coming catastrophes, and now Monica was determined to put Steve's persuasive image to work.

She had designed a portrait of the poor fellow sinking up to his neck in water. Her hope was it would send a message that the river, though beautiful and often tame, was wild and uncontrollable. If a bridge was out, or a crossing seemed too dangerous, one should turn back lest they end up like Steve.

After an hour of digging, followed by another hour of positioning the post, packing it in, and erecting the hefty wooden display, Monica was sweaty and huffing despite the cool blast of the wind. She stood and admired her work where it stood near the parking area. Once again she smiled and nodded at it as if to say, "Stand guard for me, Steve!" Then she lugged the post-digger, shovel, and tools back to the truck and hoisted them over the sides and into the bed with a loud clang.

One down.

As she got into the cab, her lungs were filled with fire. She swallowed, tossed back half a bottle of energy drink, and drove to Gatlinburg to grab a late lunch of pulled pork and chips. Wiping barbeque sauce from her cheek, Monica navigated east toward the long, arduous trail to Ramsey Cascades.

The long, narrow dirt road into Greenbrier was clouded with plumes of dust thrown up by SUVs and trucks ambling along the pothole-ridden track. Monica fell in line behind a wide-framed truck with out-of-state plates rumbling along at ten miles per hour. Monica leaned back and sighed.

"Please, Jesus," she muttered, "give me patience."

Nearly forty minutes and seven miles later, she arrived at the trailhead. It was jammed with vehicles, many parked at precarious angles on steep slopes on the lip of the bank. She was in a Park Service truck, though, and took the initiative to roll up to the colossal boulder barring passage onto the trail. She climbed out without shutting the door and limped to the back of the truck on a pair of tight, wobbling legs, her muscles taut after the long drive. She grit her teeth, stretched, and lowered the gate to remove her tools.

Monica leapt into her work, digging fiercely. But the ground here was firmer, thickly inlaid with roots from centuries of growth. Unlike Elkmont, which had been devastated by the logging industry, the terra firma of Greenbrier was a stout holdout of history, strong against all invaders. With a huff and burning cough, she threw her back into the shovel and gave it all she had.

The minutes passed. Then hours. Time and again she paused to sit on the rock and wipe her brow, struggling to catch her labored breath. Hikers passed, inquiring what she was doing, and Monica summoned the strength to tell them.

Once the hole was dug and the dirt loose enough to stab with the post-digger, she checked her watch and gasped. It was dinnertime. But there was a job to do, and she was going to finish it.

Again, the ground fought her. Every downward attack with the tool seemed to meet an azalea root as tough as titanium. Time after time she had to climb in the hole and cut through the roots with clippers and then clamber out again. By the time she had a sufficient place to put the signpost, she was gasping for air and leaning with her hands on her knees.

As she tightened the bolt fastening the sign to the post, the sun began to set. The light was fading, but in a slow manner like water rising to a boil. The last orange embers fluttered through the wind-blown trees and then vanished, and suddenly the trailhead lay under a shroud. Monica looked around, and with a sour gulp realized there was only one vehicle remaining other than hers. As she tightened the final nut onto the signpost, a couple of hikers appeared. They posed for a picture with the Ramsey Cascades Trail sign, then hurried to their car as the violet glow of sunset surrendered to the obsidian cloak of night.

Monica watched the pair of scarlet taillights fade, then turned back to Steve.

"Took you long enough," she jested to his sad, broken form. In this illustration he was crumpled at the bottom of a tall, impressive waterfall, clearly injured after his foolhardy attempt to climb the thing. Would it do the trick and dissuade would-be fools from doing the same?

Monica exhaled, her lungs burning more than ever. Perhaps working through the night wouldn't go exactly as she thought it would. Then again, maybe some coffee would change that.

The thought of a hot cup brought her smile back. She returned the gear to the truck bed, the tools slamming down with a bang. It was loud and cantankerous, but she was alone with no one to offend but the bears, and she was perfectly okay with that. Monica climbed into the truck with a grunt, then slammed the door. She jammed the key into the ignition and twisted it forward.

Nothing happened.

"Huh?" she said.

She turned it back, then forward again.

Not a sound.

She tried again, and just below the hiss of the creek she heard the *rat-tat-tat-tat* of the starter, trying and failing to get the engine going.

"Oh, come *on*," she said.

Monica tried again, but the truck sat mute. The battery was completely dead. Then she remembered how, so many hours before, she had jumped out of the truck and forgotten to shut the door in her hurry to get started. It was the only thing that made sense. With the door ajar, the dome light must have remained on, slowly draining the truck's battery until it was gone.

Monica leaned back, then pounded her head into the seat cushion. She was stuck out here, deep in Greenbrier with no one around to give her a jump.

Then she remembered her radio. Monica reached for her belt, where the radio was normally stashed.

It wasn't there.

"What the heck?" she said.

She felt along the passenger seat. Her fingers found the empty barbeque bag, damp napkins, a few wrappers—but no radio.

"Where in the world?"

She reached forward near the gearshift. Every NPS truck included a charger for the radios. Monica's hand closed around the brick-sized device and pulled it out. There was no glowing light. She twisted the knob. Nothing.

"Hello?" she said, pressing the 'transmit' button.

It was dead. Everything in the truck was dead.

Monica slammed her head back again, groaning.

How could this happen!?

She closed her eyes.

Could she hike out and try to reach cell signal? There was a ranger station near the entrance where she could get a fresh battery and even a replacement vehicle. That was almost seven miles away, though, and she wasn't sure she could walk half that distance right now.

Monica threw open the truck door and jumped out. Once again, her legs trembled, already tightening. She took a dozen steps, testing the waters.

"You've hiked seven miles before," she muttered. "Don't be a wimp, Monica."

But with each step, the weight of her day pressed down on her. Every thud of her boots carried the exhaustion of her argument with Ownby, her gut-punch with Dad, the lingering shame of abandoning Chief and the missing man, and the installation of two more Steve signs.

She stopped, standing alone in the impenetrable darkness. Crickets sang and leaves rustled with the rushing wind.

She turned around, groping in the murk until she found the truck. She climbed in once again and closed the door. Inside, all was quiet. Monica leaned back, swallowed to soothe her throat, and closed her eyes.

Her mind was ablaze with thoughts. Anger bordering on fury shot through her brain like lightning. There was so much to do, and so many reasons God should have prevented this.

Yet here she was, stuck in the depths of the Smokies, doomed to lie here and try to steal some fitful sleep.

Monica tried to burrow her way into the seat cushion. She had to rest. Her body was screaming for it, but that terrible mind of hers kept fussing.

Please, God, she begged. *Help me rest.*

A glacier of worry was grinding against her soul, merely allowing a sleep marred by endless visions of the same loved ones dying the same deaths, over and over.

After two fitful hours, her head finally slowed, her thoughts became silent, and Monica Greene discovered something akin to sleep.

25

— • —

PRAYER

*T*AP-TAP-TAP.

Monica pried her eyes open. The interior of the truck was quiet and still. Outside, however, the trees were thrashing about, pulled in every direction by the torrential wind. She blinked, rubbed her face, and glanced through the windshield at the sky. Thick gray thunderheads were brewing high above like thick, muscled arms.

Tap-tap-tap.

Monica groaned and twisted. A man was standing outside the truck, his eyes peering at her from beneath a broad-brimmed hat.

It was Ownby.

She cracked the door.

"I'm glad I found you," he said. "What happened?"

Monica nodded and yawned. "I left the door open and drained the battery. Stupid move."

"I'll give it a jump," Ownby said. "We're gonna need every vehicle."

Monica nodded again and ran her hand over her face, trying to massage herself back to life. She leaned into the seat as Ownby lifted the hoods and the attached jumper cables. After a moment he stepped back and leaned to the side.

"Start her up."

Monica obliged, sliding the key in and giving it a turn. The engine heaved, like it was chewing leather, then grumbled with power. The lights on the dash glared bright and the battery pack with the radios glowed red.

Ownby strolled around and leaned against his own vehicle, adjacent to hers.

"Thank you," she said.

"You know, we could have used you at Smokemont," he said.

A knife of guilt stabbed at her guts. "Did they find the guy?"

"Do you even care if we found him, Ranger Greene?" Ownby said, frowning at her. "Chief said you refused to join the search."

Monica scowled, the knife in her middle twisting. "Yes," she said, "of course I care. Did you find him or not?"

Ownby bit his lip and paused. "We did," he answered. "He was in the river, hypothermic and near death. We airlifted him to the university hospital. Last I heard his condition was improving."

"That's good."

"Why'd you abandon your team, Ranger?"

Monica lifted her gaze, fighting the urge to cower before the question. "I didn't," she said. "What I'm doing will save lives."

"We needed you back there and you left us," he said.

Monica's face burned with sudden fury. "I didn't want to get drawn into another errand," she declared.

"Errand? Saving a man's life is an *errand?*"

She swallowed, shame rising into her mouth. "You found him, right?" she said. "His life was saved, even without me."

With a sudden, jolting *bang!* Ownby slapped the side of the truck. "What's wrong with you, Monica? I understand that you want to save lives with these trail signs. I want that, too. But there's something desperate about you right now and it worries me. I don't know if I can trust you anymore."

She looked up at him but didn't answer. She knew he was right. Yet her fervor for her work didn't feel like a problem at the moment, so she just met his eyes with a steady glare.

"Listen to me," Ownby went on. "This may be out of line to bring up, but I know you're a Christ-follower. I am, too. And that's why I'm *especially* concerned."

The addition of her faith to the conversation lit a small fire in her, and suddenly she felt the urge to defend herself.

"What does that have to do with anything?" she said, her voice low.

"You believe in helping people because Jesus helped people. Right?"

"Sure," she said.

"Well, you're not Jesus, Monica."

The words had their intended effect, and she felt her muscles loosening as if she'd been struck in the temple. The statement reeked of insult. Was Ownby condemning her and her faults? But it also smelled of sweet truth, the kind of truth that gives freedom from all kinds of mental slavery.

The sharpness of the remark stung no matter how she took it, so she scowled and said, "Neither are you, Mike."

Then he laughed. Monica recoiled in shock, wanting to swing an arm through the open window and punch him. But Ownby just glanced at the roaring river, smiled, and shook his head.

"That's damned right," he said, still chuckling.

"What's funny?" she said.

"It's just true, that's all," he said, grinning. "I'm not God, and neither are you. So maybe you should stop tryin' to die for everyone's sins."

"What does that mean?"

"Something's gnawing at you. You're not just eager to do this work of yours—you're religious about it. And if anyone gets in your way, you treat 'em like a heretic."

Monica rolled her eyes. "Give me a break, Mike."

"No," he said, his smile vanishing in an instant. He jabbed a finger at her. "You give *me* a break, Monica. If you abandon your duty again like you did yesterday, it'll be your last act as a park ranger."

"Fine," she said.

"And the next time you're tempted to do so—because you will be, it's just who you are—I want you to do something."

She sighed. "Do what?"

"I want you to pray."

Monica cocked her head. "Pray?"

Ownby pointed the finger up to the sky. "Are you really a Christ-follower?"

"Yes."

"So you trust Him above all else?"

She narrowed her eyes. "Yes."

"Then stop your damned hurrying and trust in the Lord, Monica Greene. Quit running for a minute and pray."

She shook her head. "So I'm supposed to pray if someone's drowning or clinging to the side of a mountain?"

"For a tiny second, you can. Or," he said, raising a gray eyebrow mischievously, "is He not as strong or smart as you?" With a glance at the open hood of her truck, he sighed and grumbled, "That ought to be enough for the battery to be charged," and strolled to the engine block.

He disconnected the cables and wound them into a tight loop. "We've closed all entrances to the park, but we still have dozens of cars at multiple trailheads. I want you to meet up with Blaze at Newfound Gap. She's closing down the facilities on Clingman's, and might need help clearing out stragglers."

Monica continued to cast her most rigid frown his way. "I do pray, you know. All the time."

Ownby opened his truck door. "That may be so. But there's a difference between talking and listening."

The fatherly witticism chafed her like a fungal infection and she shook her head. "Sure. How's the weather?"

"Same as yesterday," Ownby said. "The outer bands will hit mid-afternoon."

Monica looked into the churning sky of gray smoke and gloom.

Ownby slid into his vehicle with a grunt. "Hurry up and get to Newfound Gap. I bet Blaze will be glad to see you."

He slammed the door and backed the truck away. Monica watched him go, a frown set into her face like dried Tennessee clay. A gale rocked her vehicle sideways and she steadied herself, then grabbed the gearshift.

Stop.

Ownby's voice flowed through her mind.

Pray.

"I don't need to pray," she said. "I need to get moving—"

Her obvious defiance to Ownby's words came into clear view before her, and she stopped. Monica closed her eyes and shifted back into park.

"Fine," she grumbled.

Then, with a tone salted with sleep-deprivation and impatience, she began murmuring to the Almighty, hoping He was listening.

26

—·—

Dark Clouds

ONCE HER RADIO GAINED ENOUGH JUICE TO WORK, MONICA turned it on and orders immediately began to stream out.

"...establish a barricade at Townsend Wye. Ranger Mullens, oversee evacuation of Cades Cove Campground....."

Monica glanced at the barking device as her truck bounced over the numerous potholes dotting the road out of Greenbrier. What was she to do now that a tropical storm was about to slam into the park?

On either side of the narrow gravel track, trees whipped from side-to-side, their trunks in the grip of an invisible monster. The wind shoved her truck sideways, forcing her to jerk the steering wheel back to center to keep the vehicle securely on the road.

"God," she whispered, leaning toward the windshield, "Please help us down here."

Her knuckles paled as they gripped the wheel. Monica swallowed, her throat still singed from the bitter flavors emanating from below, and navigated onto Highway 441 toward Newfound Gap and the Appalachian Trail.

While the infamous two-thousand mile footpath originates in Georgia, it gloriously bisects the Smokies along the border between Tennessee and North Carolina. Most thru-hikers opt for a northbound journey, taking advantage of the southern spring climate. But a rare few opt for the southbound journey, bringing them into the Smokies in autumn. There would undoubtedly be dozens of these brave souls on the spine of the mountains when the storm hit. Everywhere within the park the A.T. was remote, except for one place: Newfound Gap. If Monica and Blaze wanted to possibly evacuate any stranded hikers, it would have to be there.

Monica swerved into a ditch to avoid a fallen tree, then engaged the four-wheel drive and grumbled back onto the road. High winds had blown down a handful of enormous trunks, while others groaned and cracked in the violent gusts. The rushing air from the east pushed against her climb and the truck shuddered as if on the edge of a sword. Monica held the vehicle steady, inching along until she finally crested the ridge of Newfound Gap. As she pulled into the parking lot, the full brunt of the approaching storm slammed into the truck with a deafening blast.

She jerked the wheel into the lot and powered toward the lone NPS vehicle waiting there beside two silent and dark SUVs. She killed the engine and leapt out.

Blaze's short figure ran around one of the entrances to the Appalachian Trail, looping yellow "caution" tape around the iconic trail sign that led toward Charlie's Bunion.

"Blaze!" Monica called.

Blaze turned and saw her. "What are you doing up here?" she called.

"Ownby sent me!" Monica yelled, the wind screaming in her ears. "How can I help?"

"Run this trail for a half mile north and check for hikers!"

"Are you kidding?"

But Blaze tore off the end of the bright roll of tape and gave her a grave look straight in the eye. "I'll go south," she said. "There are two vehicles here with no camping permits registered to them. People are still out there."

"Got it," Monica said.

She ducked under the yellow barrier and began her run. It was all uphill and her lower body immediately burned with effort. On each side of the narrow footpath trees rocked back and forth. Black clouds spun overhead, so low that she wanted to duck to avoid their touch. White spikes of lightning broke the horizon and the growl of thunder shook her bones.

The flat trail quickly deteriorated into an obstacle course of shattered rock and exposed tree roots. Her toes scuffed the ground while the wind hissed in her ears. She turned corner after corner and spied nothing but wet dirt pooling with black water.

She slowed to a stop and leaned on a tree to catch her breath.

They're not here.

Suddenly the world exploded with fire and light and she flew backward. Her head slammed into the ground and bright sparking stars burst over her eyes.

"Agh!" she cried, gasping. Her hands patted her body, checking for burns or other wounds.

I'm alive.

Monica lifted her throbbing head and peered about. Through a haze of shooting lights, she beheld the remains of a tree just a few feet in front of her, its trunk and branches smote to dark obsidian.

She stumbled to her feet, dizzy with pain. That lightning bolt had nearly consumed her. In fact, if she hadn't stopped to rest, she would have been right at the spot that the fiery spear had hit—

The sky ignited again and an ear-splitting whine screamed in her ears. Another bolt had just hit nearby. Monica turned and ran, sprinting with every ounce of remaining energy to get back to her truck and some semblance of safety. She turned a sharp corner, scrambled down a rock formation, sliding along on her bottom, then hit the ground. Another *boom!* blasted her ears and she pounded the trail hard.

Get me back alive!

She leapt over an eroded ledge but her boot kicked into a buried rock. Her body flew forward and her legs were trapped behind her and Monica hit the ground yet again, her face sliding into the mud.

Monica spat slimy dirt from her mouth. She rolled heaving onto her side and wiped at her face. Another flash burst through the air, blinding her—*Was this it, the one that finally caught up to her?*—but the timpani of thunder shuddered somewhere in the hollow below.

A new sound rose after it, the din of tropical rain battering the forest. It came like a gray veil and the tiny pellets stung her skin with their icy teeth. She lay still as the rain enveloped her, panting for breath.

I almost died, she thought over and over. It wasn't the first time she'd touched gloves with Death, but somehow it felt different. Death, it seemed, had been studying her moves.

"Pray," she whispered, the water pouring over her face.

The sky broke open once more, the flash like a photographic negative. She had to get up. She had to get back to the truck and off this mountain before the storm killed her.

Pray.

Monica rose to a knee, flicked the droplets from her eyes, and stood on both trembling legs.

"God," she gasped.

What was there to say? She didn't want to die. That was it. She had to live. For her father, for the people of the Smokies, for herself.

Monica grabbed the nearest trunk, steadied herself, and lurched back toward the trailhead.

WHEN SHE REACHED THE GAP, Blaze was waiting in her truck. Monica ran and climbed into the passenger's seat.

"What happened to you?" Blaze asked, glancing at her in horror.

"I slipped," Monica said.

"No sign of anyone?"

Monica shook her head. Blaze turned one of the dials on the control panel. Warm air began rushing through the vents.

"Thank you," Monica whispered.

Blaze continued to stare at her. "You okay?" she said after a moment. "You seem rattled."

"I almost got struck by lightning," Monica said.

"Me, too," she said. "I love the lightning. Wish it would've got me."

Monica shook her head. Her friend couldn't be serious. "You don't mean that," she said.

Blaze grinned. "Can you imagine a more legendary death? Park Ranger gets struck by lightning trying to save stranded hikers in a hurricane."

Monica smiled and hugged her chest to warm herself. "You're already a legend. You don't need an epic death."

"If I'm a legend, then you're notorious," Blaze said. "What happened in Smokemont? And where've you been for the last twenty-four hours?"

Monica relayed the story of the dead battery at Ramsey Cascades, and Blaze burst into laughter when she described turning the key and realizing she was stuck.

"I wish I'd been there!" she grinned.

A gust of wind slammed into the side of the truck like a sledgehammer. Blaze swore and Monica yelped, grabbing the door handle beside her.

"We'd better get down," Monica said.

"No kidding."

She released the handle with trembling fingers, the adrenaline surging through her blood. Glancing at the vacant parking lot, its dark surface rippling with waves of pelting rain, she added, "I know we did all we could, but I still hate leaving."

Blaze sighed. "We tried. That's all we can do."

The truck shuddered and swayed, bludgeoned yet again. Trees rocked wildly and rain spattered the windows like bullets.

Monica peered toward the trailhead. Maybe someone would come, someone who'd been hurrying close behind her—

"I'm serious," Blaze said. "You can't blame yourself for anything that's about to happen."

"But I still don't want it to happen," Monica said.

"Me neither."

Monica gave her friend a nod, then opened the door and hustled from one cab to the other as the rain flew into her eyes. Monica wiped her face clean, then backed from her parking spot and navigated out of the parking lot.

She rolled down the mountain toward Headquarters, her foot steady on the brake. The sky was consumed by an oppressive gloom like a cauldron of tar. Monica glanced up and shivered. One couldn't behold such a sky without feeling the weight of death, and the power of nature to indiscriminately dish it out.

As she continued to descend the winds jerked the truck left and right. Monica burned the headlights as the road nearly disappeared under the blanket of horizontal rain. She came to the Alum Cave Trailhead and saw no less than five vehicles scattered across the lot.

"Oh, God," she whispered.

She considered pulling off to check the trail, to see if someone was in need of help, but Blaze's words echoed in her mind. There was also the Stranded Steve sign, freshly installed, to warn hikers of a whole litany of risks, even if it was the wrong image.

So she pumped the accelerator and blew past the dark, silent parking lot. And yet there were more vehicles at Chimney Tops and Huskey Gap Trail, eight in total. Combined with those at Alum, there were thirteen vehicles at the trailheads. She wanted to turn around. She wanted to rush up the Chimney Tops Trail and evacuate every human soul she could find. But the storm had arrived and was unleashing its hate upon them. The black skies spun into a blurred miasma of rain and wind and hail and darkness. Thunder rumbled high above, and a blinding flash burst over the valley. Monica took a long, heavy breath.

People are going to die today, she thought.

People are going to die, and there's nothing I can do about it.

27

—·—

SHELTER

AS THE RAIN HAMMERED DOWN, MONICA SAW OWNBY standing beside the road in a bright yellow rain slicker. He held two glowing traffic wands and waved them past HQ toward the maintenance area.

Monica followed the truck ahead of her to a long building with a dozen garage doors. Inside, numerous plows, wreckers, and other emergency vehicles waited for duty. She pulled her truck under the roof into the shelter of the garage and hopped out of her vehicle, her clothing still wet through. Blaze appeared beside her, similarly damp and dripping. "Well, *that* was fun," she said.

"Any idea what we do now?"

Blaze pointed across the broad gravel staging area outside the garage doors. A pair of shuttle buses were idling, their headlights glowing in the rain. "The order is to hunker down," she said. "Ride out the storm until it's safe."

Monica exhaled. It was a relief to know their work was, for the time being, done. All they could do was wait and pray.

"Are they going to come get us?" Monica asked. "I don't really want to run out there again."

"I think so," Blaze said.

Monica nodded. "Okay. In that case I'm going to make a quick phone call."

"Good luck," Blaze answered with a laugh. "Hopefully the cell towers are still working."

Monica stepped away from the rangers, found a lonely corner to herself, and pulled her phone from her pocket. It was smeared with moisture but the screen glowed brightly. She wiped it off and made the call. The other end picked up immediately and his nasal voice crackled through the speaker.

"My power is already out!"

"It's going to be okay, Dad," she said. "Just paint or something until the electricity can come back—"

"No, no!" he howled. "I can't see or eat or do much of anything! Call the power company, Monica!"

"That won't help," she said. "It's going to be out for a while. Do you have plenty of food?"

"No! I need to use the microwave!"

She ran her fingers through her hair. "Dad, we talked about this. You can't use the microwave or the refrigerator."

"Monica, I need you to come here right now," he whined. "I need you to—I need you here!"

"I can't come right now," she said, steadying her voice. "I'm still at the park and it's too dangerous to be out right now—"

"You're not coming!?" he yelled. "Why not!?"

"Dad, we talked about this."

"Why won't you come here and be with me? I'm scared and alone. Don't you care about your father!?"

She glanced at the growing cluster of colleagues. A line was forming near the buses.

"Dad, we talked about this," she said. "I told you yesterday that we had to prepare for the storm, and now we're about to ride it out. I can't—"

"Why are you abandoning me!?"

"I'm not," she snapped, any remnants of calm dissipated by her father's rage. "I'm doing my job and I would love it if you did yours."

"I'm all alone, Little Bear," he pined. "I'm your father and I'm alone. I thought you cared about me!"

"Dad, of course I care about you—"

"You're all I have left," he said. "I'm so scared to lose you!"

She looked up and saw Blaze waving at her. Everyone was boarding the shuttle buses.

"Dad, I've got to go—"

"I can't do this," he said, the stream of panic continuing. "I need you now, Monica. I need you here!"

The last rangers were climbing aboard. She began jogging toward them.

"Just hold on, Dad," she said, her voice shaking. "Ride out the storm and I'll come help you—"

"I *can't!*" he screamed. "Now get over here!"

She gasped, and in a rush of panic realized that she hadn't been breathing and was about to pass out. Monica stumbled into a pillar to regain her balance. Her hand shook and the device wiggled free and clattered to the ground, the screen cracking into a brilliant spiderweb. The speaker continued to shriek at her like a street preacher.

"I'm scared! I'm alone and I'm scared, Monica!"

Monica crouched and reached for the splintered phone. The garage had vanished and the entire world was a tiny, blinking point of light in a pit of darkness.

"I'm sorry, Dad," she said.

The voice inside the phone continued to scream until the call suddenly ended as if cut through with a knife. The words *Signal Lost* appeared.

"Monica?"

She blinked and saw Blaze's face, then looked back at the phone. The line was dead, the conversation over. Her friend put a hand on her arm.

"It's going to be okay," Blaze said. "Come on."

Blaze led her to the bus and they took a seat in silence while the smell of dank, wet fabric flooded the air.

What was she going to do? Her father had gotten this bad a few times before. The first time was just after Monica's mother left. Most recently was a few months ago when she was still working out west. He called her screaming and didn't let up for two hours. According to his doctors, Joshua Greene hadn't taken his medication in over a week.

The two halves of her brain were suddenly at war with one another. She knew that her father was wrong about her. She wasn't abandoning him. It wasn't fair of him to scream at her, and it wasn't right to demand that she drive through a tropical storm just to sit with him in the powerless dark.

On the other hand, the little child that still lived inside her had just been shamed. Not only was her father alone and scared, but he depended on her. Would it really be too much to make the drive, however harrowing, and comfort him in his terror? How was it *not* selfish to remain at the park? A man was crying out to his only daughter, and she was turning him down. These two realities tore at her, and it manifested as desperate gasping for air as if she were suffocating.

Her frame jolted as the bus rolled over the gravel, its tires thudding in and out of potholes, until they slowed to a stop and the doors opened. Monica moved without thinking, letting Blaze guide her through the blinding maelstrom. They stumbled up some steps, over a porch, and into a dimly lit cabin that smelled of sweet cedar and a rich campfire. Monica blinked the rainwater out of her eyes and looked around the room. They were standing in one of the staff residences. The furniture had been stacked against the walls to make room for row after row of cots where the rangers would ride out the tempest.

Blaze led them to a thin mattress wedged in the corner of the room and helped her down.

"What's going on?" she said, keeping her voice low. "Is everything okay?"

Monica shook her head, holding back an eruption of tears or screams.

"Is it your father?"

She nodded and wiped her nose.

Blaze gave her back a firm pat. "Is he okay?"

Monica shrugged. "No. Yes. I don't know." She hung her head and balled her hands into fists. "He's losing it, but he can still cut your heart out sometimes."

Blaze shrugged. "That's all my dad was any good at."

Monica turned to her. "I'm sorry to hear that."

Blaze smiled, her cheeks dipping to hint at tragedy. "I got the hell out of there as soon as I could. Ran away at eleven. When they caught me they put me in the foster system. *That* was a treat, let me tell you."

"My God," Monica said. "I had no idea."

"Of course you didn't," Blaze said, shrugging. "It's nobody's business, but given your current situation, I figured we had something in common: bad fathers."

"What should I do about him?" Monica said, pressing her palms into her eyes. "He wants me to go to him. Should I?"

"Hell, no," Blaze snapped. "It's crazy out there right now, and it's only going to get worse. Besides," she said, "the governor put a curfew in place for East Tennessee. No one is allowed out except cops and first responders."

"Aren't we first responders?"

"On federal land, but not anywhere else." Blaze gave her a playful pat on the back. "Looks like you're stuck here."

It was comforting to know the curfew gave her a solid reason not to go. Yet she still felt that nagging pain in her middle, twisting her on and on. Wouldn't a truly loyal daughter, a fully loving daughter, defy man's law to care for her family? Wasn't a daughter supposed to honor her father, even if he was losing his mind?

She began drumming her leg and chewing a fingernail, her brain working with furious effort. Blaze must have sensed it, because she smacked her back again.

"Hey," she said. "Let it go. I can tell you're worrying here."

"Of course," Monica admitted. "What would you do?"

Blaze cocked her head in thought. Then she gave Monica a sisterly glare. "Me? I'd take a shot of moonshine and cuss him out. But you aren't that type."

Monica smiled. "No, I'm not."

"No, you're the type to talk to the Sky Fairy about it."

Monica furrowed her brow. "The what?"

"You know," Blaze quipped, pointing up at the ceiling. "The Big Guy. The Old Bearded White Guy. The Sky Fairy."

Monica sighed. "You're right. I should be praying right now."

"Yeah," Blaze said, her face growing more and more mischievous. "Go talk to J.C. about it."

Giving Blaze's leg a slap of its own, Monica smiled at her, stood, and maneuvered around the weary, rain-soaked rangers on their creaking cots. She made her way back to the front door, grabbed the handle, and slipped outside.

28

— · —

THE STORM

T HE WIND RIPPED THROUGH THE TREES, CARRYING ALL manner of natural debris through the air. The porch was well sheltered, though, and she stepped toward a rocking chair, inspected it to see if it was dry, and sat down.

What a miracle that she could be outside during such a storm! She had endured severe weather in the Smokies before, including the tropical depression that had nearly cost her and Blaze their lives. But never had she experienced winds and rain of this magnitude. Trees bent and swung, dancing to survive the furious assault. Several were old oaks with deep, stubborn roots; they certainly wouldn't survive the vicious winds, unable to flex with the onslaught.

Just as she sat and lowered her weight into the chair, a loud crack burst from the woods nearby. She squinted to see what it was, but the darkness was too thick to be pierced. Monica leaned back, exhaled, and closed her eyes.

Suddenly a voice sounded from the other side of the porch: "I don't want to startle you."

She flicked her eyes open and turned toward the shadows. A man was sitting in another rocking chair. He leaned forward, a cigar in his hand.

It was Ownby.

"Goodness," she said.

"My apologies," he said. "I didn't think anyone else would come out here."

She glanced at the cabin door. "Too many people in there."

Ownby took a long drag of his cigar, the tip glowing orange in the darkness. "Agreed."

Monica watched him and laughed softly. "I didn't take you for a smoker," she said.

He blew a plume into the air. "I'm not," he said. "At least not regularly. Just when I'm nervous."

Monica swallowed as the air was wrenched by another loud burst from the trees. It took a while for her lungs to regain their normal cadence, especially as cracks of thunder rumbled in the sky, and the wind continued to howl like an ancient beast. Water was everywhere, running like a river over the roads.

Yet as she admired the violent beauty of the world around her, the caustic voice of her father remained in her mind. The cacophonous sounds tore at her spirit and she shuddered.

"Monica," Ownby said, suddenly breaking the silence, "I want to ask your forgiveness."

She looked and found his face, his eyes reflecting the glow of his cigar. He tapped it and the ash fluttered to the ground.

"Okay," she said.

"I crossed the barrier between professional and personal this morning. Yes, we share the same faith, but as your supervisor I shouldn't have spoken about that."

She remembered the bitterness with which she had received his words. "Thank you," she said, her voice soft. "I think I needed it, though."

"I've always seen myself as a mentor to my team members. A father, even. But it was out of line."

Monica's mouth parted at his words.

A father.

He leaned back and dragged another hit from his thickly-rolled cigar. The smoke blew behind him into the woods, but she could still smell it. It was sour like all burning plants, but there was a sweetness to it, too. She closed her eyes and remembered sitting on a hand-woven rug with her grandparents. Papaw always had a pipe clenched in his teeth. When she fell asleep in that old house, the strangely delightful smell would swirl in her nose. That same sensation flowed through her olfactory system on the porch.

"I took your advice," she said, daring to keep the discussion going, "Before I left Ramsey, I stopped and prayed."

"You did?" he said, his smile faintly visible.

"Yes," she said. "But I don't know if it made much difference."

"What do you mean?"

She shrugged. Mirroring his motion from the moment before, she waved at the surrounding monsoon. "The storm still came, didn't it?"

Ownby nodded.

"And people will still die, won't they?"

"They very well might," he answered.

"So what difference does it make?" she said, her voice rising. "Where is God in all of this?"

Ownby blew another puff into the air and flicked the ash away once more. "That all depends," he said. "What do you expect from a prayer, Monica?"

Clearly that professional boundary was behind them again. But this time she'd invited him over.

"I expect things to change," she said. "I expect God to do something."

"And what does that look like?"

"God could turn the storm away, or help us completely evacuate the park."

"Very well, let's imagine God *did* turn the storm away," Ownby said. "What happens to it?"

"It doesn't hit us."

"But where does it go? Does it magically vanish?" Ownby leaned forward. "Of course not. Say it swings north, hits West Virginia, and all those poor folks in the river valleys get flooded out."

Monica sighed. The point had been made.

But Ownby carried on. "What if it goes south? Too much rainfall in the Tennessee River means Chattanooga goes under like Atlantis."

"I get it," she said.

"The storm was comin' either way, Monica," Ownby said. "It had to hit somewhere."

"It didn't have to," she said, her cheeks growing hot. "It—it could have dissipated. Jesus spoke, and the wind and waves obeyed Him. Right?"

"Indeed they did," Ownby replied, rocking gently in his chair. "But what was Jesus's main concern?"

"Safety," she answered immediately.

And not at all to her surprise, Ownby shook his head. "No. Faith."

"Faith," she echoed, frustration rising in her chest.

Then Ownby cleared his throat. "Why are you afraid?" he recited. "How is it that you have no faith?"

"But the disciples' safety still mattered," she quickly interjected. "Jesus had to save them from the storm, didn't He?"

"Don't get me wrong," Ownby said. "Safety is important, and it's what we're charged with overseeing. But I'm talking about trust."

"Trust," she said, her eyebrows sharpening.

"Do you really put your trust in God, Monica?" Ownby asked. "Or do you use Him?"

"Use him?" she echoed. "What does that mean?"

A blinding flash lit up the forest like midday, then a rancorous boom split the air. Both flinched, but Ownby continued rocking even as the thunder rumbled up the hills.

Ownby smiled, a puff of smoke floating over his head.

"It's about the heart. If you start out with *God, give me this; God, I want that*—then where is your heart? Where is your faith?"

She took a long breath, but didn't respond.

Ownby leaned forward, the cigar held to the side. "If you lead with faith, dependence, neediness: You put your trust in God, not yourself. Then He has room to show up."

"Isn't that what I'm doing?" she said.

"I don't know," he said. "But the anxiety I see from you isn't the kind of fruit that grows with faith. God is not a tool to get things done. Yet when we surrender to Him, He gets more done than we can imagine."

Ownby leaned back, rocking once more. Monica looked out into the tumult as the squalling winds tore at the trees, sending flailing branches through the air that shone briefly in the few remaining lights powered by backup generators.

Ownby's words ate at her guts. She'd read the Gospels. She knew who Jesus was. Yet there was an element of Ownby's characterization of God that felt foreign, like she'd never really known Him to begin with, and she winced with sudden nausea. Had she believed in a "sky fairy" all along? Was her faith in nothing more than a magical force that rewarded people for being good? Every day of her life she had striven to be a good person, and she had been largely successful. So why, then, did she feel like God was in her way, an antagonist blocking her efforts to save lives?

Monica bowed her head.

"I'm exhausted, Mike," she said. "My father isn't doing well. He's very sick, and blames me for it."

Ownby frowned. "He blames you? Why?"

"I don't know. I try to take care of him, but I have a job," she said. "He doesn't work, and his social security hardly covers the bills."

"Do you pay for his expenses?" Ownby asked.

Monica lifted her head, not wanting to boast, but slowly nodded.

"Hmph," Ownby replied. "It doesn't sound like anything is your fault."

"There's more," she continued. "His kidneys are failing and he needs a donor. Guess who's the perfect match?"

Ownby's eyes went wide. "Really?"

"But I don't trust him. He refuses to listen to his doctors, flushes his meds, and eats nothing but frozen meals. I've tried everything."

"Does he think he's entitled to your kidney?"

She buried her face in her hands, and the tears began to rush through her eyes. "Probably," she whimpered.

Ownby sighed. It was a weary, grieving sigh, and Monica knew in that moment that he was on her side.

"Just because he's your father," the man proclaimed, "doesn't mean he's entitled to anything of yours. He already has your heart, doesn't he?"

She nodded, wiping fresh tears. "Of course."

"Then that's enough," he declared.

The Emergency Manager cleared his throat and extinguished the cigar, squishing the butt against the porch railing beside him. The tiny red embers flickered a moment, then died.

"Monica," he said. "May I pray for you?"

A wave of surprise crashed into her as if carried over the mountains on the winds. She trembled at the thought of her boss talking to God about her. She wanted to refuse. She wanted to cry *No!* and rush back indoors, away from this person who had somehow found his way into her personal business.

But she also wanted to say *Yes* and trust that Mike Ownby wasn't being a boss in this moment, but a caring mentor. He was asking for nothing in return. Nothing was being transacted. It went against every protective instinct within her—for how often can one truly trust a relative stranger, or a casual acquaintance, with the delicacies of one's soul?

She sat speechless, the silence swelling between them like a wound. But she drew a breath and said, her voice quivering, "Yes."

Ownby bowed his head and folded his hands together.

"Lord," he began, "I lift up your daughter, Monica Greene."

The prayer went on until she no longer thought about time. As Ownby spoke she felt dizzy, as if she had drunk a strong cocktail. Her ears went cloudy and her mind wandered into the unknowable reaches of the wild, wondering what evils she might have to resist in the coming hours.

Yet she heard everything he said, every uplifting and encouraging word. And in that moment, she realized that Mike Ownby genuinely cared about her. She had no idea what that kind of relationship was supposed to be like, and it both terrified and thrilled her.

When the prayer was done, Ownby excused himself to the cabin, leaving Monica free to tremble and wonder at the miracle she'd just experienced, all while the tempest raged around her.

29

— ◆ —

The Road

T HE STORM REFUSED TO LET UP.

Monica retreated to the crowded cabin, found an empty cot, and laid down to get some much-needed rest. It took quite a while to actually fall asleep. The howling wind shook the old structure, and the frame groaned and creaked through the long night.

When she woke, Blaze was beside her, checking the power of her radio.

The door swung wide and Ownby's voice boomed throughout the room. "Everyone up!" he called. "Sustained winds have dropped below thirty miles per hour, which means we're back in business."

Monica rose with the rest of the crew, her damp clothing still heavy and uncomfortable.

"Listen carefully," Ownby said as the rangers donned their gear and stood by. "Radio towers are down throughout the park. Apparently auxiliary power ran out a few hours ago. That means you will need line of sight for your radios to work. Cell towers are out as well," he continued. "I know you want to call your loved ones. For now, just hang in there and we'll let you know when the signal has been restored."

Monica swallowed as that familiar sick sensation poked at her guts. How had her father handled the storm? She tried to imagine him alone in the dark and shivered. She would have to hurry over to him the moment their rescue work was concluded.

"First order of business," Ownby said, "will be opening up the roads. Emergency Medical Services can't reach trailheads if there are trees everywhere. Assist maintenance in clearing obstructions. Then split into smaller teams to check for stranded hikers and campers. Remember: Transportation is key. Without it, we're cut off from support and EMS. Everyone got it?"

"Yes, sir," the rangers answered.

"Alright, let's go."

One-by-one, the standing army of Great Smoky Mountains National Park filed out of the cabin into the gray, dreary morning. The skies above continued to churn while a steady rain fell.

Monica stepped out onto the road. Downed branches were strewn as far as the eye could see. For every four or five trees still standing, one had cracked just above the roots, splitting vertically so that mighty spikes jutted into the sky like spears. The ground was invisible in places, hidden under a rippling layer of water. Monica stepped into an ankle-deep pool, gawking at the nearby river. The water crested over the roads!

"I hope the bridges are still intact," Monica said.

The rangers dragged the severed tree limbs off the pavement, and once the path was clear, they loaded onto the shuttle bus and began rolling back to the garage.

The long fence surrounding the maintenance compound lay in a mangled mess, more than a dozen fallen trees lying on it along the perimeter. A colossal oak next to the road had ripped a crater out of the earth that was filled with gushing mud and debris. The driver slowed to a crawl to carefully avoid the obstacle.

They rolled into the dark, silent building and the rangers poured out, spreading toward the fleet of park trucks. Monica flicked a lightswitch but nothing happened.

Wilde emerged from the bus with a flashlight illuminated and ran across the garage. He opened a metal box on the wall and pulled a red lever. With a sudden electronic hum, a series of lights clicked on, dimly illuminating the space. Backup generators began to roar outside.

Wilde ran back to the center of the large, open space and climbed up a step ladder, his impressive figure towering over them.

"Let's gather up!" he called. "Sevier County maintenance crews are clearing Highway 321 to the east. That way we can focus on our main roads."

He rattled off a list of ranger names and ordered them to handle Newfound Gap Road, the main highway over the mountains to Cherokee. Then he turned to Monica and Blaze.

"You two," he said. "Clear the road to Laurel Falls, then sweep the trail."

"How many vehicles are at the trailhead?" Monica asked.

"Four," he said. "We sent runners but they didn't see anyone on the trail."

"They didn't see anyone?" Blaze repeatedly, scowling. "Where the hell did they go?"

"We don't know," Wilde said. "That's what we need you two to find out. Once you find the hikers, call for help. We don't need another Little River situation."

Monica's lip curled at the veiled rebuke. But in Wilde's gaze she saw neither judgment nor condemnation, and rather something of a brotherly concern.

She nodded and held out her hand, into which Wilde placed a set of truck keys.

"Thank you," Monica said.

"We'll be fine," Blaze scowled, audibly annoyed.

They turned away and found their truck. She backed out into the rain and heard a muted splash as the rear tires descended into the brown floodwaters.

She drove along what was left of the service road. The truck shuddered on the slick surface, but the tires held strong and pushed. With a jolt, they climbed the lip of Little River Road and flattened out on the even surface.

Long, broken branches lay in pieces over the road like dead snakes. Monica drove right over them, the boughs cracking loudly under her tread. The road curved and they sped along, rolling over sticks and leaves, until the way straightened out and they could see far ahead.

Then Monica groaned. A bulky tree lay across the road, its bark plump and wet.

"That didn't take long," she said.

The tree wasn't unattended. A sturdy wrecker, its yellow lights flashing, idled beside the fallen trunk. Monica pulled alongside it and found two crewmen in white helmets.

"Need a hand?"

"You bet," one of the guys said.

Together, the four of them looped thick chains around the largest branches. Monica crouched and fed one end of the links under a bend in the trunk, which Blaze grabbed and handed back to the maintenance guys.

"That oughta do it," one said.

Monica and Blaze climbed back in their truck and watched as the wrecker shifted into gear. The engine growled like a dinosaur and the tires began to grind against the ground. Inch-by-inch, the wrecker hauled the trunk to the side of the road. The two guys reached into a rear compartment and withdrew a pair of chainsaws.

"Go on ahead!" they called, and Monica waved as she swerved around them.

Blaze peered into her side mirror. "We'll just end up waiting on them at the next tree," she said.

"Probably," Monica said. "It's better than sitting there with them trying to make small talk."

Blaze smiled. "True."

They continued west, trampling small bits of debris, and sure enough they rounded a bend and found a toppled branch of red pine. Monica slowed the truck to a stop.

"We have chainsaws of our own, right?"

"God, I hope so," Blaze said.

Blaze leapt out and headed to the rear of their truck, then reappeared with a large plastic case. Blaze flipped it open and removed the large tool.

"You want the honors?" she asked.

Monica jerked her thumb toward the tree. "Help yourself."

Blaze grinned, donned a pair of safety goggles, and made quick work of the trunk. After each cut, Monica hauled the section away, rolling it to a ditch flooded with dark, filthy water. Soon the branch had been dissected enough for them to pass. They stowed the chainsaw and returned to the cab.

They made it another half-mile down the road, but were once again forced to disembark and begin sawing a wild, gangly victim of the storm. More bush than tree, its long, gnarled branches stretched with claw-like twigs, many of which were tipped with small barbs. Monica took the chainsaw this time while Blaze worked the smaller limbs with a hedge trimmer. The work was slow, and after more than fifteen minutes of labor they heard the maintenance wrecker sputtering behind them on the road.

In all, the team cleared six trees leading to Laurel Falls Trail. One was severed twenty feet in the air, its upper half hanging over the road like a scimitar. It didn't take long to realize that this particular tree would require special attention, men in lift buckets and safety gear. The team carefully pruned away the jutting branches to form a narrow but passable lane beneath, clearing the way to the trailhead.

Monica put the pedal to the floor all the way up the hill to the popular destination for hikers and waterfall enthusiasts. When they breached the gap, Monica gasped.

"Oh, God," Blaze moaned.

Two vehicles—one car, one truck—were parked near the entrance to the trail. Two others were still where their owners had left them, situated side-by-side, but now they were barely visible except for the shimmer of metal under the colossal hulk of a toppled tree.

"You don't think anyone was in them?" Monica said, breathless.

"I hope not," Blaze said.

"What if they were sheltering from the storm?"

"I don't want to think about it."

Monica slid the truck to a halt and leapt out. They rushed to the cars and searched the mangled branches and drooping leaves for any signs of life.

"Hello?" Monica called.

Blaze echoed her, hollering from the other side.

They climbed over the outer limbs, trying to peer through what was left of the crushed windows. The roofs were both completely cratered into the seats. Every bit of glass was shattered and sprayed onto the pavement. The shards glinted like ice as Monica peered through the broken hedge. She squinted but couldn't see through the cracks in the branches.

"Anyone in there?" she yelled.

No answer.

"I say we leave it for now," Blaze said.

Monica bit her lip, trying to get a better view. The entire structure had been pancaked, and it was unlikely anyone would have survived it anyway. Had a stranded hiker taken shelter in one of these cars? What if several people were trapped there, suffering in some awful contortion? What if they could hear Monica's cries, but couldn't respond? What if—

"Monica?" Blaze said, breaking into her thoughts. "Can you hear anything?"

Monica exhaled. Every bit of her wanted to find a way in, to see if there were victims in need. But not a sound could be heard. Not a peep or tap or anything trying to communicate with the outside world. The truth was that anyone who had been in those cars was dead. It was that simple, and that meant turning away and letting go.

"Okay," she said. Then Monica rotated and clambered over the debris. She reached flat ground and pulled out her radio. "Wilde, this is Greene."

The radio burst into static, then the ranger's voice came clearly through: "Go, Greene."

"Two vehicles at Laurel Falls have been destroyed by a tree," she reported. "Unknown if anyone was inside."

"Okay," Wilde said. "If they were in there, is there any chance they survived?"

"Not really, no," she said.

"10-4," Wilde answered. "Be careful out there."

"We will," Monica answered. She was about to return the radio to the holder on her belt but paused, quickly squeezed the transmit button, and added, "Hey, Wilde?"

"Yes?"

"Any cell signal yet?"

"Nope," he said. "No cell, no phones, no power."

"Thank you."

It was worth asking. She hadn't spoken to her father in twelve hours, meaning the man had been unsupervised—and likely unhinged—for half a day. That was a lot of time trapped in his apartment, and there was no telling when she'd be able to get in touch with him again.

"Everything okay?" Blaze asked.

Monica nodded, storing the radio, and they jogged up to the trailhead and peered into the woods. The landscape was ravaged. Trees lay everywhere, crisscrossing the trail and littering the hillside. Other than the constant sway of brush in the wind, nothing was moving.

"I can't see anyone," Blaze said. "You got anything?"

"No," Monica said.

"At first I thought people were stupid for not getting back to their cars," Blaze said. "Then we found that mess back there. Now I just think they're stupid for even being here."

Monica frowned at her. Now wasn't the time to lord anything over anyone, especially those who might be fighting for their lives.

"Come on," Monica said. "Let's just find these people, no matter how stupid they are."

With one more scan of the parking area, the two rangers jogged up the trail in the shadow of the battered ridge.

30

Laurel Falls

T HE TRAIL WAS IN WORSE SHAPE THAN THE ROAD.

Tree trunks barred the passage like fallen mammoths laying heavy and crooked on the narrow pad of broken pavement.

Monica and Blaze rounded a bend with speed and startled: there were two bears right in their path! The creatures took one look at the humans, snorted, and dashed off down the slope, scattering leaves in their wake. They continued their brisk pace up the trail, pausing to climb over the fallen limbs and run up mounds of earth that had slid over the trail. It was going to take a small army of volunteers to cut and remove the blowdowns and make each of the Smokies' beloved hiking routes passable again.

The trail twisted into another hollow, the way littered with more obstacles than Monica and Blaze cared to count. With each challenge they found a way to clamber up the steep slope, move around the blockage, and then descend to the trail once more. They ran around a corner only for the path to vanish under a wall of thick, muddy earth. The entire hill had collapsed.

Not only was their way barred by mounds of dirt higher than either of them stood, but it was strewn with the naked remains of stripped trees, their branches and leaves ripped away during the violent landslide.

"Wow," Monica whispered.

"Well, this trail is officially dead," Blaze said. "Will that stop anyone from trying to hike it? Nope."

She sighed and climbed the thick brown bulge. When she reached a level spot above and looked down and said, "Come on."

Monica followed, but the whole thing felt risky. Landslides were notoriously unreliable places to maneuver. The ground was loose and the pressure of several human beings might be enough to get it moving again. She ascended cautiously, testing each step for a few seconds before giving it her full weight.

When she grabbed Blaze's hand and crawled up beside her, she wheezed, "Thanks."

"Let's just hope this thing is still here when we come back," Blaze said.

Monica felt her hands shaking. "I'd be okay if it decided to slide the rest of the way down while we're gone."

They scrambled over the decimated trunks until the pile ended and they were able to find the thin thread of trail as it reappeared on the other side. The rangers slid down, and when her boots hit the hard material, Monica felt a wave of relief flow through her like a summer breeze.

No more of that, please, she thought.

The trail tilted downward. It was all descent now to the falls. To their right, the southern flanks of Cove Mountain climbed precipitously skyward, and every tree seemed to lean down on them as if it might crack and tumble over. To the left, a sheer, steep drop fell into the Laurel Branch gorge. Monica peered over the edge, looking for any unnatural colors, the kind of dyes used in fabrics, but saw nothing.

A loud hissing began to swell in their ears, and Monica knew immediately what it was: Laurel Falls, the trail's namesake. They came to it in haste and slowed to a stop, steadying themselves on the man-made bridge at its base.

Families have always loved to wade, picnic, and enjoy the beauty of Laurel Falls. But after one too many accidental plunges down the dropoff that awaits any small child—or an intoxicated, reckless adult—the Park Service installed a permanent bridge of poured concrete. A row of cylindrical aqueducts allowed the water to flow through to the lower pool below. Thanks to this heavily reinforced engineering, the bridge at Laurel Falls had withstood the attack of the storm, even though the spitting runoff was flowing an inch deep over the walkway.

Monica and Blaze moved quickly onto the bridge, scanning the valley below.

"You see anyone?" Monica asked.

Blaze's head oscillated back and forth, checking every feasible direction. "No."

"Nothing?"

"No," Blaze repeated. "You've got to be kidding me. Where are they?"

Monica leaned over the railing toward the gorge. "Is anyone out here!?" she cried.

It was useless to shout from where she was. Her ears were flooded with deafening noise. It was impossible to hear any distant cries of the lost.

"Let's get down there," Monica said, and began lowering herself to a boulder below.

"Are you sure?" Blaze asked. "Shouldn't we check the upper part of the trail?"

"Who goes uphill during a storm?" Monica said.

Blaze shrugged. "True."

Monica continued descending, watching each step as the runoff and rain had made the surfaces wet and slick. A second waterfall poured into a surging stream at the bottom of the gorge. Normally the creek here was narrow and calm, but the abundance of rain had swollen it so wide that it filled the base of the ravine.

Monica crept her way downhill while clinging to branches and roots for support. Blaze slid after, keeping close behind.

"No one could survive down here," she declared.

"Then we need to find the bodies," Monica said. "Those vehicles didn't park themselves."

"Nope," Blaze said, that familiar edge to her voice reappearing. "A bunch of morons did."

Monica scowled. Why did Blaze have to be so dismissive? This wasn't the time for I-told-you-so's. It was time to focus on what mattered, which was helping others stay on the right side of life and death.

"Idiots or not, we have to help these people," Monica said, ducking under a rhododendron branch.

"Sure," Blaze said. "But they'll just go and do it again."

"What do you mean?" Monica said.

Her boot slipped as she stepped over a moist, mossy stone and she caught herself, trembling.

"We'll find these people, but it won't change anything," Blaze said. "We'll be out here again after the next disaster taking the exact same risks."

"Allison," Monica said, glancing back at her friend. "You're oversimplifying it. Have some compassion, for God's sake."

"Compassion?" Blaze scoffed. She stopped. Her lip curled and her eyes narrowed. "I have *plenty* of compassion. I love this place. It's my home. But these *people* keep coming and screwing it up. I'm sick of it."

Monica swallowed, the taut sensation in her chest was still throbbing. "We can't condemn people based on one mistake," she said.

Blaze drew a long breath through her nostrils, then kicked a rock into the foaming waters. "Then why do they get to condemn me? Why am I here, clinging to the side of a slippery wall, where if I lose my grip I'm dead?"

"That's why we got into this job. To end someone's nightmare."

"Not me. I told you," Blaze said, "I love this place. I hate these *people.*"

The two fell into silence. Monica wanted to respond, but nothing seemed appropriate to match her friend's indignation. She turned to the raging river, its waters dark and black with shadow and mud, running swiftly downhill. Anyone caught in them would be swept away. She had instantly put herself in harm's way, and by proxy, Blaze as well.

"I'm sorry for judging you," Monica said, her head bowed. "And I don't want anything bad to happen to you."

"It's fine," Blaze said. "Let's just find these people and get the hell out of here."

They continued their precarious wire-walk along the river's edge, keeping their boots barely above the fierce waters. They reached a small lip where the stream dumped into another pool below. Monica paused and peeked over the edge. It would be another nerve-wracking climb down the wet layers of exposed Anakeesta sandstone.

"I'll go first," Monica said. "You wait until I get to the bottom."

"Okay," Blaze agreed.

Monica crouched and squinted at the wall. Water dripped down the side while moss lay thick on the stones like green beards. What spot could hold her? Perhaps the best move at this point was just to jump. But that brought the chance of losing her balance and possibly tumbling into the stream.

"I don't know," she said, frowning. "I don't like it."

Blaze leaned over, took a look for herself, and made a sour face. "Me, neither."

"What do we do?"

Blaze removed her helmet and adjusted her ponytail, keeping the hair bound and out of her face. She replaced the helmet, attaching the chinstrap with a click, and shook her head. "Hell, Monica," she said. "I don't have a clue."

Monica sighed and took another gander over the edge. Nothing she could see brought her any hope. Just then a strange sound caught her ear.

"You hear that?" Blaze asked.

"I sure do," she whispered.

As if on cue, Monica heard it again.

"Help!" a voice said. *"Please, please help!"*

31

GORGE

THERE WAS NO QUESTION. THEIR QUARRY WAS VERY CLOSE, and to get to them Monica and Blaze would have to descend into the ravine.

"Give me your hand," Monica said. "Help me down."

The two locked hands as she squatted by the edge and lowered her leg down the exposed face. Monica's foot found a hold and pushed on it. It gave a little, and the surface was slick like ice.

"Hold tight," she said, gritting her teeth. She brought her other leg down, looked for a good step, and chose a wide shelf deep in the wall. Her upper body hung over the edge, but the spot was dry and solid. She pushed on it, found it reliable, and let go of Blaze's hand, gripping a loose root protruding from the bushy earth.

It was only about a four foot drop, but the ground sloped sharply toward the river, so she couldn't simply leap. Instead, Monica let her foot go but kept it close to the wall. She touched her toe along the rock face until another trustworthy notch held strong, then she lowered herself the rest of the way and set her boots on solid ground.

"I'll show you the holds!" Monica called up.

With smooth athleticism, Blaze swung herself over the edge and placed her hands and feet on the exact same spots Monica had used. In less than ten seconds she was beside her.

"Okay," Blaze said, blowing a loose strand of hair out of her face. "Where are they?"

Monica listened again, and sure enough the desperate voices continued to hail them. The sound was coming from deeper down the sharp gorge carved by the Laurel Branch. Monica pointed and the two continued forging downhill, weaving through the dense snarls of rhododendron and thorns choking the narrow chasm. Monica's boots skidded along a patch of mud and she threw out an arm and caught herself on a tree.

"Hello?" she called.

The response was immediate, but weak: "Hello?"

Monica and Blaze scrambled along the hill until the earth disappeared from beneath them, terminating in another lip, and the women lowered themselves and scooted over the edge. Gravity deposited them into a cove like coins into a tin, and they steadied themselves and took in their surroundings.

The branch gurgled along a wide trench. The land around it flattened into a small half-moon, the walls framed with jagged, diagonal plates of rock. On Monica's side of the water, the ledge was narrow and uninviting, the air suffocated by encroaching brambles. On the other side, a small hollow had formed, likely from the large bodies of bears seeking a cool place to rest in the hot summers. As she surveyed the little cove, Monica's breath caught in her throat.

Six human beings were clumped together in the space, all shivering, soaking wet as they sit or lie on the ground.

One of the survivors immediately saw her and rose to her knees. "Thank God!" she moaned.

It was a woman with long blonde hair matted to her scalp. Her cotton t-shirt, emblazoned with the words "Gatlinburg, TN," stuck to her mud-streaked body. Red scars marked her arms and face.

Monica made a rapid assessment of the stream and its rushing, brown waters. It looked shallow enough, likely a reason the survivors had stopped here. She dropped a leg into the water and sank up to her knee.

"I'm crossing," she announced.

"Right behind you," Blaze said.

Monica took the next step, the water rising up to her calf. The current was strong but not nearly enough to overpower her legs. She took the last three steps with confidence and emerged on the other side, kneeling beside the woman.

"I'm Monica Greene," she said, placing a hand on the woman's back. "What's your name?"

The woman lifted her head to answer and croaked out a heavy sob. She wept with vigor, releasing what must have been hours of pent up terror and suffering, wheezing to catch her breath as she wrapped her arms around the ranger's neck. Monica held her then gently pushed back so they were face to face.

"Tell me your name," she said.

"D–D–Deborah."

"Hey, Deborah. I'm going to help you out of here." Monica gave her shoulder a gentle squeeze and gestured to the other five who were perking up at the arrival of the rangers. "What are everyone else's names?"

Still shivering, Deborah listed them off one by one. In all there were three parties of hikers who had ridden out the storm. Deborah and her husband, who were both in their fifties but in admirable physical shape, had taken up the mantle of leadership during the disaster. A single woman, short and a bit overweight, had stuck close to them, and was sitting motionless with her back against the rocks, her eyes open but filled with weary haze. The other couple, two retirees in khaki shorts and bright neon shirts, sat up but moved slowly, and Monica noticed that they had wrapped bandages around their knees.

The sixth and final hiker was also a man of advanced age, but he was lying apart from the others, his balding head turned away. Monica frowned but turned her attention back to Deborah.

"What brought you to the mountains?" Monica said, crossing to the others. She took each hand to get a sense of just how hypothermic they might be, and to get a good look at their skin tone and pupils. Excessive dilation, or even contraction, indicated issues like shock, dehydration, or an impending seizure. As for the survivors' skin, Monica expected a certain amount of blood loss in the cheeks and forehead after such a long time exposed to the rain, but there were specific factors that could signal dire emergencies.

"We came for our anniversary," Deborah said. She took the hand of the man nearest her. "My husband and I honey—honeymooned here twenty years ago."

Monica flashed her a smile. "That's wonderful," she said, then resumed her inspection. The elderly man and woman were frigid and pallid with thirst and hunger, but smiling wide at the arrival of park rangers. The younger woman struggled to sit up and answer Monica's questions.

"Can you walk?" she asked.

"I dunno," the woman mumbled.

"Are you injured? Anything at all?"

The woman stared at the ground as if dumbstruck, then shook her head.

"Are you sure?" Monica said.

"I—yeah."

Monica turned and found Blaze's eyes. Blaze was tightening her nose, and Monica realized she smelled it too. A faint, sour odor filled the air.

"Did you all drink from the creek?" she asked.

"Yes," Deborah said.

"Did you filter it?"

"No," Deborah said.

"How about boiling it?"

"No. How would we do that?"

From above, she heard Blaze mutter, "Oh, give me a break...."

"Who's had diarrhea?" Monica asked, looking from person to person.

At first, they seemed shy to admit such an intimate detail, but Deborah once again did the honors for the group by whispering, "We all did."

"Next time," Monica said, "bring a filter."

Nearly every page of the National Park website warned against drinking untreated water. Even the one-dollar trail map had a thorough note about the dangers of doing so. Giardia, a nasty intestinal parasite, lived in the rivers throughout the park and regularly made life miserable for hikers who didn't treat their fluids. For these six survivors, deprived of food, sleep, warmth, and healthy water, the dehydrating effects of giardia could be fatal.

Monica reached into her pack and found a small pouch of hydrating gel. She handed it to the young, overweight woman. "Drink this," she said. "You need to replenish your fluids."

Monica retrieved a handful more and distributed them to the other survivors, each of whom accepted the silver gift with grateful, trembling hands. The only person who hadn't received one yet was the old man who continued to lie completely still, several yards away from the rest of the group. Monica crawled over to him and placed a pouch in his open, boney hand.

"Sir?" she said.

His eyes were closed, his lips parted. Monica peered at his back. Almost imperceptibly, it flexed out, and back in with steady breaths.

"Sir?" Monica repeated. "You need to drink this."

The hand didn't move. Then, with a tiny flick of the fingers, the man dropped the pouch into the dirt.

Deborah's voice rose over the din of the river. "I didn't tell you about Jack. He won't take it."

Monica lifted her gaze.

"Why not?"

"When we met him at the falls he was alone and said that's how he wanted it. To be alone."

There was nothing wrong with that, Monica thought.

But Deborah went on, explaining, "Then all of the sudden, Jack fell from the falls—at least we *thought* he fell."

Monica frowned. "What do you mean, you *thought* he fell?"

Deborah's face grew dark, the bags under her eyes purple. "He needed help, so we climbed down to him," Deborah explained. "But he refused."

"He refused," Monica echoed.

Deborah nodded but said no more.

Monica walked back to where Jack lay, crouching to get a good look at his face. The eyes were still shut, sunken in emaciated, pale flesh.

"Blaze," she said, nodding at the man. "Ten-fifty-two."

From a boulder above the group, Blaze took out her radio and squawked the ambulance code to the maintenance team down on the road.

Monica squeezed Jack's hand, rubbing it with her fingers to massage the blood back to life. "Sir," she said, speaking directly into his face, "can you hear me?"

The man's head rolled back and he blinked as if waking from a drunken stupor. "Mmm," he said.

Deborah leaned toward them. "Can you tell what's wrong with him?"

Monica took a short breath. "A lot," she said. Her fingers found his wrist and felt for a pulse. Faint and sluggish, the vein gave little report. "He's in shock," Monica continued. "Weak pulse, dehydration, exhaustion, hypothermia."

Deborah gasped.

"I'm surprised more of you aren't as bad as he is," Monica said. "We don't really have time to talk about it, but I'm amazed any of you thought it was a good idea to be out here when the storm came."

It was a rare moment of venting her starkest thoughts, but looking into the skeletal face of the man before her, Monica couldn't help dreading what was to come. The man was not strong enough to stand and walk out to the road. The journey would be perilous, too, over wild lands and blowdowns, all while trying to keep one's balance against the sharp mountain flanks. Hopefully a rescue crew could arrive and assist, but they were probably an hour or two out at the very least. The odds of this man surviving and seeing his loved ones again was minimal. There was little they could do for him until a team arrived.

"Sir," Monica said to the man, "do you think you can stand up?"

The head moved from side to side.

"We need to get you out of here," she said. "We can't move you by ourselves. You need to try."

He shook his head again, eyes still shut to the world. "No," he mumbled, his lips a faint blue. "I can't...."

Monica stood. "Can the rest of you walk?"

One by one they nodded.

"Drink those hydration gel packs I gave you," she said. "They'll give you the strength you need to get home."

"Do you have any dry clothes?" one of the women asked.

"No," Monica said. "We have emergency blankets, but those won't do much for you right now. We need to get you out of here. Let's get up and ready, everyone."

The five began to move, bending and groaning like hibernating creatures awakening after a long winter. Monica watched each, looking for signs of debilitating injury. The heavyset woman rubbed her elbows, both of which had probably been hurt. The couple with bandaged knees struggled to their feet but held steady. Deborah's husband had dried blood on his face, originating above his hairline. But they all managed to reach their feet and hold their position.

"Good," Monica said. "Now here's what's going to happen. Ranger Blaze here is going to lead you out to the road. From here, it's best just to follow the river straight down. It'll be slow and difficult, but it's much faster than trying to get back up to the trail. Once you reach the road, emergency vehicles will be able to take you to the hospital." Monica paused and took a breath, giving each of them the most confident look possible. "You're strong enough. You can make it."

Deborah smiled, took a few hobbling steps toward her, and embraced her one more time. "Thank you, Monica," she said.

"You're welcome."

As they parted, Blaze leapt down from the rock again. "Radio check," she said.

Monica hit the 'transmit' button, sent a quick test, and confirmed: Their communication was good to go.

"Take your time down there," Monica said, giving Blaze a playful smack on the back. "And don't say anything mean."

Blaze rolled her eyes. "Only if they start complaining."

That'll be in about a hundred yards, Monica thought with a weary smile.

Then Blaze glanced at Jack, lying on his side. "Remember," she said, "none of this is your fault."

Monica followed her gaze. "I know," she said. "I just hope the rescue team gets here soon."

"They will," Blaze said. "I'll see you at Headquarters. Take care of yourself."

"You, too," she said.

She watched as Blaze rallied the quintet of shivering survivors with a loud shout, jogged into the heavy brush, and began forging the way ahead.

"Count off!" Blaze cried. "Every sixty seconds, give me a count!"

The bedraggled walkers mumbled, "One"–"Two"–"Three," until all were accounted for. Monica waited until they had shuffled out of sight, then the small cove grew silent except that spatter and spit of the stream.

She turned to face the limp, motionless body of the man who was almost certainly going to die, and began pondering what she could do to save him before it was too late.

32

—·—

HOPE

"SIP ON THIS," MONICA SAID.

She knelt beside the man and pressed the squeezable pouch into his hand. The fingers hung frail and limp.

"Jack," she repeated. "You're severely dehydrated. All you have to do is put the straw in your mouth."

His narrow face stared up at the tree tops. Wisps of snowy hair clung to his head. His eyes were large and dark, gazing at the heavens with a fervent intensity. His thin lips began to move and she heard a muted mumble issuing from them. She inched closer to his face and stuck the straw out and placed it at the opening of his mouth.

"Drink," she said.

His mouth wiggled, perhaps in an effort to accept the gift. But instead he firmly shook his head.

"No," he moaned.

"Please," Monica said. "It will restore your strength."

He drew a long breath, then released it with a loud, disgusting gurgle. *There was fluid in his lungs.*

"Go away," he said, his eyes still closed. "I'm done."

"The heck you are," Monica countered. She set the pouch on the ground and withdrew the folded silver emergency blanket. With a loud crackle and pop, she opened it and laid it over him. "There," she said. "This will help you get warm."

"No, it won't," he rasped.

"What do you mean?"

He lifted his eyes and met her gaze, his head trembling.

"I'm going to die."

"No, you're not," Monica said. "Just do as I say."

He gave a weak cough and said, "It doesn't matter."

Jack's desperate situation, coupled with his certainty to succumb to it, created an overwhelming sensation like there was divine authority to it. Monica flexed her fingers in and out of a fist, then hardened her jaw and narrowed her eyes at him.

"Tell me," she said, "since you're lucid enough to give up, why doesn't it matter?"

He huffed a little, as if the conversation were draining him of all his remaining stamina. "I screwed up," he said, sniffing. "I made a mistake. Now I have to pay for it."

Monica lowered her head and propped her arms up on her knees. Was this guy serious? Had she and Blaze really come all the way out here to argue with a man about his own survival?

Then she remembered Deborah's telling of their story, of how they'd seen Jack at the base of the falls, seemingly a victim of a terrible slip-and-fall. But the way she'd said it filled in the last blank in Monica's mind.

"I'm sorry you feel that way," she said. "One mistake doesn't deserve a death sentence, though."

"That's—not true," he said, then coughed violently with a pained wince.

"Why not?"

He fidgeted under the shimmering silver space blanket, the metal material rustling like autumn leaves. "Don't you get it?" he said, struggling to form phrases without gasping. "Just leave me alone."

The blanket rose and fell in anxious plumes, like waves breaking against the sides of a boat. His breath came and went in furious, agonized blasts. His eyes opened again and glared fiercely at the sky.

"Fine," Monica said. "Should I just leave you?"

"Yes," he said. "Please."

"Think about that," she said. "What would that do to me if I just left you here? How would that change who I am?"

He grunted, a loud pant like that of a bear, then lifted his head again, the entire upper part of his body shaking. "Who cares," he growled.

Monica shuddered at the defeat in his voice. "Who cares?" she said, repeating his taunt. "I care, Jack. I found you out here. I can help you. Whether you want it or not, your life is sacred to me."

Jack's head snapped back, almost with supernatural fervor. "Shut up," he hissed. "You know *nothing* about me."

Monica shrugged. "Maybe. I know you tried to kill yourself up there by jumping from the falls. I know you didn't die, and suffered painful injuries."

He sniffed.

"I know you've given up, Jack," she said. "But those five people tried to save you. They put their lives at risk in the face of a tropical storm to save yours. And now, even after all that, you're still stubborn about it all."

"They should have left me there," he said, struggling to eject the words as his chest puffed up and down.

"Really?" Monica scolded. "You think they'd really do that, Jack?"

He mumbled again but it was impossible to know exactly what he said.

"Do you have any idea how selfish it was to come here—to Laurel Falls, of all places—to do what you did?" she said. "This is the most popular trail in the entire park. You *had* to know it would be crawling with people! But you came anyway, didn't you?"

"Please... just shut up," he said weakly.

"No. I'm not going to shut up," Monica said. "I came all the way out here to help people, and your attitude isn't making my day any easier."

Again, he grumbled something that was unintelligible and rolled over, the blanket bending under him.

"I don't care about your mistakes," she said. "I can't help you take them back. But I *can* help you see there's a future out there. There's hope if you want it. You just have to choose to believe in it."

She found herself almost out of breath from the impassioned speech. She was leaning toward him, as if he were a winded teammate in need of a pep talk.

But Jack just curled his lip into the harshest grimace she had ever seen. "You don't understand," he muttered.

Then he laid his head on the ground, breathing in short, shallow bursts.

Monica stared at him. Warm hope had been doused in an ice bath of his words. She sat back as if the weight of this man's life and death were now on her shoulders. What horrible events had happened to him to evict every bit of optimism from his heart, and any remnant of faith from his spirit? What unthinkable sins did he commit that made life so unpalatable?

Nothing could be said to change him. There wasn't a sermon in the world—at least not one Monica could think of in the tiny hollow—that would create a new heart in him, a heart with an appetite for abundant life.

Monica sighed.

"I guess there's only one thing I can do for you, Jack," she said. "I'll pray that you find comfort and peace, and that you're still with me when the rest of my team gets here."

He didn't move, and she barely heard him groan, "Don't waste your breath."

Monica grit her teeth.

"I won't," she whispered.

She bowed her head and began to whisper with fast and anxious words. There was a loud grumble and the sound of spitting, but she carried on. She prayed until time melted away, her head between her knees and her hands opened to the skies above. Every few seconds she opened her eyes and peeked at Jack's motionless form, making sure that the emergency blanket continued to rise and fall with his shallow breath, and continued her prayer.

AN HOUR LATER, the first of the rescuers appeared in the ravine below. They were WASAR, the Wilderness Area Search and Rescue unit, a team of elite volunteers who assisted the park rangers at times such as this. A man's neon green shirt shone like a beacon in the drab forest, and his yellow helmet blazed like a searchlight. Monica stood and waved as he hustled up the steep hill.

"Where is he?" the rescuer said.

Monica stepped aside and pointed. "Right here. He's not responsive, but he still has a pulse."

The WASAR volunteer rushed to Jack's side. "You're Monica Greene, right?" he said.

"Yes."

"Jeff Weatherly," he said, shining a tiny flashlight into Jack's eyes.

Three others sprinted up the steep, inhospitable terrain. Two dropped to the ground, unclipped their packs, and began removing emergency gear while the third handed Weatherly a gray tube with a hose connected to a clear plastic mask. Weatherly wrapped the elastic bands around the back of Jack's head and secured the mask so it fit snugly around the nose and mouth.

"Oxygen flowing," he said.

Two others swiftly cut away Jack's sleeve with a small pair of scissors and pushed an I.V. needle into the waxy flesh.

"What now?" Monica asked.

Weatherly glanced at his watch. "We'll let that bag get into his system. Probably thirty minutes. Hopefully that will be enough to stabilize him for the journey."

Monica nodded. "Thank you. You're miracle workers."

"Just doing the job," Weatherly said.

"The *volunteer* job," Monica added. She cast a look at Jack, eyes still closed but chest rising and falling slowly with the flow of rich oxygen. "Be careful if he wakes up," she continued. "He isn't too keen on survival."

A wave of surprise passed over the volunteer unit, but they brushed it off with professional calm. "That happens," Weatherly said. "We'll deal with him if it comes to that."

Monica smiled and nodded. Now that Jack was safely in their care, she knew she had to move on. Certainly there were more stranded souls that needed her help. There was no point in waiting around.

But the man's despair still hung over the little cove like Death's cloak, and it still seemed to be lurking and waiting for its chance to strike. What could be said? He almost certainly couldn't hear her.

Instead of speaking more words that he could ignore, Monica simply laid her hand on Jack's arm and gave it a firm squeeze. Hopefully it would send the message that life, a life where men and women volunteer to preserve the wellbeing of others, is worth fighting for.

Monica stood, thanked the volunteers once more, and turned away. She'd probably never see Jack again. Hopefully he'd make a full recovery, see his family, and atone for whatever sins had led him to give up on it all. Her role in his story was over.

But that wouldn't stop her from continuing to pray for him. As she descended the sharp, treacherous gully, heading toward her next mission to save the wounded and lost, that's exactly what she did.

33

— • —

CHIMNEYS

"ALL AVAILABLE RANGERS TO CHIMNEY TOPS TRAIL!"

It was Wilde's voice, deep and steady as ever.

"Greene here," she said as reached the saddle-shaped flat of Fighting Creek Gap. "On my way." With a quick glance at the mangled heap of smashed cars, Monica leapt into her truck and swung around with a wide u-turn.

For most of her life, Monica had been taught that she was responsible for the well-being of others. Her father, more than anyone, regularly reminded her just how crucial she was to his happiness and health. Her students, in the old days of teaching, were her charge and responsibility. The world of education would frequently proclaim just how essential she was to her students, and how without her these kids would struggle and fail. In every avenue of life, the world made it clear that Monica Greene was the last straw that could not break.

Yet with Jack, it felt different. She had done all she could. She had searched the wilderness for him, found him, and provided everything he needed to stay alive. And yet he had rejected everything Monica had for him. Thanks to this, she felt somewhat absolved of whatever his fate ended up being.

But the need to save him hadn't left her, even as she piloted her truck through the shattered forest. In the end, it had still been her who had stayed with him. Was there a word she was supposed to say that she had failed to utter, or some heroic act that she had been too cowardly to perform?

At this thought, any peace left her and she turned the steering wheel with a white-knuckled grip. She rounded the bend that passed Headquarters and suddenly gasped. Her lungs felt crushed and she grabbed the seat belt and pulled, wheezing to get a full breath.

What's happening to me? she thought.

While her eyes were studying the debris-littered road, she couldn't shake the image of Jack's hollow face from her mind. Then she blinked. Jack's visage was gone, replaced with the countenance of the woman with a weak, haunted smile.

It was the face of her mother.

Monica drew a long breath through her nostrils, her brain wavering with dizziness.

"It's not my fault," she whispered.

She tightened her grip. Sweat ran over her palms, greasing the wheel.

"It's not my fault what happens to you!" she cried.

She rubbed her eyes, hoping to purge the ghost from her mind, then slammed her boot on the accelerator and thundered up the mountain.

SHE PULLED INTO A SPACE beside three other NPS vehicles and jumped out of her truck and slammed the door. The first thing she noticed was Stranded Steve gaping at her from one of her billboards. He was clinging to the side of an exposed mountain, sweat pouring down his decrepit face, all because he'd ignored the warnings not to climb the chimneys.

Monica didn't have time to admire her work and jogged past him down the trail. She'd barely made it to the first bend in the path when she heard heavy boots and slowed to a stop.

Another ranger was running toward her: Wilde.

"What's the situation?" she asked.

Wilde's normally strong face was creased with worry, and his beard was riddled with brown clods of mud. He pointed back to the screaming river below them.

"We've got fourteen hikers stranded," Wilde said.

"Fourteen?" she exclaimed. "What about the bridges?"

"The first two are in good shape, but the third is gone."

"Gone?" she said. "What happened?"

Wilde shook his head, more distraught than she'd ever seen him before. "We don't know for sure. Trees probably fell into the river. Then the waters rose, boulders pushed it, or a tree knocked it out. Point is, it's gone."

"Who's here?"

"You, me, and Mullens. Ownby's up there, too."

Monica raised an eyebrow. "Ownby? Really?"

"He insisted," Wilde said.

"Okay. What do you need from me?"

Wilde pointed up to the parking area. "Help me get the gear from the truck."

They rushed back up the shallow steps to the parking area. In the bed of his truck lay several long, yellow-striped duffel bags. He hoisted two out and handed them to Monica who looped the straps over her shoulders. Instantly her frame dropped as eighty pounds of gear hit her.

"Oof!" she said, her knees buckling. "What's in these?"

"Cables," he said. "Harnesses, helmets, flotation devices."

"Got it," she said.

He lifted two more identical bags and placed them on a single shoulder. For a moment she thought he might be favoring one side of his body by allocating all the weight there, but then he reached in again. Monica gawked as Wilde slung two *more* bags over the other shoulder.

"First aid," he said, his voice raspier with the load. "Command tent, maps, radios – and food."

"Shouldn't we make two trips?" she said.

He shook his head. "No time."

Wobbly with the incredible burden, Wilde marched toward the trailhead. Monica followed, grunting as she built momentum with the tedious bags pulling on her shoulders.

As Wilde had described, the first two bridges were still intact; however, they definitely needed repair. High, surging waters had battered them, and an onslaught of broken limbs and shattered trunks had been slashing at the substructure for hours. The planks swayed and the bags wiggled as the straps inched toward her neck, tightening. She paused, loosened the load, and stumbled onward.

Monica and Wilde rounded a corner after the second bridge and turned to climb a steep ascent of a ridge. Water ran down the middle of the trail, chattering under the splashes of their boots.

"How much farther?" she called.

"It's the next crossing," Wilde said.

Monica nodded, gasping for breath as the grade steepened severely. Each step took exponentially more effort than the one before. Her legs burned with fresh fire while Wilde was breathing like a horse, inhaling through both his nose and mouth, summoning as much oxygen as possible to make the climb.

"You got this," she said between gulps.

"You, too," he said.

They rounded a switchback. She had carried loads like this before through the backcountry, but usually they were on her back in a pack that positioned the weight on her hips, not her shoulders. This was an entirely different struggle, a task only a cruel coach or drill sergeant would force on his minions in need of a harsh lesson about resilience and toughness—

Suddenly Wilde's entire frame buckled and he tumbled to the ground with a loud cry.

"Wilde!" she shouted.

She lifted the bags off of her and threw them down, then rushed to her fellow ranger's side. "What happened?" she said.

Still tethered to his four bags, Wilde grabbed at his foot.

"Ankle!" he said. "My ankle!"

"Did you twist it?"

He shook his head, eyes shut and face twisted in a grimace. "Sprain!"

Wilde grit his teeth, pulled up the pant leg, and rolled down the sock. Already the upper barrel of his ankle was beginning to purple and swell.

"Oh, no," he growled. Then he laid his head back and let the foot fall to the ground. "I felt something pop and then I went down. Damn it!"

Monica felt her heart beginning to thud against her ribs.

"Is there an ice pack in any of these bags?" she asked.

Wilde groaned and tried to push himself up. He patted a bag. "Here," he said. "Oh, *God!*"

She tore open the zipper. Six red-and-white boxes lay within, a bright cross on the lids. She opened one and grabbed an air-activated ice pack. She ripped open the packaging, massaged the bag, and handed it to Wilde.

"Here," she said, pulling the zipper back.

"Thanks," Wilde said, pressing it on the wounded joint. "Can you get the rest of these bags up there? I don't think I can carry one now."

"Of course I can," she said, her tone icy. "Maybe we should have taken two trips."

He scowled at her. But the wetness around his eyes told the whole story, and she immediately regretted the smart remark and softened her expression.

"I'm sorry," she said.

"It's fine," he said, panting heavily. "I was stupid. I guess I thought that I had to be the hero. Now look at me."

She smiled at him. "I feel that way all the time."

He laughed again, this time devoid of any snark. "That's why we do this job, isn't it? Otherwise they'd put us in an asylum for the crazy stuff we do."

She shrugged. "They probably would." She stood and shouldered one of the bags. "I'll be back."

His face tightened. "Please be careful, Monica," he said, wincing. "For now, you're Incident Commander."

She froze. Wilde was the acting I.C. over the Tennessee side of the rescue operation. If he was out of commission, then it had to fall to someone else.

Monica reached out a hand and took Wilde's with a loud clap.

"I'll do my best," she said.

He nodded. "I know."

"Stay on the radio," she said, releasing his grip. "Keep sending out the word. We're going to need everyone up here."

Wilde nodded, still gasping. At the moment, she knew his body was urging him to fall asleep and protect the newly injured leg. He probably wanted to throw up and pass out. He wouldn't, of course, thanks to his mighty pride, which meant his situation would be all the more miserable. She knew this because she, too, had sprained an ankle in the Grand Canyon, and had been shocked at how painful and difficult it was to do much of anything afterwards. The spirit is always willing, but the flesh can be maddeningly weak.

"Alright," she said. "I'll send a runner back for the rest of these."

"Good," Wilde said.

She took one more long look at him. He was their strongest ranger, the former Army man who could handle anything. Now he was down.

In that instant she remembered that it had been Wilde who had plucked her and Blaze from the Little River, saving their lives. It had been Wilde again who was there when she needed rescue, withstanding the noxious fumes in the mine and carrying her out. In her zeal to be the hero, she had run into life-threatening trouble each time. What would she do if disaster struck a third time, now that Wilde was on the sidelines?

"Thank you," she said.

Then she turned and began the careful journey up to the broken bridge, wavering with each step under the weight of the enormous bag.

34

—·—

THE CROSSING

MONICA TURNED A CORNER AND GASPED.

Before her was a wall of raging white water. Ashlyn Mullens stood at the edge of the spitting flume, the mist adding a distinct shine to her orange-and-blond hair. Beside her, Mike Ownby was frowning as he gazed across the gap, his arms tightly crossed.

Monica followed his gaze and dropped the bag, staring across the chasm in horror.

This is impossible.

Across the river canyon, seemingly a thousand miles away, the crowd of terrified hikers huddled together. Meanwhile, every tree by the river's edge had fallen. The distance between the two shores was easily more than seventy feet. What could they possibly use to span such a gap? The river itself was a furious maelstrom of crashing water, punctuated with the occasional chest-shaking *Boom!* as a stone would tumble and slam into another. It made Class V rapids look like a lazy river. Between her and the survivors there was nothing but loud, misty air. The river may as well have been the Atlantic Ocean.

"Monica!" Ownby bellowed. "You're here!"

"There are four more bags down the trail," she announced. She tapped Mullens on the shoulder and said, "Can you bring them the rest of the way? Check on Wilde while you're down there."

"Check on Wilde?" Mullens said. "Why?"

"He sprained his ankle."

Ownby brought a hand to his mouth. "Oh, dear," he said.

"I'll be your Incident Commander for the time being."

Mullens nodded and uttered, "Yes, ma'am," and began jogging down the trail, leaving Monica and Ownby alone beside the roiling river.

"I'm glad you're here," Monica said. "This isn't going to be easy."

He shot her a quick but weak smile. "Well, someone suggested I get into the game." He nodded up at the survivors. "Any ideas?"

"Fast-rope," she said. "But I'm guessing there aren't any helicopters available."

Ownby shook his head. "Feds won't give the green light due to the risk. Besides, I've been on the radio with the National Guard all morning and every helicopter is currently in use."

She sighed. Fast-roping was a quick and easy way to reach inaccessible places, as long as one had the aircraft, training, and cooperative weather. But after an incident several years ago in which a rescuer's life was lost, the Department of the Interior had put the brakes on it. As for available helicopters, it made sense that the National Guard was handling a thousand other crises outside the park and couldn't spare a bird at the moment.

"What about a wire crossing?" she said. "Have you noticed any strong trees that would be a good anchor?

"Not in the immediate area," Ownby said.

"Are there any other routes to that side?"

"Of course, but they're even worse," Ownby said with a frown. "Road Prong Trail is long and steep, and it's probably flooded right now. These poor souls wouldn't stand a chance. Then there's the manway from Sugarland Mountain, but who knows what condition it's in." Ownby exhaled and shook his head. "I know it doesn't seem like it, but this spot here is the best hope we have."

Monica shook her head. That couldn't be true. It was almost guaranteed that someone, ranger or hiker, would fall into the river, and anyone who fell in would be bashed into the rocks like a ragdoll.

"What about waiting it out," she said. "Can we drop supplies? Dry clothes, food, sanitary water? It may not be safe for people to cross, but equipment should be fine."

He thumbed his chin, considering. "I don't know," he said after a moment. "That assumes they can all make it that long. And we're talking a week, Monica, not days. There's a lot of moisture on the mountain." He shook his head again. "I still think we need to make this work."

"How?" she said.

Ownby shrugged. "I don't know," he said. "That's why it's your job, now."

Monica gawked at him.

Her job now?

"What does that mean?" she snapped. "Aren't you the Emergency Manager?"

He smiled. "Aren't you the Incident Commander? There's a reason I stick to the office and the UTV scene, Ranger Greene. This was never my gift of the spirit, so to speak."

Monica scowled, and in a sudden burst of anger muttered, "Then what good are you?"

She stepped past him and lifted her gaze to the far side of the stream. Not only was the threat of falling into the river real and dangerous, the idea of it alone had the potential to freeze every single survivor in their tracks. If the rangers weren't able to execute every step of the procedure with iron-clad confidence, these weak and terrified men and women couldn't be expected to trust them with their lives.

She had to make a breakthrough, and make it with swagger. Otherwise, no one would dare budge.

But how?

Alongside the shore, a stone staircase climbed the ridge behind a scrub of dogwood and curved around a trio of stumps, the shattered hilts of three trunks broken into splinters. But on the other side of the trail, somewhere near the top of the staircase, one solitary trunk remained. Maybe it could be leveraged as an anchor.

Monica turned upstream. She had to find a spot on her own side, but that wouldn't be easy. The woods were thick with rhododendron and fractured trees. The mutilated trunks created claustrophobic dens of branches with small limbs lush with dagger-like thorns. Monica stepped off the trail and slunk on all fours under a dripping black trunk.

"Careful, Monica," Ownby warned.

"I know what I'm doing," she said, and continued her foray into the wild.

The underside of the snarl quickly proved the best way to traverse it. Several smooth, rounded depressions lay under the larger tree carcasses, likely formed by bears or other mammals seeking shelter from the wet and cold. Currently they were filled with two or three inches of muddy water, but Monica was able to slip through them swiftly and make progress.

She'd ventured perhaps a hundred feet upstream before taking a hard left turn toward the water and rising to a squat. She grasped at branches and crept through the maze until the spray of the water was tickling her flesh. She paused. Could any of the trees be useful for a harness? Could she collar several of them together, gathering their combined strength and ensuring a more reliable passage? She counted two trees that were sturdy enough, then a third, a fourth, and finally a fifth. The main question was whether they'd have enough material for the job.

Monica dropped to the forest floor once more and doubled-back on her foray. A few minutes and several streaks of mud later, she regained the trail and stood, brown muck painting her uniform. Ownby was still alone, but two more bags were on the trail.

"Mullens took them one at a time," Ownby explained. "Apparently Wilde wouldn't let her carry any more at once."

"He learned that the hard way," Monica said. She pointed up the stream. "I think we might have a shot. It's not going to be easy, or completely free of risk. But it's the best chance we've got."

The man nodded, his eyes staring out over the water. They seemed to be shimmering with liquid.

"What is it?" she asked.

Ownby shook his head. "I'm sorry for letting you down, Monica." He smiled at her, the same expression on his face as when he'd prayed for her the night before on the porch. "Please tell me what I can do to help."

She shrugged. "Just help me save lives."

He nodded. "Will do."

Heavy boots began to stomp nearby, and the two parted gazes. Ashlyn Mullens appeared, running slowly with one bag over her shoulder.

"Good work," Monica said. "I hope you're ready for more."

She nodded, breathing heavily but appearing ready either way.

"Let's start with the cables," she said. "I'll take a bag, and you take one as well."

"Where are we going?" Mullens asked, staring nervously into the wall of water.

Monica nodded to the cramped rhodo clump beside them, then went to the ground and began dragging the heavy load through the mud and filth.

SHE TOOK A BOW AND ARROW from one of the bags. The shaft of the arrow shaft was specially designed to hold, drag, and carry the weight of a tow line, and Monica took a set of folded instructions tucked in a plastic bag and pushed them over the razor tip.

The package ready, Monica handed the bow to Mullens.

"Care to do the honors?" she said.

Mullens nodded gravely and took the weapon in hand. She aimed high over the river and let the arrow loose. It sailed straight into the air as if it might soar over the treetops, then angled sharply down and plummeted toward the earth. The point stabbed into the bank of lush greenery on the far side, just barely making the crossing.

"Good shot," Monica said, patting her on the back.

"Thanks," Mullens said

A pair of stranded hikers separated from the larger group and descended to the water's edge. One plucked the arrow up and tore off the instructions. Heads side-by-side, the pair read the message, waved, and flashed a thumbs-up signal.

"We're good to go," Monica said. "Let's send it."

On the near end of the line, they tied and clipped one end of the thick cable, the first wire that would support their weight as they attempted to cross. Much too cumbersome to throw or tow with a flimsy arrow, the cable would have to be hauled over manually. Monica and Mullens held it up and waved. The hikers returned the gesture and began pulling. The silver line began snaking out over the abyss.

"Hold it high!" Monica said.

They hoisted the cable over their heads as the hikers dragged it across. One drop into the violent waves could easily sever the connection between the rope and the much heavier cable, then they'd be back to square one.

The cable bowed but did not catch in the water, and soon a solid strand lay over the river, the first piece of the bridge that would hopefully deliver these men and women to safety.

"Let's anchor this off," Monica said. Together, she and Mullens passed it around the five trees she had selected. They threaded the loose end through a winch and began jacking it taut against the trunks. The ratchet clicked with each turn while the trees inched together.

Monica loaded the second arrow.

"A little less height this time," she said.

"Right," Mullens acknowledged. She aimed, pointed the projectile toward the treeline, and let it go. For a moment it looked pure, like a dart on a line straight toward the bullseye. But a whip of wind caught it, knocked the head down, and threw it right into the water. Instantly the thin guide began streaming away from their feet.

"Grab it!" Monica cried.

Mullens leapt forward, the string whistling through her fingers, then she closed her hands into fists. The string stopped with a jerk.

"Here," Monica said, and she bent over and helped Mullens haul the stubborn cord back up. The little arrow came clattering over the rocks, water dripping from both ends.

Mullens knocked the arrow once again, aimed, and fired a third missile. This shot was a hybrid of the first two, smooth and direct. It whizzed past the two leaders on the side, several steps safely below them. They scrambled to attention and began hauling the load across in haste.

Monica and Mullens wrapped the second anchor around the set of trees and tightened it with a ratchet.

"Okay," Monica said. "I'll cross with the end of the third and secure it on the other side."

"But you can't cross," Mullens said. "You're the I.C."

"I know," Monica said. "But I'm not asking you or Ownby to go first."

"Why not?"

"Because," Monica said, looking her fellow ranger in the eye, "this scares the heck out of me, and I would be a coward to ask you to do it first."

Without further protest, Monica laid her fingers on the first cord, then the second, feeling the tremulous strength within. With both hands, she closed her fingers into fists and pulled. The cords wobbled under the force.

"It needs to be tighter," she said. "Can we get a few more pounds of pressure out of ours?"

Mullens turned and worked the ratchet while Monica positioned herself high on a rock in full view of the hikers. She waved her hands until she had their attention, put her fists together, then yanked them apart as if to imply tension and pulling. On the far side, a man copied the motion, then outstretched his arm as if to say, "Make it straighter." Monica nodded, and the workers on the far side began cranking. She held the line again and felt a flutter of energy, the kinetic waves rippling up and down the braided silver steel. After a few more seconds, Monica gave the cable another shake. This time it barely moved.

She closed her eyes and took a long, heavy breath.

"Okay," she said. "Time to harness up."

AS SHE SLIPPED HER FEET THROUGH THE STRAPS, her hands began to tremble. Her eyes repeatedly turned to the churning waters. Monica swallowed, trying to force the memories and feelings away, but she blinked and saw the cold depths of the bottom of the Obed River, the faces of her parents, the screams of her father, the howling accusations of her mother—

She doubled over, coughed, and rubbed her eyes. Now was no time for haunted dreams and memories. Monica sturdied herself by standing tall and buckling the waist belt of her harness. She clipped two carabiners to a pair of thickly braided lanyards, securing her to the wire. Lifting her legs from the ground, she tested the cable's load-bearing capacity.

It held.

"Take your time," Mullens said.

Monica nodded. "Thanks."

Just above her head was a winch that would help her slide over to the far side. It would be slow going, but that would give her time to assess each element of the crossing and decide if anything needed to be adjusted in the positioning and anchoring of the cables.

Monica kicked out from the shore, sliding a few feet. Then she began to backslide as her weight dragged her back. The tiny steel teeth in the winch bit down and she stopped with a jerk, swinging gently. A mere foot below her legs the waters raged, the roar deafening in her ears.

She reached up and grabbed the wire with one hand and the winch with the other. She crept hand-over-hand a foot farther, pulling the winch along. The cable remained strong as she swung out into the void. An icy mist swirled over the depths, the tiny crystals biting her exposed skin. Her fingers shook from the fear and the cold. She drew a deep breath.

You can do it, Monica.

She dared a glance down into the swirling, watery tornado, the black depths cracking open as the foam spat into the air, and she could see flashes of boulders lying beneath like tombstones. She gulped, crept forward, and slid the winch closer to the far shore. Her arms stung from the effort and she let go for a moment, gasping.

"Jesus," she said, her voice raspy, "give me strength!"

She pulled a few inches more and paused to take a few breaths and rest. The waters thundered below. Upstream, a viscous *crack!* tore the air. Something enormous was breaking into pieces and could come careening down the valley at any time.

"Not again," she moaned.

Monica focused on the thread of wire that was keeping her on the better side of life and death, and shoved the winch onward. It seemed like millions of feet lie between her and solid earth. Never had her arms been so tired. It wasn't just the struggle of pulling her own weight—Monica prided herself on beating anyone who challenged her to a pull-up competition, and was looking forward to competing against Wilde—it was the struggle of mind over matter, of pushing out the thunder of the water and the soul-freezing treachery of the watery chute.

"Help me, God," she wheezed, and pushed the winch a few inches more.

Of course she was calling on Him now that she was exhausted. Her faith always seemed to be a last ditch effort, a safety net, a fire escape. To her, God had never been a person or a figure to be loved and enjoyed; He was, at least in the world of her lukewarm faith, a 9-1-1 call.

Yet somehow He was supposed to be her *first* call, her number one plan in all things. The truth was that she believed God was absent from the physical world and not worth calling. Yet as she dangled above the white serpentine river, its cold waters striking her with its crystal fangs, Monica wanted Him to show up in a powerful and meaningful way. It was a scorching contradiction, like heartburn from an extra helping of the Lord's Supper. She felt small and pathetic, a tiny child on a string in the hands of a furious deity, an unforgiving parent of an annoying, faithless child.

Monica reached out again, taking the frigid winch in her shivering fingers, and slid it forward.

"I'm sorry," she moaned.

She repeated the motion, moving in spite of the cold and the paralysis of frozen adrenaline. She did as she was supposed to.

"Be with me," she whispered. "Give me—strength...."

Monica leaned forward, and as she did so, she thought her arms might give out. She continued in spite of the weariness and hauled her limp body just a few feet more. She flailed with her feet, hoping to add momentum to her movement.

Then something seemed to kick back at her.

Monica opened her eyes.

The far bank was right in front of her.

A grin exploded on her cheeks. She jerked the device forward once more and pulled herself the rest of the way in one smooth, easy motion.

She'd made it!

Monica reached out and hugged the vegetation as if it was a long-lost loved one. Then she disconnected herself from the cable and clambered up the stone steps toward the shivering survivors.

35

— . —

RESCUE

A T THE TOP OF THE STEPS, ALL FOURTEEN SURVIVORS STOOD in a disorganized row, their faces brightening with hope.

"Hey, everyone," she said. "I'm going to get you out of here."

They all rushed her, wrapped their arms around her, and cheered as if God Himself had come down on a cloud to deliver them from certain death. As the group parted, a man and woman stepped forward.

"We are *so* happy to see you!" the man said. He was tall and leanly built, his muscles showing through the wet clothing.

"Yes," the woman added. "So happy!"

Monica extended a hand and shook each of theirs. "Ranger Monica Greene," she said.

"Max," the man answered.

"Eva," his partner said. She was short, not even five feet tall, but powerfully framed with strong legs and short blond hair that fell just above her shoulders. A cute birthmark on her cheek gave the impression that she was always smiling.

"We were beginning to worry that no one would come," Max said.

"We've had our hands full," Monica said. "How's everyone holding up?"

Max and Eva glanced at each other before answering. They exhaled slowly, the weight of their ordeal clear in the weariness of their gazes.

"We had actually just finished hiking her first map," Max said, nodding proudly at his wife.

Eva smiled. "It took us two years, but we did it!"

Monica grinned and said, "Congratulations!"

Many hikers make it a goal to hike all 800 miles of trails in the park; to do so is to "finish a map." Monica nodded toward the distant chimneys. "Was this your last trail?"

"This, and Road Prong," Eva said. "But by the time we finished it was starting to rain and a lot of people were wandering on the trail, unsure what to do."

"The skies opened up and things got ugly fast," Max said. "Our plan was to hike back up Road Prong to our car. It was only when we saw how many people were still out that we thought, 'We can't just leave them.'"

"You stayed to help?" Monica asked.

They turned to each other and nodded a bit sheepishly. "Yeah," Max said.

Monica couldn't help herself and gave them both a pat on the back. "You two are heroes," she said.

Max and Eva introduced Monica to each of the survivors, and once again the distinctly foul odor of diarrhea floated about the air. Out of the fourteen hikers, there were four who were clearly dehydrated and exhausted. Monica looked into their eyes and saw a similar vein of defeat she'd experienced with Jack at Laurel Falls. They would need immediate evacuation.

Monica led the first four down to the cables and explained the procedure. She took the pair of harnesses and handed them to two of the survivors.

Much to her surprise, the first two crossings went without incident. Two men slid side-by-side on the twin wires to safety and landed in the arms of the rangers waiting on the far side. Monica hauled the carabiners back up using a support line; meanwhile, the faces of more rangers began to appear on the far side. Wilde himself arrived, too, limping slowly on a pair of crutches.

Monica waved back, then turned to a pair of survivors next to her. "Just like they did," she said. "It'll be over before you know it."

The hikers strapped in, closed their eyes, and flew over the chasm in a matter of seconds. Mullens waved as they were freed, and Monica pulled the harnesses back up. She turned to the next survivor, a woman with long dark hair, and offered her the harness. The woman took a look at the device and shook her head.

"No," she said, her lip quivering. "I can't."

"It's okay," Monica said. "I was nervous too."

"No."

Eva stepped beside her and gently laid her hand on the woman's arm. "Hey, Becky," she said. "Are you scared?"

The woman nodded. A tear slipped down her cheek.

"It's okay to be scared," Eva said. "We all are."

"I can't do it, Eva," Becky said, shaking her head, her hair fluttering around her.

"You can," Eva said. "All you have to do is put on the harness and gravity will do the rest."

"I can't!" Becky cried. "I'm so scared!"

Monica put a hand on Becky's other arm. "I know you are. Everyone here is. But this is the only way to get home"

"What about this?" Eva said, trying to soothe the frightened woman. "I'll go down with you. How does that sound?"

Becky's eyes widened. "You—you would do that?"

Eva turned to Max, who was sitting on the stone steps above them. His eyes were dark and heavy, but he looked back and forth from Becky to his wife, then nodded. "Yes," he said. "Go. I'll be down soon after."

Becky slowly donned the harness and clipped it to her torso. Monica marveled at how effective Eva's efforts were as Becky slid her legs through the lanyards and hooked herself onto the second rescue cable.

"Hold on so you don't go too fast," Monica said.

Becky nodded at her, eyes enormous.

"It'll be okay," Monica added. "Physics will do the rest."

"I—I don't—I can't—"

Monica leaned over and tugged on the carabiners securing the harness to the rescue cable. They were all securely looped over the wire.

"Hold on," Monica interrupted, and without waiting for any approval from the fear-stricken Becky, she gave the woman a gentle shove.

A shrill scream filled the gully as Becky flew like a bullet over the river. The wire buckled and she seemed to surf right on the top of the frothing rapids. The strength of the anchors held, and Becky flew straight into the waiting arms of a team of rangers.

"Now that's zip-lining," Eva said with a grin.

Monica laughed. "Bet you can't do *that* in Gatlinburg."

Eva turned back to Max, blew him a kiss, and pushed off the bank, moving more methodically and cautiously. She reached the bank and stepped lightly on land. She turned, waved at Max, then disappeared into the woods.

"How many left?" Monica asked.

Max counted. "Six."

"Good," Monica said. "You've done an amazing job. Both of you."

Max smiled. "Thanks. We're happy to help."

They ushered two more hikers to the wires, a middle-aged couple from West Texas. With every step, they chatted Monica's ear off about how they get rain and storm clouds in the desert all the time and it rarely means much, which is why they got caught in the backcountry.

"We ain't no damned fools," the man said.

"Can't help it if it's different than where we're from," the woman added.

"Of course," Monica said, stifling her annoyance at their flippant attitude. "Go ahead and get in the harness and let me know when you're ready."

The two suited up and when they were hooked up to the line, Monica gave them each the go ahead. The two slid down, shrieking until they hit the far shore.

"Four more including you?" Monica said, turning back to Max with a sigh.

He nodded. "I'd like to go last, if you don't mind."

"Not at all," Monica answered. "I'd do the same."

They sent two more, a pair of girlfriends vacationing on an early fall break from the University of Kentucky. They, too, had withstood the ordeal quite well, making use of good preparation and excellent physical fitness. They went hand-over-hand down the cables without any fuss and soon had vanished in the woods below.

"That leaves me," Max said, "and Mr. Wilson."

Monica peered up the trail and spied the man of whom Max spoke. She realized that she knew next to nothing about him, and Max and Eva hadn't mentioned him either. He sat in silence next to a large tree along a flat stretch of trail, staring into the forest, his bald head reflecting the wisps of light peeking through the clouds above.

"Should I go get him?" Monica said.

"I don't know if you can," Max said. "He told me a thousand times that he's not crossing that river."

"He said that to you?"

"Over and over," Max said.

Monica nodded. "Great."

"You want me to go?" Max said.

She shook her head. A good leader didn't do that. It would be on her to convince Mr. Wilson that crossing was the best plan.

"I'll talk to him," she said.

Monica climbed up from the bank, brushed off her pants, and headed over to the place where the old man was sitting in solemn silence.

MONICA SEATED HERSELF ON THE WET GRASS beside the man. He looked at her, rubbed his nose, and hastily turned away. He was thin and unmuscled, clearly not the outdoorsy type. A thin paintbrush of white hair sprouted from his scalp. When he lowered his hand into his lap, Monica saw that the fingers were shaking.

"It's okay to be scared," she said. "I was, too."

Mr. Wilson remained motionless, watching something of interest off in the forest. A browned leaf fluttered down, thrown off its branch by a gust of wind, and brushed his cheek. The man took it in his quivering fingers and set it beside him.

"Are you here with family?" Monica said.

This question seemed to hit the mark. He gave her a partial glance, his eyes heavy, but looked away.

"If you are," she said, "they must be anxious to see you. Is there anyone who might be worried?"

She leaned toward him. It was essential that her words create definitive pictures in Mr. Wilson's mind, pictures with faces and voices that he longed to experience again. She peered at his hands which lay in his lap. A silver ring encircled a finger.

"You're married. Does your wife know you're okay?"

No answer.

Monica took a breath, then said, "If I was separated from my family, I'd definitely want to get back to them. Where are they right now?"

He sighed, his eyes heavy with exhaustion. The eyelids twitched, their scarlet interiors bright like blood.

When he finally spoke, each word was full and measured.

"I'm not going."

He turned away again.

At first a blast of dejection ran through Monica like an icy wind. But she had to stick with her tactic.

"I guess they'll be disappointed," she said, letting her tone fall. "I think it'll be especially hard when they learn how long you survived, only to give up hope at the last minute."

She paused again, hoping this would pierce his defenses. Mr. Wilson remained immobile, staring into the distance as if something fascinating were there.

She extended her arm over the river. "You know the parking lot is just past those trees? In fifteen minutes we can have you on your way to your family."

Mr. Wilson's frame rose for a moment, but fell with a swift exhalation. He bowed and shook his head.

"I'm not going across that river," he repeated.

Then he climbed to his feet and began walking up the trail, a slight limp hampering his gait.

Monica watched him, resisting the urge to run after. Another thought came to her, and thankfully it involved less footwork.

She scooped up her radio and pressed the button.

"Ownby?" she called.

"Yeah?"

"I've got a job for you."

HE DANGLED OVER THE RIVER as Monica firmed her grip on the cable. With Max assisting, they hauled Mike Ownby over the white monster of roaring water, his helmet hanging loosely on his head. Ownby glanced down at the raging bedlam, then looked to the shore with a goofy grin on his face. He crested the near bank and grabbed Monica's hands to haul himself up, laughing like a rider on a rollercoaster.

"Wow!" he said. "What a rush!"

"It's way more fun to pull yourself," Monica said. "Want to try?"

"Oh, no!" Ownby said, smiling. "I'm not like you. I couldn't arm wrestle a chicken right now."

"I'm sure you'd do fine."

The aging man held a finger up to his elbow. "Carpal tunnel. I can barely type with this hand anymore."

They made sure Ownby was standing on firm ground before unclipping him from the line.

"Where is he?" Ownby asked. "Up the trail?"

"Just a little ways," Monica said, standing at the top of the stairs. "I think he wanted to get away."

"I would, too," Ownby said. "How scared he must be."

"He's not the only one," Monica said, her hands on her hips. "I'm scared that one of our anchor trees will fail, or that he'll fight us on the way over. I wish we had a sedative."

Ownby turned to her, a scolding expression on his shaking head. "You're starting to sound like Blaze," he quipped. "Don't give up on people so easily."

He marched up the steps to follow the old road and Monica climbed after. Ownby wasn't nearly as advanced in years as Wilson, but her supervisor was much closer to the man's age than she was. Perhaps he could summon some words of wisdom that would be heard and heeded.

Monica stood beside Max and waited until Ownby reached Wilson. He said something and the two shook hands. He placed his palm on Wilson's shoulder, and the pair began ambling out of view.

"Where are they going?" Monica said.

Ownby wasn't going to seriously indulge Mr. Wilson's wild plans to get out of here by some other path? She gnawed and looked behind her to the far bank where the other rangers were staring up at her, their expressions anxious.

"Chimney team, standby," she said into the radio. "We'll be crossing momentarily."

Monica looked back up the trail. The two men were now walking toward her, side-by-side and chatting softly.

"They're coming," she said.

Max smiled. "I think your plan worked."

As the two approached, the gist of their conversation began to float into her ears.

"—then we had our *third* daughter," Wilson was saying. "I kept wondering if God would eventually give me a son. But, by golly, they kept getting more beautiful. So I said, 'Okay, Lord. I'll be a father to a bunch of girls!'"

Ownby clapped him on the shoulder. "For me, it was boys. Boy after boy until Angelica and I had five of 'em. Five! Who needs five boys in their house?"

Wilson laughed. "Someone who wants an empty cupboard!"

"No kidding!" Ownby roared. "They ate anything and everything—except salad, of course. If Angie bought a head of lettuce, that thing would just sit in the refrigerator until it turned brown."

"Mm, hmm," Wilson replied, nodding. "They didn't touch it, did they?"

"Didn't even look at it," Ownby confirmed.

"Oh, my," Wilson said, chuckling gently. "What fun kids can be."

"I'll tell ya."

The two sauntered along, and with each step Wilson ignored the ranger and her volunteer partner. Yet as they passed, Ownby turned to Monica and nodded.

We're good to go.

"Get ready," she whispered to Max.

Monica rotated to watch as Ownby led the old man to the wires. Their conversation was quickly swallowed by the thunderous river, its white rapids continuing to spew gray mist into the ravine.

"My third boy was the hardest—" Ownby was saying, opening his carabiners one at a time to secure himself to the cable.

"Middle children are never easy—" Wilson replied. The harness was in his hands, and he lifted his leg to begin putting it on. "—But you learn to— something for everyone. Right?"

"Exactly," Ownby said. "Now just slide that strap there—"

Wilson brought the thickly corded straps up to his hips. His hands grasped for the buckles and lowered his head to squint at the connection.

Monica stared, nervous energy rushing through her like a solar storm. As the harness reached Wilson's waist, she leapt forward and said, "Let's go."

She began to descend the stairs, but Ownby must have spied the movement out of the corner of his eyes, because his head snapped to her and he raised a hand and waved it back-and-forth. *Stay there*, he seemed to yell with his gesture.

Monica slid to a halt, grabbing at the bushes beside her for balance.

Max halted, breathing heavily. "What's the matter?"

"I think Ownby is trying to distract him with conversation. So far it's working."

Max raised his chin. "I wish I'd thought of that."

Ownby gave Wilson's harness a good tug. He patted him on the arm. "Lookin' good, Carl!" he cheered.

Monica lifted the radio. "Chimney team, we're sending him over."

Ownby inched toward the edge of the stairs and shouted over the blast of water below, "Take a big jump, Carl! You can do it!"

The old man, however, was doing exactly what Monica feared. He froze, his arms over his chest and legs tight together.

For a moment, she felt a wave of pity. How could he *not* be nervous? Before him was a tempest of ice, rock, and dark death. It was everything he feared, and now that he was right up against it, it was more overwhelming than ever. Wilson began to back away, one little step at a time, until his tether jerked at the wire.

"Go!" Monica shouted.

The old man turned to her and his eyes went pale.

Ownby waved his hands toward his new friend. "It's okay!" he said. "Just tell me about your baby grandson—"

The river hissed like some ancient creature hunting them in the bush. Monica shuddered as the frigid spray blasted her neck. Wilson continued to press himself against the cliff, as far from the water as possible, while Ownby reached out for him with both hands.

"Look!" Ownby said, yanking on his own tether with violent jerks. "I'm safe! I'm secure!"

Wilson began to sink to the ground again.

He's not going to move.

Monica took another few steps, moving toward him.

Ownby pointed across the water. "Carl, I'm going to go! Watch!"

Wilson took one look, then bent over and began fiddling with his straps. Monica stared.

He's trying to get out of the harness!

"Carl!" Ownby called. *"Carl!"*

The aging head lifted as if it weighed a thousand pounds. Water dripped into his heavy eyes.

"I'm going first!" Ownby cried. "Just follow me!"

Ownby took three quick steps, bent his knees, and leapt into the void. He seemed to float for a moment, the carabiner rubbing hard against the wire. But it recoiled and flexed upward, and Ownby was lifted in the air and began sliding down toward safety.

"See?" he yelled.

Once again Ownby seemed giddy, like a child. Monica smiled. She had to admire his optimism. In his mind, going about it this way was the one thing that could convince Carl Wilson to take the leap of faith necessary to save his own life.

Yet even as Ownby slowed again, sliding at a glacial pace along his wire, Wilson did not budge from the rock wall. If anything he seemed to harden, like a victim of a curse. Monica balled her hands into fists.

Someone has to save this man.

She sprang forward and covered the distance to him in just a few seconds.

"Come on," she said, sliding her hands under Wilson's armpits and hauling him up.

He went deadweight and cried, "No, no!"

"You have to trust me," Monica said. "It's going to be okay!"

"No, don't!" he screamed.

"Trust your harness!" Monica yelled right back. "Just trust it and go!"

She dragged him across the narrow footpath until she stood on the edge, the back of her boots touching nothing but air. Wilson struggled against her, but his feeble strength could not compete. She tightened her hold on his arms.

"Sir!" she said. "It's for your own good!"

"No, no, *no!* I don't want to go! I don't want to *go!*"

"Mr. Wilson, stop!"

"*No!*"

He lurched away from her, slipping out of her hands. As he did, a volcanic rush of panic exploded within her and she lashed out with an arm to catch him. Her fingers closed on the thick strap tethering Wilson to the wire and she pulled.

In that microsecond, she realized she was making a terrible choice. But it was the choice that made sense, in spite of the horrific spectacle. Wilson needed this. He wasn't going to save himself. Ownby had tried and it wasn't enough.

Monica tensed her abdominal muscles and rotated her torso with a powerful jerk. Her fists pulled, the strap went tight, and Wilson bent double as the harness wrenched him backward, sending over the edge into the dense mist with a loud cry.

She gasped. The deed was done and she could only watch as the old man tumbled through the air, legs and arms swinging as his screams melted into the cacophonous flume below.

He flew a short ways before he slid to a halt beside Ownby.

"Carl!" Ownby shouted. "Calm down!"

He reached for Wilson but the frightened man was writhing in panicked horror. He found Ownby in the chaos of his tumbling and latched onto his arms.

"Carl!" Ownby shouted again.

The old man snatched wildly and pulled Ownby so close that their cables were nearly touching.

"Help me!" Wilson shrieked.

"Just slide down, Carl!"

"Let me out!" Wilson cried. He released Ownby and snatched at this harness like a mad animal.

Monica stared in horror. "What is he doing?" she said.

"Don't!" Ownby pleaded, reaching for the desperate man. "Just a little farther—"

Then Wilson dropped. As if a trap door opened beneath him, he plummeted several feet but he threw out his arms, grabbed Ownby, and stopped with a violent jerk.

"Mike!" Monica screamed.

"What's happening?" Max yelled, clambering down the steps to stand beside her.

Monica couldn't speak, and just pointed.

Ownby rotated face-first toward the water until his body was upside-down over the raging stream. Below him, Wilson dangled with kicking feet. Then Ownby yanked one arm back, grimacing in agony, leaving Wilson hanging by a single appendage.

Carpal tunnel.

Monica scrambled to the water's edge. Could she get any closer and reach one of them?

"Help!" Wilson wheezed.

"I can't!" Ownby cried.

The radio burst to life, its crackling words barely audible. "Greene, Greene!" someone was shouting.

She couldn't answer. She'd never seen anything like this in her life and had no idea what to do—

Wilson howled again, his hand slipping. He spun for a moment and Ownby rotated with him.

Monica turned from the water and rushed back up to the wire and its anchor point on the shore. Gritting her teeth, she clipped into the line. She would have to go out there and hoist Wilson back up. It was the only way to save him. But would the cable and its anchor points hold?

She'd have to trust it. Monica gave the thick, silver cord a firm look, then gazed out over the raging white river.

God, please help me—

She leapt into the abyss. She felt her weight immediately test the strength of the wire, and for a moment she thought all of them were about to drop right into the river. She bobbed upward and she slid to a halt twenty feet from Ownby.

"I'm coming!" she called.

Wilson clung to Ownby's hand while his legs working at the pedals of an imaginary bicycle below.

Monica reached up, took the wire in her hands, and began moving toward them, pulling herself one foot at a time.

Crack!

The wire sunk right as the sound hit her ears.

"Monica!"

She turned her head. It was Max, still on the shore.

"The trees!" he yelled.

The cable dropped again.

Monica turned back to Ownby, his body twisted upside-down, holding onto Wilson. She had to get to them. She was the only one who could save them—

CRACK!

This time her stomach shot into her mouth from the brief drop and she screamed. Wilson's legs vanished into the spray. Monica shook her head and shouted, "No, no!" but there was no denying what was about to happen.

The trees were about to come down.

"Ownby!" she cried.

The man didn't turn to her, his head still swirling in gray mist mere inches about the claws of the water.

"Let him go!" Monica yelled. "Save yourself!"

The wire fell again.

"Ownby!" she called one more time.

But her boss didn't budge, his hand locked onto Wilson's arm to keep him from disappearing into the mouth of death.

"Monica, hurry!" Max bellowed from above,

She turned away from the two men and pulled herself up the sagging cable. The trees quivered, shaking the wire up and down. Her hands slipped over it, the braided strands slick with moisture.

Suddenly all sound vanished. The water, the yelling, her own desperate breathing—it all became a haunted void. It took her brain a moment to realize that something had rendered her momentarily deaf. There was only a dog-whistle whine, high and terrible and meaningless.

An enormous shadow fell over her. A jet black cloud descended like the doomsday dreams of Saint John. She grabbed her chest as the air flew from her lungs.

Then a hand appeared, jutting over the edge of the embankment. Monica lunged toward it as the cable went totally slack, spooling through her carabiners like thread. Her hand found Max's and clamped onto his fingers. The shadow passed and Max pulled her up onto flat ground.

Monica crawled to her knees, wheezing. A dark, splintered tree trunk lay over the trail, and beside it the cold and worthless wire.

She whirled and faced the river. The men were gone.

"Mike," she moaned.

The radio exploded, Wilde's voice cutting through the static. "Monica?" he yelled. "Where are they?"

She swept the chasm with her eyes. The world was a frenzy of spray and mist. The newly fallen tree shuddered in the current and the wire snaked into the depths and disappeared. The men were nowhere to be seen.

"Mike," she moaned again, sweeping the shoreline for any hope. There was no sign. The men had been swallowed whole, gulped down by the great leviathan. The river raged on, humming a dissonant, remorseless dirge.

36

— • —

EXTRACTION

M ONICA CRAWLED TO HER FEET.

She took three steps and swayed, then grabbed the mossy rocks beside her for support. With every breath, a throb was pulsing in her temples like fists, pushing her skull and chanting two awful words.

Your.

Fault.

"Mike," she sobbed.

Across the river, the rangers were loading the bow and arrow to set up a new rescue cable. Monica watched in silence, heavy with helplessness. She knew she would have to move. She couldn't just stay there, guilt-stricken. There was still work to do.

She hadn't seen him fall, but she couldn't get the idea of Ownby plummeting into the water out of her mind. Max appeared beside her.

"They're gone, aren't they," he said.

The words had a sobering effect. What had happened was a fact, and it must be reckoned with.

Monica breathed quietly through her nose. "Yes," she whispered.

"I'm sorry," Max said.

"I'm the one who's sorry," she said.

"Why?" he said.

She shook her head. "Never mind," she said. "I'm done."

The radio crackled and she heard Wilde's voice.

"Please receive the guide line, Greene."

Monica rose to her feet with a weary grunt and limped over to the newly-arrived arrow. With robotic movements, she pulled at the small string as it carried a new wire across the water. Max joined her and the two wrapped the incoming cable around a clump of small trees and tightened it with the ratchet.

"You should cross first," she said.

Max ran his fingers over the wire, then gazed up at the trees.

"It'll hold you," Monica said.

Max exhaled, then nodded.

"It's the best you can do," he said.

Max approached the edge of the steps, glanced over at her, and nodded. He donned the harness and clipped onto the new wire. He looked at Monica without a word, then stepped out over the void. He coasted several feet, then slowed to a stop over the fallen tree while the wire wobbled. Max pulled himself toward the far shore, and after a minute of slow movement, he landed and threw his arms around Eva.

Monica waited for Max to get out of the harness and stared into the river. There had to be a chance that Ownby survived. Could she bring the possibility into existence through sheer will?

Yet the swollen flume raged on, emotionless as ever, detached from the troubles and worries of humankind. Monica swallowed, the taste of bile rising in her throat, and hooked the carabiners onto the wire.

Monica closed her eyes.

"If I deserve to be punished, God," she said, "now is the time to do it."

She crouched, pushed off the block of stone. Her body flew through space, falling forever until the safety lines grabbed the wire and guided her across. Her boots hit the earth hard and she tumbled over, the tether stopping her fall. A pair of hands helped her up, and she wiped the spray from her eyes and looked to see who was helping her.

It was Wilde.

"Walk with me," he said.

They returned to the trail in silent discomfort, creeping through the tunnel of rhododendron. As they emerged on the beaten path, Monica stared numbly at the ground. Was Wilde escorting her in order to have her processed for discipline? Was he leading her to a waiting police car, her guilt already determined?

Or had he seen just how desperate the situation had truly been when Wilson, who was perfectly safe and secure in his harness, fought to escape it. Wilde must have seen how Wilson grabbed at Ownby and pulled him down, preventing him from getting free of the wire before the tree collapsed. The raw power of Mother Nature, coupled with the delicate frailty of the human body and mind, had conspired to wreak havoc that day.

Wilde hobbled along on his crutches and Monica walked beside him in silence for a quarter of a mile or so, much as they had during her tour of the park. When they reached the first bridge, Wilde stopped and looked out over the creekbed. The waters were still bright with violent foam. Up and down the shores of the stream, park staff were combing for any sign of Mike Ownby and Carl Wilson.

Wilde leaned against the wooden railing. "This is probably where they'll wash up," he muttered.

Monica nodded quickly, holding her mouth. At any moment it felt like a sob could explode out of her.

What she'd give to find Mike alive! She gazed out over the river, scanning the shores for any sign of him.

Wilde peered out in the opposite direction. He wasn't looking at her, thank God. If he dared to, it might break her. Wilde was one of those people whose gaze carried some kind of deep-seated authority with it, and she couldn't handle such a piercing look right now.

Yet for so many reasons she *did* want to be broken over it. She wanted to gush out a confession that everything was her fault. She had pushed Wilson too hard and far, and after he'd tampered with his safety gear. And then she'd ventured onto the wire, adding too much weight. The tree had come down because of her!

Monica shuddered and sunk to the boards of the bridge, gasping for breath.

Why had Ownby even been with her, but at her request! And why was Ownby on site and not coordinating at Headquarters? He was there because of her criticism. Again—*her fault!*

"Oh God," she moaned. "Forgive me!"

What was she doing here except adding chaos to an already unmanageable situation? She wasn't cut out for challenges of this magnitude. She thought she was prepared for them after leading the team at Grand Canyon. But how had that ended?

Monica tried to stifle a cry, but it broke through, piercing the air.

"Monica?" Wilde said.

She shook her head, covering her face.

Wilde knelt beside her. "It's okay," he said, his low voice. "It's not your fault."

"Yes, it is," she said.

"That's a lie," he said. "Don't believe it for a second."

But a whooshing sound had begun to fill her ears, like the rising tide of a mighty ocean. She was going to pass out. Monica leaned her head back and rubbed her swollen cheeks, trying to keep herself aware and present, just in case they found Ownby and there was something she could possibly do to save him.

Then a sharp crackling cut through the din of her head. It was the radio. The voice was obscured by static, yet painfully clear: "We found him," it said.

"Him?" Monica cried, sitting up. She snatched the radio. "Who?"

For what seemed like eternity no one answered. There was only mechanical hissing, like the voice of a basilisk about to bite its prey. Wilde stared at the radio, holding his breath.

Then the voice spoke again: "Ownby. His body has been sighted at the switchback."

"That's a half-mile downriver," Wilde said.

Monica pressed the button, her thumb throbbing. "Is he alive?" she blurted.

Again, the static sizzled in response. The voice spoke once more.

"Get a team onsite for extract, over."

She gaped at the device as the static hiss rose in volume like the drone of cicadas.

"Is he alive?" she shouted into the microphone. "Someone tell me, is he alive?"

The radio was quiet, and for a long time no one answered. Then a voice, remorseless and detached, answered, "He is ten fifty-four, over."

Monica's head fell.

Ten fifty-four.

Dead.

"I have to go," she said.

Monica scrambled to her feet and stepped over Wilde.

"Monica, wait," he urged.

But she broke into a run, tears beginning to streak her face like rain.

She rounded the bend up to the final turn leading to the parking lot. She turned a corner and shouted in surprise as she nearly bowled into another person.

It was Blaze.

"Monica?" she said. "Where are you going?"

Monica brushed the salty tears away and lifted her face.

"I can't talk, Allison," she said, waving her hands to stave off the panic. "I have to go!"

"Wait!" Blaze said, utterly confused. "Did you hear what happened to Ownby?"

Monica shook her fists and jammed her eyes shut, the horrible grief welling over like a tsunami. "I—please—just let me go!"

She pushed past Blaze, nearly shouldering her over, and ran to the parking lot. She found her truck in a blind dash, feeling for the handle and throwing open the door. The engine exploded to life and she flew out of the lot, tires screaming in protest.

"God, why did you let this happen!?" she cried.

The truck bellowed as it swung around the tight corners skirting the mountainside.

"Why!?" she screamed.

She drove like her truck was a battering ram. Her hands began to feel filthy, and she pressed them against her pants as the sobs shook her.

The sound of the hissing radio met her ears again. She was nearing the sharp turn on Highway 441 known as The Switchback, where they'd found Ownby. She punched the brakes and grit her teeth as the truck slid to a stop. Her head snapped forward, nearly butting the steering wheel.

Monica Greene sat in the truck and did not move, staring intently into the river gorge. Behind the screen of green and yellow leaves, the vivid form of an orange cot met her eyes. Four men in yellow vests were carrying it toward the water's edge.

Monica leapt out of the truck and ran to the edge of the bridge overlooking the Pigeon River. She watched in silence, trembling. Could there be any chance—any miraculous hope—that Mike Ownby wasn't completely gone and could be revived?

The men lowered the cot and stepped into the gray waters. Something was wedged between two enormous boulders. But it couldn't be Ownby. Not the man she knew who spouted clever sayings and prayed for his colleagues in the dark of a storm—

The object came free as the four workers struggled against its weight and shape. As it shifted, its features became distinct and clear, despite being hundreds of yards away behind a million green leaves.

Monica gagged as a sob shot up her throat and burst out like the cry of a dying bird. The object's head hung limp and lifeless, its long pale neck doing nothing to support itself. The four rescuers climbed out of the waves, each conveying one appendage of the dead thing until they laid it on the orange cot. When released, the arms and legs dangled like severed tree branches, fallen and broken, pointing at nothing.

She watched a minute more as the men hoisted the cot into the air and began the difficult trek out of the gorge. When the vivid orange had faded completely from sight, Monica cleared her throat, blew her nose, and weaved her dizzy way back to the truck. She wiped her tear-strewn eyes and placed her hands on the wheel. She shifted into drive and rolled the rest of the way down the mountain, her eyes glazing over as the emerald world flew by.

Monica pulled into HQ and laid the truck keys on the dash. Digging into her pockets, she found her National Park Service badge and ID card. She turned them over in her fingers, the dull metal failing to capture what little light was leaking through the clouds. She climbed out, set the items on the seat, and she slammed the door.

"I'm done," she said.

Then she got in her car and drove away.

37

—·—

CHOICE

THE CONSULTATION ROOM WAS A DRAB CLOSET WITH TWO stiff-backed chairs and hardly enough square footage for more than one person. Monica sat in one of the chairs, waiting in silence.

Twenty-four hours had passed since Mike Ownby's death. Every minute brought a thick fog of numbness, the air moist with the palpable memory of a ghost.

Despite the haze, she had found her way to her father's house, the roads of East Tennessee littered with debris from the storm. When she arrived, the house was a mess, sheets and garbage and splattered paint everywhere. Her father was nowhere to be found. She promptly sped to the hospital.

Waiting in the stuffy room, Monica bounced one of her legs, channeling the nervous energy to the floor. She took a hefty bite out of her thumbnail, drawing blood, and wiped it on her pants.

It's going to be okay, she tried to assure herself.

She checked her phone, wondering if perhaps Dr. Watt would message her about the delay, then stuffed it back in her pocket. Doctors never explained the reason for the eternal waits their patients had to suffer. They simply waltzed through the door after a quick knock and then proceeded to act as if you hadn't been waiting in a sterile room for a brief eternity.

Her phone buzzed and she fished it out. It was Blaze.

Hey girl, hope you're doing okay

We could really use you today

Monica flipped it over and sighed.

She couldn't go back. Not after what happened with Ownby. Not after her abysmal failure.

She found herself chewing the fingernail once more. How long did it take to get someone in here to talk to her? Was there something they weren't telling her? What if—

The door rattled with a pair of quick knocks, then opened. The upper half of a familiar, espresso-shaded face appeared behind a surgeon's mask. It was Dr. Watt.

"Miss Greene," she said. "How are you?"

Monica heaved a heavy breath. "I'm worn out."

"I imagine it's been hard in the park right now."

Monica sighed. "Look, I don't want to be rude," she said, "but I'd appreciate it if we could get right to it."

Watt nodded, then slowly took the mask off and set it in her lap. "Once the roads were clear, two nurses checked in on your father. They found him unconscious on the floor."

Monica nodded, swallowing.

"He nearly went into shock," Watt continued, her voice gentle, motherly. "I'm afraid the worst case scenario has come upon us much more quickly than I thought. Your father's kidneys are no longer working."

"I figured," Monica said.

"When we spoke before, I was hopeful he could turn it around," Watt said. "However, your father did not take his prescribed medication. And with the storm, we weren't able to administer dialysis treatment."

"Okay," Monica said. "Anything else?"

"Yes," Dr. Watt went on. "We had him evaluated by one of our clinical psychiatrists. You've probably been wondering if anything might be—" she paused, probably searching for the proper term "—*off*."

"Off?" Monica echoed.

"His emotional outbursts," the doctor continued. "Do you ever feel like your father is two different persons? Kind, fatherly, and loving one minute, then excessively impatient and abusive the next?"

Monica felt the air stop in her throat. "That sounds *exactly* like my father," she whispered.

"Textbook borderline personality disorder and bipolar disorder," Watt said. "And since he's never been treated for these mental illnesses—"

"Mental illnesses?" Monica interjected.

Watt nodded. "Border personality and bipolarism both qualify as mental illnesses and require treatment. I wanted to test him, but he refused. However, it wasn't hard to guess and our analyst simply made the confirmation."

Monica sighed. "Great. He's a certified headcase. Any more bad news?"

Watt fiddled with the mask strings, working them between her fingers. She seemed to do an assessment of Monica, eying her up and down. Then she cocked her head a little to the side.

"It all depends on your decision."

Monica narrowed her eyes. "What decision?"

"The donation," Watt said.

"The donation you told him about," Monica shot back.

Watt's expression remained motionless. "What do you mean? I told him nothing."

"You told him it was an option, and that I was an ideal donor!" Monica said. "All week he's been screaming about what an awful daughter I am since I'm not immediately cutting myself open and handing him my organs. Do you have any idea what that's like? What kind of pressure that puts on a person?" Monica threw up her hands. "Why would you do that?"

Watt frowned. "I didn't tell him," she replied matter-of-factly. "He must have presumed it."

Monica lowered an eyebrow. "How?"

"Well, your father asked about treatment options. I listed all the ones I'd prefer him to choose but he began asking about donations. He pushed hard, Miss Greene. And in that pushing, he started asking if you were a potential donor. I refused to answer, but I'm afraid my refusal was taken as a 'yes.'"

"So what you're telling me," Monica continued, "is that he hasn't followed your instructions—which was a non-negotiable for me—and he's successfully put himself in a position where the only path forward is this kidney transplant. Right?"

Watt was silent a moment. "He hasn't followed the instructions," she said. "That is accurate."

"And I'm the only available donor?"

The doctor closed her eyes. "Given your father's age, condition, other complicating factors—"

"Just answer me," Monica interrupted.

Watt drew a long breath through her nostrils, then let it out slowly. "Yes. You are the only available donor."

Monica bent double and buried her face in her hands. She wanted to scream so loud that every patient in the hospital would hear her. She wanted to throw open the door and run from the hospital and the mountains and Tennessee. How could this be happening? What had she done wrong to make the universe crush her like this? Every hour that she'd been here, she'd tried to help others; so far, the only reward she was reaping was failure.

Dr. Watt shifted in her chair and cleared her throat. "Miss Greene," she said, "may I make a suggestion?"

Monica shrugged. "Fine."

"You don't have to do this."

Monica leaned back and snorted. It was the laugh of one condemned to the gallows.

"I *don't?*" she said.

"Of course not," Watt said. "I hope I haven't made it seem like you have no choice in this matter. As your father's primary doctor, all I can do is assess his situation and describe available paths to recovery. At this point, my job is just to say that he needs a new kidney."

Monica felt stupid, not quite able to follow the doctor's meaning. "Huh?" she said.

Watt leaned forward. Then, with a lowered voice, she said, "I am not—and will not—tell you what to do with your body, Miss Greene. That is entirely up to you. And one more thing: No one will judge you either way. This is not a fair position to be in. You need to do what you believe is best."

Monica stared Dr. Watt in the face. The words made perfect sense as they passed through Monica's ears, but they didn't seem real. It sounded like a lie, the kind of lie Satan whispers to encourage selfish indulgence.

She leaned back and ran her fingers through her hair, still dirty from the day before. "What should I do?" she asked.

Dr. Watt shook her head. "I can't tell you that. I *can* tell you that no matter what decision you make, you'll never be one-hundred percent sure it was the right one."

Monica laughed again, mirthless as if Death himself had cracked a joke. "Great," she said.

"This may be inappropriate to share," Watt said, "but three years ago, I lost my mother to cancer. The last weeks were...." She didn't finish the sentence, trailing off and letting the words die without a conclusion. Watt closed her eyes while her lips curved into an empathetic smile. "I'll just say, your predicament reminds me of my own."

Monica exhaled, her eyes heavy, as Dr. Watt went on, "I mean it. Whatever choice you make, you'll have something to regret and then have to find a way to forgive yourself. That's how this works."

She stood and threaded the mask back over her ears. "Now," she said, "I have to speak to some other families. Go ahead and think about it. If you want to visit your father in the meantime, he's in the ICU."

Monica nodded. "Thank you."

Dr. Watt turned the handle, stepped halfway out, then paused and turned back.

"I'm serious, Monica," she added. "Give yourself grace. If you don't, you might never have peace again."

Then she slipped back through the portal and the door shut behind her.

38

— · —

THE ONE

T HE LAST PERSON SHE WANTED TO SEE AT THAT MOMENT was her father.

She took the elevator to the main floor and walked toward the entrance to a little chapel. The light was dim, radiating through a colorful stained glass cross that felt out of place in the white and gray world of modern medicine. There was a plain, square window in the corner through which natural light splashed over the maroon carpet. She strolled towards it and found a door to a small sitting garden, and gladly helped herself to some fresh air.

The outdoors were lush with humid atmosphere, a stark change from the climate-controlled building. She removed her jacket and found a seat on a small concrete bench. The moment her bottom hit the surface, the burden of her tension released, and her tears began to fall.

What was the right decision? How was she supposed to make a wise choice about such a weighty matter? Her head throbbed. It was all too much and she just wanted to lie down and sleep.

Breathe, Monica, she told herself. *Focus on what matters.*

Her hand fell to her side, rubbing the flesh where one of her precious internal organs sat invisible. In her line of work, it wouldn't be wise to limit herself to a single functioning kidney. One bad incident could put her on her deathbed. Making the donation would almost certainly limit her ability to work in the field.

This was enough to make up her mind for her. Yet there was another piece of the decision-making puzzle that really set her against the idea: Her father's behavior.

She'd always known there was illness in his mind. She hated the term—her father wasn't a psychopath—but still, the criteria fit. Back in Detroit, Monica had taught students who suffered from personality disorders. It was like teaching two completely different people trapped in the same body. On one day, the child might be polite, accommodating, and eager to please; the next, he or she would try to bite your fingers off and burn the school down. And while her father wasn't threatening to physically hurt her or commit arson, he did exhibit violent changes in his attitude. How else was she supposed to feel when her father showed gushing love, only to follow it with scathing hate?

Monica bowed her head and exhaled, trying to let all these details escape her. Then she closed her eyes and remembered the night on the porch with Mike Ownby.

Just because he's your father, she recalled him saying, *doesn't mean he's entitled to anything of yours.*

She shoved her palms into her eye sockets and moaned, "Oh, Mike."

Ownby had done something unthinkable, at least from her perspective: he'd actually listened to her that night. He also apologized for crossing the line and speaking at a personal level about his faith. Then prayed for her, *with* her permission, and asked for nothing in return.

More words came to her, these about her father, as if carried on the wind over the Tennessee River: *He already has your heart, doesn't he?*

At this she sobbed, covering her mouth. "Of course he does!" she exclaimed, struggling to hold it all back.

She stood and yanked the door open and shouldered her way back into the chapel. At the front of the room, perched on a narrow lectern, was a thick, ornamental Bible. The pages were thin and crackled at her touch. There was a verse she wanted to find, a crucial word immersed in the waters of memory she needed to find....

Monica flipped through the pages, the paper snapping one at a time. Then she found it.

"For I was hungry and you gave me something to eat," she murmured. "I was thirsty and you gave me something to drink, I was a stranger and you invited me in, I needed clothes and you clothed me, I was sick and you looked after me, I was in prison and you came to visit me."

She looked up from the book, toward the dim colors twittering in the stained glass cross.

And if you needed a kidney, she thought, *would I give it to you?*

A part of her burned, as if her thoughts could touch the red of a stove and pull away in shocking pain. This couldn't be the answer. If anything, she was cherry-picking lines out of the Bible to soothe a deep, lifelong wound that needed a more nuanced solution.

But there wasn't time for nuance. Her father was close to death. As far as she knew, a machine was filtering his toxins, and would continue to do so until the rest of his organs shut down. And when it happened, there would only be one person who could have stopped it.

Monica collapsed on the carpeted dais like an overstuffed hiking pack. She lay there weeping without restraint or worry. She cried for her father. She cried for Ownby. She cried for herself.

And she cried because she couldn't truly know what God was telling her to do.

But she had to do something. No one else could.

Monica buried her face in the floor and screamed.

WHEN THE ELEVATOR DOORS OPENED, Monica marched straight toward the nurse's station.

"I need to see Dr. Watt," she declared.

"Just a moment," explained the young RN, who couldn't have been more than twenty-five. "She's seeing another—"

"*Now,*" Monica ordered.

This roused the unfortunate young woman from her seat, and she rushed down the hall and ducked into a patient's room. A few seconds later, Dr. Watt appeared and hurried down the hall.

"Yes?" she said. "Did you talk to your father?"

Monica shook her head. "No."

"Well, I think you should speak to him before—"

"Tell me one thing," Monica snapped. "Will you treat his mental illness?"

Watt blinked, apparently stunned by the bluntness of the inquiry. "Of course," she said.

"You'll treat it, and make sure he takes his medication?"

"Well, we'll do our best—"

"No," Monica said. "I need a solid answer. He doesn't listen to me now, and he won't listen to me later. Either you force him to undergo treatment for his mental health or I walk. Because I'm not letting you put my precious kidney into someone in his condition. Understand?"

Dr. Watt stepped backward, giving herself a few more inches of space. She steadied herself on the nurse's station and swallowed.

"Yes," she said. "We would—we would have to put him in a permanent care residence, which he has said over and over he will never do—"

"Do it," Monica said. "My kidney, my rules."

Dr. Watt nodded. "I agree with you one hundred percent."

"Good," Monica said. "Now let's get this over with."

"What do you mean?"

"The kidney transfer."

The doctor shook her head. "I didn't mean—we have to prep the area, schedule the anesthetist and surgical team—"

"Now," Monica interrupted. "I want to do the damned thing now."

Watt's mouth dropped. "It won't be easy to arrange, Miss Greene."

Monica crossed her arms.

"I don't care," she said. "I want to get this over with."

Dr. Watt studied her for a moment, the muscles in her face twitching and tightening, perhaps trying to decipher what was really happening in Monica's head. But after nearly a minute of careful staring, she sighed.

"Okay," she said. "I'll get right on it."

Monica crossed her arms. "Good."

39

ANGEL

THE HOSPITAL GOWN TOUCHED HER KNEES. IT WAS FIRMLY starched yet frigidly thin, like tulle in a harsh winter wind. She reached to her back, the ends of the strings in her fingers, and fumbled to tie them together. As she did so, she looked up and found her face gaping back at her from the cold recesses of a mirror. At the sight she froze, let the strands fall, and stared.

Her eyes were those of a phantom. Dark, hollow trunks inhabited by weary orbs like spider eggs. A long brown track of mud was still tattooed on one of her cheeks. Her flesh seemed thinner than ever before, her collar bone jutting out and forming a long, dark shadow.

She tried not to think about what was going to happen, and what it would mean longterm for her career and personal safety. For now, she had one goal: Ready her body for the donation.

Monica hadn't spoken to her father yet. She didn't want his input, emotional or otherwise. Whether he was manic and gushing with gratitude, or depressive, spewing insults and codependent slander, she didn't want to deal with it. She would give her father this immeasurable gift and show him this ultimate act of love, the one thing she could do to satisfy him and give him life. Maybe then she would qualify as a worthy child.

Monica stepped forward until her nose was almost touching its twin in the luminous glass. The burrowed eyes trembled, beholding the haunted depths within.

She had made her choice. And yet, what she was doing felt wrong. How could it be wrong to save her father's life?

Gazing into the sunken portals to her soul, Monica gulped down a puddle of bile. The donation wasn't her failure. Her failure had occurred long before in the crucible of childhood. Somehow she had chosen to be the person she was, and that choice was fatally flawed. There was no going back to that moment, either, for the river of time flows one direction, regardless of monsoon or drought. She had failed to keep her mother sober. She had failed to keep her parents together. She had failed to protect her rangers. And so far, she had failed to support her father.

In the midst of all this, she was supposed to keep her faith and follow God. Now, as she gazed at the ghost of herself, she knew: She couldn't even grasp that love for herself. How in the world would she ever learn to share it with others?

She sucked a deep breath and let it out as if it were her last. She turned, tied the strings of her gown, and laid her hand on the door handle of the bathroom.

Then her phone buzzed, breaking the silence of the sterile room.

Just ignore it.

Yet part of her was overcome with curiosity, and she reached for her folded khakis on the counter, reached in the pockets, and checked the caller.

It was Blaze.

All at once, a dozen different reactions flowed through her and her hand began to shake. It was as if every desire to answer, to ignore it, to throw the phone, to put her uniform back on—all of it—began to flow down her arm and flood her fingers with lightning.

It continued to ring, displaying a picture of Blaze on the screen, who had posed for her portrait by scowling to ensure the picture was a dud. Monica couldn't help but crack a limp smile. Typical Blaze.

"Hey," she said, bringing the phone to her ear.

"You're alive," Blaze said, her drawl pulling at the end of each word. "Where *are* you?"

"The hospital," Monica said.

"What? Are you hurt?"

"No. It's my dad."

"Is he okay?"

Monica glanced at the door separating her from the surgery prep room. "No, he isn't. His kidneys aren't working."

"Damn, I didn't know. Do they have him on dialysis?"

"Yeah," she said. "It's pretty much the only thing keeping him alive right now."

"Wow. That's awful."

Blaze paused, and Monica exhaled in relief at the stretch of quiet. The last thing she wanted to do was rehash her decision with yet another person. In fact, she was hoping that this could mean the call was about to end—

"Is he stable?" she asked.

"I don't know," Monica said. "Apparently he's been like this for a few days."

"Really—a few days?" Blaze said, the worry suddenly gone from her voice. "So you could leave for a while?"

Monica narrowed an eyebrow. "What?"

"Look," Blaze said, "I know you're upset about what happened to Ownby. We all are. But nobody thinks you're to blame."

Monica rotated and faced the mirror again, staring at herself as she listened to Blaze. "Why are you telling me this?"

"It wasn't your fault, Monica," she said. "It was an accident. A tragedy. Nobody is blaming you."

"I don't care if anyone's blaming me."

"Great," Blaze said. "Come back, then."

"I can't. I just told you—"

"You said he's stable, right?" Blaze interrupted. "Look, we're worn out. We've been going nonstop for forty-eight hours, some for seventy-two or more. The rescue teams are spread thin, trying to help all around the park."

"I can't leave, Allison," Monica tried to interject, "See, I'm—"

"There's a family that's stranded," Blaze said. "A mother and three kids."

Monica closed her eyes. In the darkness, the image of a woman with a subtle, suppressed smirk appeared before her, flanked by three little human forms.

"Okay. What am I supposed to do?"

"They're trapped on the far side of the Little River," Blaze said. "We know because their vehicle is still parked at the trailhead, but no one has seen them for three days."

"Three days?"

"They went out the night before the storm and they've been out there since."

Monica took a long breath, trying to keep herself calm. "A mother and three kids?" she said.

"Yes," Blaze said. "Wilde's running point as a temporary Emergency Manager, but even he's getting desperate. People are injured and exhausted. We need fresh legs."

Monica shook her head. "I'm pretty far from fresh, Allison."

"Stop it," Blaze said. "You're one of our best. And other than me, you're also the only available ranger who is trained in fast-roping."

Monica frowned. It shouldn't matter that she was trained in fast-roping. The practice had been deemed unsafe by the park service after an operation went awry.

"I don't understand," she murmured.

"We got the green light to drop," Blaze said. "After what happened to Ownby, the park superintendent has been appealing nonstop for permission. Apparently they said yes, but only in extreme post-tropical storm scenarios."

"Wow," Monica said, her surprise tainted by disbelief.

"I know," Blaze said. "We're all shocked, too. But we need to move fast before the feds decide it's no longer necessary."

"Okay," Monica said. "Take care of yourself out there."

"You're not listening to me," Blaze said. "You're the only other ranger who's fast-rope certified."

"What about Mullens?"

"She's out from a rattlesnake bite."

Monica scowled. "So the only way to reach these people is to jump out of a helicopter?"

"We've tried everything. There's just no way over that river," Blaze explained.

"Have you tried a backcountry bushwhack? You know, get around it?"

"It's not just the Little River," Blaze shot back, starting to sound annoyed. "The tributaries are flooded, too. Goshen Prong is basically a lake right now. That family party is entirely cut off and the only way we can reach them is from above. We need to do it now."

Monica's head fell. For a tortured moment she stared at her bare feet on the cold, tile floor, her mind rushing back to the woods, trying to imagine the Little River Trail. For three days, a mother and three children had been hunkering, trying to survive. Yet no sign of them had been seen nor heard. How could anyone be sure they were still alive? If they weren't, she would be risking her father's safety to locate four corpses.

Was it worth it?

"I want to help, I really do," Monica said. "But I can't. My father needs me right now."

"Monica," Blaze said, "I get it. But if your dad can make it a day or two, then we need you to come back."

"I don't think he can," Monica said. "He could die at any moment, and I can't be responsible for that."

"Didn't you say he's stable?"

"Barely," Monica said. "I promise, when I'm done here, I'll help in any way I can."

For a moment, she heard only silence, broken by Blaze's quiet breathing. Finally she said, "Fine, I hope your father gets better," and the call went dead.

"Allison?" Monica said.

She pulled the phone away and the screen was black as a grave. She sighed and stowed the phone in the pocket of her pants.

Was she making a mistake? Should she put the donation on hold and try to help the family trapped in the backcountry? Could her father possibly make it another twenty-four hours without the gift of her internal organ?

Suddenly the door to the bathroom opened with a metallic squeal, and Monica saw Dr. Watt's face appear in the mirror.

"Everything okay?"

Monica didn't move. "I think so," she whispered.

Dr. Watt smiled. "It's okay to be nervous. You're in good hands."

Monica drew a long breath, letting the oxygen tickle her nerves. Then she let it out through pursed lips.

"How is he?"

Watt glanced behind her. "Still with us, thankfully," she said.

Monica nodded. Her teeth found her lower lip and started working at it. Then, her hands trembling, she said, "Is he stable?"

Dr. Watt sighed. "All I can say is the sooner we do this for him, the better."

Monica sighed. Then she lifted her head. "Okay. I'm ready."

SHE FOLLOWED DR. WATT OUT OF THE RESTROOM to find her father lying flat on a gurney in a pale preparation room. Beside him, a large contraption hummed and hissed as tubes snaked out from under her father's blankets.

That machine is his kidney right now, she thought with a shudder.

The door closed behind her, and he lifted himself with a grunt.

"Little Bear!" he wheezed.

She smiled and walked toward him with slow, shaky steps.

"Hey, Dad."

His eyes were wide, shining opals. "I can't believe you're doing this," he said.

Her smile felt as if little lead weights had been pinned to her cheeks. She gently stroked his arm and said, "Yes, I am."

"I'm—I'm so thankful," he said, his breathing slow and raspy.

"Of course."

"When Dr. Watt told me—when she said you'd do it, I—I couldn't believe—"

She wanted to shut him up. If he kept talking, she thought she might pass out. "Dad, please," she said. "Can we just let it be?"

But he beamed at her, the harsh halogen lights glimmering in his wet eyes. "You're my angel."

Monica shuddered as if the word itself was charged with static electricity that raised her hair and sent prickles up and down her flesh. She glared at him.

"Dad...."

What was it about that word? Whatever it was, it was making her dizzy, and she backpedaled until her legs hit the edge of a hospital bed parallel to her father's. She sat and rubbed her temples.

"You know, Little Bear," the old man went on, "I can't help but feel that you shouldn't—oh, what am I saying—you shouldn't be doing this."

She raised her head and stared at him, her eyelids falling to send him a hard expression. "Dad, we both know that's a lie."

"A lie?" he said. "I—I don't understand what you mean."

"Don't you remember all the calls?" she said. "The voicemails? You *definitely* think I should be doing this."

"I—I don't know what you're talking about," he stammered.

"You don't remember?" she said. "You don't recall screaming at me for being an ungrateful daughter?"

He wiggled his hand, as if the gesture sufficed for an apology. "That wasn't me," he said. "Not the *real* me. I love you! I would never—I didn't *mean* to say—"

"You didn't *mean* to?" she said.

"I'm sorry, I skipped my doses, you see—which you said not to do—but I wasn't in my right mind."

"Really?" she said. "Exactly *when* are you in your right mind?"

"That's not fair, Little Bear."

"Not fair?" she said, suddenly yelling. "Not *fair!?*"

Dr. Watt appeared like a messenger from heaven. "Hey, you two," she said. "How are we getting on?"

Her father began to speak, but Monica interrupted him. "We're getting on great," she snapped. "Can we get this over with, please?"

"Yes," Watt said. "We're ready when you are."

"Great," Monica said. "Put me under."

"Monica, please," her father said. "Don't be angry with me."

Monica shot him a look of razor blades. "Dad, stop."

"It's not my fault," he opined. "I—I miss your mother."

"Dad," she whispered. "Please...."

"I miss the times we were together," he went on. "The three of us on our trips to the mountains. Goodness, what adventures we used to have. And the days we'd go to the park and I'd paint while your mother would sing. Do you remember her voice, Little Bear? She'd fill that park with music lovelier than birdsong."

Monica took a breath but it caught in her throat. The corners of her vision darkened, and her ears swirled with sounds of the ocean.

"And," her father went on, "do you remember that day in the canoe? On the Obed River?"

She turned her head, searching for Dr. Watt. Across the room, she spied the form of a person with a white coat. She reached out and groaned, "Put me under, please...."

Dr. Watt's voice sounded distant, like it was underwater, and said, "Please give us ten to fifteen minutes, Miss Greene...."

"We saw so many beautiful things that day," her father droned on. "And then you—you were so little and wild, sweet thing—you shook that boat side-to-side, you wanted so badly to have your own adventure."

Monica fell back, wheezing. The room clouded over in a sickly brown darkness, and a skeletal hand of ice tightened its cold claws around her neck.

"And then we went over the edge! Both your mother and I. And goodness, it was cold!"

He laughed, but the sound of his cackle was far away, like a coyote cry rippling over the hills.

"So there we stayed for god-knows-how long, waiting for you to paddle to us. I thought we'd die of hypothermia. And your mother, my goodness, she was so patient with you. So patient, she was—like an *angel*...."

Monica's breath stopped in her throat. The face of that woman, her self-serving grin carved into water-stained stone, flashed before her.

Then she saw no more.

40

TWENTY-FOUR HOURS

SHE WOKE AND SHIVERED, HER BODY DRENCHED IN SWEAT. She blinked and saw Dr. Watt standing beside her, looking down with a heavy look.

"Miss Greene," she said. "Are you okay?"

Monica immediately swung her gaze back and forth, searching. "Is he here? I don't want to be in the same room as—"

"It's just me and my assistant," Dr. Watt said.

Still suspicious, Monica checked her surroundings again and indeed saw only the doctor and a young, thin nurse in a pastel smock.

"Ugh," she said, swallowing to coat her throat with saliva. She ran a hand over her face and rubbed her eyes. "I passed out, didn't I?"

"It happens," Dr. Watt said. "Lots of people get anxious before a big surgery like this."

Monica scowled, rubbing her cheeks. "You think I passed out because of the surgery?"

Dr. Watt crossed her arms. "I know this isn't easy," she said. "Personal issues aside, we need to act soon. If your father doesn't receive a transplant, he's going to—"

"I know, I know," Monica said. "He'll die."

The doctor stared at her, her eyes solid as granite. "I can't change your family's story, Miss Greene. That's up to you and your father. All I can tell you is that he doesn't have long to live if he doesn't get this transplant."

Monica sighed. "I know."

"But," Dr. Watt continued, "it's obvious there's a lot of unhealed trauma between you. It's also clear that whoever your mother is, her absence is a major part of the picture. I really think you and your father should look into a counselor."

Monica felt as if two black holes had collided out in the universe and their galaxy-destroying impact had rushed through her. Once more she felt sick and a familiar slithering chill ran up her throat. She coughed.

"We're fine," she muttered.

"No," Dr. Watt said. "You're not. You're far from fine. I'm worried about you, Miss Greene."

Monica closed her eyes at these words. Suddenly she was no longer in the hospital, but on the windy trailhead of Ramsey Cascades. A thin, gray-haired man was with her, smiling as he connected a pair of jumper cables to the battery of her truck—

"Did you hear me?" Dr. Watt said. She leaned in and put a hand on Monica's shoulder, squeezing it like a worried sister. "I'm concerned about you."

"Why?"

Dr. Watt studied her a moment, then took her hand back, leaving her flesh cool where it had been resting.

"You just passed out after your father started talking about your mother," Dr. Watt said. "Clearly a lot has happened, and the two of you—you and your father, I mean—haven't dealt with it."

"What is there to deal with?" Monica asked.

"Whatever made this happen," Watt said, gesturing toward the hospital bed. "Clearly your father's words upset you on a deep level."

"So what, now?"

Dr. Watt shook her head. "I don't know. But I think there's a lot for you to consider, Miss Greene. Why don't you go in and talk to your father?"

The very suggestion of the thing made her want to swear louder than ever. Her tongue held it back, though, and she simply winced. "I'd rather not."

Dr. Watt crossed her arms once more. "Monica Greene," she declared, "I will not clear you for this procedure until you go talk to your father."

Monica gaped at her. "What?"

"Go talk to him," Dr. Watt said, gesturing to the pair of steel doors behind her.

"Now?"

"Now."

Monica's mouth fell. She had to wonder if this was a bluff, a proud attempt by the doctor to cross over into psychology or the priesthood. But Dr. Watt held her ground, her eyes fixed emphatically on the patient.

"Fine," Monica declared.

With that, she sat up and inched off the table. Steadying herself with one hand, she found her balance and marched toward the steel doors. They opened at her approach, revealing the shape of her father in the adjacent room.

As the doors reconnected them, Monica couldn't help but notice Joshua Greene watching every step she took. His eyes were wide, perhaps with concern—or was it calculated measurement to gauge his own chances in the matter?

Monica couldn't tell, and her weariness made it harder than ever to judge. Every instinct in her soul screamed to put up a defense, to keep him at arm's length. Out of all his manipulations, the decision to bring up her mother—to recall that moment in the river, that day when the canoe tipped and she nearly killed her mother and father—was more devious than any before.

Monica approached his bed with slow steps.

"Are you okay?" he asked. He studied her, his eyes quivering.

Monica began to answer, but thought better of it and paused. She bowed, then shook her head.

"No, Dad," she said. "I'm not."

"Oh," he said softly, his voice seemingly filled with paternal compassion. Then he said no more.

Monica glanced at him, frowning. Was he unsure how to turn this to his advantage? Or was he genuinely worried for her?

She let him simmer. Speaking felt too dangerous, too vulnerable. It was already proving unwise to reveal her feelings to him, given his propensity to twist and turn them like dials. Now, having blacked out in front of him, Monica knew that it would be impossible to keep her true thoughts captive.

"I don't know what to say, Dad."

"Well, what do you need?" her father asked.

She noticed his tenor was calm. How was he able to control his rampant emotions when it suited him? Good God, she thought, how exhausting is it to play chess against someone with such a mind!

Monica reached out and took his hand. "I want you to be better," she said, giving it a squeeze.

"Oh, Little Bear," he said, smiling up at her. "You love me so well."

The words washed over her like the rising tide. But also like an ocean's swell, she knew that a consummate rip current was ready to yank her into dangerous waters.

"I appreciate that. But Dad," she said, her voice low, "I need you to listen to me right now."

"Yes," he said, nodding with a bright smile. "I'm listening."

"I need you—I need you to—"

She stopped mid-sentence.

What was she about to say? Myriad possibilities lay before her, multiple futures that were hovering on the surface of her tongue. Which one would she speak into being?

She swallowed, praying that the false ones, the evil realities borne of selfishness and cruelty, would sink down to her stomach and meet a foul acidic doom. She closed her eyes.

Jesus, give me strength.

Monica opened her eyes. The face of her father lay before her, shriveled and sunken.

"I need you," she said, each word paced out like the lines of a poem, "to wait for me."

Her father's eyes stretched wide. "What do you mean?"

Monica took a deep breath and let it out with a gust. "I need you to wait for me," she said. "There's a family out there that needs my help, and I can't do it with only one kidney."

Suddenly he began to squirm, the tubes flailing like tentacles. "But—but Monica!" he protested.

"I'm the only one who can rescue them," she said, squeezing his hand again, "and there's a good chance you'll be okay long enough for me to do this."

She stood and began moving toward the bathroom where her street clothes lay folded and ready when her father shrieked, "What are you doing!?"

"I'm doing what's right," she said, turning back to him. "And I'll come back. I promise."

The man writhed in his bed. "Doctor!" he wailed. "*Doctor!*"

Watt flew through the door. "What is it?"

"Don't let her go!" he cried. "She's going to let me die!"

"What do you mean?" Dr. Watt said, incredulous.

He continued to thrash and a pair of his tubes jerked loose, filling the room with deafening alarms.

Monica froze. The piercing screams stabbed her ears and the urge to stop and return to the surgery came flooding back. There was an obvious need right in front of her. Why not stay and tend to it?

But she'd seen this act too many times before. Her father, so sweet and charming one moment, had been demonically transfigured into something else entirely. Monica put her hand on the bathroom door. "I'll be back," she said as Watt silenced the heinous noise. "Just give me some time."

Dr. Watt gaped at her. "What time, Miss Greene?" she said. "We are ready *now.*"

"I know," Monica said. "But I can't do this. Not yet."

A pair of nurses rushed to Joshua Greene's side as Dr. Watt strode across the room until her face was inches from Monica's.

"You do realize," she said, breathing heavily, "that your father might not make it that long."

Monica took a breath, but nodded. She glanced at her father as he continued shaking in the throes of his tantrum. "I do," she said. "But that's not my fault."

"You're the only available donor," Dr. Watt said.

"I know," she said. "But a stranded family needs help and I'm the only available ranger."

"*Little Bear!*" her father howled.

Monica and Watt locked gazes, and in that moment Monica felt an understanding pass between them. Dr. Watt nodded.

"I promise I'll be back," Monica said. "Give me twenty-four hours."

"No!" her father bellowed. "Don't you leave me!"

Dr. Watt looked back at her patient, who was still quaking as if possessed. "You promise?" she said. "I have to reschedule everything."

Monica nodded. "Just keep him alive, and I'll come back as soon as I can."

Dr. Watt glanced at the bed and the gyrating man. "I'll try."

<h1 style="text-align:center">41</h1>

— • —

<h2 style="text-align:center">THE DROP</h2>

THE SKIES HAD LIGHTENED OVER THE HOURS AS STRANDS OF gold pushed through the clouds. To spite the renewed hope, pockets of rain continued to fall as the lingering arms of the storm slowly dissipated and broke over the land.

For Monica, the mood felt wholly appropriate to the situation. The world was draped in a shroud, all living things suspended on the precarious edge of a blade, and any firm gust of stubborn wind could topple them into the depths below.

She wiped a sheen of sweat from her brow, speeding along the highway toward the mountains.

What if he dies? she thought.

Monica hardened her eyes toward the horizon. The choice had been made; there was no point in doubling back now. Her father was in the hands of doctors and hemodialysis. The lost mother and her three children, however, had no one to help them except Monica and Blaze.

With her foot to the floor, a part of her felt complete, as if she had found the missing piece to an old jigsaw puzzle that had never been whole. She was holding it in her fingers now, gazing at it, wondering at its story. But it wasn't in place yet. There was still work to be done. The work of a park ranger.

She arrived at headquarters with a screech of her tires and parked. Across the massive front of the HQ building, a small city of tents stood high, as if the government had decided to hold a massive yard sale. The silhouettes of a dozen park staff dashed among the awnings, working on folding tables.

The power must still be out, Monica thought.

She climbed out and jogged through the wannabe craft fair. She ducked under a large tent and saw a man and woman standing at a nearby table. They both turned at the sound of her bootsteps.

"Look who it is!" cried Allison Blaze, her face a mix of shock and delight.

Wilde managed a wry smile before turning back to the table, moving gingerly to favor a foot wrapped in a walking boot.

"I'm here," Monica said. "I'm ready to go."

Blaze pulled her into a tight hug, and a cascade of joyful sensations rushed through Monica's body.

"How's your father?" Blaze said as they parted.

Monica shook her head. "Not good. But Lord willing, he'll make it long enough. So tell me: What's the situation?"

Blaze rotated so all three of them could observe the table where a topographical map of the Little River area lay. Yellow adhesive notes were placed all over it with dates and times.

Wilde pointed at the tiny markers. "Still no sign of the family," he said. "These are locations we've visually checked. And here—" he said, sliding his finger to a point along the river "—is where we attempted to cross with a high-suspension UTV. One of the tires got wedged between two underwater boulders and it wouldn't budge. We towed it out and tried again, and the second time it nearly rolled over. The current was too strong."

"At least you tried," Monica said. "Tell me about the family."

Wilde pointed to another table and Blaze retrieved a small stack of printed papers. "There's some good news here. This family camps a lot, so they should know what they're doing."

Blaze handed the papers to Monica. The first was a permit from the previous month.

"Usually the husband is with them," Blaze said, pointing to the details. "But he's out of the country on business, according to friends and family."

Monica read the first name. "Tiffany Campbell."

"That's the mother," Blaze said. "Thirty-six years old, five feet nine inches tall, long black hair."

Monica flipped to the next paper. It was another camping permit with several details penned in a hurried scrawl.

"Are these the kids?" she asked.

Blaze nodded. "Three of them. Ericka, twelve years old. Crystal, nine. And Xavier, five."

Monica swallowed. "Five years old," she whispered.

"Yeah," Blaze said. "But it sounds like Tiffany has done her fair share of backcountry camping, so hopefully these kids are still in decent shape."

"Yet there's still no sign of them," Monica said.

Wilde broke in with a resounding, "No."

The severity of his tone sent a tremor through Monica, and she found his gaze. "What's worrying you?" she said.

"Everything," he scowled. "Three days and no sign from them. That's very concerning, and I don't like the idea of dropping more people out there."

Blaze sneered and a playful glance at Wilde. "He's been against this from the beginning. But thankfully it's the only option."

Wilde continued to lean over the map and scrutinized the undulating lines marking the harsh terrain. "Unfortunately, that's currently true," he said. "But I am going to be on that helicopter the entire time you two are on the ground. If anything goes wrong, I'll make sure you're picked up right away."

"Okay then," Monica said, facing Blaze. "Where's our ride?"

"North Carolina," Blaze said. "Our bird is a National Guard chopper. Right now they're extracting hikers from Hazel Creek. They probably won't be here for another hour."

"Well, we'd better get it done soon. I don't want to drop after sunset."

Wilde cleared his throat, and both women waited for whatever the man seemed to have to say. But he was merely tugging at his beard and looking into the sky. The sun had fallen behind Cove Mountain, its fiery orange arms throwing shadows over the valley.

"You're not dropping after sunset," he said. "But we're cutting it close."

Monica nodded. "Close is good enough for me."

"Me, too," Blaze said.

"Are your packs ready?" Wilde asked.

Blaze said, "Yes. I'll have Monica double check hers while we wait."

Wilde picked up the radio and made the call. The rangers were ready to go.

THE HELICOPTER TOUCHED THE GROUND and Monica and Blaze ducked through the open door into its belly. Behind them, Wilde hobbled aboard, helped by a cane. Inside, a National Guardsman handed her a headset as the whine of the rotors reached a screaming pitch. She landed in a seat, then tugged the safety strap over her shoulder and snapped it home. She unclipped her helmet and set it in her lap so she could fit the bulky earphones over her head. As she did, the roar of the metal machine was swallowed by an eerie, underwater wind. A voice burst to life as the captain spoke from the front. "You secure, Ranger?"

Monica checked her restraint, then flashed a thumbs up.

Blaze slid into the seat across from her and snapped her belt in place then stuck her thumb toward the sky. "I'm good!"

Wilde jostled into a seat, then gave the go-ahead.

"We're all clear," the Guardsman said into the headset.

The blades churned faster, sending shuddering jolts through the craft. A spasm fluttered in Monica's throat but she calmed it with a quick swallow. The chopper wavered gently, as if in nervous anticipation of leaving the ground, then lifted off. Monica peered out the open door as the green grass, dyed to the shade of a blood orange by the descending sun, fell away beneath them. It was beautifully terrifying.

When Monica began learning how to perform search and rescue, she quickly realized it required going places that human beings didn't normally travel. Those places often had no infrastructure: No roads, landing strips, shelters, or anything for dozens, even hundreds of miles. Rescuing lost hikers required flying over the barren landscape and then reaching the survivors by whatever means necessary. Sometimes that could be achieved via a UTV or Jeep. Other times it meant procuring a helicopter. Yet growing wings didn't always mean the victims could simply be simply plucked out of the wilderness and flown to safety. Many of the places where hikers ended up stranded or injured couldn't accommodate a six million dollar aircraft. That meant fast-roping, a technique that was fraught with risk.

The helicopter nosed south, rising so rapidly that Monica's stomach began to flop. She leaned to the side so she could peer out the open side of the Blackhawk UH-60 as it climbed the flanks of Sugarland Mountain. As far as the eye could see, the Great Smoky Mountains stretched east and west. The lesser ridges descended like long velvet curtains of green and gold. The hurricane had blown away the last vestiges of summer and soaked the land with the bittersweet waters of autumn.

Monica leaned back as winds shook the vehicle like a round of cannon fire. She held her breath and grabbed the strap bisecting her chest, trying not to look afraid.

Blaze didn't seem to notice the turbulence and chatted busily with the National Guardsman. Wilde stared out the window, his face stoic as marble. As if he sensed Monica's gaze, he turned.

"I'll have the pilot do a sweep and check for heat signatures," he said.

Monica nodded. "Got it."

"If the family isn't at the campsite," Wilde went on, "the two of you should proceed downriver, due north. Stay together and don't do any bushwhacking unless I say so."

Monica sent him a thumbs up as Blaze leaned toward the window, her jaw working at a piece of gum. Then, as if satisfied, she settled back in her seat and crossed her arms, smiling.

"You feeling confident?" Monica said.

Blaze grinned. "I'm about to jump out of a helicopter. I feel great!"

Monica began to laugh but the chopper topped out, giving their bellies a jolt. They flew over the knifelike vertebrae of Sugarland Mountain, stuttering in the jetstream, then nosed down once more, practically diving into the Little River drainage. Monica grabbed her gut and swallowed again.

"Thirty seconds out," the pilot called.

Monica tore open the pockets of her cargo pants and removed a thick pair of gloves from the pouches. "Glove up!" she called.

The coverings were heavy and insulated, specifically designed for fast-roping. Anyone who has tried to grab a quick-moving rope knows how easy it is to suffer burns; as long as she got a decent grip with her boots, the gloves would protect her from the friction.

She pulled them over her fingers as the pilot announced, "Twenty seconds!"

Monica wrapped both hands around her straps. The chopper swayed, rocking in a cradle of violent winds that were pouring over the peaks into the valleys below like water swirling into the spout of a funnel. The metal hull shrieked, the noise slicing through the headset. Then a low, terrible groan began to rumble under them.

"Ten seconds!"

Monica leaned forward, grabbing ahold of the coiled rope lying on the floor, her hands shaking as the helicopter continued to gyrate in the rushing air. Blaze mimicked her. The aircraft swung sideways, slamming to a lateral halt and throwing everyone to the side. The hull steadied, rotating slowly from its fading momentum, then finally held still.

The Guardsman gave the signal, jabbing his finger toward the yawning door.

Monica ripped off the headset and set her helmet in its place, looping the chinstrap around her cheeks. With a swift pinch of the clasps, she released her harness and pushed the entire spool of rope out the side of the chopper. It unfurled like a firehose. She crawled to the edge and cradled the rope with her legs. Then, with a last glance at Wilde, Monica slid out into thin air.

Immediately she dug her feet into the thick cord to slow her fall. Heat radiated through the gloves but cooled as she slowed. Her heart hammered against her ribs, but she exhaled and felt her body settle into a gentle, controlled slide down the rope. Soon she'd be on the ground and could begin the search for Tiffany and the kids—

Suddenly the rope wrenched away from her as a blast of wind shook the atmosphere, and she flew sideways as the helicopter fought the buffeting gusts. Her arms held firm but she swung wildly beneath the thudding rotors and her legs slipped free.

Monica gave a cry of terror, dangling from the trembling rope as the wind rushed past her.

Then the helicopter swayed again, yanking the rope from her hands. She plummeted into the darkness, her screams masked by the roar of the blades.

42

—•—

SHOT IN THE DARK

*N**O! NO!*

Monica groped with desperate hands, her gloves slapping at the rope without securing it.

I'm falling too fast!

She swiped again and felt the cord against her inner arm. Instantly, she squeezed her arms into a taut knot, clasping the rope against her body. White hot fire burst over her flesh, little more than a layer of khaki protecting her skin. Everything was still rushing past her—tree tops, shuddering topiaries of small emerald leaves, thick black trunks of swaying lumber. Monica gasped and squeezed harder. The same terrible stovetop singe ripped through her shirt, burning the skin on her forearms, chest, stomach, thighs, calves, ankles....

"Stop!" she screamed, and clutched with all her might. Then she looked down.

I'm going to hit!

Monica twisted her legs and bent her knees right before she slammed into the ground like a bag of concrete. Right as her feet made contact with the hard-packed dirt of the campsite, muscle memory took over and she launched herself forward. She tucked her head, rolling on her shoulder, and when she came to a stop, Monica lay on her side, gasping for breath. Vertical spikes of searing pain throbbed across her arms and abdomen. Panting, dizzy, and tasting blood, she gasped, "I'm down."

For a moment she rested, catching her breath and letting the adrenaline pass. Then she stood, wobbling under the weight of the rescue pack, and craned her neck to look up at the helicopter. Blaze was descending over her, also struggling with her speed, but she slowed her plunge in time and leapt from the rope, landing deftly on both feet.

The cord began climbing back up as the Guardsman hauled it in. The task took a good thirty seconds as the aircraft continued to work against the violent winds, but soon the rope was gone and the helicopter bird flew out of sight, its rotors continuing to pound in their ears.

For a moment Monica and Blaze stood in silence, catching their breath and peering into the quiet of the forest. The mission before them loomed enormous.

Monica turned to the west. The light was fading fast, and the canopy of trees was only making it darker. It was time to get started.

"Let's go," she said, and they stepped into the wild.

CAMPSITE 30 WAS BROAD AND FLAT, the last level ground before the mountain began its steep ascent to Clingman's Dome. The Little River Lumber Company had ceased its logging efforts once it reached this point, and thus the trail terminated here as well. Monica climbed up the hill and immediately spotted a pair of tents beside a rusted fire ring. The bright nylon shimmered against the dim background of forest.

"There," she announced, pointing.

They sprinted up the narrow access path that connected the subunits of the campsite and crawled over a downed tree.

"Check the blue tent," Monica said, pointing. "I'll take the red."

Even as she hurried up on the site, it was obvious that no one was there. The flaps were open, waving like flags in the wind and slapping against the sides. A large branch had fallen on the red one and it was buckled in the middle. Monica dropped to the ground and stuck her head inside. Her hands hit a wet sleeping bag that disappeared into the impression of the branch.

"Hello?" she called.

No one answered. As far as she could tell, there was no sign of human presence in the ruptured shelter. She pressed against the entire length of the sleeping bag to be sure, but only felt the cold squish of saturated goose down.

"Tiffany!" she called.

After waiting for a reply that did not come, she jogged over to Blaze who was inspecting both sides of the other tent, a blue structure ravaged by the claws of fallen branches that had raked the nylon to ribbons.

"Any sign of them?"

Blaze pulled her head out of the tent and held up an object. It was a single child-sized University of Tennessee baseball cap.

"Is there anything else?"

Blaze shook her head. "Just two abandoned sleeping bags. Everything else is gone."

"Okay," Monica said. "It seems like everyone survived the storm and hiked out. Let's head downstream." She leaned into the radio and sent a call to Wilde.

"I've got heat signatures," Wilde responded, the radio crackling.

"Where?"

"North of your position," Wilde said. "One mile."

"How many people?"

The radio was silent a moment, then Wilde said, "Looks like four. We need to circle around again." The communication cut out for a moment, then it flared back with Wilde mid-sentence, grumbling to the pilot: "—I don't care about the damned wind shear, take us around again."

Blaze took the lead this time, flying over the fallen tree toward the exit of the campsite only to run head-on into the upper waters of the Little River. The water rushed past like a bullet.

With a heavy breath, she inched up to the water's edge. The white train couldn't have been roaring more loudly or fiercely. Hundreds of gallons were rushing past her each second. The sheer power was enough to throw her down the slope and slam her body into a boulder.

Monica closed her eyes and quickly whispered, "Please protect me." Then she lifted her leg and pressed down. The moment her boot hit the water, it shifted to the left and her entire sense of balance was destroyed. She jabbed out with the pole to steady herself as her boot wavered in the water. Then it finally landed and her weight shifted into the river. Monica gasped, trembling with shooting adrenaline as it fired lightning through her body.

Keep going.

She pressed hard into the poles, bent her knee, and lunged out with the other leg. Just like before, the water slapped it away and she had to lean against her supports and pray the river didn't topple her over.

"You're almost there!" Blaze yelled from behind her.

Monica nodded and looked down at the water, only for the white spray to spit in her eyes. She focused on her next spot. The foam rushed flat over the bottom, meaning there were no rocks or logs to force it up into a swell. She lifted and stomped, the splash soaking her entire lower body, and her boot landed on the creek bottom.

Solid.

Another step. The river still yearned to shove her over and smash her head open, but Monica stabbed with the poles and kept herself upright. She brought her right leg forward, slammed it down, wobbling a bit as the rushing waters plowed harder, then lunged forward and threw herself onto dry land.

Monica clambered out and turned and watched Blaze copy her exact movements, taking slow, precise steps through the deluge. She emerged and laughed.

"That's the stupidest thing I've ever done!"

Monica extended a hand and helped her climb over a boulder. "At least we made it. Come on."

They resumed their stride, jogging down the trail as darkness began to fall over the forest.

"Wilde," Blaze said. "Any update on the heat signatures?"

"Yes," he answered, his voice breaking up through the tinny radio. "They're still there, about a mile north of your position."

"Good!" Monica said.

"I do have some bad news," Wilde continued. "We're running out of light up here. Pilot says we have to land and replace the batteries in our infrared goggles."

"Got it," Monica said. "We'll keep moving until we hear from you again."

She broke into a jog down the littered pathway. Shadows crept over the land, cloaking everything in a palpable black mist rendering them blind and weary. Monica snapped on her headlamp but it barely added any light. She slowed her pace just in time to stop before running into a hulking trunk lying over the trail.

"Whoa," she said.

Her light poured over the saddleback of the tree.

"Look," Blaze said. Her own headlamp was aimed above Monica's head. A scrap of pink nylon fabric fluttered on the end of a branch, its surface speared through. Monica smiled.

"We're on the right path," she said, catching her breath.

They resumed their downhill trek. The trail was no longer a path, but a mess of shattered branches and poking twigs jutting out of the earth like fingers. Monica picked her way through, high-stepping to avoid snags and stumbles.

"So," Blaze said as the light completely vanished, "what'd you tell your father?"

"What do you mean?" Monica asked, wiping sweat from her eyes.

"When you left," she said. "I'm guessing you didn't just leave him."

Another drip of salty liquid dribbled into Monica's eye. Annoyed, she flicked it out with her finger. "I told him I'd be back in twenty-four hours."

"How'd he take it?"

Her boots crushed a branch with a loud crunch. It was as if an endless heap of forest trash had been slashed down by some vandal to bar their passage.

"Not well," Monica said. "Why do you ask?"

"I don't know," Blaze said. "That couldn't have been easy. Sure, your dad treats you like he has dibs on your entrails. But still, he *is* your dad."

Monica drew a deep breath and let it out loudly. "Yup."

"Do you love him?"

"Of course," Monica answered. "Why wouldn't I?"

"See," Blaze said, her voice twanging mischievously, "that's the difference between you and me. I don't love my dad."

"Not even a little?" Monica said, glancing behind her.

"Nope," Blaze said, smiling weakly. "He was a monster. And as much as I tried to love him, he made it impossible."

"My father isn't a monster," Monica said, crawling over a downed tree. "He's just untreated, and it makes him say some monstrous things."

"I get it," Blaze said. "I *wish* the junk between my dad and me was that tidy. But it isn't. And that's why I don't love my father, and you do."

Blaze added nothing more, and the only sound in Monica's ears was that of their boots crushing pinecones and twigs underfoot, and the ever constant roar of the river. The sun vanished, and the only illumination came from their headlamps. The dark hung thick about them like a hood, and nothing they did could penetrate it beyond a few feet in front of their sweating faces.

"How far have we gone?" Monica asked.

"Point-five," Blaze replied.

"Tiffany?" she called.

No answer.

The trail angled back toward the edge of the water, abutting a sharp drop down to the raging foam. Its howling roar continued to flood her ears, but then a new sound appeared for the first time in nearly an hour. It was barely audible under the deafening sibilance of the water. It found her and she stopped suddenly, and just as soon as her ears had begun to adjust to it, it was gone.

"What?" Blaze asked, still right behind her.

"Wait," Monica said.

There was nothing for a moment. Then it came again, low and weary, like a person moaning in sadness or pain.

"They're here!" Monica said. "I think they're in the river!"

Once again, the adrenaline spigots began to gush and every bit of her body vibrated with tense energy. The Campbells were close—she could feel it!

She rushed forward, hopping over a low-lying tree branch that had fallen on the trail, and ran to the edge of the path as it swept over the river below.

"Tiffany?" she cried. "*Tiffany!*"

The groaning sound resumed, and this time it was louder, closer, and deeper. In fact, it was so deep that she felt her chest rumbling from the vibrations. She swung her head, searching the waters for some sign of the survivors in the midst of the waters, clinging to a rock or branch. Then the deep rumbling sounded again, and it rose to a chest-shaking growl.

"Monica!" she heard behind her.

She leaned closer to the river. The family had to be here! Why else would she be hearing—

The obvious answer suddenly appeared in her brain like popcorn exploding. Monica turned her head. The growling continued.

With a sudden bark, the sound erupted into agonized grunts. Monica's mouth fell. "God," she whimpered, "please...."

Her light passed over the waters, then landed on an enormous cloud of dark fur. Standing before her, teeth bared and paws stamping at the ground, was a three hundred-pound black bear, flanked by three squealing cubs.

43

THE FAMILY

*D*ON'T PANIC.

Monica took a slow backward step, her boot skidding on the slick muddy bank. The bear seemed to take this retreat as a sign of weakness and crept forward, snarling. The eyes glowed like pearls in the bright glare of the headlamps, but the body was dark and ragged with debris.

"Whoa, bear!" Monica yelled.

She stepped again and found a root with her heel, and pressed against it.

"Get back!" Blaze yelled, rushing up beside Monica.

They threw their arms in the air and yelled. The bear swatted, throwing mud about itself, growling. Long claws raked the earth and sent pebbles skittering everywhere.

"Go away!" Monica yelled. "Leave us alone"

It always felt childish to her, but yelling at bears remained the best form of defense. As long as the creatures believed that humans were a threat, they wouldn't attack. It was all Monica could do to make herself threatening, and the bear ignored her shouts, marching toward her, its head low and rigid.

Blaze raised her arms and stomped her feet. "Go away, bear! *Go away!*"

The bear stamped and growled, huffing like an enormous St. Bernard.

"Go away!" they hollered again.

The bear charged. It was swift and silent, a blur of darkness like a bat swooping from above.

Monica shouted in terror and stumbled backward. The bear stopped just short of her, slapping its paws against the ground like thunder. Then it grunted, its gruff voice furious with a deafening *Huff, huff, huff!*

A bluff charge.

"Go, bear!" Monica screamed. *"Go!"*

It lunged at them again, mere inches from her face.

Huff, huff!

Monica took both trekking poles and gripped them like spears, then thrust them at the bear's snout. "Go, *go!*"

"Go!" Blaze yelled, swinging her sticks as well. "Leave us alone!"

The bear stamped and growled, filled with rage. It stood up on its hind legs, swatting at the air and opening its powerful jaws, the teeth shining with saliva. It swung an arm and Monica saw the dull claws flying toward her and she ducked. A blast of wind blew over her head as the tremendous appendage flew past. Then the bear came down with a crash and leered at her again.

"Go!" she cried. "Bear, just go!"

She raised her trekking poles, trying not to cower and give the bear any sense that she was afraid. Monica filled its face with the sharp end of her poles and its mouth continued to open and close, issuing more *huff huff* sounds while slashing the earth with its claws and leaving deep gouges.

But it lowered its head and pivoted the long body around, showing them its backside. It ran back to the cubs who were watching curiously from the rocks, their adorable ears perched atop their heads like fuzzy cookies. At the return of their mother, the three little ones scampered about, yipping with delight.

Then they retreated, leaving Monica sitting on the ground, heart hammering its way out of her chest. The mother bear and her cubs trudged across the trail, slipped into the foliage, and vanished into a hollow.

As if released from a hangman's noose, Monica gasped, her body struggling to relax. The fight-or-flight juices continued to surge through her. She massaged the bridge of her nose as a flood of pain seized her face.

"Check the creek for the Campbells, would you?" she said, her voice labored. "Maybe the bears were drawn to them."

Blaze obliged without a word, moving cautiously to the water's edge and scanning the white creek with their lamps. After a minute of surgical inspection, she turned and muttered, "Nothing."

Monica pulled herself up. Every muscle vibrated like a spring ready to uncoil. She was beginning to wonder if her body might break the next time it was tested.

Blaze returned from the bank, her eyes glowing like half-moons.

"You think Tiffany and her kids had any encounters like that?"

Monica exhaled slowly and shook her head. "God, I hope not."

"Hard to imagine that situation," Blaze said, her gaze turning back to where the creature had just stood. "Two mothers, both trying to protect their kids. That'd be quite the standoff."

"Let's get going," Monica said. "Make sure to watch for those bears in case Mama is still mad at us."

They returned to the trail and resumed a slow jog. Monica took out her radio.

"Wilde," she called. "Are you back in the air?"

The radio hissed for a while with no answer.

They covered a half-mile or so when the trail abruptly disappeared, leading straight to a treacherous dropoff that fell into a broad sweep of the river. She blinked, gawking into the black abyss where dirt was supposed to be. What had happened?

"Where's the trail?" she said.

"Here," Blaze said. She was crouching and holding the long arm of a maple branch aloft so they could pass under it. "A few years ago, heavy rains rerouted the river. It's almost impossible to find the new trail if you don't already know where it is."

"Apparently," Monica said.

Blaze led the way, ducking under the low-ceilinged tunnel. Monica followed and gaped at the battered path, its narrow passage obstructed by collapsed trees with branches rising like medieval spikes. Every ten or twenty feet they faced another wall in the haunted labyrinth of wooden death. Every turn led to a booby-trapped dead end, and it seemed to take forever to find the right path through the smothered ruins.

They finally stepped out of the trees and stood once again on a broad, well-worn road covered in broken, leafy twigs and innumerable acorns. Monica looked behind and saw a nearly identical dropoff where the trail had been washed away on the north side.

The rescuers plodded along once again, occasionally pausing to shout the names of their quarry. No answers came except the rustle of the trees and the breath of the wild river. As they reached the end of a long, gradual bend, they spied the distant silhouette of a trail sign.

There was a piece of bright pink cloth on it.

Monica broke into a sprint all the way up to the sign. As she neared it, the object came into focus. It was a t-shirt, curled into a roll and tied around the top of the post.

"What does that mean?" Blaze said, running up to the post beside her.

Monica frowned and squeezed the fabric. Bulbs of clear water dribbled out, running down the darkened wood sign.

"They came this way," Monica said.

She turned to her right where the Rough Creek Trail led away, disappearing into the rhododendron wrapped around Sugarland Mountain.

"They wouldn't go that way, would they?" she asked.

"No," Blaze answered, shaking her head. "It's steep, overgrown, and you can't go far before reaching tough creek crossings."

"So there's no chance they took that route," Monica said.

Blaze shook their heads. "Very unlikely," she said.

Monica turned back to the pink flag hanging limp and sodden against the trail sign. "So it means they came this far, and possibly wanted to leave a marker in case anyone came after them. Does that make sense?"

"I don't know," Blaze said. "Imagine you're stuck out here for days. No cell, no internet. Your batteries are dead. You keep trying to find a way out, but constantly backtrack to the same junction. What if they marked it to remember that they've already been here?"

Monica nodded. "That makes sense." She leaned into her radio once more. "Wilde, come in!"

There was no reply.

"Where the heck are they?" Monica scowled.

Now that they knew the family was nearby, she was suddenly more fearful than ever before that they would pass by and not know it. She needed eyes in the sky.

"Tiffany!" she called.

Blaze joined in, repeatedly yelling her name, but they heard no reply from the fathomless wilderness.

They came upon Campsite #24, a normally pleasant hamlet tucked in the confluence of two branches of the river. Today, however, it was a mud patch, the brown earth only recently exposed after days of flooding. Blaze gave the camp a quick look, but turned back with a shake of her head.

"There's no one here," she said.

Monica sighed. The heaviness of defeat was beginning to wear on her. They had been moving for roughly two hours against the dense oppression of night through a jungle of shattered woodlands.

The path led to a creek crossing that mostly resembled a swift rice paddy, so they stepped in up to their calves and forged ahead through the bog. Trees poked out of the water, their roots invisible. Monica halted a moment to gather her bearings. Without the trail they could lose their position. She peered through the murk, a faint mist rising over the gurgling waters. At the edge of her light, she could barely spot the beige sheen of runny earth emerging from below. She gestured toward it and led the way, lifting her legs to avoid any underwater obstacles like roots and stones.

The trail appeared again, its brown carpet shimmying out of the depths. From there, it skirted the lip of land while the river cut a deep scar, forming a cliff that ran dangerously close to their boot steps. Monica scanned the trail for any clue that the Campbells had made it this far, scouring the bank where they had beached, searching up and down in case they had finished their crossing somewhere else. But there was nothing to be seen, no unnatural neon fabrics to be found.

"There's nothing on the river's edge," Monica announced.

"Or on the trail," Blaze called.

Monica sighed. Were they going too far? What if they kept moving north but the Campbells were lost or trapped upstream?

"I don't feel good about that crossing," Monica said. "I have a hard time imagining them making it."

"Me, too," Blaze agreed. "Are we sure they're not out there now, in the river?"

It was worth a look. Monica crept down the bank once more and stepped ankle-deep into the foaming boil. She didn't want to venture too far without a secure cable to keep her tied to land, but it was worth moving farther out to cast her light into the midst of the stream. If the Campbells were out there, their screams would no doubt be swallowed up by the constant roar of the river. That was one reason why hikers were advised to carry a whistle. While one could run out of energy and even lose their voice, a whistle could work longer and more effectively than a human voice box. Did Tiffany think to pack one?

Monica stepped out, her legs sinking up to the knees.

"Careful!" Blaze called. "Do you want to rope in?"

"No," Monica said, swinging her light over the distant waters. "I just need a second—"

Suddenly the radio exploded with ear-splitting violence.

"*—they're right below you, right below—*"

Monica grabbed the device.

"Repeat, Wilde, repeat!" she cried. "Where are they?"

"Right below—"

The sound cut out a moment, then returned with a mechanical rattle. "Greene, Greene!"

It was Wilde, alright. Monica pressed her 'transmit' button and simply said, "Greene here. Go."

"They're right below you," Wilde repeated.

"The Campbells?"

"Yes," Wilde said. "One, maybe two hundred feet."

Monica turned and rushed toward the shore. "On land?"

"No," Wilde said. "They're in the river."

Monica stared at the radio. "*In* the river?"

"Ten-four."

There wasn't anything else to say. Monica grabbed Blaze's outstretched hands, climbed back up to the trail, and began sprinting.

44

— · —

COLD

T HE RIVER THUNDERED BESIDE THEM.

Monica ran until Wilde radioed, "Beside you!" then she slowed to a stop. She slid down the steep bank, the mud giving way under her weight and dumping her into the edge of the raging river. She passed her headlamp over the creek, its surface a frothing cauldron of brown branches flying about in the black brew.

There was no sign of the Campbells.

"Wilde!" Monica yelled over the holler of the water. "I can't see them!"

"Trust me!" came the reply. "They're out there!"

Monica squinted. Her light barely reached the middle of the river, but she discerned the faint form of several trees that had fallen and jammed into some boulders like broken statues.

Blaze slid down beside her. By the time her boots splashed down, she had unstrapped her pack and was fishing for rope. Monica did the same, removing a cord of one hundred feet from her pack.

"Here," Blaze said, running the end of her lanyard to the body of a young, yellow buckeye tree. She secured the line, then brought the other end to Monica.

Monica turned to the river. It was a dark, shrouded channel of chaos. Every step would be an unknown. They'd have to be patient, no matter how dire the Campbells' situation might be.

Monica clicked her radio. "We're ready to go in, Wilde."

"Go," Wilde ordered. "They're still there."

Monica rotated and looked at her partner. Blaze was leaning back on the bank, the cord coiled around her arm.

"I've got you," Blaze said.

Monica nodded, then turned and took a long, slow breath.

She lifted her leg and stuck it out into the Little River. The current grabbed it and tugged. She was ready, resisting and forcing it upstream. Thrusting both hiking poles down, she wobbled forward, her boots sliding over the smooth stones with broad tops like bowling balls. The tread hit bottom and she wavered, then steadied herself.

One step at a time.

Polar water soaked her from the waist down, and the chill spread into her chest and down her arms. Her fingers began to tremble. "You can do this," she said, shivering. A glacial wind flew down the mountain, running along the track of the stream, and blew right into her face. She continued walking, one slippery step at a time.

The water climbed up to her elbows and wrapped its arms around her. Monica grit her chattering teeth and leaned against the current, keeping her balance in spite of the raging torrent. Her light had begun to discover what lay in the midst of the river, too. Just as she had started to see, a pair of once-mighty trunks lay cracked and battered, their broad forms piercing the waters and creating great white flanges of foam. Each lay at an angle, jutting into the impenetrable dark of the night sky.

Monica trudged toward them, sweeping her light back and forth, praying for a sign of the Campbells. There was nothing.

"Tiffany!" Monica cried. "Where are you!?"

The spit and spray flew in her eyes, and the waters churned in a whirlpool. She blinked the fluid away just as something moved in the shadows, a pale orb the size and shape of a human face.

"Tiffany!"

The visage vanished but Monica knew what she had seen. The image of the emaciated survivor hovered in her sight like a photograph, paralyzing her for a moment, and a harsh wave of hopelessness flew with the winds and water to overwhelm her. Monica narrowed her eyes and took a dozen slow, careful steps. The pale shape reappeared and its features sharpened into a woman's thin, weakened face. It was Tiffany Campbell.

She was standing in the river, the waters rising up to her neck. Her hair was long and straight, tied in a short ponytail. When fully healthy, she was probably an athletic woman with a complexion the color of hot chocolate. But now she could be mistaken for a ghost, even as Monica came closer.

Tiffany turned and met Monica's gaze. The eyes were heavy and sullen. Exhaustion had emptied her, and the remorseless icy waters were draining her of the will to live.

Monica startled: she couldn't see any of the children.

Where were they!?

Monica scrambled forward. She knew she had to stay patient, but with Tiffany in sight, she could barely restrain herself from sprinting through the water. Her legs threw themselves forward with terrible determination. She was going to save that woman no matter what.

I bet there's room in that clever mind of yours to talk to the Lord.

"There's no time," she said as if Mike Ownby were in the river beside her.

She forced her way toward the withered woman trapped in the frigid waters, defying the wall of water moving against her.

"I'm coming!" Monica cried.

Tiffany's face barely flinched in response. Monica pushed harder, spurning the furious rapids with every step. Adrenaline shot through her veins at the thought of Tiffany's horrible fate.

There was no time to lose!

Monica lunged forward with a bold step, unworried about what might be at the bottom. Her boot found a submerged stone, landed, and suddenly slid right over it. She wobbled, throwing her arms out.

She was going to fall!

Monica stabbed with a trekking pole. Her body toppled over, the current snatching her and closing its jaws. The pole responded just like her boot: It skidded against a rock and skated right on.

With a cry of surprise, Monica toppled over and plunged into the depths.

She released her poles and clawed to grab at anything she could. Her body spun as it shot through the water and her fingers slipped off everything they touched.

She felt a texture in the water, rough and firm—a branch!—but it proved too slick. Monica swung her arms again just as she slammed into a tree. Her torso stabbed with pain and the impact spun her like a twig in the current.

Then the world exploded. Her vision burst white like a machete had been driven right into her skull. Her arms and legs went limp, she exhaled the last of her breath, and all became dark and silent.

45

— · —

ABYSS

T HE PAIN VANISHED.

The sun blazed high above as Monica sat in the belly of the canoe, her hand trailing out the side. Her fingers cut a small 'V' in the surface of the Obed River. High beyond the peak of the canyon, a flock of birds rode swiftly on the air, their cries sweet gracenotes punctuating the rattle of the oars against the gunnels.

Behind her, a woman was steering the boat in silence. The man before her was wordless, too.

How long had they been like this, not speaking? She couldn't tell. She glanced behind her and saw the woman staring off into the distance, a contented smile set between her plump cheeks.

She felt the touch of a slimy plank of wood in the river. She shook her hand and rubbed the green goo on her shorts.

Her mother's voice broke the quiet.

"What are you doing, Little Bear?"

Monica turned and looked into the woman's face. It was no longer smiling. Instead, it had twisted into a strange frown, one eye glaring more harshly than the other.

"I touched something gross."

"And what'd you do with it? Wipe it on your pants?"

Monica turned around, ashamed.

"Well, did you?" the woman insisted.

"Yes," Monica whispered. She tucked both hands in her lap and bowed her head.

"You're gonna ruin them," the woman spat.

"I'm sorry, Mama," Monica said.

"If you ruin those shorts, I'll slap the hell out of you, young lady."

Monica pushed her head down even further, burying it in her chest. The man before her was utterly silent.

The woman wasn't done. "You gonna answer me?"

"It didn't leave a stain," Monica protested softly. "They're okay."

"No, they're not!" the woman roared. "You ruined your good pair, didn't you!?"

Monica shook her head. "They're fine. I swear!"

But the shorts were clearly stained, the faded pink khaki now smeared with the residue of frog spawn. The woman's eyes went wide and seemed to fill with fire at this infraction.

Then she stood. Instantly the canoe lurched to the left, then to the right. Monica grabbed both gunnels and shrieked in surprise.

"What the hell is wrong with you?" the woman said.

Finally, the man turned around and muttered, "Please, Naomi, just let it go—"

She ignored him and stepped forward. The canoe shimmied back and forth and a loud clanging rattled the back of the boat. Monica managed to see a glass bottle fly through the air before it hit the deck and smashed into a hundred jagged shards. A puddle of brown liquid began to spread at the woman's feet. She startled, paused, and stared at the remnants below.

"It's okay, Naomi," the man said. "She didn't mean any harm."

The woman was undeterred. The terrible glare rose again, finding little Monica. It was an otherworldly glare, a look brought about by devilish devices. The little girl had no clue what to do.

"Mama," she whimpered. "I'm sorry."

"Sorry?" the woman sneered. "You'll *be* sorry. I said I'd slap the hell out of you, and I'm gonna do it right—"

The woman took another step and the canoe teetered. Monica grabbed both gunnels for dear life, and without a thought she jerked with all her might. The canoe swiveled and both adults tumbled out of the boat and into the river.

"Monica!" the man cried.

"What did you *do!?*" the woman screamed.

Monica leaned over the edge, the boat wobbling. "Daddy!" she yelled. "Mommy!"

The man's long black hair was matted to his flesh. "Little Bear!" he shrieked. "What were you thinking?"

"I don't know!" she cried.

"Help us get back in!"

She turned and searched the boat for an oar or life jacket. But the canoe was barren, empty of anything that could help. Everything had fallen in except her. She scrambled back to the edge and stretched out her hand. The man paddled toward her, his head dipping under once or twice before he reached her. Then he caught her grasp and began hauling himself back into the canoe.

"Where's your mother!?" he bellowed.

Monica stared at him. "I—I had to help you—"

The man leaned over and screamed, spit flying and spattering her face, "Help your mother!"

Monica gasped and peered into the river. Sure enough, the woman was bobbing in and out of the water. She raised an arm but her head vanished below the surface. A moment later she reappeared, screamed, and then slipped below once more, leaving only an unfinished howl.

"Do something!" her father bellowed. "This is your fault, Little Bear!"

The words he spoke pierced her ears like arrows. With that, she didn't think any further. There was only one thing to do.

Monica threw herself off the side of the canoe.

She paddled toward her mother and reached her in mere seconds. She grabbed the woman's wrist to lead her back to the boat. But the woman screamed and pawed at Monica's shoulder like a drowning animal. Then she shoved with all her might.

Before Monica could comprehend what had happened, she was underwater. She kicked and opened her eyes to see if the woman was indeed sinking beside her.

She wasn't.

Instead, Monica floated in the ether and watched the shimmering image of the woman rising to the surface. She reached the long shadow of the canoe and disappeared with a circular ripple. The man had helped her in.

Monica continued to watch. Her muscles wouldn't move.

Shouldn't you swim to the surface, too?

But she didn't. She remained there, her arms and legs weightless as the river wrapped her in its watery blankets. She stared and watched for a sign from above.

Wouldn't the woman come back for her?

Wouldn't she reach down and pluck the child back up?

The face did not reappear. Only the distant, ocre sun, devoid of passion or loyalty, looked down through the shifting waters like an abstract painting.

Monica touched the riverbed, her bottom resting on a garden of weeds. Should she swim up? She certainly needed to breathe, didn't she?

But she couldn't make herself move. The surface seemed so far away, so difficult to reach. Wasn't it her fault she was down here, anyway? Shouldn't this be her new home, this pleasant and lonely abyss?

A shadow came over the sun and swept it away. Gloom covered the canyon, and she shivered as the water went cold.

Go back.

The shadow blotting out the sun narrowed to a long thin oval, the form of the man's head. It was her father, looking for her.

But her arms and legs didn't want to work. A mysterious force had bled them of their willpower. Despite this atrophy, a feeling that she would come to understand much later in life, she forced each joint to bend, each appendage to plant and push, and within seconds her face broke the surface. The man grasped her with trembling hands and helped her clamber back into the belly of the boat, right where she'd been moments before.

Monica lay on her back gasping for breath. Water trickled from her ears and all she heard for a time was the hollow moaning of the river.

Then a voice broke through, cold and laden with blame.

"I almost died—because of *you.*"

Monica grabbed her chest, desperate to breathe.

"I'm sorry—Mama Bear—" she wheezed.

She stared into the heavens, searching for the birds. They had flown away, off to a distant perch. She exhaled and closed her eyes.

"I'm sorry, Mama."

46

— · —

MOTHER

S OMETHING WAS TUGGING AT HER ARMPITS.

She blinked and water swept into her eyes. Her head was a universe of pounding pain and her hands instantly flew to her temples to ease the throbbing, but her muscles barely registered, leaving her arms to hang limply into the waves like dead vines.

The Little River raised its voice once again, the defiant hissing cutting through the liquid in her ears. She heard it and a shiver of terror rippled through her—she knew where she was, and that something terrible had happened—yet her mind continued to lie in the bottom of the boat.

"Mama?" she sputtered, water running over her lips and cheeks. "Mama—"

A swell rose over her head, drowning her words. She spat and coughed.

"I've got you!" someone said.

She turned her head but another wave spilled into her eyes.

"Where— how—"

"Hang on, Monica!"

Liquid flowed into her ears each time she dipped in the current. She blinked and winced at the rippling fire in her head.

"What about—the Campbells?" she managed to ask before another whitecap hit her in the mouth.

"You're almost safe," her rescuer said. "Stay with me."

She recognized the voice. *Blaze.*

How long had she been unconscious? How long had she been sinking into the depths of her tortured memory, waiting for someone to save her?

"Leave me," she moaned. "You have to help them—"

"Shut up, Greene!"

Fingers dug into the crooks of her armpits, working against the relentless current. Then the pressure under her arms suddenly abated and she sensed the firmness of land against her back. She let her head fall, the helmet barely hanging on by the chinstrap.

"Look at me, Monica," Blaze said, crawling over her. A headlamp shone directly in Monica's eyes, the blinding flares stabbing into her brain like spikes. She jerked away with a moan.

"I know it hurts, but I need to check you for a concussion." Blaze squinted from behind the wall of white light. "Oh, it's a concussion alright."

Monica licked her lips and twitched at another jolt of cranial pain. "I'm fine," she grumbled. "Let's just go help that family."

"Don't be stupid," Blaze said, shaking her head. "You almost died."

Monica rolled her head back weakly. "I'm always almost dying," she muttered.

"Of course you are," Blaze said with a guffaw. "It's like you *want* to sacrifice yourself."

The moment her friend's words had been spoken, Monica felt every muscle in her body go slack, and she thought she'd sink through the mud like the entire earth had become quicksand. It wasn't that simple, she wanted to say.

But the repeated jabs of knifing pain behind her eyes silenced her and Monica exhaled, trying to expel the agony one breath at a time.

Blaze grasped Monica's chinstrap with gentle hands and wiggled the helmet loose. "Here," she said, pressing a cold compress into Monica's hand. "Put this on your head."

Monica nodded and grimaced as she raised her hand and set the compress on her scalp. She could feel the massive bump through the material.

"How can I help?" Monica said through gritted teeth.

"Spot me," she said. "Then pull the kids in when I signal that they're hooked to the rescue line."

Blaze laid the spooled rope in Monica's lap. She took it with her free hand. "Okay," she said.

"One more thing," Blaze added as she took her first step into the writhing waves. "Don't you dare follow me."

Monica sighed and a hot spear shot through her brain. "I won't," she said.

Blaze turned and began her march into the black sea, her headlamp slowly fading as she moved toward the invisible jungle of broken trees.

"Dear God," Monica whispered, her lips quivering, "please help us."

Her head pulsed with blinding pain once again and she yelped. She adjusted the compress, moving it around the swollen bulb.

If I hadn't been wearing this helmet, she thought, *that collision would have split my head wide open.*

It was a thought both humbling and horrifying. How had she gotten into this mess? She'd been making great progress, trodding along one careful step at a time. And then....

She remembered seeing the woman, her flesh ashen like the wax of a candle.

The words of her departed mentor flooded her mind.

I bet there's room in that clever mind of yours to talk to the Lord.

"Okay, Big Guy," she said. "It looks like you forced me to sit down."

She pushed herself up, her muscles tingling with ache, and looked over the river. Blaze's light had grown dim in the thin sheen of mist hovering over the river.

"Please protect her, Lord," she whispered. "Please be with my friend."

She looped the rope around her hand and felt it shudder with Blaze's distant, jarring steps.

Suddenly the light vanished.

Monica leaned forward, her head shooting with the sudden movement.

Where did she go?

"God, *please*," she moaned.

Darkness shrouded the entire river valley. She was alone on the riverbank, the solitary light of her headlamp shining weakly into the bleak world of shadow.

"Jesus," she whispered, "please do something."

Thirty seconds passed. All was still black and void.

"You have to save them," she said, her lips shaking. "You have to save them, because I— I can't."

Can't.

The word left her mouth, large and palpable like a chunk of unchewed meat. Her entire being felt lighter, as if the weight of her gear and the water and her wounds were no longer sodden with the spit of the devil.

Monica bowed her head, and before she knew it a small sob had dribbled out of her.

"I can't," she repeated.

Then the sob morphed into a half-laugh, half-weep, her spirit consumed with a strange truth she couldn't quite name. Instead, all she could do was shake her head and wipe away the tears from her smiling cheeks.

She bowed her head again, exhaled deeply, and closed her eyes.

The face of her mother appeared, as if she was hovering over the river like a ghost. Monica opened her eyes and saw nothing except the photographic negative, like a picture of a murder scene.

She closed her eyes.

The canoe again, lurching to the side. The jarring clatter of shattering glass. A hundred shards lay glittering at the woman's feet.

Pieces of the day's bottle.

Monica opened her eyes. Everything was still a screen of darkness. There was no sign of her partner's headlamp. Yet her mind was still in the dream, immersed in the river of the past.

"She brought it with her," Monica said, her lips moving slowly. "On a canoe trip. A *family* canoe trip."

Monica bit her lip and bowed her head yet again.

"She was drunk."

The image before her shifted. It was no longer the woman hovering over the waters, but a man, his thin face and heavy eyes beholding her with terrible shame.

She pressed her lips together as they trembled. Then she said, her voice guttural, "Dad knew."

Monica Greene lifted her head. Suddenly the world was no longer clad in a pall. A new sun had risen in her mind, a massive star with terrific power to send light into every dark place and make it shine like the dawn.

All her life she believed she'd nearly killed her parents. She believed that, because Mama Bear's little girl had nearly ended her life, the woman had taken to drinking.

Yet she'd been an addict all along.

Monica stood to her feet, wobbling on the uneven ground.

"Oh, God," she whimpered, fresh tears running down her cheeks.

The moment she was finished speaking, light reentered the world. Far in the distance, a tiny headlamp appeared over the waters, its white cone sweeping back and forth to illuminate the cresting rapids.

Monica wrapped the rope tight against her forearm, the cord biting into her still-tender skin. Someone was on the line, and as they inched closer to the shore, she reeled them in. Monica began to distinguish an adult-sized figure in the water, her bony fingers clinging to the rope.

It was Tiffany Campbell.

Monica splashed into the rocky creek, gasping with excitement. "You're almost here!" she called.

Her face began to come into view, cast in stark shadows by Monica's head-lamp. The ranger hauled on the rope until Tiffany was in arm's reach. Monica lifted the waterlogged woman up the bank to the level trail surface. They finally reached it, gasping for breath, and she lowered Tiffany to the ground. Monica collapsed and crawled beside her.

"You're safe," she gasped.

Gazing at the woman's face, Monica began to perceive the depths of suffering this woman had gone through. Tiffany's cheeks were sunken to the bone. A thin neck barely connected her head to the shoulders. Her once espresso-rich skin was pale, like the belly of beached fish. And as she lay back, eyes wide, there was barely enough breath moving in and out of her lungs to keep her alive.

"You need oxygen," Monica said. She turned to Blaze's pack and dug into it, locating a small tank with a silicone mask. She laid the triangular barrier on Tiffany's face and turned a knob on the tank, starting the flow of rich air.

Tiffany shuddered at the rush of cool, medicinal oxygen. "You're going to be okay," Monica said, rubbing the woman's arm.

She glanced back at the river. Blaze's headlamp had disappeared again. Wherever the family had been finding refuge, it was cut off from direct line of sight.

Monica turned back to Tiffany and smiled, despite the tiny explosions in her skull.

"We're going to get you out of here," she said.

Tiffany closed her eyes and drew a deep breath, her chest rising slowly.

"It's going to be okay," Monica said.

She checked the river again. Darkness remained.

I bet there's room in that clever mind of yours to talk to the Lord.

Monica smiled, the muscles in her cheeks somehow sore like the rest of her body. Then she dropped her head and began to murmur a desperate plea to the Almighty for mercy. It only lasted ten seconds or so. She squeezed Tiffany's hand, then released it.

Beneath the mask, the weary mother's mouth began to move.

Monica lifted the device a mere millimeter and leaned her ear close. "What is it?" she said.

Tiffany swallowed and licked her lips. Then, unmistakably, she said, "Amen."

Monica replaced the mask and smiled. She exhaled, looked back over the dark waters, and waited.

47

CHILDREN

I T WASN'T LONG BEFORE THE SOLITARY HEADLAMP REAPPEARED far away over the distant waters.

Monica grasped Tiffany's hand and tenderly lifted it.

"Can you hold the mask?" she asked.

Tiffany nodded with tiny flicks of her head, and placed her palm on the silicone pyramid. Monica checked that the seal was intact, then turned back to the river and slid down the bank.

Across the waves, the light bobbed back and forth as the rescuer took careful, deliberate steps. Was it possible she'd somehow gathered all three kids and had them with her?

Monica's heart swelled at the possibility, but she knew there was just no way. Carrying one child across the depths would be hard enough. Conveying three? Impossible.

Each minute passed like an eon as Monica collected the rope inch by inch. She pressed her lips together, narrowed her eyes, and concentrated everything on the work at hand.

Blaze's steps became audible, splashing louder than the din of water, and her figure staggered into view.

By her side was a terribly skinny girl whose head barely broached the top of the waters. Her hair had probably been beautifully braided and adorned with beads several days ago; now it was a tattered mess, littered with twigs and leaves and clumps of mud. Her face was heavy but her eyes bright, anxiously searching the shore.

"Monica, can you help?" Blaze yelled.

"Yes!" Monica cried, and rose to her feet. An immediate blast of pain slammed her head like a hammer and she wobbled, grabbing at a branch for balance. She found it, held herself steady, and then lurched into the swells toward her friend.

"I've got Crystal with me," Blaze gasped.

Monica reached and took the girl's arm. "Come here, I've got you!" she said.

"Mama!" the girl cried.

"She's here!" Monica yelled. "Your mother's right here!"

The gaunt girl let go of her rescuer and ran forward in the darkness. "Mama!" she sobbed.

Tiffany set the mask to the side and reached out with both arms. "My baby!" she wailed, and the two embraced, lying together on the ground.

Monica looked away from them, back to Blaze, who was leaning with her hands on her knees, her feet still immersed in the river. "Are you okay?"

Blaze didn't answer. She panted in exhaustion, her chest rising and falling in great heaves.

"Blaze?"

The woman shook her head. "No," she said. "I'm not okay."

"Are the others still out there?"

Blaze nodded. "Xavier was too scared."

Monica remembered her list of names.

Xavier, five.

"What about Ericka?" she said.

Blaze gulped another swallow of air, let it out, and said, "She stayed with him. She wouldn't leave her brother all alone."

Monica drew a long breath as the concussion hammered her skull. Wincing, she exhaled and watched her partner. Blaze was absolutely gassed. The journey through the river had taken everything from her.

But there were still two kids out there. Someone had to go get them.

Monica lowered her face, staring at the border of mangled earth as it spewed white foam. Could she risk it?

Please God, give me wisdom.

She reached out and took the rope in her hands. Her fingers unclipped the carabiners and pulled them toward herself.

"What are you doing?" Blaze said.

Monica snapped the titanium ovals to her harness. "I'm gonna get the kids."

"No. We need support. I'm calling Wilde."

"What about Ericka and Xavier?"

Blaze spat into the river and stood tall. Only then could Monica see that her friend's face was a twisted snarl of fury. "No," she said. "You're concussed, and I'm not going out there again."

Monica's mouth fell. "What are you talking about?"

Blaze stabbed a finger toward the river. "No one is walking out there again. The next person who does is going to die."

"What?" Monica gasped. "Tiffany made it! You and Crystal, too!"

"Barely," Blaze scowled. "I nearly slipped a million times. I'm cut up every-where—razor sharp branches, slippery rocks, and it sounds like a tree's about to fall on my head—I'm sorry, Monica, but kids are going to have to ride it out."

"Ride it out?" Monica echoed, incredulous. "We'd be abandoning them to die."

"They have to wait!" Blaze exploded. "I'm not going out there again! I won't make it!"

"You don't have to, Blaze," Monica said.

Blaze's face was red as hot blood. "And neither are you!" she cried. "Call Wilde, tell him we need the helicopter!"

"The wind is too strong," Monica said, her voice as calm as possible. "Do you really think they could hold steady enough to get two scared kids out of here?"

"Fine," Blaze said, panting in desperation. "Then they'll wait. They made it this long, what's another few hours?"

"We can't do that to them," Monica said.

"Yes, we can," Blaze insisted. "I'm not going back out there."

Her friend's words echoed in her ears like shattering glass. Yet the fiery anger in Blaze's face, and the forcefulness of her words, gave Monica pause, and she cocked her head and frowned.

"It's okay, Allison," she said, "I understand."

"Good," Blaze said. "Call Wilde and tell him to get us the hell out of here."

"No, not that," Monica said. "I understand that you're scared."

"Scared?" Blaze said. "*Scared?* What are you talking about?"

"I'm frightened, too, believe me," Monica continued. "And I promise you: I don't want to die today. But if that's what I'm called to, then I'm prepared for it."

"Shut up with that crap," Blaze hissed, her hands balling into fists. "You're not going."

Monica crouched and grabbed the rescue rope. With a quick motion, she clipped herself in. Then she tossed the compress aside and scooped up her helmet.

"What the hell are you doing?" Blaze howled. "Stop it!"

"I'm getting the kids."

"No! Don't go out there!"

Monica held up a hand. "I didn't leave my father's deathbed just to abandon them."

"You won't make it," Blaze seethed. "If you go out there you're as good as dead, Greene."

"Maybe so," Monica said. She placed her helmet back on her head, and as it touched the scalp, her head came alive once more with pangs of pain. She pulled the strap around her jaw and snapped it in place. "But I'm still going to try."

"Don't be stupid, Greene! Don't die for nothing!"

Monica drew a slow breath and let it out with pursed lips. She grabbed a pair of harnesses for the kids and held them out in front of her.

"Nothing?" she said.

Blaze's frown wriggled in anger, but she held her tongue as Monica clipped the harnesses to her belt and stepped toward the shore.

"Hold that rope with all you've got," Monica said. "With any luck, there will be three of us on the other end of it."

Blaze sighed, then stomped ashore and snatched up the line. She looped it around her hands with a grunt of disapproval. "Fine," she said.

Monica wanted to scold her again, to chide her for surrendering her bravery in the face of tremendous fear. But as Blaze collapsed and rested her arms on her knees, Monica felt nothing but pity. She swallowed and forced her face into a smile.

"Hey," she said, trying to flash a grin Blaze's way. "It's going to be okay."

Blaze merely shook her head in defeat.

Monica turned away. Such pessimism would do nothing but poison her. With a final deep breath, one that she hoped was filled with holy anointing, she faced the river and descended into the rushing deluge.

48

FLOOD

WITH EACH CAUTIOUS STEP, MONICA WHISPERED A PRAYER.

"Don't leave me," she said. "Don't forsake me."

The words had hardly left her mouth when the careening waters attempted to hurl her downstream. She tightened her grip on the trekking poles and pushed forward.

"Be with me. Give me strength."

She found a rhythm as she moved, creating a familiar and reliable pattern. Lift the foot, steady it in the current, probe forward. Find even ground, lean into trekking poles, shift weight.

Repeat.

"Help me to trust you, God."

Monica wanted to look back to the shore so she could gauge her progress. But doing so felt like folly, the kind of twisting motion that would throw her off balance.

There was only one way: Forward.

"Give me your patience, Holy Spirit."

Monica duplicated her pattern, breathing calmly and focusing on the rhythm. It was the only way through the tempestuous waters. Panic had no place. Fear must be shunned. These were mortal enemies to her mission.

"Give me courage like yours, Jesus."

Monica lifted her head to check her surroundings and saw the hulking masses of the fallen trees not too far ahead of her. They lay enormous and black, soaked with moisture. One lay at an angle like a ramp, propped up against another and tapering to a narrow point over the depths. This must have been the obstacle that blocked her view of Blaze's headlamp.

Monica altered her path, aiming to the left. She peered at the colossal wreck, the bark stripped away as the water slowly ate at the inner strands.

Lift, steady, probe.

Ground, lean, shift.

Repeat.

"You are my strength and my shield."

The arduous move forced her upstream, millions of gallons resisting every inch she tried to gain. She strained against the river while her head reignited in splitting pain and flashes of white. More than anything, she wanted to sleep. Her teeth gritted, Monica lifted a leg and forced it forward.

She passed the tree and gazed into a little cove. A third tree lay flat in the waters, smeared black with moss. The waters swirled in a maelstrom of bubble and foam. Monica limped into its midst, aided by the fierce push of the current, and quickly reached the tree.

"Ericka!" she cried. "Are you there?!"

A hand waved and Monica turned to illuminate the oldest Campbell child. She was a pre-teen, tall and lanky. Her expression was shockingly alert, the eyes sharply focused on the ranger.

"Blaze?" the girl called.

"I'm Monica," Monica answered. "Monica Greene."

Ericka glanced into the river, her mouth falling into a frown. "Where's Blaze? Is she okay?"

"She's fine," Monica called. "Crystal's fine, too. They made it to the shore. Blaze needed to rest."

Upon hearing that her sister was safe, the girl sprung into action. She turned around, swinging her legs over the log, and as her body shifted Monica could see a tiny boy huddled behind her.

Ericka leaned toward her brother. "Okay, Lil Cookie," she said. "It's time for us to go!"

The boy, whom Monica presumed to be Xavier, shook his head.

"We gotta go, little man," the eldest sister said.

He shook his head again, eyes huge and wet with fear.

"Listen, Lil Cookie," she said. "When we get home, you can have a whole box of Oreos. But you have to get off this tree and go with Miss Greene here."

At this, the boy's eyes turned to the ranger. He stared at her for a second, then looked back at the sister. "A whole box?" he said, his voice tiny.

Ericka nodded. "A whole box."

The boy stretched out his hand and closed all but one of his fingers. "Pinky promise?"

Ericka extended her own little finger, interlocked it with her brother's, and shook it.

Monica smiled as Ericka scooted down the trunk and the boy followed, mirroring his sister's actions. The fear of the raging river withered under the power of a well-structured pinky promise.

"Are you Xavier?" Monica asked.

"We all call him Lil Cookie," Ericka said. "That's all he ever wants to eat."

"Lil Cookie?" Monica said, grinning at him. "I love cookies. My favorite kind is Thin Mint. What's yours?"

He studied her a moment, perhaps weighing trust against suspicion. But after a second he murmured, "Oreos," and the corners of his mouth wiggled into a smile.

"Here's what we're going to do," Monica said. She unclipped two harnesses from her belt, one medium-sized and one small, and held them up to the kids. "Before you get it in, put these on. They'll help you stay safe."

Ericka swiftly donned hers, threading her thin legs through the loops. She turned to assist little Xavier and said, "He won't have to walk, will he?"

Monica took a winded, nervous breath. Now that she had walked the entire way here, she knew there was no way a five-year-old child would ever be able to resist the power of the river. She'd have to carry him, which meant spending strength holding him *and* sacrificing one of her points of contact with the ground.

"I'll carry him," she said. "But I'm going to need your help. I only have two trekking poles. One's for me and one's for you. But I'll need you close to me, because carrying your brother isn't going to be easy."

The girl nodded. "Okay."

Monica unclipped the second rope and attached it to Ericka's harness. Then she used a carabiner to hook Xavier to her own straps.

"Are you ready?" she asked.

Ericka looked into the swirling black waters. "I'm scared. But I want to see my mom."

Monica reached and took her hand. "Me, too."

THE FIRST TWENTY FEET OF THE MARCH took an eternity. Pressing against the current's relentless phalanx, Monica struggled to keep her balance as she clutched Xavier to her chest and leaned desperately into the flow. Ericka wobbled like a novice wire-walker and swung her free arm, grabbing Monica and pulling. Monica yelled, "Let go!" and tried to maintain her sense of harmony between the current and gravity.

After several near-falls and multiple moments when her adrenal glands emptied themselves, Monica thought she might collapse from exhaustion. But they were still deep in the river and a long way from shore.

"God," she said, gasping, "please help us."

She took the lead, moving one cautious step at a time as she regained her rhythm. This time, though, with the added burden of Xavier, she had to test each step multiple times, working her boot around to guarantee that the foothold would be solid and secure when she shifted all of her weight. Worse, the little boy was constantly twisting in sheer terror, making the balancing act even harder. As he shifted his head from her left shoulder to her right, she felt her body giving way to the current. She yelled, shoved against her pole and shuddered until she finally found her balance again.

"Please, don't wiggle like that," she said, trying to keep her voice calm.

"I'm scared!" Xavier wailed. "I want Mommy!"

"She's just ahead," Monica said with ragged breath. "We're going to her."

"I want Mommy now!"

Ericka spoke up from the rear and said, "We'll see her soon, Lil Cookie. Be patient."

"I'm scared!"

"We all are," Monica said. "Just hold still and we'll be there soon."

"No, no!" he cried. "I'm scared!"

"Hey," Ericka said. "He loves stories. Can you tell him a story, maybe?"

Tell him a story?

Monica wheezed as her foot slid over a slimy stone and she tightened her core muscles to keep her balance. How was she supposed to tell the kid a story while concentrating on their harrowing passage?

"I don't know if I can—" she stammered.

"Please tell me a story," the boy said. "Please!"

"Maybe I can," Ericka said.

But the hesitancy in the girl's voice made it clear that she could not. The only thing that Ericka should be thinking about was making it back to land in one piece.

Head throbbing, with white lights bursting across her vision yet again, Monica closed her eyes. She executed her rhythm once more, moving a few feet closer to the shore, then licked her lips.

"Have you ever heard of Bigfoot?" she said.

"Bigfoot?" the boy asked. "No."

"I've heard of Bigfoot!" Ericka replied. "He's like a gorilla man, right?"

"No one knows for sure just *what* he is," Monica said, trying to keep her voice from shaking. Her boot touched a muck-coated stone, and in her exhaustion she nearly let her weight fall on it. She stalled, held her leg high, then probed further and found flat ground.

"Big step there," Monica said back to Ericka.

"Bigfoot has big steps?" Xavier asked.

"He sure does," Monica said, lining up her next lunge. "His feet are huge—bigger than a bear's! And he's enormous, too. Some say he's eight feet tall."

"Whoa!"

"You can hear his footsteps from a mile away," Monica said.

Her own feet weaved between a garden of rocks on the creek bed below. For a panicked second, her boot wedged between two and wouldn't budge. She squeezed the handle of her pole, leaning on it, and worked the shoe loose.

"Sometimes campers find a creature has visited their campsite and taken all their food," Monica went on. "They think it's a bear, but they find their pack sitting on the ground, zipper open, and just the food missing. Would a bear be so polite?"

"No," Xavier cried. "It was Bigfoot!"

Suddenly the bedlam of the rushing stream was ripped open with an ear-shattering *crack!* Monica immediately froze and turned her head toward the source, somewhere in the invisible darkness upstream.

"What was that?" Ericka cried.

For a few seconds nothing more could be heard over the constant babble of hurrying water. But a deep, vibrating groan rose out of the earth under them. Then the air exploded again in a series of sudden bursts like gunshots.

Monica's eyes went wide.

A tree is coming down.

"Go," she said. "Fast, but careful!"

Lift, steady, probe. Ground, lean, shift.

The earth shook as if it was breaking open to welcome the apocalypse. Thunder cascaded down the river valley, hammering eardrums and shaking ribs. Monica caught herself as she swayed in the rippling current, shifted Xavier to her other arm, and took another precarious step forward. As she leaned into this new position, the waves rose, swelling above her navel.

"You okay, Ericka?" she called.

She heard the girl spitting and coughing.

"It went over my head!" she said.

"Keep your balance, no matter what—"

Another swell struck her, carrying new force with it.

Monica angled her headlamp upstream. The light fizzled as it hit the impenetrable obsidian of night. She waited as her eyes adjusted to the shimmering surface of the river to see what devilry was being prepared for them.

"Why are you stopping?" Ericka complained, spewing out water again.

"Just wait," Monica said.

Nothing seemed amiss other than the heightened crests of the rushing rapids. Monica squinted.

How far away had that tree been?

Monica craned her neck to get a better look at their complete surroundings, as it was always possible that there was something she hadn't noticed—

It was right above them.

The first tree had slammed into another, knocking it into the river. The impact had slowed its fall, but it was picking up speed again and careening toward them.

"Get beside me!" Monica screamed. "On my left!"

She turned to grab Ericka.

"What's happening?" the girl cried.

"Mommy!" Xavier howled.

"Come here!" Monica yelled, still watching as the tree slowly toppled toward them, ripping its last roots free from the dirt. "When I say, take a deep breath!"

"What?" Ericka shouted.

"Trust me!"

Ericka sobbed, wrapping her arm around Monica's waist. Monica steadied herself, twisting her boots into the clay bottom. The towering battering ram was plummeting in slow motion. The earth moaned as a hundred roots ripped free from bedrock, and the tree slammed down with a deafening *boom!* that sent up another volley of waves slapping cold water into their faces.

"Get ready!" Monica ordered.

The trunk gave way to the pull of the river. It loomed over them like a gray scythe, long and soulless, ready to cut them down. It tumbled in the waves until it picked up speed, matching the pace of the current.

Monica dug her fingers into Xavier's side. "Ready?" she shouted.

"I'm scared!" Ericka screamed.

The tree charged right toward them.

They had three seconds.

Monica spied the white flecks of lichen shining bright as water splashed the ashen bark.

Two. It was about to cut them in half—

"Now!"

Monica grabbed Ericka's collar and yanked her down with all the strength her arms could muster. Her head ducked under just as the tree rolled into them. Monica felt both children struggling but she held as tight as possible.

Then her entire world became unspeakable pain, like a red hot sword had been driven into her hip. She was wrenched off her feet and hurled down, her face slamming into the rocky bottom. In that instant she released both kids as the tree rolled over her. The colossal weight lifted and she found herself spinning in the current. She snatched about for the rope to possibly steady herself, and her fingers found it and closed. She jerked hard to twist her body upright, tightened her fingers on her trekking pole, thrust it down, and fumbled to a standing position again.

"Ericka!" she yelled through a mouthful of water.

A wave of nausea struck and she doubled over, vomiting. Her vision fogged, pulses of blinding heavenly light pushing the backs of her eyeballs.

Xavier's body seesawed to the surface and he coughed, weeping between convulsions. Monica pawed at him with her free hand until she had a strong hold on him.

"I— I got you— Lil Cookie," she mumbled.

She staggered forward, her boot slipping off a stone. Monica gasped, wavered drunkenly, and blinked. Her side was on fire, like a stick of dynamite had exploded in her flesh.

Ericka's voice burst from the racket, shouting, "Monica!"

Monica turned, almost flopping backward into the water.

"Are you okay?"

"What happened!?" Ericka said.

"A tree—fell...," Monica said, dreamlike. "You, Ericka— you lead now...."

"What?" The girl stumbled up beside her, staring at her face in shock. "I can't lead!"

Monica licked her lips. Everything was tilted, sliding and spinning. If only she could just lie down and sleep....

"I don't feel good," she managed to say.

I'm going to drop Xavier.

"Take your brother...."

Her hand fumbled blindly at the harness. In her mind it was a million miles away. It wasn't even her hand working with the clip anymore. It belonged to someone else, someone who wasn't about to bleed to death in the middle of this godforsaken river.

"I can't!" Erica cried.

"Yes, you can," Monica said. "You have to."

She gazed into the young girl's eyes, trying to convey strength. But she had none left. As they stood side-by-side, contemplating the next move, she vaguely saw Ericka glance at her abdomen. Her face fell like it had seen a corpse.

"You're bleeding," she gasped.

"Please," Monica said. "Take him."

Her arms trembled. She couldn't hold him any longer, and she'd be damned if she dropped him in the river.

"I'll go with you, Sissie!" Xavier said.

Then Monica felt a tremendous lightness. Xavier was in his sister's hands, and Monica knew that the budding heroine would have the grit to convey him safely to shore. She had to, because the ranger no longer could.

Her work was over.

"Here," Monica said.

She slipped the helmet off and pressed it onto Ericka's head. "Clip the chinstrap," she said.

"But you need it," Ericka said.

"No. You do," Monica said, her voice faint. Her hands found the carabiner securing her to the shore. Her thumb fumbled with the catch until it broke loose.

"Take this," she said, holding it out.

With a slow, wordless extension of her arm, Ericka took the device and hooked onto her own harness.

"Good," Monica mumbled, smiling weakly. "Now go."

Ericka stared back. Her eyes glimmered with brewing tears. Xavier looked back and forth between his sister and the ranger.

"Thank you," Ericka whispered.

Then she turned to resume the long, trudging sojourn to the shore, leaving Monica alone in the raging Little River.

Monica remained upright, watching in silence. It was done. She had given everything. A family had been saved just in time.

She breathed heavily, wincing at the hot irritation. *What of your father?* she thought.

"I'm sorry... Papa Bear," she said. "I didn't mean for this to happen."

She reached down and placed a hand on her side, flinching at the touch. Her entire palm returned scarlet, illuminated by the pale, vanishing light of her lamp as it crept toward the shore on Ericka's head.

The darkness grew around her. This wasn't how she thought things would end. Then again, how *did* she think they'd come to a close? Would she die in old age, lying beside some lifelong lover she hadn't yet met? Perhaps she'd succumb to a uniquely feminine disease, like her grandmother who passed away of cervical cancer. She'd never really thought about it. Regardless, the answer had been revealed, and there was nothing to do now but accept it.

Monica swayed as the physical world slid farther and farther away from her. On the distant shore, she could barely make out the silhouette of the twelve-year-old girl carrying her younger brother in her arms, stumbling toward land after a death-defying journey through the sea.

"Okay, God," she sighed as the pain forked through her like lightning. "I guess I'm done."

She no longer felt the need to remain balanced. Her body was seeming to slide away from her. Her essence, her soul, whatever ethereal being had resided in the mortal shell of Monica Greene, was receding from the waters, looking down at the woman standing cold and alone and in pain.

You'll be okay, she whispered to herself. *You did your best.*

Monica exhaled again, and closed her eyes.

Then she let herself slip under the surface.

49

AFTERMATH

WHEN SHE OPENED HER EYES AND IMMEDIATELY SAW THE face of her father, she knew she was dead.

Orange light was streaming through window blinds, casting vertical shadows on the wall. The air was warm and the smell of roses and phlox filled her nose. Every sense told her this was heaven. For how else could she and her father be in the same place at the same time, beholding one another? She had died and now they were both in Paradise, free from their burdens and suffering.

"Oh, Little Bear," he said, his voice gruff but his eyes sparkling.

"Hey, Dad," she groaned.

Monica raised an arm to rub her face, but as she did she felt a tight pinch against her skin. She looked and saw a web of I.V. tubes tangled around her skin. Only then did she notice the beeping sounds of innumerable machines.

She wasn't in heaven. She was in a hospital bed covered with a thin checkered gown and stark white sheets. A markerboard hung directly across from the bed, her name written on it. Her physician, whose name was clearly scrawled with fresh black ink, was Dr. Watt.

"I'm alive?" she murmured.

At this, her father covered his mouth and trembled, tears of joy dripping over his cheeks. He took her hand and clasped it tight in his.

"Yes, you are, thank the Lord!" he said.

Monica laid her head back on the thin pillow. "How did I—?"

Joshua Greene shook his head. "I don't know all the details," he said. "But that gal you were out there with went out after you and pulled you in."

"Blaze," Monica said, stunned.

"She had to resuscitate you," he said. "And you nearly bled to death!" This broke him up again and he dropped his head and pressed her hand to his face.

"So I *was* dead," Monica said.

Her father nodded and sniffled in response. Perhaps the knowledge was too terrible for him to utter aloud. She watched him with pity, but also gratitude that he did indeed love her so much.

"What about you?" she said.

Only now did she notice that he was in a wheelchair, a network of tubes and wires surrounding him. Two thin oxygen pipes coiled about his nostrils.

"I'm okay," he said softly.

"What about your kidneys?" she asked.

"I've done everything you asked," he said, nodding. "Absolutely everything."

Despite the groggy emergence from near-death, her brain had snapped to attention the moment her father began speaking about his obedience to her wishes.

"Really?" she said. "Even dialysis?"

"Oh, yes," he said, scowling and shaking his head. "It's a hellish experience, let me tell you. But I'm doing it, and they tell me it's the only thing keeping me alive at the moment."

Monica narrowed her eyes. "Meds?"

He nodded. "Yes."

"Everything?"

"Of course."

"Without complaining?"

He opened his mouth to speak again, but stopped himself. He smiled, a Cheshire Cat's grin. "No," he said. "But I'm working on that."

Monica continued to scrutinize him with her gaze, looking for any crack in the presentation. "How about therapy?"

"I do a little physical therapy each day," he said. "Dr. Watt wants me to up it a bit, and I'm—"

"No," Monica interrupted. "I mean counseling."

"Counseling," he echoed.

"Yes," she said. "For your mental health."

Suddenly she was no longer the broken patient recovering from a brush with the afterlife. She was the doubting daughter, the traumatized caregiver diligently sniffing for any sign of a lie. And it seemed she still had good reason to be skeptical. Her father was obviously wrestling with his answer. Several times he started a sentence but aborted after just a word or two. He scratched the back of his neck and looked away, toward the window.

"Dad," she said. "Look at me."

"I am, Little Bear," he complained.

"No," she said, staring directly into his pupils. "Look at me."

Perhaps remembering that his daughter had nearly been taken from him, the man did as told. His eyes found hers and pulsated, nervous for so many reasons. She knew how hard this must be for him. To have almost lost her, and then to have her back in a heartbeat. She wasn't the only victim here, even if she was the most wounded.

Monica took his hand. "I know you love me," she said.

"Oh," he quickly replied. "I do, Little Bear, I do!"

"Wait," she said. "Just listen."

Monica paused and swallowed, preparing herself to form several difficult sentences.

"All my life, I've felt responsible for Mom," she said, continuing to bore her gaze into his. "And you haven't helped."

A shockwave seemed to ripple through him, but she continued speaking before he could interrupt and defend whatever he felt needed defending.

"It's not my fault that she's an alcoholic," Monica declared. "And it wasn't my fault that she nearly drowned in the Obed River during our canoe trip. She'd been drinking all morning and afternoon. It was her fault that we tipped. It was her fault that we nearly drowned."

"Monica," her father began to say, "what does this have to do with—"

"You took her side."

His eyes went wide.

"I— no, I would *never*—"

"Dad," she said, cutting through his objections, "you took her side because you were afraid of her. Throughout your entire marriage you let her run over you, yet you knew she was an addict the whole time."

"Monica—"

"Then she abandoned us," Monica continued, her voice rising. "She abandoned us because she loved her bottles more than you or me. And my entire life, I believed it was my fault because of that day on the river."

Her father's mouth parted, but he didn't speak.

Monica let the words marinate, breathing through her nostrils as the machines sang their mechanical songs.

"All I've ever tried to do was save people," Monica said. "But in reality, I was trying to save Mom. I believed I almost killed her, and that she drank to numb the trauma. But it was a lie. And you went along with that lie, Dad."

"Little Bear," he whimpered, his spirit clearly beaten down. "I didn't mean to hurt you—"

"But you did, Dad," she said. "And now we need to deal with it. Do you understand?"

"Sure, sure, yes," he said, answering perhaps too quickly.

"I'm not sure you do," Monica said. "Do you understand that everything in our lives is the way it is because we haven't dealt with this? Can you even begin to comprehend how messed up our relationship is—how messed up *I* am—because of all this?"

His eyes fell and he didn't answer.

"Listen to me," she repeated. "I love you. You are my father. But I can't save you. I can't save you and I can't save Mom either. And I shouldn't have to."

Once again, Monica left the words out in the open. They needed to breathe, like a fragrance sprayed into a musty room. She watched her father take it all in. Accepting responsibility can be hard enough. Taking ownership of enabling the addictions and abuse of a loved one is nearly impossible. She was asking quite a lot of her father.

But it had to be asked. For too long had these things been unspoken and unresolved. The conversation could no longer be about microwave meals, pills, and whether her kidney should become his kidney. Perhaps a time would emerge for these conversations. For now, however, they needed to talk about Mama Bear, and how Joshua Greene had chosen to enable his wife's addiction and not to stand up for his daughter.

The man's head fell, bent almost ninety degrees at the neck. If her words were heavy, their effect had formed a chain pulling him toward the floor. But as close to death as he was, he fought to lift his head again. He took Monica's hand, gave it a squeeze, and kissed it. He held it there for a long time. She didn't know how long, and didn't want to count.

But their embrace had a pleasant aura, like incense. His tears baptized her knuckles, the salty drops running down her arm into her I.V. sites with a slight sting.

Finally, he lifted his head, wiping his eyes.

"You're right," he said, perforating the long silence. "You can't save me."

At first she just wanted to nod, appreciating that he was on the same wavelength as her. But something about his tone struck her as ironic, and she raised an eyebrow. "What do you mean?"

Her father exhaled, then laid a finger gently on her side.

"You can't save me," he said. "That tree nearly ripped your kidney out right there in the river. It was horribly damaged and Dr. Watt had to remove it."

"What?" she said.

Her hand flew to her hip. A rampart of bandages was there to shield it. Monica gasped.

"So," her father continued, "when you say you can't save me, you're absolutely right. You only have one kidney now, and you need it a heck of a lot more than I do."

Monica stared at him, her mouth open.

"Oh, Dad!" she finally said. "I'm so sorry!"

"Stop," he said, rubbing her arm. "If you'd given it to me, you'd have saved one selfish life. But you gave it to four people, including those kids, and saved their lives instead." He settled back in his wheelchair with a satisfied smile. "I'd say," he went on, "you did exactly what God would want you to."

With a knock at the door, the nurse appeared.

"Mr. Greene?" he said. "Your next treatment is in fifteen minutes. Would you like me to take you?"

Her father sighed, then smiled wryly at his daughter. "Duty calls."

"Thank you," Monica said, a tear slipping down her cheek.

"No," Joshua said. "Thank *you.*" He kissed her hand again. As the nurse wheeled him to the door, her father never took his eyes away from Monica.

"I'll be fine, Little Bear," he said, winking. "There's still a chance they'll find a donor. But even if they don't, I'm okay. As long as God wants me here, I'll be okay."

Monica smiled, and blew him a kiss from the confines of her hospital bed. "I love you, Papa Bear," she said.

He caught the kiss and blew one back. "I love you, too, Little Bear."

He rolled out the door, and was gone.

50

— • —

EMERGENCY MANAGER

TWO WEEKS CAME AND WENT BEFORE MONICA STEPPED FOOT in Great Smoky Mountains National Park. Finally clear to return to work, Monica drove to Headquarters, slid into the handicap space, and hooked her temporary disabled tag on her rearview mirror. She climbed out, wincing in constant discomfort at the never-ending ache in her side.

The parking lot was packed and the lawn empty, all the equipment long since returned to its rightful place inside the building. The storm was becoming a distant memory. The park had reopened and the roads were cleared, their lanes swept of any and all obstructions.

But artifacts of the damage were everywhere, and one couldn't travel more than a hundred feet on the roads without seeing a downed tree that had been sawed into enormous logs and dragged into the ditches. Monica limped along the sidewalk, leaning on a cane, and pulled open the front door.

A chorus came from all directions: "Surprise!"

Monica startled at the sudden explosion of noise. The halls and offices were stuffed with park staff. A banner hung from the ceiling bearing the words, "Welcome Back!" Helium-filled balloons polka-dotted the walls. At the front of the group were two familiar faces, one tall and bearded, the other short and fierce.

"Hey, you two," Monica said, smiling at them.

Blaze rushed forward and wrapped her arms around her. "I'm so glad to see you," she said.

They parted and Monica said, "I guess we're even on saving one another's lives."

"Oh, no," Blaze said. "Saving yours was a *lot* harder!"

Monica laughed, her face souring at the jolts of pain it caused. "Thank you, Allison," she said.

"Don't count on it again," Blaze said. "If your body hadn't have gotten caught on a big tree branch, I'd never have reached you in time."

"I'll definitely be more careful from now on," Monica said, gesturing to her side.

She turned and saw Wilde's thick hand before her. She took it for a powerful shake and looked in his eyes, finding warmth and respect residing there.

"Remarkable work," he said. "Truly inspirational."

"Thank you," Monica said.

"Inspirational?" Blaze said, scoffing. "Hell, call it like it is, Chris. She's a badass lady boss."

"I'm just glad I'm still around," Monica said.

"So are we," Blaze said. "Now—since we're celebrating, can we drink on the job now?" She leaned over and opened the lid of a large cooler that was sitting in the hallway. "Who wants a beer!?"

"Just one each," Wilde yelled. "We still have a job to do, and for some of you that involves driving."

Monica smiled as her colleagues filed by and helped themselves to a beverage. Each patted her on the shoulder or shook her hand, sharing an affirming remark. It was refreshing, and she chose to accept the show of appreciation, even if she had plenty of questions about her own choices along the way. More than anything, she wanted to ask about how they were going to memorialize Mike Ownby.

"Can I sit down and talk about something with you?" she said, turning to Wilde who was supervising the cooler. "I need a break."

"Oh, sure," he said. "Come this way."

Wilde stepped around her, trusting the contents of the cooler to the general wisdom of the National Park Service, and led her down the hall, limping to favor his recovering ankle. Monica hobbled after, leaning into the cane to accommodate the constant throbbing in her hip.

She arrived at a doorway to an office with an empty desk. Wilde walked in and swept a stack of files and a laptop off the surface.

"You can sit here," he said. "I've been using this office, but only temporarily."

Monica scanned the room with her eyes, and a pit of sorrow filled her stomach.

It was Ownby's office.

She shook her head and whispered, "I can't."

Wilde stared back at her. "Please," he said. "Take a seat."

"No. Not after what happened."

Wilde stepped to the high back armchair and spun it so it was ready to accept its next occupant. "You know," he said, "back when you first told him about your Preventive Search and Rescue ideas, Ownby told me: She's the one for this job when I retire."

Monica felt her eyes growing hotter by the second, and knew what was coming. "He didn't retire," she said softly. "He died."

"I know you think it's your fault, Monica," he said, nodding toward the chair. "But you need to let that go. Mike wanted this to be yours."

"No," she said again. Then the tears began to flow like water down a wall of rock.

"It's your decision," Wilde said, stepping away from the chair. "But let me tell you: I don't belong here. I like it out there."

At this, he jerked his head toward the window. While the immediate exterior of the office was a well-manicured lawn, not far off were the thick forests in which a million mysteries awaited, mysteries that Wilde no doubt longed to uncover.

Monica bowed a moment, smiled, then lifted her head again to look him full in the face. "I'll give it a try," she said. "Just for a minute."

Leaning on the cane, Monica worked her way around the desk and lowered herself into the chair. The leather grunted and crackled at her presence.

"How does it feel?" a new voice said.

Monica turned to the door and saw Blaze leaning against the frame.

"Awkward," Monica said.

"It looks good on you," Blaze said.

Wilde nodded. "Not bad."

Monica sighed and leaned back, letting the chair absorb her. It groaned quietly, then was silent.

"I don't know, guys," she said. "It feels too soon. I miss him."

Wilde sat opposite her. "I know," he said. "We've already held a service, and I know you'll want to do more to honor him now that you're back. But Monica," he said, leaning forward, "the job needs to be done, and I can't think of anyone more qualified—and passionate—than you."

Monica exhaled and let the words permeate her spirit. She had been an Emergency Manager before, and she would be lying to herself if she said she hadn't wanted the Smokies role all along. But not in this way. Not at the cost of a man's life.

Monica bit her lip. Wilde was right that the job needed to be done. But was she truly the person for it?

"Look," she said, forming her thoughts carefully, "I know I can do it. But I don't know if I should."

Blaze scowled. "Oh, hell. Of course you should."

"But Ownby—" Monica began.

Wilde raised a hand to silence her. "You need to let that go."

"How can I?" she said. "I just don't know—"

"Let it go," Wilde insisted, leaning over the desk. "It wasn't your fault."

Monica stared at him. She blinked and felt a cold tear dribble down her cheek. "Do you really believe that?"

Wilde crossed his arms and nodded. "Yes."

"Everyone does," Blaze said. "You didn't pull Ownby into the river. You didn't push the tree over. You did none of those things. Stop killing yourself over bad luck and other people's choices, Monica."

As she drew another breath, her lungs felt like they might collapse and never hold air again. But with a trembling chest, she exhaled slowly, bowed her head, and nodded.

"Okay," Monica whispered.

"Good," Wilde said, standing from his seat. "We need a leader with experience and willpower. Is that you, Monica Greene?"

Monica swallowed. She was a leader. She had the experience and the will. And more than that, she had learned important lessons at a terrible cost. More than anything, the wisdom born of pain placed a mandate on her to use them well, and for the good of others.

Monica sat up and the leather chair huffed as the air shifted. "If you want me to lead you," she said, "I will."

Wilde simply smiled but Blaze burst out cheering and clapping.

"Okay!" Blaze said. "Then tell us: What's next, Madam Emergency Manager?"

Monica laughed at her friend's celebration and the absurdity of it all, and then straightened her face.

"Well, during my time in the hospital I've been thinking about Stranded Steve," she said. "I think we need to retire him."

"What?" Blaze said.

Monica nodded and rubbed her chin. "It didn't work, did it? Why were so many people still on Little River, Chimney Tops, and Alum Cave during the storm? We posted signs there, but people still went out on the trails."

"That's true," Blaze said.

"Let's leave the signs in place for now," she said. "But I'd like to try a different approach."

"Like what?" Wilde said.

Monica shrugged. "Where does everyone get their information these days?"

Wilde sighed, shaking his head. "The damned internet."

Monica grinned. "Exactly. The damned internet. Let's tap some younger resources. Interns. Local college students. Let's see if we can't get a presence going on social media."

"Social media?" Wilde replied, his voice laden with dread.

"Oh, relax, old man," Blaze teased, slapping his arm. "The woman wants nerds, let's get her nerds."

Then Blaze threw her a faux salute.

"And Allison," Monica continued, dropping her eyebrows at her friend, "go easy on the drinks."

"What?" Blaze said, feigning innocence. "I'm responsible!"

"You better be."

Wilde put a hand on Blaze's arm. "I'll keep an eye on her."

Then, as the two turned to withdraw down the hallway, Blaze snarled, "The *hell* you will, Christian Wilder Webber. I'm a grown woman and I can take care of myself...."

Monica chuckled as the banter of her friends drifted down the hall, and she leaned back in the chair.

The numb shock of what had just transpired continued to flood her body. This wasn't her chair. Heck, given the events of her past, it felt like she didn't have a right to even be in the same room as this chair.

Yet here she was, the newly appointed Emergency Manager of Great Smoky Mountains National Park. Her friends trusted her. Her colleagues respected her. And despite the things that had gone wrong, dozens of lives had been saved.

She exhaled, inspecting the broad oak desk before her. While Wilde had cleared his materials from it, a folded piece of paper was still sitting in the middle. It was labeled, "To Ranger Monica Greene." She took it and opened it.

Dear Ranger Greene, it read.

Thank you for saving my father's life. He has been dealing with severe depression ever since the death of his wife. I had no idea he would attempt to take his life at Laurel Falls, but that's exactly what he tried to do the day the storm hit. My father has been in a losing fight with painkillers for years. We've stood by his side but it hasn't been easy. Your hard work and sacrifice seem to have made a massive difference in his attitude. He wanted to thank you himself, but is afraid to speak to you face to face. I hope this note will suffice. Thank you for saving his life.

Sincerely,

Angela Blackstone (Daughter of Jack Cooper)

Monica folded the note and leaned back, the leather cracking beneath her.

"Good for you, Jack," she murmured to herself, and let her gaze drift to the window.

The lawn surrounding Headquarters lay verdant and green, no longer marred by the damage of the storm. Its lush grasses were properly cut, forming a picturesque scene for all passersby, and there were plenty of passersby to speak of. Now that sufficient time had passed since the tempest and the cleanup, tourists had returned to the Smokies, flooding it with their eager eyes and ubiquitous cameras. Trucks, SUVS, and motorcycles paraded past, hurrying on to Cades Cove, Newfound Gap, or whatever exotic destination awaited them in the wild.

Yet danger was everywhere. It always would be, even if there wasn't a hurricane waiting to inundate the mountains. Even as Monica was safe in her office enjoying the view, someone could be setting out on a trail without proper gear, appropriate training, and ample common sense. Much work was to be done if she was going to be a success as the new Emergency Manager. How could she possibly live up to the example of her predecessor, who put his trust in her before giving his life in the name of saving others? How could she make Preventive Search and Rescue a regular protocol in the park? And how could she bolster the resources of the ranger team and properly train and equip them to do their work safely?

There was much to be done. Too much, in fact, for one afternoon's contemplation. Already her head was beating with pain from the effort, and Monica began to massage her temples.

Am I really the right person for this? she wondered. *Or am I just destined to fail?*

Monica turned her gaze back to the lawn. Perhaps her worst fears were right. Maybe this was too much for her and she had no chance at success.

A flash of motion caught her eye. Monica leaned forward and gawked out the window. A mother bear, thick with a heavy diet of acorns and berries, was dashing across the road. A trio of cubs followed, lolloping with an adorable gait across the pavement.

Dozens of vehicles slid to a halt and several tourists even threw open their doors to step out and catch the spectacle on camera. But as soon as they had appeared, the family of bears was gone, led by its mother into the wilderness.

"Good luck, Mama," Monica said with a smile.

Monica stared at the patch of emerald forest where the bears had vanished moments before. While a few of the tourists were stubbornly intent on getting another photo opportunity, traffic had resumed its hurried train, zipping by much too quickly.

Monica settled back in the chair, breathing rapidly.

Mama.

She stood and bent into the handle of her cane. Trying to hide the hitch in her step, she walked down the hall toward the doors. Blaze was sitting on the cooler, a can of beer in her hand. She glanced up and took a long swig, grinning.

"Ready for a drink?"

Monica flashed her a smile. "No, thanks. I'll be back in a bit."

"Where are you going, boss?"

"I've got something I have to do," she said.

"Okay," Blaze said. "Should I have maintenance start removing those Stranded Steve signs this week?"

Monica paused as her hand touched the door to the Park Headquarters building. She shrugged. "No rush."

Blaze cocked her head, dragged on her beer again, and said, "Sounds good to me."

Then Monica stepped outside.

51

— • —

THE BEGINNING

THE LEAVES HAD FADED TO BROWN AND WERE FLUTTERING to the ground like wax paper. All was peaceful as they often are in autumn, a way that makes death somewhat beautiful, celebrating the cycle of the seasons.

Monica sat outside a cafe and watched a nearby tree shed its leaves one at a time, tricking through the air onto the sidewalk, waiting for a passerby's foot to provide a delightful crunch. She exhaled, doing everything in her power to regulate her breathing, and sipped a mug of hot tea. For Monica, coffee was normally the rule, but today she needed a beverage that wouldn't get her too jittery. That meant tea, which packed a slightly less caffeinated punch.

Monica leaned over the table and shivered as a gust of wind rushed up the street. It was midday, but the first chills of October were making their presence known. She glanced at the time.

12:08.

Monica bit her lip.

She peered up and down the sidewalk for any sign of the coming guest. She'd gone to great lengths to arrange this meetup. It hadn't been easy. Her father, for one, had been of little help. He didn't know the first place to look or the right number to call. Besides, Monica had thought, she wanted him to devote his energy to his treatment, and to building a legitimate case for rising to the top of the kidney donor list.

After a barrage of calls to shelters in nearby cities, she tracked her target to Asheville. A bustling, eclectic city, Asheville was like many other upper-middle class urban regions with a subterfuge of high art and ritz that hid the rampant poverty no one wanted to talk about. Its homeless population could be found along its main streets, lurking near dumpsters or in alleys throughout the downtown stretch.

It was here that she found who she was looking for.

Monica sipped her tea and swallowed. She checked her phone for the time again.

12:14.

Would the woman even show up? Surely she had thought things through, too. Even addicts had moments of clarity, epochs of sobriety. Certainly in a deep place in her heart, buried under the rubble of ruined pride and broken dreams, a pocket of truth had remained. Would the woman be willing to take that truth in her hands and speak openly of it? Would she be able to ask forgiveness, to own her actions and entrust her hope to the Savior she once taught her young daughter about?

Monica couldn't tell, and so she gnawed incessantly at her lip.

12:22.

Monica bowed and remembered her mentor's haunting words.

Pray.

She began to mumble at a low volume so as to not scare her fellow coffee shop patrons.

"God, I love my mother. I want to forgive her. Please heal our relationship...."

Another bundle of brown leaves fell to the ground, popping underfoot like bubble wrap as couples strolled down the sidewalk. Monica glanced up and soaked in the amber glow of the day. Lovers laughed together, nuzzling and cuddling against the inaugural cold. Lone men and women, accompanied only by their laptops or books, enjoyed the quiet solitude.

Monica sighed.

Maybe she wasn't coming. Could that be okay? Would it be too hard to live with yet another disappointment?

12:28.

What was she supposed to expect? The woman had used her like a marionette, pulling every string to make her addiction look like someone else's fault. She had hooked Monica's father, baiting him and manipulating him to evade any accountability for decades. Why would today be any different?

"God," she said, ducking once again, "I know I expect too much. I want you to work like a magician. But I know you're powerful. I know you're good. Please—just give me peace."

Monica opened her eyes and lifted her head. That was all she truly wanted. Peace. To exist among the brokenness of her life without being poisoned by it. To acknowledge her wounds without hating them.

Peace.

She took a long breath, let it out, and sipped her tea once more. She replaced the cup, and as it hit the saucer with a clink, Monica looked down the sidewalk again.

She saw her.

A woman was walking in her direction. She was much shorter than Monica, but her face was similarly shaped. Her hair was cropped close to the head, much like Monica's own cut.

Her mouth fell.

The woman shuffled up to the table, staring back. Her eyes seemed weighted with the heaviness of life and its terrible turns, and she sniffed.

"You're—" she said, her words slightly hampered by an aberration of speech, "you're—a grown woman!"

Then she smiled, a subdued kind of grin. It was as if she wanted to fully enjoy all that life had to offer, all that motherhood had to provide, but couldn't surrender herself to it without giving something precious away. It compressed her cheeks into little cherries, red with the cold.

Monica stood, towering over her. "Are you—sober?" she asked weakly.

The woman nodded, her head moving slowly. "Two days," she whispered in reply. Then she shrugged a little, as if she knew that it wasn't good enough.

Monica shuddered. "Two days?"

The woman nodded, her head shaking.

Only two days?

Should she go through with this? Was there any sign of real commitment here? Or was it all another setup, another trap that Monica would never truly escape?

Two days, she thought.

It was a start.

Monica stepped forward and wrapped the woman in her arms. Their bodies shared a world of warmth, and the connection immediately began to soothe a deep, deep wound in Monica's heart.

She exhaled. Then, her voice quivering, she said, "I've missed you, Mama Bear."

An unspeakable peace began to flow through her. It was outside her realm of understanding, but she was grateful for it. They parted, and she saw the woman's lips spread into a smile of relief.

"I've missed you, too," the woman said.

Monica gestured to the table and chairs. "Would you like to sit down?"

The woman nodded, and they took their places around the tea kettle. With her mother listening, Monica began to speak, sharing her story and her heart.

She didn't stop for a long, long time.

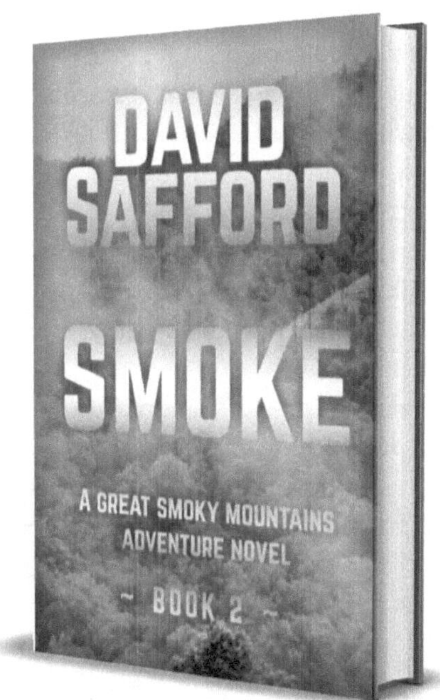

AS WILDE LOWERED HIMSELF INTO THE CAVE, a blast of subterranean wind blew into his face and he shivered on instinct. With a quick shake of his arms, he ducked and aimed the headlamp into the dark recesses of the cave below him.

Long, gray rocks rose from the shadows like dragon teeth, their edges smoothed by millennia of erosion. Grasping at little ledges, Wilde placed his feet one at a time, slowly resting his weight on them to see if they would hold. He ducked his head with another step, grabbed a hold of another jutting boulder and squatted. A spray of water, falling from the cliffs above, spattered the top of his head and trickled down the rocks below.

"Hello?" he called into the darkness.

There was a muffled shuffle. "Is someone there?"

"My name is Christian Webber! I'm a ranger!" Wilde beckoned. "I'm coming down, but I need you to stay where you are!"

"Hurry!" cried the voice. "I... I don't know if I can hold on!"

Wilde gave the rope a little tug. He looked up at the entrance to the cave, the surface light already a distant shimmer. "Pay out the line," he said.

Blaze's head appeared, blotting out the light behind. "You're already at twenty feet."

"Gonna need a lot more," he said.

He turned back and resumed motion, stepping slowly to maintain his balance. Water rushed in thin tendrils along the path, gurgling mindlessly.

"This is ugly," Wilde whispered to himself, struggling to find the next safe place to plant his foot. He flashed the headlamp in every direction to get a sense of the shape of this place. There were, of course, no flat surfaces upon which to walk, for caves don't erode and evolve in ways habitable to humans. Instead, explorers must become like ancient amphibians, sliding over the massive slates, carefully feeling their way along and moving only when the earth would let them.

With this cave, it was no different. It was a narrow labyrinth of jagged teeth and razor blades, all dripping and slippery and cold in the suffocating dark. The only way forward was a thin chute perforated by countless blades jutting toward the faint glow of the sun. In spite of the jagged pockets of stone, many stretches of the cave wall were smooth and featureless, black membranes slick as ice.

One of those smooth stretches was right below him.

"Give me a little resistance!" he called.

"Why?" Blaze answered.

"I'm gonna slide!"

"You've got to be kidding me."

Looping the rope around his leg and arm, Wilde stepped off the rocks and placed his backside on the steeply slanted surface. Immediately he began to slip over the undulating stone at tremendous speed. Wilde shoved his boots down as the bumps punched at his buttocks.

"Blaze!" he called.

Then his hands snapped as the rope caught on his wrist with a sudden jerk, and he came to a stop. His body swung to the side, pivoting around the clip and the harness. He clawed at the cave wall to bring himself back upright, his breath quick and heavy.

"Good catch," he called.

"Are you crazy!?" she replied, her voice thin and echoing through the hall of stone.

"Yeah," he said, "a little."

Wilde wiped a film of sweat from his forehead and took three long, slow breaths.

You got this.

After another inspection, he found that the underground space was broader here, though the grade of his descent wasn't leveling out at all. If anything, it seemed to bend itself into a wall.

"You okay down there?" he yelled into the depths.

"Yes, yes!" a shrill voice came in reply. "Please hurry!"

Wilde grit his teeth. He needed to keep moving, and the voice wasn't far. He pressed his fingers into the rock and lowered himself, his arm wiggling. Even if each finger only gave him a millimeter of support, it would do.

"Keep talking to me," Wilde said. "I'm moving toward you."

"I'm going to fall!" cried the invisible victim. "Oh, God!"

Wilde moved slowly, traversing the wall, and suddenly his boots landed on solid ground. He bowed his head and the lamp illuminated a small plateau jutting out from the wall, about the size of a small car. In the middle of it, leaning against the jagged prow of rock, was a bright green day pack.

No one was there.

"I found your pack!" he called, placing both feet on the cave floor. "Where are you?"

"Here, here!" the voice cried.

Wilde strode over the stone tabletop and crouched over the far edge, squinting down.

The cave fell away before him like a cliff to Hell. It was a sheer drop, with only a few precious knobs of stone to grasp onto before sliding to one's certain death. The trickling stream sprayed into the abyss where it splattered the ground far below, someone in the invisible depths.

Wilde squinted into the weak pool of light. Someone was clinging to the wall about fifty feet down, dangling helplessly and gazing up at him with large, terrified eyes.

It was a fully grown man.

"I'm coming to get you!" Wilde yelled.

"Hurry!" the man said. "I can't hold on much longer!"

Wilde leaned over the edge and stared at the surface he would have to hold onto. It was flat, slick, offering only the faintest toe and finger holds. He would have to rely on the rope.

He gave it a tug and shouted, "Pay it out, Blaze!"

The rope slackened for a moment and he reeled it in.

Then it went completely taut.

"I need more!" he called.

"That's it!" he heard her cry from far above. "We can have more to you in... three minutes!"

He craned his neck, glancing down at his quarry.

"Can you hold on for three more minutes?"

"No!" the man wailed, panting like a winded dog. "I don't want to die!"

Wilde yanked on the cord. Something didn't feel right. It was as if he was being held by a machine, not by a sensitive, reactionary human.

It's caught on a stone.

It had probably happened when he'd slid down, or when he traversed the wall toward the stone tabletop. But it didn't matter. His target was still fifty feet below him, likely to lose his grip in minutes.

Or seconds.

Wilde peered down again.

"You okay?"

"No!" the man cried, panting in desperation. "I'm slipping!"

"I'll be right there," Wilde said, his voice cracking.

His own words had betrayed him. Was there a fate worse than falling to one's death in a cave, all alone in total, impenetrable darkness? What if he survived the fall, living for days or even weeks on a starving belly that taught him the deepest meaning of suffering and slow, inexorable death?

Focus.

The ranger twisted back, reaching up toward the cave entrance far above, and whipped the thin cord of rope in the air. Maybe he could free it from whatever obstruction it had found....

The rope flew down to him in a loose pile.

Yes!

Wilde scooped it up and looped it around his hand so he could pay it out as he descended.

"You got me, Blaze?" he hollered.

Her reply bounced off the cavern walls, echoing as if in a tin can. "Yeah!"

Wilde crawled over the lip of the plateau and let his body slide down the starkly vertical cliff. Glancing down, he searched for his first toehold. He lowered himself a little more, putting all his weight on it.

Good.

"Oh please," the man below him wailed. "I don't wanna die!"

"Neither do I," Wilde said. "Hang in there."

He lowered the next foot, pushing with his toe. His foot slid and kicked into empty space and he nearly lost his grip.

"Agh!"

Wilde clutched the wall, gasping.

Dear God!

Shaking, he probed with the foot again and found another minuscule notch about three feet below him. Gritting his teeth, he let his weight carry him down until he was putting nearly everything on the little nook of slippery stone.

It held.

"You got this, Wilde," he whispered to himself.

He took another daring step.

There was nothing.

He kicked wide, running his boot over the surface. There had to be something. Some tiny depression or crevice for him to wedge his boot.

Nothing.

He looked up at the rope. It lay loosely over the lip of the plateau, but only had a few more feet to offer him.

"I can't hold on!" the man cried.

"I'm going as fast as I can," Wilde snapped.

The victim was just below him, maybe fifteen feet more, his face pale with terror. He dangled from trembling hands, his fingers dug into two small pockets of stone while the rope chewed into the flesh of his sweaty palm.

Wilde unspooled the rope until it choked his wrist. He kicked his boots toward the victim. He was merely a foot away from him.

"Can you grab my boot?" Wilde called, craning his neck to look down at his quarry.

But the man shook his head. "If I let go, I'll fall!"

"You need to reach for me!" Wilde said. "I don't have any more rope!"

"What do you *mean* you don't have any more rope!?" the man cried.

"I mean, I don't have any!" Wilde said. "Now, climb!"

The man looked up at him, his eyes heavy with weariness and fear. His lower lip fluttered like a white flag in the wind.

"I'll try," he moaned.

"Good," Wilde said, stretching his fingers toward the man. "You can do it."

But Wilde didn't believe it. If this guy had any reserves of heroic strength, they must have been spent holding onto that wall for the hours he'd been down here.

The man's knuckles trembled as he grunted. But he gave up almost instantly, his elbows barely bent, and he let himself sink down until his arms stretched above his head while his body dangled below, his head hanging in defeat.

Wilde exhaled, fighting back his own sense of defeat.

I have to get down to him.

But how?

Looking back at the rock face, Wilde studied the rope. He only needed a foot or two of length to reach the guy. Then he pointed the headlamp at his legs, which were propped up against the surface to keep him steady.

Just one foot more.

Then Wilde began to laugh. He knew exactly what to do, even if it was brazenly stupid.

"What's so funny, man!?" the victim below cried.

"I'm going to help you," Wilde said. "Don't worry."

Gritting his teeth, Wilde hauled himself back up the cave wall until enough of the lifesaving rope was slack again. He crossed one leg over it, looping like he had with his forearm, over and over until the rope was spooled about his leg in a helix. There was only one thing left to do.

"Blaze!" he yelled.

"Yeah?"

"Hold on!"

Wilde grinned for a moment as he imagined Allison's horrified face at the thought of what he was about to do.

Then, with one sickening glance down, he let go of the wall.

~

Smoke: A Great Smoky Mountains Adventure Novel - **Coming Fall 2023!**

Smoke launches in October of 2023 and follows Ranger Christian "Wilde" Weber's quest to locate a missing boy who has disappeared while hiking with his family. On his dangerous backcountry quest, Wilde will tread into the most treacherous realms of the park where ancient secrets are hiding, praying to never be discovered.

Fire debuts in October 2024 and tells the story of Ranger Allison Blaze as she hunts for a deadly arsonist who is setting fires throughout the park, threatening visitors and wildlife. Her mission gets even harder as she and her husband Travis enter the world of foster parenting, forcing Blaze to make impossible choices between the park she loves and the daughters she has chosen to raise.

To join the adventure and get updates on all the Great Smoky Mountains Adventure news, releases, events, and more, go to: DavidSafford.com/Adventure

The Ten Essentials

Since the 1930s, The Ten Essentials have been the go-to packing list for any hiker or adventurer. These items comprise the minimum necessary gear you need to survive an outdoor situation and practically guarantee that you will be ready if something goes wrong.

Each of these "systems" can be easily purchased at an outdoor supplier like REI, a common retailer like Walmart, or online through Amazon, Backcountry, or other similar sites. Before heading out on your next adventure, I highly recommend filling out your adventure pack with a reliable piece of gear in each of the following systems:

1. **Navigation:** Pack a map and compass, and be familiar with how to use them. Waterproof maps are preferred as they won't crumble and disintegrate in the rain. While many hiking apps exist (I use Avenza and others, like FKT-holder Nancy East, recommend Gaia GPS), these depend on your phone's battery which can quickly die in parts of the backcountry with no cell signal.

2. **Light:** Bring a headlamp, as this frees your hands from carrying a flashlight. Pack extra batteries as well and store them in a watertight plastic bag. Do not rely on your cell phone's flashlight!

3. **First Aid:** At a minimum, load your first aid kit with bandages and antibacterial ointment. Many hikers also include ibuprofen to prevent swelling and moleskins to avoid blisters.

4. **Sun Protection:** Sunscreen and a good hat are enough to tackle this essential, though sunglasses can be very helpful especially when hiking above the treeline.

5. **Knife/Repair Kit:** Depending on your gear needs, you'll need some kind of small pocketknife to cut thread, fabric, or tape. Some hikers include duct tape (it fixes everything), thread, or floss. A sewing needle isn't a bad idea for longer adventures where gear could deteriorate and break down.

6. **Fire:** If you want to survive overnight or in the cold, fire is a must. Pack a lighter, matches, tinder, and/or a stove. Practice fire building methods, preferably in wet conditions; the Smokies are technically a tropical environment and much of the wood is damp throughout the park.

7. **Shelter:** If worse comes to worst, you'll need shelter in a pinch. This can be a small bivvy or tarp; at the very least, a large garbage bag with an air slit can get the job done.

8. **Extra Food:** Pack your anticipated calories and carbs, then pack a few more. It's easy to underestimate how tiring it can be to hike in the mountains. The human body needs calories to function, and if you don't prepare then you may find yourself too exhausted to protect yourself. Jeff Woody (former FKT holder) recommends 300 calories per hour that you are hiking.

9. **Extra Water/Filter:** Water is the most important thing for your body to function in the wild. For every hour you plan to hike, pack at least 24 ounces of water. If the temperature/humidity is high, pack more. In addition to water, bring a reliable filter. Many Smokies hikers (myself included) use the Sawyer Squeeze, a simple device for safely filtering your drinking water. Lastly, sometimes water alone isn't enough, as your body needs electrolytes. Sweating causes them to leave your body, and replenishing them is crucial. Avoid energy drinks like Gatorade, and instead opt for a packet or gel that can be mixed with your water and provide essential energy during your adventure.

10. **Extra Clothes:** Bring rain gear and additional socks to complete this safety system. An entire change of clothes isn't necessary as long as you pack sufficient lightweight raingear.

Acknowledgments

Telling a story of this scope and magnitude requires a team of dedicated adventurers. I am indebted to a great many of them.

First and foremost, thank you to my partner, wife, and love for supporting me in the writing of this book. Thank you for encouraging me, letting me bounce ideas off you around the dinner table, and most of all for helping edit the final manuscript. I love you, Natalie, and I am so grateful for you.

Along with my wife I must give thanks and glory to my savior, Jesus Christ. I know it's cliche for public figures to give a shout out to God or Jesus, and I don't want this to fall prey to those tired tropes. Instead, I'll just say that I'm still amazed that you could love a sinner like me. Thank you for forgiving me and all the hot mess that comes with me, and thank you for calling me to try to tell stories that authentically incorporate your love and goodness.

A team of beta readers shared hours of their time to review the first draft and provide priceless insight as to what worked and what didn't. Thank you to Michael Scott, Sandy Juker, April Bly, Lori Palmer, Elizabeth Aulds, Sarah Sorgius, and Natalie Lein for your time, talent, and selfless asssistance.

To learn more about Smoky Mountain adventures, I've relied on the experience and wisdom of several incredible hikers and park staff:

- Liz Hall, the park's Emergency Manager, generously shared her time and insight to help me fact-check a number of details about search and rescue. In many ways, she inspired the character of Monica Greene.

- Jeff Wadley, member of the Backcountry Unit: Search and Rescue (BUSAR) graciously walked me through the nitty gritty of search and rescue, including how logistics and infrastructure are put in place to support workers in remote corners of the park. You can read his book about plane crashes in the Smokies here.

- Jeff Woody, one-time holder of the Smokies 900 Fastest Known Time, provided invaluable insight into how hikers maintain health and nutrition during long-distance adventures.

- Benny Braden, founder of Responsible Stewardship, stands as an example of physical strength, mental toughness, and spiritual maturity, having used hiking in the Smokies to overcome unbelievable trauma. His example, writings, and videos served as essential research on this project.

- Gretchen "Braids" Pardon sets the mold for Smoky Mountain storytelling with her honest and inspirational vlogs. While I have yet to work with her, I am grateful to be a follower and fan, and I frequently use her YouTube videos to research trails, campsites, and other locations in the park that I have yet to visit.

- Johnny Osborne is one of the leaders of the Hiking in the Smokies Facebook group, and I am grateful to him for his many videos and posts about the park. As with "Braids," Johnny on the Trail is a go-to source of Smoky Mountain information, adventure, and knowhow.

Finally, I must give a shout out to my teammates at The Write Practice (https://thewritepractice.com) for cheering me on during this journey. Joe Bunting is a matchless leader and writing coach, and I am honored to work with him. Everyone wanting to write their own book should visit The Write Practice and be a part of what Joe is doing to help writers tell their stories!

Font and Formatting

Title font is Bebas Neue, an Open Source font family originally designed as a single font by Ryoichi Tsunekawa.

Back cover font is Glacial Indifference, an Open Source font licensed under the SIL Open Font License, Version 1.1.

Internal formatting and fonts provided via Atticus.io under legal licenses.

Cover and jacket photographs by David Safford, editing with G.I.M.P. open source software.

Map of Great Smoky Mountains National Park provided by National Park Service in the public domain.

ABOUT THE AUTHOR

David Safford is an American novelist, teacher, and writing coach. When he isn't working with students, telling stories, or playing with his two children, he can be found in the mountains and trails enjoying the wonders of God's creation. He lives with his family in East Tennessee. Learn more at http://DavidSafford.com.